Richard Montanari is a novelist, screenwriter and essayist. His work appears regularly in national and regional publications across the US, and he is also the author of the internationally acclaimed thrillers *Kiss of Evil*, *Deviant Way*, *The Violet Hour* and *The Rosary Girls*, all of which were published in more than twenty countries. Richard lives in Cleveland, where he is currently working on his next novel featuring Kevin Byrne and Jessica Balzano.

For more about Richard Montanari, visit the author's website at www.richardmontanari.co.uk

Praise for Richard Montanari

'In this high body count chiller from the author of *The Rosary Girls*, Jessica Balzano and Kevin Byrne are up against a savagely inventive serial killer . . . A grisly, atmospheric thriller'   *Publishers Weekly*

'If Gustav Mahler had been a novelist instead of a composer, he might have written something like *The Rosary Girls* . . . Montanari is very good at getting you to think you're one step ahead of the cops. Don't flatter yourself. It's highly unlikely you'll come close to figuring out whodunit before anybody in the book does'   *Philadelphia Inquirer (Editor's Choice)*

'Incredible . . . Ranks with *The Silence of the Lambs* and *Kiss the Girls* . . . A breath-taking rollercoaster ride full of plot twists and suspense that keeps the reader begging to know what's next'   *CelebrityCafe.com*

'A no-holds-barred thriller that thrusts the reader into the black soul of the killer . . . those with a taste for Thomas Harris will look forward to the sure-to-follow sequel'   *Library Journal*

'An utterly savage and frightening thriller . . .'   *New Mystery Reader*

'If you like the gritty suspense thrillers of Thomas Harris, your prayers have been answered'   *Book of the Month Club*

THE SKIN GODS

RICHARD MONTANARI

William Heinemann: London

Published in the United Kingdom in 2006 by William Heinemann

3 5 7 9 10 8 6 4 2

Copyright © Richard Montanari 2006

The right of Richard Montanari to be identified as the author of this work has been asserted by him
in accordance with the Copyright, Designs and Patents Act, 1988

William Heinemann
The Random House Group Limited
20 Vauxhall Bridge Road, London, SW1V 2SA

Random House Australia (Pty) Limited
20 Alfred Street, Milsons Point, Sydney, New South Wales 2061, Australia

Random House New Zealand Limited
18 Poland Road, Glenfield
Auckland 10, New Zealand

Random House (Pty) Limited
Isle of Houghton, Corner of Boundary Road & Carse O'Gowrie, Houghton 2198, South Africa

The Random House Group Limited Reg. No. 954009
www.randomhouse.co.uk

A CIP catalogue record for this book is available from the British Library

Papers used by Random House are natural, recyclable products made from wood grown in
sustainable forests. The manufacturing processes conform to the environmental regulations of the
country of origin

Printed and bound in Great Britain by
Mackays of Chatham plc, Chatham, Kent

ISBN 97804 3401395 1 (from January 2007)
ISBN 0 43401395 1

For the men and women of the
Philadelphia Police Department.

Brìgh gach cluiche gu dheireadh.

THE SKIN GODS

1

"WHAT I REALLY WANT TO DO IS DIRECT."

Nothing. No reaction at all. She stares at me with those big Prussian blue eyes, waiting. Perhaps she is too young to recognize the cliché. Perhaps she is smarter than I thought. This is either going to make the task of killing her very easy, or very difficult.

"Cool," she says.

Easy.

"You've done some acting. I can tell."

She blushes. "Not really."

I lower my head, raise my eyes. My irresistible look. Monty Clift in *A Place in the Sun*. I can see it working. "Not really?"

"Well, when I was in junior high we did *West Side Story*."

"And you played Maria."

"Not hardly," she says. "I was just one of the girls at the dance."

"Jet or Shark?"

"Jet, I think. And then I did a couple of things in college."

"I knew it," I say. "I can spot a theatrical vibe a mile away."

"It was no big deal, believe me. I don't think anyone even noticed me."

"Of course they did. How could they miss you?" She reddens even more deeply. Sandra Dee in *A Summer Place*. "Keep in mind," I add, "lots of big movie stars started out in the chorus."

"Really?"

"Naturellement."

She has high cheekbones, a golden French braid, lips painted a lustrous coral. In 1960 she would have worn her hair in a bouffant or a pixie cut. Beneath that, a shirtwaist dress with a wide white belt. A string of faux pearls, perhaps.

On the other hand, in 1960, she might not have accepted my invitation.

We are sitting in a nearly empty corner bar in West Philadelphia, just a few blocks from the Schuylkill River.

"Okay. Who is your favorite movie star?" I ask.

She brightens. She likes games. "Boy or girl?"

"Girl."

She thinks for a few moments. "I like Sandra Bullock a lot."

"There you go. Sandy started out in made-for-TV movies."

"Sandy? You know her?"

"Of course."

"And she really made TV movies?"

"Bionic Showdown, 1989. The harrowing tale of international intrigue and bionic menace at the World Unity Games. Sandy played the girl in the wheelchair."

"Do you know a lot of movie stars?"

"Almost all of them." I take her hand in mine. Her skin is soft, flawless. "And do you know what they all have in common?"

"What?"

"Do you know what they all have in common with *you*?"

She giggles, stamps her feet. "Tell me!"

"They all have perfect skin."

Her free hand absently goes to her face, smoothing her cheek.

"Oh yes," I continue. "Because when the camera gets really, really close, there's no amount of makeup in the world that can substitute for radiant skin."

She looks past me, at her reflection in the bar mirror.

"Think about it. All the great screen legends had beautiful skin," I say.

"Ingrid Bergman, Greta Garbo, Rita Hayworth, Vivien Leigh, Ava Gardner. Movie stars live for the close-up, and the close-up never lies."

I can see that some of these names are unknown to her. Pity. Most people her age think that movies began with *Titanic,* and movie stardom is defined by how many times you've been on *Entertainment Tonight.* They've never been exposed to the genius of Fellini, Kurosawa, Wilder, Lean, Kubrick, Hitchcock.

It is not about talent, it is all about fame. To people her age, fame is the drug. She wants it. She craves it. They all do, in one way or another. It is the reason she is with me. I embody the promise of fame.

By the end of this night I will make part of her dream come true.

THE MOTEL ROOM is small and dank and common. There is a queen-size bed, and gondola scenes on delaminating Masonite nailed to the walls. The blanket is mildewed, moth-eaten, a frayed and ugly shroud that whispers of a thousand illicit encounters. In the carpeting lives the sour odor of human frailty.

I think of John Gavin and Janet Leigh.

I paid cash for the room earlier today in my midwestern character. Jeff Daniels in *Terms of Endearment.*

I hear the shower start in the bathroom. I take a deep breath, find my center, pull the small suitcase out from underneath the bed. I slip on the cotton housedress, the gray wig, and the pilled cardigan. As I button the sweater, I catch a glimpse of myself in the dresser mirror. Sad. I will never be an attractive woman, not even an old woman.

But the illusion is complete. And that is all that matters.

She begins to sing. Something by a current girl singer. Her voice is quite pleasant, actually.

The steam from the shower slithers under the bathroom door: long, gossamer fingers, beckoning. I take the knife in hand and follow. Into character. Into frame.

Into legend.

2

THE CADILLAC ESCALADE SLOWED TO A CRAWL IN FRONT OF Club Vibe: a sleek, glossy shark in neon water. The thumping bass line of the Isley Brothers' "Climbin' Up the Ladder" rattled the windows of the SUV as it rolled to a stop, its smoked-glass windows refracting the colors of the night in a shimmering palette of red and blue and yellow.

It was the middle of July, the slick belly of summer, and the heat burrowed beneath the skin of Philadelphia like an embolism.

Near the entrance to Club Vibe, on the corner of Kensington and Allegheny streets, beneath the steel ceiling of the El, stood a tall, statuesque redhead, her auburn hair a silken waterfall that graced bare shoulders before cascading to the middle of her back. She wore a short spaghetti-strap black dress that embraced the curves of her body, long crystal earrings. Her light olive skin glistened under a thin sheen of perspiration.

In this place, at this hour, she was a chimera, an urban fantasy made flesh.

A few feet away, in the doorway to a shuttered shoe repair shop, lounged a homeless black man. Of indeterminate age, he wore a tattered wool coat despite the merciless heat, and lovingly nursed a nearly empty bottle of Orange Mist, holding it tightly to his breast as one might nestle a sleeping child. Nearby, his shopping cart waited as a trusted steed, overflowing with precious urban plunder.

At just after two o'clock the driver's door of the Escalade swung open, spilling a fat column of pot smoke into the sultry night. The man who emerged was huge and quietly menacing. His thick biceps strained the sleeves of a royal blue double-breasted linen suit. D'Shante Jackson was a former running back for Edison High in North Philly, a steel girder of a man not yet thirty. He stood six three and weighed a trim and muscular 215 pounds.

D'Shante looked both ways up Kensington and, assessing the threat as nil, opened the rear door of the Escalade. His employer, the man who paid him a thousand dollars a week for protection, stepped out.

Trey Tarver was in his forties, a light-skinned black man who carried himself with a lithe and supple grace, despite his frame's ever-expanding bulk. Standing five eight, he had broached and passed the two-hundred-pound mark years earlier and, given his penchant for bread pudding and shoulder sandwiches, threatened to venture much higher. He wore a black Hugo Boss three-button suit and a pair of Mezlan calfskin oxfords. Each hand boasted a pair of diamond rings.

He stepped away from the Escalade and flicked the creases on his trousers. He smoothed his hair, which he wore long, Snoop Dogg style, although he was a generation-plus away from legitimately copping hip-hop fashion cues. If you asked Trey Tarver, he wore his hair like Verdine White of Earth, Wind & Fire.

Trey shot his cuffs and surveyed the intersection, his Serengeti. K&A, as this crossroads was known, had had many masters, but none as ruthless as Trey "TNT" Tarver.

He was about to enter the club when he noticed the redhead. Her luminous hair was a beacon in the night, her long shapely legs a siren call. Trey held up a hand, then approached the woman, much to the dismay of his lieutenant. Standing on a street corner, especially *this* street corner, Trey Tarver was in the open, vulnerable to gunships cruising up both Kensington and Allegheny.

"Hey, baby," Trey said.

The redhead turned to look at the man, as if noticing him for the first time. She had clearly seen him arrive. Cool indifference was part of the tango. "Hey, yourself," she said, finally, smiling. "You like?"

"Do I *like?*" Trey stepped back, his eyes roaming her. "Baby, if you was gravy I'd *sop* ya."

The redhead laughed. "It's all good."

"You and me? We gonna do some bidness."

"Let's go."

Trey glanced at the door to the club, then at his watch: a gold Breitling. "Gimme twenty minutes."

"Gimme a retainer."

Trey Tarver smiled. He was a businessman, forged by the fires of the street, schooled in the bleak and violent Richard Allen projects. He pulled his roll, peeled a Benjamin, held it out. Just as the redhead was about to take it, he snapped it back. "Do you know who I am?" he asked.

The redhead took half a step back, hand on hip. She gave him the twice-over. She had soft brown eyes flecked with gold, full sensuous lips. "Let me guess," she said. "Taye Diggs?"

Trey Tarver laughed. "That's right."

The redhead winked at him. "I know who you are."

"What's your name?"

"Scarlet."

"*Damn.* For real?"

"For real."

"Like that movie?"

"Yeah, baby."

Trey Tarver considered it all for a moment. "My money better not be gone with the wind, hear'm saying?"

The redhead smiled. "I hear you."

She took the C-note and slipped the bill into her purse. As she did this, D'Shante put a hand on Trey's arm. Trey nodded. They had business to attend to in the club. They were just about to turn and enter when something caught the headlights of a passing car, something that seemed to wink and glimmer from the area near the homeless man's right shoe. Something metallic and shiny.

D'Shante followed the light. He saw the source.

It was a pistol in an ankle holster.

"The fuck is *this?*" D'Shante said.

Time spun on a crazy axis, the air suddenly electric with the promise of violence. Eyes met, and understanding flowed like a raging current of water.

It was on.

The redhead in the black dress—Detective Jessica Balzano of the Philadelphia Police Department's Homicide Unit—took a step back and in one smooth, practiced motion, pulled the badge on a lanyard from inside her dress, and slipped her Glock 17 out of her purse.

Trey Tarver was wanted in connection with the murder of two men. Detectives had staked out Club Vibe—as well as three other clubs—for four straight nights, hoping for Tarver to surface. It was well known that he did business in Club Vibe. It was well known he had a weakness for tall redheads. Trey Tarver thought he was untouchable.

Tonight he got touched.

"Police!" Jessica yelled. "Let me see your hands!"

For Jessica, everything began to move in a measured montage of sound and color. She saw the homeless man stir. Felt the weight of the Glock in her hand. Saw a flutter of bright blue—D'Shante's arm in motion. A weapon in D'Shante's hand. A Tec-9. Long magazine. Fifty rounds.

No, Jessica thought. *Not my life. Not this night.*

No.

The world uncoiled, shot back to speed.

"Gun!" Jessica yelled.

By this time Detective John Shepherd, the homeless man on the stoop, was on his feet. But before he could clear his weapon, D'Shante spun and slammed the butt of the Tec into his forehead, stunning him, flaying the skin over his right eye. Shepherd collapsed to the ground. Blood spurted, cascaded into his eyes, blinding him.

D'Shante raised his weapon.

"Drop it!" Jessica yelled, Glock leveled. D'Shante showed no sign of compliance.

"Drop it, now!" she repeated.

D'Shante drew down. Aimed.

Jessica fired.

The bullet slammed into D'Shante Jackson's right shoulder, exploding the muscle and flesh and bone into a thick, pink spray. The Tec flew from his hands as he spun 360 and collapsed to the ground, shrieking in surprise and agony. Jessica inched forward and kicked the Tec over to Shepherd, still training her weapon on Trey Tarver. Tarver, hands up, stood near the mouth of an alley that cut between the buildings. If their intel was accurate, he carried his .32 semi-auto in a holster at the small of his back.

Jessica looked over at John Shepherd. He was stunned, but not out. She took her eyes off Trey Tarver for only a second, but that was long enough. Tarver bolted up the alley.

"You all right?" Jessica asked Shepherd.

Shepherd wiped the blood from his eyes. "I'm good."

"You sure?"

"*Go.*"

As Jessica sidled up to the alley entrance, peering into the shadows, back on the street corner D'Shante pulled himself into a sitting position. His shoulder oozed blood between his fingers. He eyed the Tec.

Shepherd cocked his .38 Smith & Wesson, aiming it at D'Shante's forehead. He said: "Give me a fucking reason."

With his free hand, Shepherd reached into his coat pocket for his two-way. Four detectives were sitting in a van, half a block away, waiting for the call. When Shepherd saw the casing on the rover, he knew they would not be coming. When he had fallen to the ground, he smashed the radio. He keyed it. It was dead.

John Shepherd grimaced, glanced up the alley, into the darkness.

Until he could get D'Shante Jackson frisked and cuffed, Jessica was on her own.

THE ALLEY WAS littered with derelict furniture, tires, rusting appliances. Halfway to the end was a T-junction, leading to the right. Her gun low, Jessica still-hunted down the alley, hugging the wall. She tore the wig from her head; her newly cut short hair was spiky and wet. A slight breeze cooled her a few degrees, clearing her thoughts.

She peered around the corner. No movement. No Trey Tarver.

Halfway down the alley, on the right, the window of an all-night Chinese takeout poured out dense steam, pungent with ginger, garlic, and green onions. Beyond, the clutter formed ominous shapes in the gloom.

Good news. The alley dead-ended. Trey Tarver was trapped.

Bad news. He could be any one of those shapes. And he was armed.

Where the hell is my backup?

Jessica decided to wait.

Then a shadow lurched, darted. Jessica saw the muzzle flash an instant before she heard the report. The bullet slammed into the wall just a foot or so over her head. Fine brick dust fell.

Oh God, no. Jessica thought about her daughter, Sophie, sitting in some bright hospital waiting room. She thought about her father, a retired officer himself. But mostly she thought about the wall in the lobby of the police administration building, the wall dedicated to the department's fallen officers.

More movement. Tarver ran, low, toward the end of the alley. Jessica had a shot. She stepped into the open.

"Don't move!"

Tarver stopped, hands out to his side.

"Drop your weapon!" Jessica shouted.

The back door to the Chinese restaurant suddenly flew open. A busboy stepped between her and her target. He brought a pair of huge plastic garbage bags out of the restaurant, obscuring her line of sight.

"Police! Get out of the way!"

The kid froze, confused. He looked both ways up the alley. Beyond him, Trey Tarver spun and fired again. The second shot smashed into the wall over Jessica's head—closer this time. The Chinese kid dove to the ground. He was pinned down. Jessica could no longer wait for backup.

Trey Tarver disappeared behind the Dumpster. Jessica hugged the wall, heart pounding, Glock out front. Her back was soaking wet. Well trained for this moment, she ran through the checklist in her mind. Then she threw the checklist out. There *was* no training for this moment. She edged toward the man with the gun.

"It's over, Trey," she yelled. "SWAT's on the roof. Give it up."

No reply. He was calling her bluff. He would go out with a blaze, becoming a street legend.

Glass broke. Were there basement windows into these buildings? She looked to her left. Yes. Steel casement windows; some barred, some not.

Shit.

He was getting away. She had to move. She reached the Dumpster, put her back to it, lowered herself to the asphalt. She peered beneath. There was enough light to see a silhouette of Tarver's feet if he was still on the other side. He wasn't. Jessica edged around, saw a mound of plastic garbage bags and loose refuse—piled drywall, paint cans, discarded planks of lumber. Tarver was gone. She scanned the end of the alley, saw the broken window.

Had he gone through?

She was just about to return to the street and bring in the troops to search the building when she saw a pair of dress shoes emerging from beneath the pile of stacked plastic garbage bags.

She drew a deep breath, tried to calm herself. It didn't work. It might be weeks before she actually calmed down.

"Get up, Trey."

No movement.

Jessica found her wind, continued: "Your Honor, because the suspect had taken two shots at me already, I couldn't take a chance. When the plastic moved, I fired. It all happened so fast. Before I knew it, I had emptied my entire mag into the suspect."

A rustling of plastic. *"Wait."*

"Thought so," Jessica said. "Now, very slowly—and I mean *very* slowly—place the gun on the ground."

After a few seconds, a hand slid out, a .32 semi-auto ringed on a finger. Tarver put the gun on the ground. Jessica picked it up.

"Now get up. Nice and easy. Hands where I can see them."

Trey Tarver slowly emerged from the pile of garbage bags. He stood, facing her, hands out to his sides, eyes darting from left to right. He was going to challenge her. After eight years on the force, she knew the look. Trey Tarver had seen her shoot a man not two minutes ago, and he was going to *challenge* her.

Jessica shook her head. "You don't want to fuck with me tonight, Trey," she said. "Your boy hit my partner and I had to shoot him. Plus, you shot at *me*. What's worse, you made me snap a heel on my best shoes. Be a man and take your medicine. It's over."

Tarver stared at her, trying to melt her cool with his jailhouse burn. After a few seconds, he saw the South Philly in her eyes and realized it wouldn't work. He put his hands behind his head and interlaced his fingers.

"Now turn around," Jessica said.

Trey Tarver looked at her legs, her short dress. He smiled. His diamond tooth glimmered in the streetlight. "You first, bitch."

Bitch?

Bitch?

Jessica glanced back up the alley. The Chinese kid was back in the restaurant. The door was closed. They were alone.

She looked at the ground. Trey was standing on a discarded two-by-six. One end of the board was perched precariously on a discarded paint can. The can was inches from Jessica's right foot.

"I'm sorry, what did you say?"

Cold flames in his eyes. "I said 'You first, *bitch.*' "

Jessica kicked the can. At that moment, the look on Trey Tarver's face said it all. His expression was not unlike that of Wile E. Coyote at the moment the hapless cartoon character realizes the cliff is no longer beneath him. Trey crumpled to the ground like wet origami, on the way down smacking his head on the edge of the Dumpster.

Jessica looked at his eyes. Or, more accurately, the whites of his eyes. Trey Tarver was out cold.

Oops.

Jessica rolled him over just as a pair of detectives from the Fugitive Squad finally arrived on the scene. No one had seen anything and, even if they had, Trey Tarver didn't exactly have a big fan club in the department. One of the detectives tossed her a pair of handcuffs.

"Oh yeah," Jessica said to her unconscious suspect. "We gonna do some bidness." She clicked the cuffs shut on his wrists. "Bitch."

THERE IS A time for police officers, after a successful hunt, when they decelerate from the chase, when they assess the operation, congratulate each other, grade their performance, brake. It is a time when morale is at its peak. They went where the darkness was and emerged into the light.

They gathered at the Melrose Diner, a twenty-four-hour spoon on Snyder Avenue.

They had taken down two very bad people. There was no loss of life, and the only serious injury came to someone who deserved it. The good news was that the shooting, as far as they could tell, was clean.

Jessica had been a police officer for eight years. She was in uniform for the first four, followed by a stint on the Auto Unit, a division of the city's Major Case Squad. In April of this year she had joined the Homicide Unit. In that short time she had seen her share of horrors. There was the young Latina woman murdered in a vacant lot in Northern Liberties, rolled into a rug, put on top of a car, and dumped in Fairmount Park. There was the case of the young man lured into the park by three of his classmates only to be robbed and beaten to death. And there was the Rosary Killer case.

Jessica wasn't the first or only woman in the unit, but anytime someone new joins a small, tightly knit squad in the department there is the requisite distrust, the unspoken probationary period. Her father had been a legend in the department, but those were shoes to fill, not walk in.

After her incident debriefing, Jessica entered the diner. Immediately the four detectives who were already there—Tony Park, Eric Chavez, Nick Palladino, and a patched-up John Shepherd—got up from their stools, put their hands against the wall, and assumed the position in tribute.

Jessica had to laugh.

She was in.

SHE IS HARD TO LOOK AT NOW. HER SKIN IS NO LONGER PERFECT, but rather torn silk. The blood pools around her head, nearly black in the dim light thrown from the trunk lid.

I look around the parking area. We are alone, just a few feet from the Schuylkill River. Water laps the dock—the eternal meter of the city.

I take the money and put it into the fold of the newspaper. I toss the newspaper onto the girl in the trunk of the car, then slam the lid.

Poor Marion.

She really was pretty. She had about her a certain freckled charm that reminded me of Tuesday Weld in *High Time*.

Before we left the motel, I cleaned the room, tore up the room receipt, and flushed it down the toilet. There had been no mop, no bucket. When you shoot on a shoestring, you make do.

She stares up at me now, her eyes no longer blue. She may have been pretty, she may have been someone's idea of perfection, but for all she was, she was no Angel.

The house lights are down, the screen flickers to life. In the next few weeks the city of Philadelphia will hear a great deal about me. It will be said that I am a psychopath, a madman, an evil force from the soul of hell. As the bodies fall and the rivers run red, I will receive some horrendous reviews.

Don't believe a word of it.

I wouldn't hurt a fly.

Six days later

SHE LOOKED COMPLETELY NORMAL. SOME MIGHT EVEN SAY friendly, in a doting, spinster-aunt sort of way. She stood five three and could not have weighed more than ninety-five pounds in her black spandex one-piece and pristine white Reeboks. She had short, brick-red hair and clear blue eyes. Her fingers were long and slender, her nails groomed and unpainted. She wore no jewelry.

To the outside world, she was a pleasant looking, physically fit woman nearing middle age.

For Detective Kevin Francis Byrne, she was a combination Lizzie Borden, Lucrezia Borgia, and Ma Barker, all wrapped up in a package resembling Mary Lou Retton.

"You can do better than that," she said.

"What do you mean?" Byrne managed.

"The name you called me in your mind. You can do better than that."

She *is* a witch, he thought. "What makes you think I called you a name?"

She laughed her shrill, Cruella De Vil laugh. Dogs three counties away cringed. "I've been at this almost twenty years, Detective," she said.

"I've been called every name in the book. I've been called names that aren't even scheduled in the *next* book. I've been spat upon, swung upon, cursed in a dozen languages, including Apache. I've had voodoo dolls made in my likeness, novenas offered up for my painful demise. I assure you, there is no torture you could possibly conjure that has not been wished upon me."

Byrne just stared. He had no idea he was that transparent. Some detective.

Kevin Byrne was two weeks into a twelve-week physical therapy program at HUP, the Hospital at the University of Pennsylvania. He had been shot at close range in the basement of a house in Northeast Philadelphia on Easter Sunday. Although he was expected to make a full recovery, he had learned early on that phrases like *full recovery* usually involved a lot of wishful thinking.

The bullet, the one with his name on it, had lodged in his occipital lobe, approximately one centimeter from his brain stem. And even though there was no nerve involvement, and the damage was all vascular, he had endured nearly twelve hours of cranial surgery, six weeks of induced coma, and nearly two months in the hospital.

The offending slug was now encased in a small Lucite cube and sitting on his nightstand, a macabre trophy courtesy of the Homicide Unit.

The most serious damage came not from injury to his brain, but rather from the way his body had twisted on the way to the floor, an unnatural wrenching of the lower back. This move had caused damage to his sciatic nerve, the long nerve that runs from each side of the lower spine, through deep in the buttock and back of the thigh, and all the way down to the foot, connecting the spinal cord with the leg and foot muscles.

And while his laundry list of ailments was painful enough, the bullet he took to his head was a mere inconvenience compared with the pain generated by the sciatic nerve. Sometimes it felt like someone was running a carving knife up his right leg and across his lower back, stopping along the way to twist at various vertebrae.

He was free to return to duty as soon as the city doctors cleared him, and as soon as he felt ready. Until then, he was officially IOD: injured on duty. Full pay, no work, and a bottle of Early Times every week from the unit.

While his acute sciatica was about as much agony as he had ever endured, pain, as a way of life, was an old friend. He had tolerated fifteen years of savage migraine headaches, ever since the first time he had been shot and nearly drowned in the icy Delaware River.

It had taken a second bullet to rid him of the malady. Although he wouldn't recommend getting shot in the head as a therapy for migraine sufferers, he wasn't about to second-guess the cure. Since the day he had been shot for the second—and hopefully final—time, he hadn't suffered a single headache.

Take two hollow points and call me in the morning.

Still, he was tired. Two decades on the force of one of the toughest cities in the country had drained his will. He had put in his time. And although he had faced some of the most violent and depraved people east of Pittsburgh, his current antagonist was a petite physical therapist named Olivia Leftwich and her bottomless bag of tortures.

Byrne was standing along one wall of the physical therapy room, against a waist-high bar, his right leg propped parallel to the floor. He held the position, stoically, despite the murder in his heart. The slightest movement lit him up like a Roman candle.

"You're making great improvements," she said. "I'm impressed."

Byrne glared daggers at her. Her horns receded and she smiled. No fangs visible.

All part of the illusion, he thought.

All part of the con.

ALTHOUGH CITY HALL was the official epicenter of Center City, and the historical heart and soul of Philadelphia was Independence Hall, the city's pride was still Rittenhouse Square, located on Walnut Street between Eighteenth and Nineteenth streets. Although not as well known as Times Square in New York City, or Picadilly Circus in London, Philadelphia was rightfully proud of Rittenhouse Square, which remained one of the city's toniest addresses. In the shadow of posh hotels, historic churches, towering office buildings, and fashionable boutiques, on a summer day, at noontime, the crowds on the square were enormous.

Byrne sat on a bench near the Barye sculpture *Lion Crushing a Serpent* in the center of the square. He had been nearly six feet tall in eighth grade, and had grown to his height of six three by the time he was a junior in high school. In his time in school and in the service, and in all of his time on the force, he had used his size and weight to his advantage, many times shutting down potential trouble before it began by merely standing up.

But now, with his cane, his ashen complexion, and the sluggish limping gait caused by the pain pills he took, he felt small, unimportant, easily swallowed by the mass of humanity on the square.

As with every time he left a physical therapy session, he vowed never to go back. What kind of therapy actually makes the pain worse? Whose idea was this? Not his. See you around, Matilda the Hun.

He distributed his weight on the bench, finding a reasonably comfortable position. After a few moments he looked up and saw a teenaged girl crossing the square, weaving her way through the bike boys, the businessmen, the vendors, the tourists. Slender and athletic, feline in her movement, her fine, nearly white-blond hair was pulled back into a ponytail. She wore a peach sundress and sandals. She had dazzlingly bright aquamarine eyes. Every young man under the age of twenty-one was thoroughly captivated with her, as were far too many men over twenty-one. She had about her a patrician poise that can only come from true inner grace, a cool and enchanting beauty that said to the world that this was someone special.

As she got closer, Byrne realized why he knew all this. It was Colleen. The young woman was his own daughter and, for a moment, he nearly hadn't recognized her.

She stood in the center of the square, looking for him, hand to her forehead, shielding her eyes from the sun. Soon she found him in the crowd. She waved and smiled the slight, blushing smile that she had used to her advantage her whole life, the one that got her the Barbie Bike with the pink-and-white handlebar streamers when she was six; the one that got her into the chichi summer camp for deaf kids this year, the camp her father could barely just afford.

God, she is beautiful, Byrne thought.

Colleen Siobhan Byrne was both blessed and cursed with her mother's incandescent Irish skin. Cursed, because she could sunburn in minutes on a day like this. Blessed because she was the fairest of the fair, her skin nearly translucent. What was flawless splendor at the age of thirteen would surely blossom into heart-stopping beauty as a woman in her twenties and thirties.

Colleen kissed him on the cheek, and hugged him closely—but

gently, fully aware of his myriad aches and pains. She thumbed the lipstick off his cheek.

When had she started wearing lipstick? Byrne wondered.

"Is it too crowded for you?" she signed.

"No," Byrne signed back.

"Are you sure?"

"Yes," Byrne signed. "I love crowds."

It was a bald-faced lie, and Colleen knew it. She smiled.

Colleen Byrne had been deaf since birth, caused by a genetic disorder that had planted far more obstacles in her father's path than her own. Where Kevin Byrne had wasted many years lamenting what he had arrogantly considered a handicap in his daughter's life, Colleen had simply attacked life full-on, never once slowing down to bemoan her alleged misfortune. She was an A student, a terrific athlete, highly proficient in American Sign Language, as well as being an expert lip-reader. She was even learning Norwegian Sign Language.

A lot of deaf people, Byrne had learned a long time ago, were very straightforward in their communication, not wasting their time on a great deal of pointless, inhibited conversation the way hearing people did. Many operated on what was jokingly referred to as DST—Deaf Standard Time—a reference to the notion that deaf people tend to be late, owing to their penchant for long conversations. Once they got going, it was hard to shut them up.

Sign language, although highly nuanced in its own right, was, after all, a form of shorthand. Byrne did his best to keep up. He had learned the language when Colleen was still very young, had taken to it surprisingly well, considering what a lousy student he had been in school.

Colleen found a spot on the bench, sat down. Byrne had stopped at a Cosi and picked up a pair of salads. He was pretty sure that Colleen was not going to eat—what thirteen-year-old girl actually ate lunch these days?—and he was right. She took the Diet Snapple out of the bag, worked off the plastic seal.

Byrne opened the bag, began to pick at his salad. He got her attention and signed: "Sure you're not hungry?"

She gave him the look: *Dad.*

They sat for a while, enjoying each other's company, enjoying the warmth of the day. Byrne listened to the dissonance of summertime sounds around them: the discordant symphony of five different types of music, the laughter of children, the high spirits of a political argument coming from somewhere behind them, the endless traffic noise. As he had so many times in his life, he tried to imagine what it was like for Colleen to be in a place like this, the deep silence of her world.

Byrne put the remainder of his salad back in the bag, got Colleen's eye.

"When do you leave for camp?" he signed.

"Monday."

Byrne nodded. "Are you excited?"

Colleen's face lit up. "Yes."

"Do you want me to give you a ride there?"

Byrne saw the slightest hesitation in Colleen's eyes. The camp was just south of Lancaster, a pleasant two-hour ride west of Philadelphia. The delay in Colleen's answer meant one thing. Her mother was going to take her, probably in the company of her new boyfriend. Colleen was as poor at concealing emotions as her father was practiced at it. "No. I've got it covered," she signed.

As they signed, Byrne could see people watching them. This was nothing new. He used to get upset about it, but had long since given that up. People were curious. A year earlier, he and Colleen had been in Fairmount Park when a teenaged boy who had been trying to impress Colleen on his skateboard had hopped a rail and wiped out big time, crashing to the ground right near Colleen's feet.

As he picked himself up, he tried to make light of it. Right in front of him, Colleen had looked at Byrne and signed: *What an asshole.*

The kid smiled, thinking he had scored a point.

There were advantages to being deaf, and Colleen Byrne knew them all.

As the businesspeople began to reluctantly make their way back to their offices, the crowd thinned a little. Byrne and Colleen watched a brindle-and-white Jack Russell terrier try to climb a nearby tree, harassing a squirrel vibrating on the first branch.

Byrne watched his daughter watching the dog. His heart wanted to burst. She was so calm, so even. She was becoming a woman right before his eyes and he was scared to death that she would feel he had no part in it. It had been a long time since they lived together as a family, and Byrne felt that his influence—that part of him that was still positive—was waning.

Colleen looked at her watch, frowned. "I've got to get going," she signed.

Byrne nodded. The great and terrible irony of getting older was that time went way too fast.

Colleen took their trash over to a nearby trash can. Byrne noticed that every breathing male within eyeshot watched her. He wasn't handling this well.

"Are you going to be okay?" she signed.

"I'm fine," Byrne lied. "See you over the weekend?"

Colleen nodded. "I love you."

"I love you, too, baby."

She hugged him again, kissed him on the top of his head. He watched her walk into the crowd, into the rush of the noontime city.

In an instant she was gone.

HE LOOKED LOST.

He sat at the bus stop, reading *The American Sign Language Handshape Dictionary,* a very important reference book for anyone learning to speak American Sign Language. He was attempting to balance the book on his knees while at the same time trying to fingerspell words with his right hand. From where Colleen stood, it appeared that he was speaking in a language either long dead or not yet invented. It certainly wasn't ASL.

She had never seen him at the stop before. He was nice looking, older—the whole world was older—but he had a friendly face. And he looked pretty cute fumbling his way through the book. He glanced up, saw her watching him. She signed: "Hello."

He smiled, a little self-consciously, but was clearly excited to find someone who spoke the language he was trying to learn. "Am . . . I . . . that . . . bad?" he signed, tentatively.

She wanted to be nice. She wanted to be encouraging. Unfortunately, her face told the truth before her hands could form the lie. "Yes, you are," she signed.

He watched her hands, confused. She pointed to her face. He looked up. She rather dramatically nodded her head. He blushed. She laughed. He joined in.

"You've really got to understand the five parameters first," she signed, slowly, referring to the five basic strictures of ASL, that being handshape, orientation, location, movement, and nonmanual signals. More confusion.

She took the book from him and flipped to the front. She pointed out some of the basics.

He skimmed the section, nodding. He glanced up, formed a hand, roughly, into: "Thanks." Then added: "If you ever want to teach, I'll be your first pupil."

She smiled and said: "You're very welcome."

A minute later, she got on the bus. He did not. Apparently he was waiting for another route.

Teaching, she thought as she found a seat near the front. Maybe someday. She had always been patient with people, and she had to admit she got a good feeling when she was able to impart wisdom to others. Her father, of course wanted her to be president of the United States. Or at least attorney general.

A few moments later, the man who would be her student got up from the bus stop bench, stretched. He tossed the book into a trash can.

It was a scorcher of a day. He slipped into his car, glanced at the LCD screen of his camera phone. He had gotten a good image. She was beautiful.

He started the car, carefully pulled out into traffic, and followed the bus down Walnut Street.

5

THE APARTMENT WAS QUIET WHEN BYRNE RETURNED. WHAT else would it be? Two hot rooms over a former print shop on Second Street, nearly Spartan in furnishings: a worn love seat and distressed mahogany coffee table, a television, a boom box, and a stack of blues CDs. In the bedroom, a queen-size bed and a small, thrift-store nightstand.

Byrne flipped on the window air conditioner, made his way to the bathroom, split a Vicodin in half, swallowed it. He splashed cool water on his face and neck. He left the medicine cabinet open. He told himself it was to avoid splashing water on it, thereby avoiding the necessity to wipe it down, but the real reason was that he wanted to avoid seeing himself in the mirror. How long had he been doing *that*, he wondered?

When he returned to the living room he slipped a Robert Johnson disc into the boom box. He was in the mood for "Stones in My Passway."

After the divorce, he had come back to the old neighborhood: the Queen Village section of South Philadelphia. His father had been a longshoreman, a Mummer of citywide fame. Like his father and uncles, Kevin Byrne was, and would always remain, a Two-Streeter at heart. And although it took a while to get back into the rhythms of the neighborhood, the older residents wasted no time in making him feel at home with the three standard South Philly questions:

Where you from?

Did you buy or rent?

Do you have any children?

He had thought, briefly, of plunking down a chunk for one of the recently rehabbed homes at Jefferson Square, a newly gentrified area nearby, but he wasn't sure that his heart, unlike his mind, was still in Philadelphia. For the first time in his life, he was a man untethered. He had a few dollars put away—over and above Colleen's college fund—and he could go and do whatever he pleased.

But could he leave the force? Could he turn in his service weapon and badge, turn in his papers, take his retirement ID, and simply walk away?

He honestly did not know.

He sat on the love seat, ran through the cable channels. He thought about pouring himself a tumblerful of bourbon and just riding the bottle until nightfall. No. He wasn't a very good drunk these days. These days, he was one of those morbid, ugly drunks you see with four empty stools on either side of him in a crowded tavern.

His cell phone beeped. He pulled it out of his pocket, stared at it. It was a new camera phone that Colleen had gotten him for his birthday, and he wasn't quite familiar with all the settings yet. He saw the flashing icon and realized that a text message had come in. He had just gotten a handle on sign language, now there was a whole new vernacular to learn. He looked at the LCD screen. It was a text message from Colleen. Text messaging was the hottest thing among teenagers these days, but especially for deaf teenagers.

This was an easy one. It read:

TY 4 LUNCH :)

Byrne smiled. *Thank You For Lunch.* He was the luckiest man in the world. He typed:

YW LUL

The message meant: *You're Welcome Love You Lots.* Colleen messaged back:

LUL 2

Then, as always, she signed off by typing:

CBOAO

The message stood for *Colleen Byrne Over And Out.*

Byrne closed the phone, his heart full.

The air conditioner finally began to cool off the room. Byrne considered what to do with himself. Maybe he'd take a ride down to the Roundhouse, hang around the unit. He was just about to talk himself out of that idea when he saw that there was a message on his answering machine.

What was it, five steps away? Seven? At the moment, it looked like the Boston Marathon. He grabbed his cane, braved the pain.

The message was from Paul DiCarlo, a star ADA in the district attorney's office. Over the past five years or so, DiCarlo and Byrne had made a number of cases together. If you were a criminal on trial, you didn't want to look up one day and see Paul DiCarlo enter the courtroom. He was a pit bull in Perry Ellis. If he got you in his jaws, you were fucked. Nobody had sent more killers to death row than Paul DiCarlo.

But the message Paul had for Byrne this day was not good. One of his quarry, it seemed, had loosed itself: Julian Matisse was back on the street.

The news was impossible, but it was true.

It was no secret that Kevin Byrne took a special interest in cases involving the murders of young women. He had felt this way ever since the day Colleen was born. In his mind and heart, every young woman was forever somebody's daughter, somebody's baby girl. Every young woman, at one time, had been that little girl who learned to hold a cup with two hands, had learned to stand up, sea-legged, five tiny fingers on the coffee table.

Girls like Gracie. Two years earlier, Julian Matisse had raped and murdered a young woman named Marygrace Devlin.

Gracie Devlin was nineteen years old the day she was killed. She had curly brown hair that fell in soft ringlets to her shoulders, a light dusting of freckles. She was a slight young woman, a freshman at Villanova. She favored peasant skirts and Indian jewelry and nocturnes by Chopin. She died on a frigid January night in a filthy, abandoned movie theater in South Philadelphia.

And now, by some profane twist of justice, the man who took her dignity and her life was out of prison. Julian Matisse had been sentenced to twenty-five years to life and he was being released after two years.

Two years.

The grass had only grown fully on Gracie's grave this past spring.

Matisse was a small-time pimp, a sadist of the first order. Before Gracie Devlin, he had spent three and a half years in prison for cutting a woman who had refused his advances. Using a box cutter, he had slashed her face so savagely that she had required ten hours of surgery to repair the muscle damage, and nearly four hundred stitches.

Following the box cutter attack, when Matisse was released from Curran-Fromhold prison—after serving only forty months of a ten-year sentence—it didn't take long for him to graduate to homicide. Byrne and his partner Jimmy Purify had liked Matisse for the murder of a Center City waitress named Janine Tillman, but they were never able to find any physical evidence tying him to the crime. Her body was found in Harrowgate Park, stabbed and mutilated. She had been abducted from an underground parking lot on Broad Street. She had been sexually assaulted both pre- and postmortem.

An eyewitness from the parking lot came forward and picked Matisse out of a photo lineup. The witness was an elderly woman named Marjorie Samms. Before they could find Matisse, Marjorie Samms disappeared. A week later they found her floating in the Delaware River.

Supposedly Matisse had been staying with his mother after his release from Curran-Fromhold. Detectives staked out Matisse's mother's apartment, but he never showed. The case went cold.

Byrne knew that he would see Matisse again one day.

Then, two years ago, on a freezing January night, a 911 call came in that a young woman was being attacked in an alleyway behind an abandoned movie theater in South Philadelphia. Byrne and Jimmy were eating dinner a block away and took the call. By the time they reached the scene, the alley was empty, but a blood trail led them inside.

When Byrne and Jimmy entered the theater, they found Gracie on the stage, alone. She had been brutally beaten. Byrne would never forget the tableau—Gracie's limp form on the stage in that frigid theater, steam rising from her body, her life force departing. While the EMS rescue was on the way, Byrne frantically tried to give her CPR. She had breathed once, a slight exhalation of air that had gone into his lungs, the existence leaving her body, entering his. Then, with a slight shudder, she died in his arms. Marygrace Devlin lived nineteen years, two months, and three days.

The Crime Scene Unit found a fingerprint on the scene. It belonged to Julian Matisse. With a dozen detectives on the case, and more than a little intimidation of the low-life crowd with whom Julian Matisse consorted, they found Matisse huddling in a closet in a burned-out row house on Jefferson Street, where they also found a glove covered in Gracie Devlin's blood. Byrne had to be restrained.

Matisse was tried and convicted and sentenced to twenty-five years to life in the state penitentiary at Greene County.

After Gracie's murder, Byrne walked around for many months with the belief that Gracie's breath was still inside him, that her strength impelled him to do his job. For a long time, he felt as if it were the only clean part of him, the only piece of him that had not been sullied by the city.

Now Matisse was out, walking the streets, his face to the sun. The thought made Kevin Byrne sick. He dialed Paul DiCarlo's number.

"DiCarlo."

"Tell me I heard your message wrong."

"Wish I could, Kevin."

"What happened?"

"You know about Phil Kessler?"

Phil Kessler had been a homicide detective for twenty-two years, a divisional detective ten years before that, a loose cannon who more than once had put a fellow detective in jeopardy with his inattention to detail or ignorance of procedure or general lack of nerve.

There were always a few guys in the Homicide Unit who were not very good around dead bodies, and they usually would do whatever they had to do to avoid going out to a crime scene. They made themselves available to go get warrants, round up and transport witnesses, work stakeouts. Kessler was just this sort of detective. He liked the idea of being a homicide detective, but the actual homicide itself freaked him out.

Byrne had worked only one job with Kessler as his primary partner, the case of a girl found in an abandoned gas station in North Philly. It turned out to be an overdose, not a homicide, and Byrne couldn't get away from the man fast enough.

Kessler had retired a year ago. Byrne had heard that the man had late-stage pancreatic cancer.

"I heard he was sick," Byrne said. "I don't know much more than that."

"Well, the word is he doesn't have more than a few months," DiCarlo said. "Maybe not even that long."

As much as Byrne didn't like Phil Kessler, he didn't wish such a painful end on anyone. "I still don't know what this has to do with Julian Matisse."

"Kessler went to the DA and told her that he and Jimmy Purify planted the bloody glove on Matisse. He gave a sworn statement."

The room began to spin. Byrne had to steady himself. "What the fuck are you *talking* about?"

"I'm only telling you what he said, Kevin."

"And you *believe* him?"

"Well, number one, it's not my case. Number two, the Homicide Unit here is looking into it. And three, no. I don't believe him. Jimmy was the most stand-up cop I ever knew."

"Then why does this have traction?"

DiCarlo hesitated. Byrne read the pause as meaning something even worse was coming. How was *that* possible? He found out. "Kessler had a second bloody glove, Kevin. He turned it over. The gloves belonged to Jimmy."

"It's pure fucking bullshit! It's a setup!"

"*I* know it. *You* know it. Anybody who ever rode with Jimmy knows it. Unfortunately, Conrad Sanchez is representing Matisse."

Jesus, Byrne thought. Conrad Sanchez was a legend in the public defender's office, a world-class obstructionist, one of the few who'd decided long ago to make a career out of legal aid. Now in his fifties, he had been a public defender for more than twenty-five years. "Is Matisse's mother still alive?"

"I don't know."

Byrne never got a handle on Matisse's relationship with his mother, Edwina. He'd had his suspicions, though. When they were investigating Gracie's murder, they obtained a search warrant for her apartment. Matisse's room was decorated like a little boy's room: cowboy shades on the lamps, *Star Wars* posters on the walls, a Spider-Man bedspread.

"So he's out?"

"Yeah," DiCarlo said. "They released him two weeks ago pending the appeal."

"Two *weeks*? Why the hell didn't I read about it?"

"This is not exactly a shining moment in the commonwealth's history. Sanchez found a sympathetic judge."

"Do they have him on a monitor?"

"No."

"This fucking *city*." Byrne slammed his hand into the drywall, caving it in. *There goes the security deposit,* he thought. He didn't feel even a slight ripple of pain. Not at that moment, anyway. "Where's he staying?"

"I don't know. We sent a pair of detectives out to his last-known, just to show him a little muscle, but he's in the wind."

"That's just great," Byrne said.

"Listen, I've got to be in court, Kevin. I'll call you later and we'll plot a strategy. Don't worry. We'll put him back. This charge against Jimmy is bullshit. House of cards."

Byrne hung up, rose slowly, painfully to his feet. He grabbed his cane and walked across the living room. He looked out the window, watched the kids and their parents on the street.

For a long time, Byrne had thought that evil was a relative thing; that all sorts of evil walked the earth, each in its own shoes. Then he saw Gracie Devlin's body, and knew that the man who had done that monstrous thing was the embodiment of evil. All that hell would allow on this earth.

Now, after contemplating a day and a week and a month and a lifetime with nothing to do, Byrne had moral imperatives in front of him. All of a sudden there were people he had to see, things he had to do, regardless of how much pain he was in. He walked into the bedroom, pulled open the top drawer of his dresser. He saw Gracie's handkerchief, the small pink silk square.

There is a terrible memory in this cloth, he thought. It had been in Gracie's pocket when she was murdered. Gracie's mother had insisted Byrne take it the day Matisse was sentenced. He removed it from the drawer and—

—her screams echo in his head her warm breath enters his body her blood washes over him hot and glossy in the frigid night air—

*—*stepped back, his pulse now slamming in his ears, his mind deep in denial that what he had just felt was a recurrence of a frightful power he believed was part of his past.

The prescience was back.

MELANIE DEVLIN STOOD at the small barbecue on the tiny back patio of her row house on Emily Street. The smoke rose lazily from the rusting grill, mingling with the thick, humid air. A long-empty bird feeder sat atop the crumbling back wall. The tiny terrace, like most so-called back-yards in Philly, was barely big enough for two people. Somehow she had managed to fit a Weber grill, a pair of sanded wrought-iron chairs, and a small table on it.

In the two years since Byrne had seen Melanie Devlin, she had gained thirty pounds or so. She wore a yellow short set—stretch shorts and a horizontal-striped tank top—but it was not a cheerful yellow. It was not the yellow of daffodils and marigolds and buttercups. It was instead an angry yellow, a yellow that did not welcome the sunshine but rather attempted to drag it into her shattered life. Her hair was short, perfunctorily cut for summer. Her eyes were the color of weak coffee in the midday sun.

Now in her midforties, Melanie Devlin had accepted the burden of sorrow as a constant in her life. She did not fight it any longer. Sadness was her mantle.

Byrne had called and said he was in the neighborhood. He had told her nothing further.

"You sure you can't stay for dinner?" she asked.

"I have to get back," Byrne said. "But thanks for the offer."

Melanie was preparing ribs on the grill. She poured a good amount of salt into her palm, sprinkled it on the meat. Then repeated it. She looked at Byrne, as if to apologize. "I can't taste anything anymore."

Byrne knew what she meant. He wanted to establish a dialogue, though, so he responded. If they chatted for a while, it would make it easier to tell her what he had to tell her. "What do you mean?"

"Since Gracie . . . died, I lost my sense of taste. Crazy, huh? One day, it just disappeared." She dumped more salt on the ribs, quickly, as if in penance. "Now I have to put salt on everything. Ketchup, hot sauce, mayonnaise, sugar. I can't taste food without it." She waved a hand at her figure, explaining her weight gain. Her eyes began to swell with tears. She wiped them away with the back of a hand.

Byrne remained silent. He had observed so many people deal with grief, each in their own way. How many times had he seen women clean their houses over and over after a loss to violence? They fluffed the pillows endlessly, made and remade the beds. Or how many times had he seen men wax their cars beyond reason, or mow their lawns every day? Grief stalks the human heart slowly. People often feel that, if they remain in motion, they might outrun it.

Melanie Devlin stoked the briquettes on the grill, closed the lid. She poured them both a glass of lemonade, sat on the tiny wrought-iron chair opposite him. Someone a few houses down was listening to a Phillies game. They fell silent for a while, feeling the punishing heat of the afternoon. Byrne noticed that Melanie was not wearing her wedding ring. He wondered if she and Garrett had divorced. They certainly wouldn't be the first couple ripped apart by the violent death of a child.

"It was lavender," Melanie finally said.

"Excuse me?"

She glanced at the sun, squinted. She looked back down, spun the glass in her hands a few times. "Gracie's dress. The one we buried her in. It was lavender."

Byrne nodded. He hadn't known this. Grace's service was closed-casket.

"Nobody got to see it, because she was . . . you know," Melanie said. "But it was very pretty. One of her favorites. She was fond of lavender."

Suddenly it occurred to Byrne that Melanie knew why he was there. Not exactly why, of course, but the tenuous thread that bound them—the death of Marygrace Devlin—had to be the reason. Why else would he stop by? Melanie Devlin knew that this visit had something to do with Gracie, and probably felt that if she talked about her daughter in the gentlest of manners, it might ward off any further pain.

Byrne carried that pain in his pocket. How was he going to find the courage to take it out?

He sipped his lemonade. The silence became awkward. A car rolled by, its stereo blasting an old Kinks song. Silence again. Hot, empty, summer silence. Byrne shattered it with what he had to say. "Julian Matisse is out of prison."

Melanie looked at him for a few moments, her eyes stripped of emotion. "No he's not."

It was a flat, even statement. For Melanie, saying it made it so. Byrne had heard it a thousand times. It wasn't as if the person had misunderstood. It was a stall, as if making the statement might cause it to be true, or, given a few seconds, the pill might become coated or smaller.

"I'm afraid so. He was released two weeks ago," Byrne said. "His conviction is being appealed."

"I thought you said that—"

"I know. I'm terribly sorry. Sometimes the system . . ." Byrne trailed off. There really was no explaining it. Especially to someone as scared and angry as Melanie Devlin. Julian Matisse had killed this woman's only child. The police had arrested the man, the courts had tried him, the prisons had taken him and buried him in an iron cage. The memory of it all—although never far from the surface—had begun to fade. And now it was back. It wasn't supposed to be this way.

"When is he going back?" she asked.

Byrne had anticipated the question, but he simply did not have an answer. "Melanie, a lot of people are going to be working very hard on that. I promise you."

"Including you?"

The question made the decision for him, a choice with which he'd been wrestling since he'd heard the news. "Yes," he said. "Including me."

Melanie closed her eyes. Byrne could only imagine the images playing out in her mind. Gracie as a little girl. Gracie in her junior high school play. Gracie in her casket. After a few moments, Melanie stood up. She seemed unhooked in her own space, as if she might float away at any second. Byrne stood up, too. It was his cue to leave.

"I just wanted to make sure you heard it from me," Byrne said. "And to let you know that I'm going to do everything I can to get him back where he belongs."

"He belongs in hell," she said.

Byrne had no argument to answer this.

They stood facing each other for a few uncomfortable moments. Melanie put out her hand to shake. They had never hugged—some people simply didn't express themselves that way. After the trial, after the funeral, even when they said goodbye on that bitter day two years earlier, they had shaken hands. This time, Byrne decided to chance it. He did it as much for Melanie as himself. He reached out and gently pulled her into his arms.

At first, it appeared as if she might resist, but then she fell into him, her legs all but quitting her. He held her closely for a few moments—

—she sits in Gracie's closet with the door closed for hours and hours on end she talks baby talk to Gracie's dolls she has not touched her husband in two years—

—until Byrne broke the embrace, a little shaken by the images in his mind. He made his promises to call soon.

A few minutes later, she walked him through house to the front door. She kissed him on the cheek. He left without another word.

As he drove away, he looked in the rearview mirror one last time. Melanie Devlin stood on the small front stoop of her row house, watching him, her heartache born anew, her cheerless yellow outfit a cry of anguish against a backdrop of callous red brick.

HE FOUND HIMSELF parked in front of the abandoned theater where they had found Gracie. The city flowed around him. The city didn't remember. The city didn't care. He closed his eyes, felt the icy wind as it cut across the street that night, saw the fading light in that young woman's eyes. He had grown up Irish Catholic, and to say he was lapsed was an understatement. The destroyed human beings he had encountered in his life as a police officer had given him a deep understanding of the temporary and brittle nature of life. He had seen so much pain and misery and death. For weeks he had wondered if he was going to go back on the job or take his twenty and run. His papers were on the dresser in the bedroom, ready to be signed. But now he knew he had to go back. Even if it was for just a few weeks. If he wanted to clear Jimmy's name, he would have to do it from the inside.

That evening, as darkness embraced the City of Brotherly Love, as the moonlight crested the skyline, and the city wrote its name in neon, Detective Kevin Francis Byrne showered and dressed, slid a fresh magazine into his Glock, and stepped into the night.

6

SOPHIE BALZANO, EVEN AT THE AGE OF THREE, WAS A BONA FIDE
fashion maven. Granted, when left to her own devices and given free rein
over her clothes, Sophie was likely to come up with an outfit that ran the
entire spectrum from orange to lavender to lime green, from checks to
plaid to stripes, fully accessorized, all within the same ensemble. Coor-
dinates were not her strong suit. She was more of a freewheeling kind of
gal.

On this sweltering July morning, the morning that was to begin an
odyssey that would take Detective Jessica Balzano into the mouth of madness and beyond, she was late, as usual. These days, mornings in the Balzano house were a frenzy of coffee and cereal and gummy bears and lost
little sneakers and missing barrettes and mislaid juice boxes and snapped
shoelaces and traffic reports on KYW on the twos.

Two weeks earlier, Jessica had gotten her hair cut. She'd worn her
hair at least to her shoulders—usually much longer—ever since she was
a little girl. When she had been in uniform, she had tied it in a ponytail
almost constantly. At first, Sophie had followed her around the house,

silently evaluating the fashion move, giving Jessica the eye. After a week or so of intense scrutiny, Sophie wanted her hair cut, too.

Jessica's short hair had certainly helped in her avocation as a professional boxer. What began as a lark had taken on a life of its own. With what seemed like the whole department behind her, Jessica had a record of 4–0 and was starting to get some good press in the boxing magazines.

What a lot of women in boxing didn't understand is, you have to keep your hair short. If you wear your hair long, and keep it in a ponytail, every time you even get tapped on the jaw your hair flies, and the judges give your opponent credit for landing a clean, hard shot. Plus, long hair has the potential to come loose during the fight and get in your eyes. Jessica's first knockout came against a girl named Trudy "Kwik" Kwiatkowski who, in the second round, paused for a second to brush the hair from her eyes. The next thing Kwik knew, she was counting the lights on the ceiling.

Jessica's great-uncle Vittorio—who acted as her manager and trainer—was negotiating a deal with ESPN2. Jessica didn't know if she was more scared of getting in the ring or getting on television. On the other hand, she didn't have JESSIE BALLS on her trunks for nothing.

As Jessica got dressed, the ritual of retrieving her weapon from the hall closet lockbox was missing, as it had been for the past week. She had to admit that she felt naked and vulnerable without her Glock. But it was standard procedure for all officer-involved shootings. She had been on the desk for nearly a week, on administrative leave pending an investigation of the shoot.

She fluffed her hair, applied a bare minimum of lipstick, glanced at the clock. Running late again. So much for schedules. She crossed the hall, tapped on Sophie's door. "Ready to go?" she asked.

Today was Sophie's first day at a preschool not far from their twin row house in Lexington Park, a small community in the eastern section of Northeast Philadelphia. Paula Farinacci, one of Jessica's oldest friends and Sophie's babysitter, was taking her own daughter, Danielle.

"Mom?" Sophie asked from behind the door.

"Yes, honey?"

"Mommy?"

Uh-oh, Jessica thought. There was always a Mom/Mommy preamble whenever Sophie was about to ask a tough question. It was the toddler version of the perp-stall—the technique that knuckleheads on the street used when they were trying to cook an answer for the cops. "Yes, sweetie?"

"When is Daddy coming back?"

Jessica was right. *The* question. She felt her heart drop.

Jessica and Vincent Balzano had been in marriage counseling for almost six weeks and, although they were making progress, and although she missed Vincent terribly, she was not quite ready to allow him back into their lives. He had cheated on her and she was not yet able to forgive him.

Vincent, a narcotics detective working out of Central detectives division, saw Sophie whenever he wanted, and there wasn't the bloodletting there had been in those weeks after she'd introduced his clothing to the front lawn via the upstairs bedroom window. Still, the rancor remained. She had come home and discovered him in bed, in their house, with a South Jersey skank named Michelle Brown, a gap-toothed, saddlebag tramp with frosted hair and QVC jewelry. And those were her selling points.

That was nearly three months ago. Somehow, time was easing Jessica's anger. Things weren't great, but they were getting better.

"Soon, honey," Jessica said. "Daddy's coming home soon."

"I miss Daddy," Sophie said. "Awfully."

Me, too, Jessica thought. "Time to go, sweetie."

"Okay, Mom."

Jessica leaned against the wall, smiling. She thought about what a huge, blank canvas her daughter was. Sophie's new word: *awfully.* The fish sticks were *awfully* good. She was *awfully* tired. It was taking an *awfully* long time to get to Grandpa's house. Where did she get it? Jessica looked at the stickers on Sophie's door, her current menagerie of friends—Pooh, Tigger, Eeyore, Piglet, Mickey, Pluto, Chip and Dale.

Jessica's thoughts of Sophie and Vincent were soon replaced with thoughts about the incident with Trey Tarver, and how close she had come to losing it all. Although she would never admit it to anyone—especially another cop—she had seen that Tec-9 in her nightmares every night since the shooting, had heard the crack of the slug from Trey Tarver's weapon hitting the bricks above her head in every backfire, every slammed door, every television show gunshot.

Like all police officers, when Jessica suited up before each tour, she had only one rule, one overriding canon that trumped all others: to come home to her family in one piece. Nothing else mattered. As long as she was on the force, nothing else ever *would*. Jessica's motto, like most other cops, was as follows:

You draw down on me, you lose. Period. If I'm wrong, you can have my badge, my weapon, even my freedom. But you don't get my life.

Jessica had been offered counseling but, seeing as it was not mandatory, she declined. Perhaps it was the Italian stubbornness in her. Perhaps it was the Italian *female* stubbornness in her. Regardless, the truth of the matter—and it scared her a little—was that she was fine with what happened. God help her, she had shot a man, and she was fine with it.

The good news was that in the ensuing week, the review board had cleared her. It was a clean shoot. Today was her first day back on the street. In the next week or so there would be the preliminary hearing for D'Shante Jackson, but she felt ready. On that day she would have seven thousand angels on her shoulder: every cop in the PPD.

When Sophie came out of her room, Jessica could see that she had another duty. Sophie was wearing two different-colored socks, six plastic bracelets, her grandmother's clip-on faux-garnet earrings, and a hot pink hooded sweatshirt, even though the mercury was supposed to reach ninety today.

While Detective Jessica Balzano may have been a homicide detective out there in the big bad world, in here she had a different assignment. Even a different rank. In here, she was still the commissioner of fashion.

She took her little suspect into custody and marched her back into her room.

THE HOMICIDE UNIT of the Philadelphia Police Department was sixty-five detectives strong, working all three tours, seven days a week. Philadelphia was consistently in the top twelve cities nationwide when it came to the homicide rate, and the general chaos and buzz and activity in the duty room reflected it. The unit was on the first floor of the police administration building at Eighth and Race streets, also known as the Roundhouse.

As Jessica pushed through the glass doors, she nodded to a number of officers and detectives. Before she could round the corner to the bank of elevators she heard: " 'Morning, Detective."

Jessica turned to the familiar voice. It was Officer Mark Underwood. Jessica had been in uniform about four years when Underwood came to the Third District, her old stomping grounds. Fresh-faced and fresh out of the academy, he had been one of a handful of rookies assigned to the South Philly district that year. She had helped train a few officers in his class.

"Hey, Mark."

"How are you?"

"Never better," Jessica said. "Still at the Third?"

"Oh yeah," Underwood said. "But I've been detailed to that movie they're making."

"Uh-oh," Jessica said. Everyone in town knew about the new Will Parrish flick they were shooting. That's why every wannabe in town was heading to South Philly this week. "Lights, camera, attitude."

Underwood laughed. "You got that right."

It was a pretty common sight in the past few years. The huge trucks, the big lights, the barricades. Due to a very aggressive and accommodating film office, Philadelphia was becoming a hub for movie production. Although some officers considered it a plum detail to be assigned to security for the duration of the shoot, it was mostly a lot of standing around. The city itself had a love–hate relationship with the movies. Quite often it was an inconvenience. But then there was Philly pride.

Somehow Mark Underwood still looked like a college kid. Somehow *she* was already over thirty. Jessica remembered the day he joined the force like it was yesterday.

"I heard you're in the Show," Underwood said. "Congratulations."

"Captain by forty," Jessica replied, inwardly wincing at the word *forty*. "Watch and see."

"No doubt." Underwood looked at his watch. "Gotta hit the street. Good seeing you."

"Same here."

"We're getting together at Finnigan's Wake tomorrow night," Underwood said. "Sergeant O'Brien's retiring. Stop by for a beer. We'll catch up."

"Are you sure you're old enough to drink?" Jessica asked.

Underwood laughed. "Have a safe tour, Detective."

"Thanks," she said. "You, too."

Jessica watched him square his cap, sheathe his baton, make his way down the ramp, skirting the ever-present row of smokers.

Officer Mark Underwood was a three-year vet.

Man was she getting old.

WHEN JESSICA ENTERED the duty room of the Homicide Unit, she was greeted by the handful of detectives hanging on from the last-out shift, the tour that began at midnight. Rare was the shift that ran only eight hours. Much of the time, if your shift began at midnight, you managed to get out of the building around 10:00 AM, then head right over to the Criminal Justice Center, where you waited in a crowded courtroom until the afternoon to testify, then caught a few hours' sleep, then returned to the Roundhouse. It was for reasons like these, among many others, that the people in this room, this building, were your true family. The rate of alcoholism supported that fact, as did the rate of divorce. Jessica had vowed to become a statistic of neither.

Sergeant Dwight Buchanan was one of the day-watch supervisors, a thirty-eight-year veteran of the PPD. He wore every minute of it on his badge. After the incident in the alley, Buchanan had arrived on the scene and taken Jessica's weapon, directing the mandatory debriefing of an officer involved in a shooting, running liaison with Internal Affairs. Although he was not on duty when the incident occurred, he had gotten out of bed and rushed down to the scene to look out for one of his own. It was moments like this that bound the men and women in blue in a way most people would never understand.

Jessica had worked the desk for nearly a week and was glad to be back on the Line Squad. She was no house cat.

Buchanan handed her back her Glock. "Welcome back, Detective."

"Thank you, sir."

"Ready for the street?"

Jessica held up her weapon. "The question is, is the street ready for me?"

"There's someone here to see you." He pointed over her shoulder. Jessica turned around. There was a man leaning against the assignment desk, a big man with emerald-green eyes and sandy hair. A man with the bearing of someone stalked by powerful demons.

It was her partner, Kevin Byrne.

Jessica's heart fluttered for a moment as their eyes met. They had only been partnered a few days when Kevin Byrne had been shot this past spring, but what they had shared that terrible week was so intimate, so personal, that it went beyond something even lovers felt. It spoke to their souls. It appeared that neither of them, even over the course of the past few months, had time to reconcile these feelings. It was unknown whether Kevin Byrne was going to return to the force and, if he did, whether or not he and Jessica would be partnered again. She had meant to call him in the past few weeks. She had not.

The bottom line was that Kevin Byrne had taken one for the company—had taken one for Jessica—and he deserved better from her. She felt bad, but she was really glad to see him.

Jessica crossed the room, arms out. They embraced, a little awkwardly, separated.

"Are you back?" Jessica asked.

"The doctor says I'm on forty-eight, off forty-eight. But yeah. I'm back."

"I can hear the crime rate dropping already."

Byrne smiled. There was sadness in it. "Got room for your old partner?"

"I think we can find a bucket and a crate," Jessica said.

"That's all us old-school guys need, you know. Get me a flintlock and I'll be all set."

"You got it."

It was a moment Jessica had both longed for and dreaded. After the bloody incident on Easter Sunday, how would they be together? Would it, *could* it, be the same? She had no idea. It looked like she was going to find out.

Ike Buchanan let the moment play out. When he was certain it had, he held up an object. A videocassette. He said: "I want you two to see this."

7

JESSICA, BYRNE, AND IKE BUCHANAN HUDDLED IN THE CRAMPED snack room that held a bank of small video monitors and VCRs. After a few moments, a third man entered.

"This is Special Agent Terry Cahill," Buchanan said. "Terry is on loan from the FBI's task force on urban crime, but just for a few days."

Cahill was in his midthirties. He wore the standard-issue navy-blue suit, white shirt, burgundy-and-blue-striped tie. He was fair-haired, combed and collegial, good-looking in a J.-Crew-catalog, buttondown kind of way. He smelled like strong soap and good leather.

Buchanan finished the introductions. "This is Detective Jessica Balzano."

"Nice to meet you, Detective," Cahill said.

"Same here."

"This is Detective Kevin Byrne."

"Good to meet you."

"My pleasure, Agent Cahill," Byrne said.

Cahill and Byrne shook hands. Cool, mechanical, professional. You could slice the interagency rivalry with a rusty butter knife. Cahill then turned his attention back to Jessica. "You're the boxer?" he asked.

She knew what he meant, but still it sounded funny. Like she was a dog. *You're the schnauzer?* "Yes."

He nodded, apparently impressed.

"Why do you ask?" Jessica asked. "Plan on getting out of line, Agent Cahill?"

Cahill laughed. He had straight teeth, a single dimple on the left. "No, no. I've just done a little boxing myself."

"Professional?"

"Nothing like that. Golden Gloves mostly. Some in the service."

Now it was Jessica's turn to be impressed. She knew what it took to square off in the ring.

"Terry is here to observe and make recommendations to the task force," Buchanan said. "The bad news is that we need the help."

It was true. Violent crime, across the board, was up in Philadelphia. Still, there wasn't an officer in the department who wanted any outside agencies butting in. *Observe,* Jessica thought. *Right.*

"How long have you been with the bureau?" Jessica asked.

"Seven years."

"Are you from Philadelphia?"

"Born and raised," Cahill said. "Tenth and Washington."

The whole time, Byrne just stood back, listening, observing. This was his style. On the other hand, he'd been on the job more than twenty years, Jessica thought. He had a lot more experience distrusting feds.

Sensing a territorial skirmish, good-natured or otherwise, Buchanan inserted the tape into one of the VCRs and hit PLAY.

After a few seconds, a black-and-white image rolled to life on one of the monitors. It was a feature film. Alfred Hitchcock's *Psycho,* the 1960 film starring Anthony Perkins and Janet Leigh. The picture was a little grainy, the video signal blurry around the edges. The scene that was cued up on the tape was well into the film, beginning where Janet Leigh, having checked into the Bates Motel, and having shared a sandwich with Norman Bates in his office, was preparing to take a shower.

As the film unspooled, Byrne and Jessica glanced at each other. It was clear that Ike Buchanan wouldn't have called them in for a horror classic morning matinee but, at the moment, neither detective had the slightest clue what this was all about.

They continued to watch as the movie rolled on. Norman removing the oil painting from the wall. Norman peeking through the crudely cut hole in the plaster. Janet Leigh's character—Marion Crane—undressing, slipping on her robe. Norman walking up to the Bates house. Marion stepping into the bathtub and shutting the curtain.

Everything seemed normal until there was a glitch in the tape, the type of slow, vertical roll produced by a crash edit. For a second the screen went black; then a new image appeared. It was immediately clear that the movie had been recorded over.

The new shot was static, a high-angle view of what looked like a motel bathroom. The wide-angle lens showed a sink, toilet, bathtub, a tile floor. The light level was low, but there was enough brightness thrown by the fixture above the mirror to illuminate the room. The black-and-white image had a coarse look to it, like the image produced by a web-cam or an inexpensive camcorder.

As the tape continued, it appeared that someone was in the shower with the curtain pulled closed. The ambient sound on the tape yielded the faint noise of water running, and every so often the shower curtain billowed out with the movement of whoever was standing in the tub. A shadow danced on the translucent plastic. Beneath the sound of the water was a young woman's voice. She was singing a song by Norah Jones.

Jessica and Byrne looked at each other again, this time with the knowledge that this was one of those situations when you know you are watching something you shouldn't be seeing, and by the very fact that you were watching it, something bad was imminent. Jessica glanced at Cahill. He seemed riveted. A vein pulsed in his temple.

On the screen, the camera remained stationary. Steam emerged from above the shower curtain, slightly blurring the top quarter of the picture with condensation.

Then, suddenly, the bathroom door opened and a figure entered. The slender person appeared to be an elderly woman with gray hair pulled back into a bun. She wore a flower-print calf-length housedress and a dark cardigan sweater. She held a large butcher knife. The woman's face was not visible. The woman had a man's shoulders, a man's deportment and bearing.

After a few seconds' hesitation the figure drew back the curtain, and it became clear that there was a naked young woman in the shower, but the angle was too steep, and the picture quality too poor, to even begin to as-certain what she looked like. From this vantage, all that could be deter-mined was that the young woman was white and probably in her twenties.

Instantly the reality of what they were watching settled upon Jessica like a pall. Before she could react, the knife held by the shadowy figure descended upon the woman in the shower over and over, ripping at her flesh, slicing her chest, arms, stomach. The woman screamed. Blood spouted, splashing the tile. Gobbets of torn tissue and muscle slapped the walls. The figure continued to viciously stab the young woman, over and over and over, until she slumped to the floor of the tub, her body a horrible crosshatch of deep, gaping wounds.

Then, as quickly as it began, it was over.

The old woman ran from the room. The showerhead washed the blood down the drain. The young woman didn't move. A few seconds later there was a second crash edit, and the original movie resumed. The new image was the extreme close-up of Janet Leigh's right eye as the camera began to turn and move backward. The film's original soundtrack soon returned to Anthony Perkins's chilling scream from the Bates house:

Mother! Oh God Mother! Blood! Blood!

When Ike Buchanan shut off the tape, silence embraced the small room for nearly a full minute.

They had just witnessed a murder.

Someone had videotaped a brutal, savage killing and inserted it into the precise place in *Psycho* where the shower scene murder occurred. They had all seen enough true carnage to know that this was not some special-effects footage. Jessica said it out loud.

"This is real."

Buchanan nodded. "It sure looks like it. What we just watched is a dubbed copy. AV is going over the original tape now. It's of a little better quality, but not much."

"Is there any more of this on the tape?" Cahill asked.

"Nothing," Buchanan said. "Just the original movie."

"Where is this tape from?"

"It was rented at a small video store on Aramingo," Buchanan said.

"Who brought it in?" Byrne asked.

"He's in A."

THE YOUNG MAN sitting in Interview Room A was the color of sour milk. He was in his early twenties, had close-cropped dark hair, pale amber eyes, fine features. He wore a lime-green Polo shirt and black jeans. His

229—a brief report detailing his name, address, place of employment—revealed that he was a student at Drexel University and worked two part-time jobs. He lived in the Fairmount section of North Philadelphia. His name was Adam Kaslov. The only prints on the videotape were his.

Jessica entered the room, introduced herself. Kevin Byrne and Terry Cahill observed through the two-way mirror.

"Can I get you anything?" Jessica asked.

Adam Kaslov offered a thin, bleak smile. "I'm okay," he said. There was a pair of empty Sprite cans on the scarred table in front of him. He had a piece of red cardboard in his hands, twisting it and untwisting it.

Jessica placed the *Psycho* videocassette box on the table. It was still in a clear plastic evidence bag. "When did you rent this?"

"Yesterday afternoon," Adam said, his voice a little shaky. He had no police record and this was, perhaps, the first time he had ever been in a police station. A Homicide Unit interrogation room no less. Jessica had made sure to leave the door open. "Maybe three o'clock or so."

Jessica glanced at the label on the tape housing. "And you got this at The Reel Deal on Aramingo?"

"Yes."

"How did you pay for this?"

"Excuse me?"

"Did you put this on a credit card? Pay cash? Have a coupon?"

"Oh," he said. "I paid cash."

"Did you keep the receipt?"

"No. Sorry."

"Are you a regular there?"

"Kind of."

"How often do you rent movies at that location?"

"I don't know. Maybe twice a week."

Jessica glanced at the 229 report. One of Adam's part-time jobs was at a Rite Aid on Market Street. The other was at the Cinemagic 3 at Penn, the movie theater near the Hospital of the University of Pennsylvania. "Can I ask why you go to that store?"

"What do you mean?"

"You live only half a block from a Blockbuster."

Adam shrugged. "I guess it's because they have more foreign and independent films than the big chains."

"You like foreign films, Adam?" Jessica's tone was friendly, conversational. Adam brightened slightly.

"Yeah."

"I like *Cinema Paradiso* a lot," Jessica said. "One of my favorite movies of all times. Ever see that one?"

"Sure," Adam said. Even brighter, now. "Giuseppe Tornatore is great. Maybe even the heir apparent to Fellini."

Adam was beginning to relax somewhat. He had been twisting that piece of cardboard into a tight spiral, which he now put down. It looked stiff enough to be a swizzle stick. Jessica sat in the battered metal chair opposite him. Just two people talking, now. Talking about a vicious homicide someone had videotaped.

"Did you watch this alone?" Jessica asked.

"Yeah." There was a morsel of melancholy in his answer, as if he had recently broken off a relationship and was accustomed to watching videos with a partner.

"When did you watch it?"

Adam picked up the cardboard swizzle stick again. "Well, I get off work at my second job at midnight, I get home around twelve thirty. I usually take a shower and eat something. I guess I started it around one or one thirty. Maybe two."

"Did you watch it straight through?"

"No," Adam said. "I watched up until Janet Leigh gets to the motel."

"Then what?"

"Then I shut it off and went to bed. I watched . . . the rest this morning. Before I left for school. Or, before I was *going* to leave for school. When I saw the . . . you know, I called the cops. Police. I called the *police*."

"Did anyone else see this?"

Adam shook his head.

"Did you tell anybody about it?"

"No."

"Was this tape in your possession the whole time?"

"I'm not sure what you mean."

"From the time you rented it until the time you called the police, did you have possession of the tape?"

"Yes."

"You didn't leave it in your car for a while, leave it with a friend, leave it in a backpack or a book bag that you hung on a coatrack somewhere public?"

"No," Adam said. "Nothing like that. I rented it, took it home, and put it on top of the TV."

"And you live alone."

Another grimace. He *had* just broken up with someone. "Yes."

"Was anyone in your apartment when you were at work yesterday evening?"

"I don't think so," Adam said. "No. I really doubt it."

"No one else has a key?"

"Just the landlord. And I've been trying to get him to fix my shower for, like, a year. I doubt he would come around without me being there."

Jessica made a few notes. "Have you ever rented this movie from The Reel Deal before?"

Adam looked at the floor for a few moments, thinking. "The movie or this particular tape?"

"Either."

"I think I rented the DVD of *Psycho* from them last year."

"Why did you rent the VHS version this time?"

"My DVD player is broken. I have an optical drive in my laptop, but I don't really like watching movies on a computer. The sound kind of sucks."

"Where was this tape in the store when you rented it?"

"Where *was* it?"

"I mean, do they display the tapes on racks there, or do they just have empty boxes on the racks and keep the tapes behind the counter?"

"No, they have actual tapes on display."

"Where was this tape?"

"There's a section called Classics. It was in there."

"Are they displayed alphabetically?"

"I think so."

"Do you recall if this movie was right where it was supposed to be on the rack?"

"I don't remember."

"Did you rent anything else along with this?"

Adam drained of what little color remained in his face, as if the idea, the very notion, that other tapes might contain something this horrible was a possibility. "No. That was the only one."

"Do you know any of the other customers there?"

"Not really."

"Do you know anyone else who may have rented this tape?"

"No," he said.

"Here's a tough one," Jessica said. "Are you ready?"

"I guess so."

"Do you recognize the young woman on the tape?"

Adam swallowed hard, shook his head. "Sorry."

"That's okay," Jessica said. "We're just about done for now. You're doing great."

This dislodged a crooked half smile from the young man. The fact that he was going to leave soon—the fact that he was going to leave at *all*—seemed to lift a heavy yoke from his shoulders. Jessica made a few more notes, glanced at her watch.

Adam asked: "Can I ask *you* something?"

"Sure."

"Is that part, like, *real*?"

"We're not certain."

Adam nodded. Jessica held his gaze, looking for the slightest sign that he might be hiding something. All she found was a young man who stumbled onto something bizarre and, probably, terrifyingly real. Talk about your horror movie.

"Okay, Mr. Kaslov," she said. "We appreciate you bringing this in. We'll be in touch."

"Okay," Adam said. "Are we done?"

"Yes. And we'd appreciate it if you didn't discuss this with anyone for the time being."

"I won't."

They stood, shook hands. Adam Kaslov's hand was ice.

"One of the officers will walk you down," Jessica added.

"Thanks," he said.

As the young man walked out into the duty room of the Homicide Unit, Jessica glanced at the two-way mirror. Although she couldn't see through it, she didn't have to read Kevin Byrne's face to know they were in total agreement. Chances were good that Adam Kaslov had nothing to do with the crime committed on the tape.

If, in fact, a crime had actually been committed.

———

BYRNE TOLD JESSICA he would meet her in the parking lot. When he found himself relatively alone and unobserved in the duty room, he sat at one of the computers, ran a check on Julian Matisse. As expected, there was nothing current. There had been a break-in at Matisse's mother's house a year earlier, but nothing involving Julian. Matisse had been in prison for the past two years. His list of known associates was outdated as well. Byrne printed off the addresses anyway, tore the sheet from the printer.

Then, although he may have been screwing up another detective's work, he dumped the computer's cache and erased the PCIC history for the day.

ON THE GROUND floor of the Roundhouse, in the back, was a lunchroom with a dozen or so battered booths, a dozen tables. The food was passable, the coffee was forty-weight. A bank of vending machines held down one wall. Large windows with an unobstructed view of the air-conditioning units held down the other.

As Jessica grabbed a pair of coffees for her and Byrne, Terry Cahill walked into the room, approached her. The handful of uniformed cops and detectives scattered around the room gave him the casual, appraising eye. He really did have *fed* written all over him, right down to his highly polished yet sensible cordovan oxfords. Jessica would bet that he ironed his socks.

"Got a second, Detective?"

"Just," Jessica said. She and Byrne were on their way to the video store where the *Psycho* tape had been rented.

"I just wanted to tell you that I won't be riding with you this morning. I'll run what we have through VICAP and the other federal databases. See if we get a hit."

We'll try to get by without you, Jessica thought. "That would be very helpful," she said, suddenly aware how patronizing she sounded. Like herself, this guy was just doing his job. Luckily, it appeared as if Cahill hadn't noticed.

"Not a problem," he replied. "I'll try to hook up with you in the field as soon as I can."

"Okay."

"Great to be working with you," he said.

"You, too," Jessica lied.

She capped the coffees and made her way to the door. At the door she caught her reflection in the glass, then looked beyond, racking her focus, at the room behind her. Special Agent Terry Cahill was leaning against the counter, smiling.

Is he checking me out?

8

THE REEL DEAL WAS A SMALL, INDEPENDENT VIDEO STORE ON Aramingo Avenue near Clearfield, shoehorned between a Vietnamese takeout and a nail salon called Claws and Effect. It was one of the few mom-and-pop video stores in Philadelphia not yet put out of business by Blockbuster or West Coast Video.

The grimy front window held posters of Vin Diesel and Jet Li movies, cascaded over a decade of teen romantic comedies. There were also sun-leached black-and-white head shots of fading action stars: Jean-Claude Van Damme, Steven Seagal, Jackie Chan. One corner of the window bore a sign proclaiming WE CARRY CULT AND MEXI-MONSTERS!

Jessica and Byrne entered.

The Reel Deal was a long, narrow space, with videotapes lining both walls and a two-sided rack down the center. The racks had handmade signs above them, plaques denoting genre: DRAMA, COMEDY, ACTION, FOREIGN, FAMILY. Something called ANIME took up a third of one wall. A glance at the CLASSICS rack showed a full range of Hitchcock movies.

In addition to the movies for rent were racks of microwave popcorn, soft drinks, chips, film magazines. On the walls above the tapes were curling movie posters, mostly action and horror titles, with a few Merchant-Ivory one-sheets sprinkled in for class.

To the right, next to the entrance, was the slightly elevated checkout counter. The movie running on the monitor mounted on the wall was a 1970s slasher flick Jessica didn't immediately recognize. The requisite scantily clad coed was being chased through a dark basement by a knife-wielding, mask-wearing psychopath.

The clerk behind the counter was in his late teens. He had long dirty-blond hair, kneehole jeans, a Wilco T-shirt, a spike wristband. Jessica couldn't tell which iteration of grunge he was emulating: the original Neil Young version, the Nirvana/Pearl Jam nexus, or some new breed of which she, at the ancient age of thirty, was not familiar.

There were a handful of browsers in the store. Beneath the cloying smell of strawberry incense was the faint aroma of some pretty good pot.

Byrne showed the clerk his badge.

"Whoa," the kid said. His bloodshot eyes darted to the beaded doorway behind him and to what was, Jessica was fairly certain, his small stash of weed.

"What's your name?" Byrne asked.

"My *name?*"

"Yeah," Byrne said. "That's the thing other people call you when they want to get your attention."

"Uh, Leonard," he said. "Leonard Puskas. Lenny, actually."

"Are you the manager, Lenny?" Byrne asked.

"Well not, like, officially."

"Meaning, like, what?"

"Meaning I open and close and do all the ordering and all the other work around here. All for minimum wage."

Byrne held up the outer box for the copy of *Psycho* that Adam Kaslov had rented. The Audio Visual Unit still had the original tape.

"Hitch," Lenny said, nodding. "A classic."

"You're a fan?"

"Oh yeah. Big time," Lenny said. "Although, I never really got into his political stuff in the sixties. *Topaz, Torn Curtain.*"

"I see."

"But *The Birds? North by Northwest? Rear Window?* Awesome."

"What about *Psycho,* Lenny?" Byrne asked. "Are you a fan of *Psycho?*"

Lenny sat up straight, wrapped his arms around his chest, straitjacket style. He sucked in his cheeks, clearly getting ready to do some sort of impression. He said: "I wouldn't hurt a fly."

Jessica exchanged a glance and a shrug with Byrne. "And who was that supposed to be?" Byrne asked.

Lenny looked crushed. "That was Anthony Perkins. That's his line from the end of the movie. He doesn't actually say it, of course. It's a voice-over. Actually, technically, the voice-over says *Why, she wouldn't even hurt a fly,* but—" Lenny's look of hurt instantly morphed into one of horror. "You've *seen* it, haven't you? I mean . . . I didn't . . . I'm a *real* stickler on spoilers."

"I've seen the movie," Byrne said. "I've just never seen anyone do Anthony Perkins before."

"I can do Martin Balsam, too. Wanna see?"

"Maybe later."

"Okay."

"This tape is from this store?"

Lenny squinted at the label on the side of the box. "Yeah," he said. "That's ours."

"We need to know the rental history of this particular tape."

"No prob," he said in his best Junior G-Man voice. This was going to be a great story around the bong later. He reached under the counter and took out a thick spiral notebook, began to turn over pages.

As he flipped through the book, Jessica noted that the pages were stained with just about every condiment known to man, and a few blots of unknown origin she didn't even want to think about.

"Your records aren't computerized?" Byrne asked.

"Uh, that would require software," Lenny said. "And *that* would require an actual expenditure."

It was clear that there was no love lost between Lenny and his boss.

"It's only been out three times this year," Lenny finally said. "Including the rental yesterday."

"To three different people?" Jessica asked.

"Yeah."

"Do your records go back farther?"

"Yeah," Lenny said. "But we had to replace *Psycho* last year. The old tape broke, I think. That copy you have there has only been out three times."

"Doesn't seem like a lot of rentals for a classic," Byrne said.

"Most folks take out the DVD."

"And this is your only copy of the VHS version?" Jessica asked.

"Yes, ma'am."

Ma'am, Jessica thought. *I'm a ma'am.* "We'll need the names and addresses of the people who rented this tape."

Lenny looked left and right, as if a pair of ACLU lawyers with whom he might confer on this matter might flank him. Instead, he was flanked by life-size cardboard cutouts of Nicolas Cage and Adam Sandler. "I don't think I'm allowed to do that."

"Lenny," Byrne said, leaning in. He crooked his finger, motioning him to lean closer. Lenny did. "Did you notice the badge I showed you when we walked in?"

"Yeah. I saw that."

"Good. Here's the deal. If you give me the information I asked for, I'll try and overlook the fact that it smells a little bit like Bob Marley's rec room in here. Okay?"

Lenny leaned back. It appeared as if he was unaware that the strawberry incense didn't completely cover the aroma of the reefer. "Okay. No prob."

While Lenny looked for a pen, Jessica glanced at the monitor on the wall. A new movie was running. An old black-and-white noir with Veronica Lake and Alan Ladd.

"Do you want me to write these names down for you?" Lenny asked.

"I think we can handle it," Jessica replied.

In addition to Adam Kaslov, the two other people who had rented the movie were a man named Isaiah Crandall and a woman named Emily Trager. They both lived within three or four blocks of the store.

"Do you know Adam Kaslov well?" Byrne asked.

"Adam? Oh yeah. Good dude."

"How so?"

"Well, he has good taste in movies. Pays his late fees without a hassle. We talk independent film sometimes. We're both Jim Jarmusch fans."

"Is Adam in here a lot?"

"I guess. Maybe twice a week."

"Does he come in alone?"

"Most of the time. Although I did see him in here once with an older woman."

"Do you know who she was?"

"No."

"Older as in how old?" Byrne asked.

"Twenty-five maybe."

Jessica and Byrne exchanged a glance and a sigh. "What did she look like?"

"Blond, pretty. Nice body. You know. For an older gal."

"Do you know either of these other people well?" Jessica asked, tapping the book.

Lenny turned the book, read the names. "Sure. I know Emily."

"She's a regular?"

"Kind of."

"What can you tell us about her?"

"Not much," Lenny said. "I mean, we don't hang or anything."

"Whatever you can tell us would be most helpful."

"Well, she always buys a bag of cherry Twizzlers when she rents a movie. She wears a little too much perfume but, you know, compared with the way some of the people who come in here smell, it's actually kind of nice."

"How old is she?" Byrne asked.

Lenny shrugged. "I don't know. Seventy?"

Jessica and Byrne exchanged another glance. Although they were fairly certain that the "old woman" on the tape was a man, crazier things had happened.

"What about Mr. Crandall?" Byrne asked.

"Him I don't know. Hang on." Lenny brought out a second notebook. He thumbed to a page. "Yeah. He's only been a member here about three weeks."

Jessica wrote it down. "I'm also going to need the names and addresses of all the other employees."

Lenny frowned again, but didn't even bother trying to object. "There are only two of us. Me and Juliet."

At this, a young woman poked her head out between the beaded curtains. She had clearly been listening. If Lenny Puskas was the poster boy for grunge, his co-employee was the poster girl for Goth. Short and stocky, about eighteen, she had purple-black hair, deep burgundy fingernails, black lipstick. She wore a long lemon vintage taffeta dress, Doc Martens, and thick white-rimmed glasses.

"That's fine," Jessica said. "I just need home contact information for both of you."

Lenny scribbled down the information, handed it to Jessica.

"Do you rent a lot of Hitchcock films here?" Jessica asked.

"Sure," Lenny said. "We've got most of them, including some of the early ones like *The Lodger* and *Young and Innocent*. But, like I said, most people rent the DVDs. The older movies look a lot better on disc. Especially the Criterion Collection editions."

"What are the Criterion Collection editions?" Byrne asked.

"They put out classic and foreign films in remastered versions. Lots of extras on the disc. Real quality stuff."

Jessica made a few notes. "Is there anybody you can think of who rents a lot of Hitchcock movies? Or someone who has been asking for them?"

Lenny thought about it. "Not really. I mean, not that I can think of." He turned and looked at his coworker. "Jools?"

The girl in the yellow taffeta dress swallowed hard and shook her head. She wasn't handling a visit from the police all that well.

"Sorry," Lenny added.

Jessica glanced at all four corners of the store. There were two surveillance cameras at the back. "Do you have tapes from these cameras available?"

Lenny snorted again. "Uh, no. Those are just for show. They're not connected to anything. Between you and me, we're lucky there's a lock on the front door."

Jessica handed Lenny a pair of cards. "If either of you think of anything else, anything that might be connected to this tape, please give me a call."

Lenny held the cards as if they might explode in his hands. "Sure. No prob."

The two detectives walked the half block to the department-issue Taurus, a dozen questions floating. At the top of this list was whether or not they were actually investigating a homicide. Homicide detectives in Philadelphia were funny that way. There was always an overflowing plate in front of you, and if there was even the slightest chance that you were off on a hunt over what was actually a suicide or an accident or something else, you generally bitched and moaned until you were allowed to pass it off.

Still, the boss had handed them a job, and off they had to go. Most homicide investigations began with the crime scene and the victim. Rare was the case that began at a point before that.

They got in the car and headed off to interview Mr. Isaiah Crandall, classic film buff and potential psychotic killer.

Across the street from the video store, shadowed in a doorway, a man watched the drama unfold inside The Reel Deal. He was unremarkable in all ways, except in his capacity to adapt to his surroundings, like a chameleon. At this moment he might be mistaken for Harry Lime in *The Third Man*.

Later in the day he might be Gordon Gekko in *Wall Street*.

Or Tom Hagen in *The Godfather*.

Or Babe Levy in *Marathon Man*.

Or Archie Rice in *The Entertainer*.

For when he stepped before his public he could be many men, many characters. He could be a doctor, a dockworker, the drummer in a lounge band. He could be a priest, a doorman, a librarian, a travel agent, even a law enforcement officer.

He was a man of a thousand guises, skilled in the arts of dialect and stage movement. He could be whatever the day called for.

This, after all, was what actors do.

9

AT ROUGHLY THIRTY-THREE THOUSAND FEET OVER ALTOONA, Pennsylvania, Seth Goldman finally began to unwind. For a man who had found himself inside an airplane an average of three days a week for the past four years—they had just taken off from Philadelphia, heading to Pittsburgh, they'd be returning in only a few hours—he was still a white-knuckle flier. Every bump of turbulence, every raised aileron, every air pocket filled him with dread.

But now, in the well-appointed Learjet 60, he began to unwind. If you had to fly, sitting in a rich butter-cream leather seat, with burl wood and brass appointments around you, and a fully stocked galley at your disposal, was definitely the way to go.

Ian Whitestone was sitting at the rear of the jet, shoes off, eyes closed, headphones on. It was at times like these—when Seth knew where his boss was, with the day's activities planned and security in place—that he allowed himself to relax.

Seth Goldman was born thirty-seven years ago as Jerzy Andres Kiedrau, hardscrabble-poor in Muse, Florida. The only son of a sassy, opinionated woman and a black-hearted man, he had been an unplanned, unwanted late-life baby, and from the first days he could remember, his father had reminded him of this.

When Krystof Kiedrau wasn't beating his wife, he was beating and berating his only son. Some nights the arguments got so loud, the blood-letting became so brutal, that young Jerzy had to flee the trailer, running far into the low scrub fields that bordered the trailer park, coming home at dawn covered with sand beetle bites and the welts of a hundred mos-quito stings.

During those years, Jerzy had one solace: the movies. He had worked odd jobs, scrubbing down trailers, running errands, cleaning pools, and as soon as he had enough for a matinee, he would hitchhike to Palmdale and the Lyceum Theater.

He recalled many afternoons in the cool darkness of the theater, a place where he could lose himself in the world of fantasy. Early on he realized the power of the medium to transport, to exalt, to mystify, to terrify. It was a love affair that never ended.

When he returned home, if his mother was sober, he would discuss the film he had seen with her. His mother knew all about the movies. She had once been an actress, having appeared in more than a dozen films, making her debut as a teenager in the late 1940s under the stage name Lily Trieste.

She had worked with all the important directors of noir—Dmytryk, Siodmak, Dassin, Lang. The shining moment in her career—a career that mostly had her lurking in shadowed alleys, smoking unfiltered cigarettes with a slew of nearly handsome men sporting thin mustaches and double-breasted notch-lapel suits—had been a scene with Franchot Tone, a scene where she uttered one of Jerzy's favorite lines of noir dialogue. Standing in the doorway to a cold-water walk-up, she had stopped brush-ing her hair, turned to the actor, who was being led away by the authori-ties, and said:

"I spent the morning washing you out of my hair, baby. Don't make me give you the brush."

By the time she reached her midthirties, the industry cast her aside. Not wanting to settle for the crazy-aunt roles, she moved to Florida to live with her sister, and it was there she met her future husband. Her ca-reer had long been over by the time she'd given birth to Jerzy at the age of forty-seven.

At fifty-six, Krystof Kiedrau was diagnosed with advanced cirrhosis of the liver, the result of drinking a fifth of bottom-shelf whiskey every

day for thirty-five years. He was told that if he drank another drop of alcohol, he could fall into an alcohol-induced coma, which could ulti-
mately prove fatal. For a few months, the warning had scared Krystof
Kiedrau into abstinence. Then, after losing his part-time job, Krystof had
tied one on and come home blind drunk.

He beat his wife mercilessly that night, the final blow, one that drove
her head into a sharp cabinet handle, pierced her temple, causing a deep
gash. By the time Jerzy got home from his job sweeping up the auto body
shop in Moore Haven, his mother had bled to death in the corner of the
kitchen, and his father was sitting in his chair, half a bottle of whiskey in
his hand, three full bottles at his side, his grease-stained wedding album
in his lap.

Fortunately for young Jerzy, Krystof Kiedrau was too far gone to
stand up, let alone light into him.

Late into the night Jerzy poured his father glass after glass of whiskey,
at times helping the man bring the filthy tumbler to his lips. By midnight,
with two bottles left, Krystof began to drift in and out of a stupor, and
could no longer hold the glass. Jerzy then began to pour the whiskey directly down his father's throat. By four thirty, his father had consumed a
total of four full fifths of alcohol, and at exactly five ten that morning he
fell into an alcohol coma. A few minutes later he took his final foul
breath.

A few hours later, with both his parents dead, the flies already seek-
ing out their decaying flesh in the stifling confines of the trailer, Jerzy
called the police.

After a brief investigation, during which Jerzy said barely a word, he
was placed into a group home in Lee County where he learned the art of
persuasion and social manipulation. At eighteen he went to Edison Community College. He was a quick study, a brilliant student, and he attacked his studies with a fervor for knowledge he had never known was
within him. Two years later, his associate's degree in hand, Jerzy moved
to North Miami, where he sold cars by day and earned his bachelor's degree at night at Florida International University. Eventually he worked
his way to sales manager.

Then one day a man walked into the dealership. An extraordinary-
looking man: slender, dark-eyed, bearded, brooding. He reminded Seth
of a young Stanley Kubrick in his guise and carriage. The man was Ian
Whitestone.

Seth had seen Whitestone's lone low-budget feature film and, although it had been a commercial flop, Seth had known that Whitestone would move on to bigger and better things.

As it turned out, Ian Whitestone was a huge fan of noir. He knew Lily Trieste's work. Over a few bottles of wine they had discussed the genre. By morning's light, Whitestone hired him as a production assistant.

Seth knew that a name like Jerzy Andres Kiedrau wouldn't get him too far in show business, so he decided to change it. The last name was easy. He had long considered William Goldman one of the screenwriting gods, had admired his work for many years. And if anyone made the connection, assuming that Seth was in some way related to the writer of *Marathon Man, Magic,* and *Butch Cassidy and the Sundance Kid,* he would not go out of his way to disabuse them of the notion.

Hollywood, after all, turned on illusion.

Goldman was easy. The first name was a little harder. He decided to take a biblical name to make the Jewish illusion complete. Although he was about as Jewish as Pat Robertson, the deception didn't hurt. One day, he took out a Bible, closed his eyes, opened it at random, and stabbed a page. He would take the first name he came across. Unfortunately, he didn't really look like a Ruth Goldman. Nor did he favor Methuselah Goldman. His third stab was the winner. Seth. Seth Goldman.

Seth Goldman would get a table at L'Orangerie.

In the past five years he had risen quickly at White Light Pictures. He had begun as a production assistant, doing everything from setting up craft service, to shuttling extras, to picking up Ian's dry cleaning. Then he helped Ian develop a script that was to change everything, a supernatural thriller called *Dimensions.*

Ian Whitestone's screenplay made the rounds, but because of his less-than-stellar box-office record, everyone turned it down. Then Will Parrish read it. The superstar actor who had made his name in the action genre had been looking for a change. The sensitive role of the blind professor appealed to him, and within a week the film was green-lighted.

Dimensions became a worldwide sensation, grossing more than six hundred million dollars. It put Ian Whitestone instantly onto the A-list. It turned Seth Goldman from a lowly PA to Ian's executive assistant.

Not bad for a trailer rat from Glades County.

Seth flipped through his binder of DVDs. What to watch? He wouldn't be able to see all of the film before they landed, whatever he chose, but whenever he had even a few minutes of downtime, he liked to fill it with a movie.

He decided on *Les Diaboliques,* the 1955 film with Simone Signoret; a film about betrayal, murder, and above all secrets—something Seth knew all about.

For Seth Goldman, the city of Philadelphia was full of secrets. He knew where blood had stained the earth, where the bones were buried. He knew where evil walked.

Sometimes, he walked with it.

FOR ALL THAT VINCENT BALZANO WAS NOT, HE *WAS* A DAMN
good cop. In his ten years as an undercover narcotics officer, he had put
together some of the biggest busts in Philadelphia's recent history. Vincent was already an undercover legend due to his chameleon-like ability
to move through drug circles on all sides of the table—cop, junkie,
dealer, snitch.

His Rolodex of informants and garden-variety skeeves was as thick as
anyone's. Right now, there was one particular skeeve Jessica and Byrne
were interested in. She hadn't wanted to call Vincent—their relationship teetered on the wrong word, the casual reference, the misplaced
emphasis—and the marriage counselor's office was probably the best
place for them to interact at this point.

Still, there was a case on the wheel, and sometimes you had to overlook personal issues for the job.

As she waited for her husband to come back to the phone, Jessica
thought about where they were in this strange case—no body, no suspect, and no motive. Terry Cahill had run a VICAP search, which yielded
nothing similar to the MO of the *Psycho* tape. The FBI's Violent Criminal

Apprehension Program was a nationwide data center designed to collect, collate, and analyze crimes of violence, specifically murder. The closest hits on Cahill's search were videotapes made by street gangs that recorded initiation rites of new recruits making their bones.

Jessica and Byrne had interviewed Emily Trager and Isaiah Crandall, the two people besides Adam Kaslov who had rented *Psycho* from The Reel Deal. Neither interview yielded much. Emily Trager was *well* over seventy and walked with an aluminum walker—a little detail Lenny Puskas had neglected to tell them. Isaiah Crandall was in his late fifties, short, and Chihuahua-jumpy. He worked as a short-order cook at a diner on Frankford Avenue. He nearly fainted when they showed him their badges. He didn't strike either detective as the type with the kind of stomach needed to do what was done on that tape. He certainly wasn't the body type.

Both had said that they watched the movie, start to finish, and there was nothing out of the ordinary. A call back to the video store revealed that both had returned the film well within the rental period.

The detectives ran both names through NCIC and PCIC, retrieving nothing. Both were clean. Ditto on Adam Kaslov, Lenny Puskas, and Juliet Rausch.

Somewhere between the time Isaiah Crandall had returned the film and the time Adam Kaslov took it home, someone had gotten the tape and replaced the famous shower scene with one of their own.

The detectives did not have a lead—without a body, a lead was not likely to fall into their laps—but they did have a direction. A little digging revealed that The Reel Deal was owned by a man named Eugene Kilbane.

Eugene Hollis Kilbane, forty-four, was a two-time loser, a petty thief and pornographer, an importer of hard-core books, magazines, films, and videotapes, along with various and sundry adult sex toys and devices. Along with The Reel Deal, Mr. Kilbane owned a second independent video store as well as an adult bookstore and peep show on Thirteenth Street.

They had paid a visit to his "corporate" headquarters—the back of a warehouse on Erie Avenue. Bars on the windows, shades down, door locked, no answer. Some empire.

Kilbane's known associates were a Who's Who of Philly scumbags, many of whom plied the drug trade. And in the city of Philadelphia, if you sold drugs, Detective Vincent Balzano knew you.

Vincent came back to the phone in short order with a location that Kilbane was known to frequent, a Port Richmond dive bar called The White Bull Tavern.

Before hanging up, Vincent offered Jessica backup. As much as she hated to admit it, and as weird as it might sound to anyone outside law enforcement, an offer of backup was, in its way, kind of sweet.

She declined the offer, but it went into the reconciliation bank.

THE WHITE BULL Tavern was a stone-front hovel near Richmond and Tioga streets. Byrne and Jessica parked the Taurus and approached the tavern, with Jessica thinking: *You know you're entering a tough place when the door is held together with duct tape.* A sign on the wall next to the door proclaimed CRABS ALL YEAR!

I'll bet, Jessica thought.

Inside they found a cramped, dark bar, dotted with neon beer signs and plastic light fixtures. The air was thick with stale smoke and the high-sweet redolence of cheap whiskey. Beneath that was something reminiscent of the primate reserve at the Philly Zoo.

As she stepped in and her eyes adjusted to the light, Jessica mind-printed the layout. A small room with a pool table to the left, fifteen-stool bar to the right, a handful of rickety tables in the center. Two men sat on stools, midbar. A man and a woman talked at the far end. Four men played nine-ball. She had learned her first week on the job that the first order of business upon entering a snake pit was to ID the snakes, and plot your exit.

Jessica immediately made Eugene Kilbane. He stood at the other end of the bar, sipping coffee, talking to a bottle blonde who, a few years ago, and in some other light, might have had a shot at pretty. In here, she was as pale as the cocktail napkins. Kilbane was thin and rawboned. He had dyed black hair and wore a wrinkled gray double-breasted suit, a brassy tie, pinkie rings. Jessica made him based on Vincent's description of his face. She noted that about a quarter of the man's upper lip, on the right side, was missing, replaced by ridged scar tissue. It gave him the appearance of a constant snarl, surely something he didn't have any desire to renounce.

As Byrne and Jessica made their way to the rear of the bar, the blonde slid off her stool and walked into the back room.

"My name is Detective Byrne, this is my partner, Detective Balzano," Byrne said, holding up his ID.

"And I'm Brad Pitt," Kilbane said.

Due to his partial lip, *Brad* came out *Mrad*.

Byrne ignored the attitude. For the moment. "The reason we're here is that, in the course of an investigation we're working on, we ran across something in one of your establishments we'd like to talk to you about," he said. "You are the owner of The Reel Deal on Aramingo?"

Kilbane said nothing. He sipped his coffee. Stared straight ahead.

"Mr. Kilbane?" Jessica said.

Kilbane turned his gaze to her. "I'm sorry, what did you say your name was again, honey?"

"Detective Balzano," she said.

Kilbane leaned a little closer, running his eyes up and down her body. Jessica was glad she wore jeans and not a skirt today. Still, she felt like she needed a shower.

"I mean your first name," Kilbane said.

"Detective."

Kilbane smirked. "Cute."

"Are you the owner of The Reel Deal?" Byrne asked.

"Never heard of it," Kilbane said.

Byrne kept his cool. Barely. "I'm going to ask you one more time. But you should be aware that three is my limit. After three, we move the party to the Roundhouse. And my partner and I like to party well into the evening. In fact, some of our preferred guests have been known to stay in that cozy little room overnight. We like to call it Hotel Homicide."

Kilbane took a deep breath. There was always a moment with tough guys when they had to weigh the posture against the outcome. "Yeah," he said. "That's one of my businesses."

"We believe that one of the tapes available at that store might contain evidence of a rather serious crime. We believe that someone may have taken the tape off the shelf within the past week or so and recorded over it."

Kilbane did not visibly react to this at all. "Yeah? And?"

"Can you think of anyone who might have done something like that?" Byrne asked.

"Who, me? I wouldn't know anything about that."

"Well, we'd appreciate it if you'd give this matter some thought."

"Is that right?" Kilbane asked. "What could possibly be in it for me?"

Byrne took a deep breath, exhaled slowly. Jessica could see the muscle working on the side of his jaw. "You would have the gratitude of the Philadelphia Police Department," he said.

"Not good enough. Have a nice day." Kilbane leaned back, stretched. When he did so, he exposed the two-finger handle of what was probably a game zipper in a sheath on his belt. A game zipper was a razor-sharp knife used for field-dressing game. Seeing as they were nowhere near a hunting preserve, Kilbane was most likely carrying it for other reasons.

Byrne very deliberately looked down, staring at the weapon. As a two-time loser, Kilbane understood. Mere possession of this item would bust him back on a parole violation.

"Did you say The Reel Deal?" Kilbane asked. Penitent now. Respectful.

"That would be correct," Byrne replied.

Kilbane nodded, looked at the ceiling, feigning profound thought. As if that were possible. "Let me ask around. See if anyone saw anything suspicious," he said. "I have a *varied* clientele at that location."

Byrne put both hands up, palms heavenward. "And they say community policing doesn't work." He dropped a card on the bar. "I'll expect a call, one way or another."

Kilbane didn't touch the card, didn't even look at it.

The two detectives glanced around the bar. No one was blocking their exit, but they were definitely in everyone's periphery.

"*Today,*" Byrne added. He stepped to the side, motioned for Jessica to leave ahead of him.

As Jessica turned to walk away, Kilbane slipped his hand around her waist and roughly pulled her toward him. "Ever been in the movies, baby?"

Jessica had her Glock holstered on her right hip. Kilbane's hand was now just inches away from her weapon.

"With a body like yours I could make you a fucking star," he continued, holding her even more tightly, his hand moving ever closer to her weapon.

Jessica spun out of his grasp, planted her feet, and threw a perfectly aimed, perfectly leveraged left hook to Kilbane's midsection. The punch caught him just in front of his right kidney, landing with a loud splat that seemed to echo throughout the bar. Jessica stepped back, fists up, more out of instinct than any battle plan. But this little skirmish was over. When you train at Frazier's Gym, you know how to go to the body. The one punch took Kilbane's legs.

And, it appeared, his breakfast.

As he doubled over, a rope of foamy yellow bile spurted from beneath his destroyed upper lip, just missing Jessica. Thank God.

After the blow, the two thugs sitting at the bar went on high alert, all puff and chest and bluster, fingers twitchy. Byrne held up a hand that fairly shouted two things. One, *Don't fucking move.* Two, *Don't fucking move an* inch.

The room went jungle-nervous as Eugene Kilbane tried to find his wind. He took a knee on the filthy floor instead. Dropped by a 130-pound girl. For a guy like Kilbane, it probably didn't get much worse than that. Body shot, no less.

Jessica and Byrne edged toward the door, slowly, fingers on the snaps of their holsters. Byrne speared a cautionary forefinger at the miscreants around the pool table.

"I warned him, right?" Jessica asked Byrne, still backing up, talking out of the side of her mouth.

"Yes, you did, Detective."

"It felt like he was going for my weapon."

"Clearly, a very bad idea."

"I had to hit him, right?

"No question about that."

"He's probably not going to call us now, is he?"

"Well, no," Byrne said. "I don't think he is."

OUT ON THE street, they stood by the car for a minute or so, just to make sure that none of Kilbane's crew were going to take this thing any farther. As expected, they did not. Jessica and Byrne had both encountered a thousand men like Eugene Kilbane in their time on the job—small-time hustlers with little fiefdoms, staffed with men who feed off the carrion left by real players.

Jessica's hand throbbed. She hoped she hadn't injured it. Uncle Vittorio would kill her if he found out she was punching people for free.

As they got in the car and headed back to Center City, Byrne's cell phone rang. He answered, listened, closed it, said: "Audio Visual has something for us."

THE AUDIO VISUAL UNIT OF THE PHILADELPHIA POLICE DEPART-
ment was located in the basement of the Roundhouse. When the crime
lab had moved to its bright new facilities on Eighth and Poplar, the AV
Unit was one of the few sections that remained behind. The unit's main
function was to provide audiovisual support services to all the other
agencies in the city—supplying cameras, TVs, VCRs, photographic
equipment. They also provided news composites, which meant they
monitored and taped the news 24/7; if the commissioner or chief or any
of the brass needed something, they had instant access.

Most of the unit's work in support of the detective divisions was in
the area of analyzing surveillance video, although the occasional audio-
tape of a threatening phone call came along to spice things up. Video surveillance tapes were, as a rule, recorded with a time-lapse technology
that allowed twenty-four hours or more of imagery to fit on a single
T-120 VHS cassette. When these tapes were played back on a normal
VCR, the movements were so fast that they could not be analyzed.
Hence, a time-lapse VCR was needed to view the tape in what would be
real time.

The unit was busy enough to keep six officers and one sergeant hopping every day. And the king of surveillance video analysis was Officer Mateo Fuentes. Mateo was in his early thirties—slender, fashion-conscious, impeccably groomed—a nine-year veteran of the force who lived, ate, and breathed video. You asked him about his personal life at your peril.

They assembled in the small editing bay near the control room. Above the monitors was a yellowing printout.

YOU VIDEOTAPE IT, YOU EDIT IT.

"Welcome to *Cinema Macabre,* detectives," Mateo said.

"What's playing?" Byrne asked.

Mateo held up a digital photograph of the *Psycho* videotape housing. Specifically, the side that held a short strip of silver-colored tape.

"Well, first off, this is old security tape," Mateo said.

"Okay. What does this breakthrough substantiation impart to us?" Byrne asked with a wink and a smile. Mateo Fuentes was well known for his prim and business-like manner, along with his Jack Webb delivery. It masked a frisky side, but you had to get to know him.

"I'm glad you proffered this interrogative," Mateo said, playing along. He pointed to the silver band on the side of the tape. "This is an old-school loss-prevention tag. Maybe early-nineties vintage. The newer versions are a lot more sensitive, a lot more effective."

"I'm afraid I don't know the first thing about this," Byrne said.

"Well, I'm no expert, either, but I'll tell you what I know," Mateo said. "The system, as a whole, is called EAS, or Electronic Article Surveillance. There are two main types: the hard tag and the soft tag. The hard tags are those bulky, plastic tags they put on leather jackets, Armani sweaters, Zegna dress shirts, et cetera. All the good stuff. That kind of tag has to be taken off with a device once you pay for the item. Soft tags, on the other hand, have to be desensitized by swiping them over a pad or with a handheld scanner that tells the tag, essentially, it's okay to leave the store."

"What about videotapes?" Byrne asked.

"Videotapes and DVDs, too."

"Which is why they hand them to you on the other side of those—"

"Pedestals," Mateo said. "Right. Exactly. Both types of tags work on an RF frequency. If the tag hasn't been removed, or if it hasn't been desensitized, and you walk past the pedestals, the beepers go off. Then they tackle you."

"And there's no way around that?" Jessica asked.

"There's *always* a way around *everything.*"

"Like how?" Jessica asked.

Mateo lifted a solitary brow. "Plan on doing a little shoplifting, Detective?"

"I've got my eye on a sweet pair of black linen Blahniks."

Mateo laughed. "Good luck. Stuff like that is protected better than Fort Knox."

Jessica snapped her fingers.

"But with these dinosaur systems, if you wrap the whole item in aluminum foil, it could possibly fool the old security sensors. You could even put the item against a magnet."

"Coming and going?"

"Yes."

"So someone who wrapped a videotape in aluminum foil, or put it up against a magnet, could get it out of the store, keep it for a while, then rewrap it and sneak it back in?" Jessica asked.

"It's possible."

"All without being detected?"

"I believe so," Mateo said.

"Great," Jessica said. They had been concentrating on people who had rented the tape. Now the possibilities opened up to just about everyone in Philadelphia with access to Reynolds Wrap. "What about a tape from one store going into a different store. Say, a Blockbuster tape being sneaked into a West Coast Video?"

"The industry isn't standardized yet. It's pushing for what they call *tower-centric* systems as opposed to *tag-centric* setups so that detectors can read multiple tag technologies. On the other hand, if people knew that these detectors only catch about sixty percent of the thefts, they might get a little bolder."

"What about taping over a prerecorded tape?" Jessica asked. "Is that difficult?"

"Not in the least," Mateo said. He pointed to a small indentation on the back of the videocassette. "All you have to do is put something over this."

"So if a person took the tape out of the store wrapped in foil, they could take it home and record over it—and if no one tried to rent it for a few days, no one would know it was gone," Byrne said. "Then all they would have to do is rewrap it in foil and sneak it back in."

"That's probably true."

Jessica and Byrne looked at each other. They weren't just back to square one. They weren't even on the board yet.

"Thanks for making our day," Byrne said.

Mateo smiled. "Hey, do you think I would call you down here if I didn't have something good to show you, *capitán, mi capitán?*"

"Let's see it," Byrne said.

"Check this out."

Mateo spun in his chair and hit a few buttons on the dTective digital console behind him. The dTective system converted standard video to digital, and allowed technicians to manipulate the image directly from the hard drive. Instantly, *Psycho* began to roll on the monitor. On the monitor, the bathroom door opened and the old woman entered. Mateo rewound it until the room was empty again, then hit PAUSE, freezing the image. He pointed to the upper left-hand corner of the frame. There, on the top of the shower rod, was a gray splotch.

"Cool," Byrne said. "A smudge. Let's put out an APB."

Mateo shook his head. *"Usted de poca fe."* He began to enlarge the image, which was fuzzy to the point of near obscurity. "Let me sharpen this a little."

He hit a sequence of keys, his fingers blazing over the keyboard. The picture became slightly sharper. The small smudge on the shower rod was now a little more recognizable. It appeared to be a rectangular white label with black ink on it. Mateo hit a few more keys. The image became larger by about 25 percent. It began to look like something.

"What is it, a boat?" Byrne asked, squinting at the image.

"A *river*boat," Mateo said. He brought the picture to a slightly higher degree of clarity. It was still very blurred, but it became apparent that there was a word beneath the graphic. A logo of some sort.

Jessica took out her glasses, slipped them on. She leaned closer to the monitor. "It says . . . Natchez?"

"Yes," Mateo said.

"What is Natchez?"

Mateo spun around to a computer, one hooked up to the Internet. He typed in a few words, hit ENTER. In an instant, the monitor showed a website displaying a much clearer version of the graphic on the other screen: a highly stylized riverboat.

"Natchez, Inc., manufactures plumbing and bathroom fixtures," Mateo said. "I believe this is one of their shower rods."

Jessica and Byrne exchanged a glance. After a morning of chasing shadows, this was a lead. Small, but a lead nonetheless.

"So do all the shower rods they make have that logo there?" Jessica asked.

Mateo shook his head. "No," he said. "Look."

He clicked over to the catalog page for shower rods. The rods themselves had no logos or markings on them of any kind. "My guess is that what we're looking at is some kind of tag that identifies the item to the installer. Something they're supposed to peel off when they're done putting it up."

"So what you're saying is that this shower rod was recently installed," Jessica said.

"That would be my deduction," Mateo said in his strange, precise manner. "If it had been in there awhile, you'd think the steam from the shower might have made it slip off. Let me get you a printout." Mateo hit a few more keys, starting the laser printer.

While they were waiting, Mateo poured a cup of soup from his thermos. He opened a Tupperware container in which he had two neatly stacked columns of saltines. Jessica wondered if he ever actually went home.

"I hear you're working with the suits on this," Mateo said.

Jessica and Byrne exchanged another glance, this one suffixed with a grimace. "Where did you hear that?" Jessica asked.

"From the suit himself," Mateo said. "He was down here about an hour ago."

"Special Agent Cahill?" Jessica asked.

"That would be the suit."

"What did he want?"

"Only everything. He asked a lot of questions. He wanted deep background on this."

"Did you give it to him?"

Mateo looked mortified. "I'm not that easy of a lay, Detective. I told him I was working on it."

Jessica had to smile. PPD *über alles*. Sometimes she loved this place and everyone in it. Still, she made a mental note to rip Agent Opie a new asshole the first chance she got.

Mateo reached over, retrieved the photo printout of the shower rod. He handed it to Jessica. "I know it isn't much, but it's a start, *sí?*"

Jessica kissed Mateo on the top of the head. "You rock, Mateo."

"Tell the world, *hermana.*"

THE LARGEST PLUMBING supply company in Philadelphia was Standard Plumbing and Heating on Germantown Avenue, a fifty-thousand-square-foot warehouse of toilets, sinks, bathtubs, shower stalls, and just about every other conceivable fixture. They carried high-end lines such as Porcher, Bertocci, and Cesana. They also carried less expensive fixtures like those manufactured by Natchez, Inc., a company based, not surprisingly, in Mississippi. Standard Plumbing and Heating was the only distributor in Philadelphia to carry the product.

The sales manager's name was Hal Hudak.

"That's the NF-5506-L. A one-inch OD aluminum L-style," Hudak said. He was looking at a printout photograph taken from the videotape. It was now cropped to show only the top of the shower rod.

"And it's made by Natchez?" Jessica asked.

"That's correct. But it's a fairly low-end fixture. Nothing too fancy." Hudak was in his late fifties, balding, puckish, as if everything had the potential to amuse. He smelled like Cinnamon Altoids. They were in his paper-besieged office overlooking the chaotic warehouse floor. "We sell a lot of Natchez fixtures to the federal government for its FHA housing."

"What about hotels, motels?" Byrne asked.

"Sure," he said. "But you won't find this in any of the expensive or midrange hotels. Not even in the Motel 6 variety, either."

"Why is that?"

"Mainly because the fixtures in those popular economy motels get a lot of use. It doesn't make good business sense to use budget fixtures. They'd be replacing them twice a year."

Jessica made a few notes, asked: "Then why would any motel buy them?"

"Between you, me, and the switchboard operator, the only kind of motels that might install these fixtures are the ones where people don't tend to stay overnight, if you know what I mean."

They knew exactly what he meant. "Have you sold any of these recently?" Jessica asked.

"Depends on what you mean by recently."

"In the last few months."

"Let me see." He hit a few keys on his computer keyboard. "Yeah. I've got a small order three weeks ago from . . . Arcel Management."

"How small of an order?"

"They ordered twenty shower rods. The aluminum L-style. Just like your picture."

"Is the company local?"

"Yes."

"Was the order delivered?"

Hudak smiled. "Of course."

"What does Arcel Management do exactly?"

A few more keystrokes. "They manage apartments. A few motels, I think."

"Motels of the by-the-hour variety?" Jessica asked.

"I'm a married man, Detective. I'd have to ask around."

Jessica smiled. "That's okay," she said. "I think we can handle that."

"My wife thanks you."

"We'll need their address and phone number," Byrne said.

"You got it."

WHEN THEY GOT back to Center City they stopped at Ninth and Passyunk, flipped a coin. Heads meant Pat's. Tails, Geno's. It was heads. At Ninth and Passyunk, lunch was easy.

When Jessica returned to the car with the cheesesteaks, Byrne shut his phone, said: "Arcel Management manages four apartment complexes in North Philly, as well as a motel on Dauphin Street."

"West Philly?"

Byrne nodded. "Strawberry Mansion."

"And I suppose it's a five-star property with European spa and championship golf course," Jessica said, slipping into the car.

"Actually, it's a no-tell called the Rivercrest Motel," Byrne said.

"Did they order those shower rods?"

"According to the very accommodating, honey-voiced Miss Rochelle Davis, they did indeed."

"And did the very accommodating, honey-voiced Miss Rochelle Davis happen to tell the probably-old-enough-to-be-her-father Detective Kevin Byrne how many rooms there are at the Rivercrest Motel?"

"She did."

"How many?"

Byrne started the Taurus, pointed it west. "Twenty."

SETH GOLDMAN SAT IN THE ELEGANT LOBBY OF THE PARK HYATT, the graceful hotel that occupied a few of the upper floors of the historic Bellevue Building at Broad and Walnut streets. He reviewed the day's call sheet. Nothing too heroic. They had met with a reporter from *Pittsburgh Magazine* for a brief interview and photo session, and had immediately returned to Philadelphia. They were due on set within an hour. Seth knew that Ian was somewhere in the hotel, and that was a good thing. Although Seth had never known Ian to miss a shot, he did have a habit of disappearing for hours on end.

At just after four o'clock Ian got off the elevator, followed by his child's nanny Aileen, who was holding Ian's six-month-old son, Declan, in her arms. Ian's wife, Julianne, was in Barcelona. Or Florence. Or Rio. It was hard to keep track.

Aileen was trailed by Ian's production manager, Erin.

Erin Halliwell had been with Ian for less than three years, but Seth had long ago decided to keep an eye on her. Prim and curt and highly efficient, it was no secret that Erin wanted Seth's job, and were it not for the fact that she was sleeping with Ian—thereby unwittingly creating a glass ceiling for herself—she would probably have it.

Most people think that a production company like White Light employed dozens, maybe scores, of full-time employees. The truth was, there were only three: Ian, Erin, and Seth. This was all the staff necessary until a film went into production; then the real hiring began.

Ian spoke briefly with Erin, who spun on her highly polished sensible heels, threw an equally polished smile at Seth, and stepped back onto the elevator. Ian then ruffled little Declan's fluffy red hair, crossed the lobby, glanced at one of his two watches—the one on local time. The other was set to Los Angeles time. Math was not Ian Whitestone's strong suit. He had a few minutes. He poured a cup of coffee, sat across from Seth.

"Who's up?" Seth asked.

"You are."

"Okay," Seth said. "Name two films that each starred two actors who were both Oscar-winning *directors.*"

Ian smiled. He crossed his legs, ran a hand over his jaw. He was looking more and more like the fortyish Stanley Kubrick all the time, Seth thought. The deep-set eyes, backed by a mischievous twinkle. The expensive, casual wardrobe.

"Good one," Ian said. They had been playing this trivia game on and off for nearly three years. Seth had yet to stump the man. "Four Oscar winning actor-directors. Two films."

"Right. But keep in mind they won their Oscars for directing, not acting."

"Post-1960?"

Seth just glared. As if he would supply a clue. As if Ian would *need* a clue.

"Four *different* people?" Ian asked.

Another glare.

"Okay, okay." Hands up in surrender.

The rules were as follows: The person asking the question gave the other person five minutes to answer. There would be no consulting with a third party, no Internet access allowed. If you could not answer the question in five minutes, you owed the other person dinner at the restaurant of his choice.

"Give?" Seth asked.

Ian glanced at one of his watches. "With three minutes to go?"

"Two minutes and forty seconds," Seth corrected.

Ian looked at the ornate vaulted ceiling, rummaging his memory. It appeared as if Seth had finally bested him.

With ten seconds to go Ian said: "Woody Allen and Sydney Pollack in *Husbands and Wives*. Kevin Costner and Clint Eastwood in *A Perfect World*."

"Damn."

Ian laughed. He was still batting a thousand. He rose, grabbed his shoulder bag. "What is Norma Desmond's phone number?"

Ian always said *is* in regard to film. Most people used the past tense. To Ian, film was always in the moment. "Crestview 5-1733," Seth replied. "What name did Janet Leigh sign in under at the Bates Motel?"

"Marie Samuels," Ian said. "What is Gelsomina's sister's name?"

This was an easy one, Seth thought. He was familiar with every frame of Fellini's *La Strada*. He had first seen it at the Monarch Art when he was ten years old. He still got teary when he thought of it. All he needed was to hear the mournful wail of that trumpet in the opening credits and he started to bawl. "Rosa."

"*Molto bene,*" Ian said with a wink. "See you on set."

"*Sí, maestro.*"

SETH GRABBED A cab and headed to Ninth Street. As they drove south, he watched the neighborhoods change, from the bustle of Center City to the sprawling urban enclave of South Philadelphia. Seth had to admit that he liked working in Philadelphia, Ian's hometown. Despite all the pressure to formally move the offices of White Light Pictures to Hollywood, Ian had resisted.

Within minutes they came across the first police cars and street barricades. The production had closed down Ninth Street for two blocks in each direction. By the time Seth arrived on the set, everything was in place—the lights, the sound package, the security presence needed for any shoot in a major metropolitan area. Seth showed his ID, skirted the barricades, and slipped into Anthony's. He ordered a cappuccino and stepped back onto the sidewalk.

Everything was running like clockwork. All they needed was their leading man, Will Parrish.

Parrish, the star of the hugely successful 1980s prime-time ABC comedy-action series *Daybreak,* was riding the crest of a comeback of sorts, his second. In the 1980s he had been on every magazine cover, on every TV talk show, on virtually every transit ad in every major city. His smirking, wisecracking *Daybreak* character was not all that different from his own, and by the late 1980s he was the highest-paid actor on television.

Then came *Kill Game,* an action film that catapulted him to A-list status, the film grossing nearly $270 million worldwide. It was followed by three equally successful sequels. In between, Parrish made a number of romantic comedies and small dramas. Then there was a slump in big-budget action films and Parrish wasn't getting the scripts. Almost a decade passed before Ian Whitestone put him back on the map.

In *The Palace,* his second film with Whitestone, he played a widowed surgeon treating a young boy who'd been badly burned in a fire set by the boy's mother. Parrish's character, Ben Archer, was performing skin-graft operations on the boy while slowly discovering that his patient was clairvoyant, and that nefarious government agencies wanted to get their hands on him.

This day the shot was a relatively easy one, logistically speaking. Dr. Benjamin Archer walks out of a restaurant in South Philly and sees a mysterious man, a man in a dark suit. He follows.

Seth took his cappuccino and stood on the corner. They were about half an hour from the shot.

For Seth Goldman, the best part of a location shoot—any shoot, but especially a city location shoot—was the women. Young women, middle-aged women, rich women, poor women, housewives, college students, workingwomen—they stood on the other side of the barricades, enthralled at the glamour of it all, mesmerized by celebrity, lined up like sexy perfumed ducks at a gallery. In major cities, even the gaffers got laid.

And Seth Goldman was far from a gaffer.

Seth sipped his coffee, ostensibly marveling at the efficiency of the crew. What he was really marveling at was the blond woman standing on the other side of the barricade, right behind one of the police cars blocking the street.

Seth edged his way over toward her. He spoke softly into his two-way radio, to no one at all. He wanted to get her attention. He moved closer and closer to the barricade, just a few feet from the woman now. He was wearing a Joseph Abboud navy blazer over a white, open-collar polo shirt. He oozed importance. He looked good.

"Hi," the young woman said.

Seth turned, as if he hadn't noticed her. She was even prettier up close. She wore a powder-blue dress and low white heels. She wore a string of pearls and matching earrings. She was about twenty-five. Her hair was gold-tipped by the summer sun.

"Hi, there," Seth replied.

"Are you with . . ." She waved her hand at the crew, the lights, the sound truck, the set in general.

"The production? Yes," Seth said. "I'm Mr. Whitestone's executive assistant."

She nodded, impressed. "This is really exciting."

Seth looked up and down the street. "Yes, it is."

"I was here for the other movie, too."

"Did you like the film?" Fishing, and he knew it.

"Very much." Her voice rose in pitch a little when she said this. "I thought *Dimensions* was one of the scariest movies I've ever seen."

"Let me ask you something."

"Okay."

"And I want you to be completely honest with me."

She held her hand up in a three-finger pledge. "Girl Scout promise."

"Did you see the ending coming?"

"Not in the *least*," she said. "I was completely surprised."

Seth smiled. "You said the right thing. Are you sure you're not from Hollywood?"

"Well, it's true. My boyfriend said he knew it all along, but I didn't believe him."

Seth frowned dramatically. "Boyfriend?"

The young woman laughed. "*Ex*-boyfriend."

Seth grinned at the news. This was going extremely well. He opened his mouth, as if to say something, but then thought better of it. Or at least, that was the scene he was playing. It worked.

"What is it?" she asked, circling the hook.

Seth shook his head. "I was going to say something, but I'd better not."

She cocked her head at a slight angle, began to color. Right on cue. "What were you going to say?"

"You'll think I'm being too forward."

She smiled. "I'm from South Philly. I think I can handle it."

Seth took her hand in his. She didn't tense up or pull away. This was also a good sign. He looked into her eyes and said:

"You have very pretty skin."

THE RIVERCREST MOTEL WAS A TUMBLEDOWN, TWENTY-UNIT pay and play on Thirty-third and Dauphin streets in West Philly, just a few blocks from the Schuylkill River. The motel was single-story, laid out in an L-shape with a weed-blotted parking lot and a pair of out-of-order soda machines flanking the door to the office. There were five cars in the lot. Two of them were on blocks.

The manager of the Rivercrest Motel was a man named Karl Stott. Stott was a hard fifty, late out of Alabama, with an alcoholic's damp lips, pitted cheeks, and a pair of navy tattoos on his forearms. He lived on the premises, in one of the rooms.

Jessica handled the interview. Byrne hovered and glared. They had worked out this dynamic in advance.

At just past four thirty, Terry Cahill arrived. He hung back in the parking lot, observing, making notes, walking the property.

"I think those shower rods were installed two weeks ago," Stott said, lighting a cigarette, his hands a little shaky. They were in the motel's small, shabby office. It smelled like warm salami. On the walls were posters of some of Philadelphia's major attractions—Independence Hall,

Penn's Landing, Logan Square, the art museum—as if the clientele who frequented the Rivercrest Motel were tourists. Jessica noted that someone had drawn a miniature Rocky Balboa on the art museum steps.

Jessica also noticed that Karl Stott already had a cigarette burning in the ashtray on the counter.

"You've got one going already," Jessica said.

"Pardon me?"

"You've already got one lit," Jessica repeated, pointing to the ashtray.

"Jesus," he said. He butted out the old one.

"A little nervous?" Byrne asked.

"Well, *yeah,*" Stott said.

"Why is that?"

"What, you kidding? You're from *Homicide.* Homicide makes me nervous."

"Have you murdered someone recently?"

Stott's face contorted. "What? *No.*"

"Then you have nothing to worry about," Byrne said.

They would run a check on Stott anyway, but Jessica red-lined it in her notebook. Stott had done time, she was sure of it. She showed the man a still photograph of the bathroom.

"Can you tell if this picture was taken here?" she asked.

Stott squinted at the photo. "It sure looks like one of ours."

"Can you tell which room it might be?"

Stott snorted. "You mean like, is it the presidential suite?"

"Excuse me?"

He gestured at the dilapidated office. "This look like the Crowne Plaza to you?"

"Mr. Stott, I have a deal for you," Byrne said, leaning across the counter. He got to within a few inches of Stott's face. His granite gaze held the man there.

"What's that?"

"Lose the attitude, or we will shut this place down for the next two weeks while we examine every tile, every drawer, every switch plate. We will also record the license plate of every car that pulls into this lot."

"That's a deal?"

"Believe it. And a good one, too. Because right now, my partner wants to bring you down to the Roundhouse and stick you in a holding cell," Byrne said.

Another laugh, but not nearly so derisive this time. "What is this, good cop, bad cop?"

"No, this is bad cop, worse cop. Those are the only choices you're going to get."

Stott stared at the floor for a few moments, leaning slowly back, extricating himself from Byrne's orbit. "I'm sorry, I'm just a little——"

"Nervous."

"Yeah."

"So you said. Now, back to Detective Balzano's question."

Stott drew a deep breath, then replaced the fresh air with a lung-rattling draw on his cigarette. He stared at the photograph again. "Well, I can't really tell which room it is, but the way the rooms are laid out, I'd say this was an even-numbered room."

"Why is that?"

"Because the toilets are back-to-back here. If this was an odd-numbered room, the tub would be on the other side."

"Can you narrow it down at all?" Byrne asked.

"When people check in for, you know, a few hours, we try to give them rooms five through ten."

"Why is that?"

"Because they're on the other side of the building from the street. Lots of times, people like to be discreet."

"So if the room in this photograph is one of those, it would be six, eight, or ten."

Stott looked at the water-stained ceiling. He did some serious ciphering in his head. It was clear that Karl Stott had a few problems with math. He looked back at Byrne. "Yeah."

"Do you recall any problems with your guests in those rooms over the past few weeks?"

"Problems?"

"Anything unusual. Arguments, disagreements, any loud behavior."

"Believe it or not, this is a relatively quiet place," Stott said.

"Are any of those rooms occupied right now?"

Stott looked at the corkboard with the keys on it. "No."

"We're going to need the keys to six, eight, and ten."

"Sure," Stott said, hooking the keys off the board. He handed them to Byrne. "Can I ask what this is all about?"

"We have reason to believe that a serious crime was committed in one of your motel rooms in the past two weeks," Jessica said.

By the time the detectives reached the door Karl Stott had lit another cigarette.

ROOM NUMBER SIX was a close, musty space: lopsided queen-size bed with a busted frame, splintered laminate nightstands, stained lamp shades, cracked plaster walls. Jessica noticed a ring of crumbs on the floor around the small table by the window. The worn, dirty oatmeal-colored carpeting was mildewed and damp.

Jessica and Byrne both snapped on a pair of latex gloves. They checked the doorjambs, doorknobs, switch plates, looking for visible blood evidence. Given the amount of blood generated by the murder on the videotape, the possibility of splatters and smears throughout the motel room was great. They found none. None that was visible to the naked eye, that is.

They entered the bathroom, flipped on the light. After a few seconds, the fluorescent fixture over the mirror flickered to life, settling into a loud hum. For a moment, Jessica's stomach lurched. The room was identical to the bathroom on the *Psycho* tape.

Byrne, at six three, looked at the top of the shower rod with relative ease. "Nothing here," he said.

They poked around the small bathroom—lifting the toilet seat, running a gloved finger around the drain in both the tub and the sink, checking the grout in the tile around the tub as well as in the folds of the shower curtain. No blood.

They repeated the procedure in room eight, with similar results.

When they entered room ten, they knew. It was nothing obvious, or even something that most people would have noticed. They were seasoned police officers. Evil had walked here, and the malevolence all but whispered to them.

Jessica flipped on the light in the bathroom. This bathroom had been recently cleaned. There was a slight film on everything, a thin layer of grit left from too much cleanser and not enough rinse water. They had not found this coating in the other two bathrooms.

Byrne checked the top of the shower rod.

"Bingo," he said. "We've got our tag."

He held up the still photograph taken from the freeze-frame of the video. It was identical.

Jessica followed the sight line from the top of the shower rod. On the wall, where the camera must have been mounted, was an exhaust fan, located just a few inches from the ceiling.

She retrieved the desk chair from the other room, dragged it into the bathroom, stood on it. The exhaust fan had clearly been tampered with. Some of the enamel paint was chipped away from the two screws that held it in place. It appeared that the grate had recently been removed and replaced.

Jessica's heart began to race with that special rhythm. There was no other feeling in law enforcement like it.

TERRY CAHILL STOOD near his car in the Rivercrest Motel parking lot, talking on his cell phone. Detective Nick Palladino, who was now assigned to the case, began a canvass of the few neighboring businesses as they waited for the Crime Scene Unit. Palladino was about forty, roughly handsome, old-school South Philly Italian—meaning he ate his salad at the end of the meal, had a copy of Bobby Rydell's greatest hits in the tape deck in his car, and didn't take down his Christmas lights before Valentine's Day. He was also one of the best detectives in the unit.

"We need to talk," Jessica said, approaching Cahill. She noticed that, even though he was standing directly in the sun, and the temperature had to be in the mideighties, he had his suit coat on, tie up, and there wasn't a single drop of sweat on his face. Jessica was ready to dive into the nearest pool. Her clothes were sticky with perspiration.

"I'll have to get back to you," Cahill said into the phone. He closed it, turned to Jessica. "Sure. What's up?"

"You want to tell me what's going on here?"

"I'm not sure what you mean."

"It was my understanding that you were here to observe and make recommendations to the bureau."

"That's correct," Cahill said.

"Then why were you down in the AV Unit before we were briefed on the tape?"

Cahill looked at the ground for a moment, sheepish, caught. "I've always been a bit of a video nut," he said. "I'd heard you have a very good AV Unit and I wanted to see for myself."

"I'd appreciate it if you cleared these things with me or Detective Byrne in the future," Jessica said, already feeling the anger begin to diminish.

"You're absolutely right. It won't happen again."

She really hated it when people did that. She had been ready to go upside his head, and he instantly took all the wind out of her sails. "I'd appreciate it," she repeated.

Cahill glanced around the area, letting his scolding dissipate. The sun was high and hot and merciless. Before the moment became awkward, he waved a hand in the general direction of the motel. "This is really good casework, Detective Balzano."

God, the feds were arrogant, Jessica thought. She didn't need him to tell her that. The break had come from Mateo's good work with the tape, and they had simply followed up. On the other hand, maybe Cahill was just trying to be pleasant. She looked at his earnest face, thinking: *Lighten up, Jess.*

"Thanks," she said. And left it at that.

"Ever think about the bureau as a career?" he asked.

She wanted to tell him that it would be her second choice, right after monster truck driver. Besides, her father would kill her. "I'm pretty happy where I am," she said.

Cahill nodded. His cell phone rang. He held up a finger, answered. "Cahill. Yes, hi." He glanced at his watch. "Ten minutes." He closed the phone. "Got to run."

There goes the investigation, Jessica thought. "So we have an understanding?"

"Absolutely," Cahill said.

"Okay."

Cahill got into his fed car, slipped on his fed aviator sunglasses, tossed a fed smile her way, and, observing all traffic laws—state and local— pulled onto Dauphin Street.

As JESSICA AND Byrne watched the Crime Scene Unit unload their equipment, Jessica thought of the popular television show *Without a Trace.* Criminalists loved that term. There was *always* a trace. The officers in the CSU lived for the fact that nothing ever vanished completely. Burn it, soak it, bleach it, bury it, wipe it down, chop it up. They'd find something.

Today, along with the other standard crime scene procedures, they were going to perform a Luminol test in the bathroom of room ten. Luminol was a chemical that revealed blood traces by causing a light-producing chemical reaction with hemoglobin, the oxygen-carrying element in blood. If trace blood evidence was present, Luminol, when viewed under a black light, would produce a chemiluminescence, the same phenomenon that causes fireflies to glow.

In short order, with the bathroom dusted for prints and photographs taken, the CSU officer began to spritz the liquid on the tile surrounding the tub. Unless the room had been washed down repeatedly with scalding-hot water and bleach, blood evidence would remain. When the officer was finished, he plugged in the UV arc lamp.

"Lights," he said.

Jessica flipped off the bathroom light, closed the bathroom door. The CSU officer turned on the black light.

In an instant, they had their answer. There was no trace evidence of blood on the floors, the walls, the shower curtain or the tile, no minute telltale specks of evidence.

There was blood *everywhere*.

They had found the killing ground.

"WE'RE GOING TO need the registration records for that room for the past two weeks," Byrne said. They were back in the motel's office and, for any number of reasons—not the least of which was that there were now a dozen members of PPD at his formerly quiet place of illicit business—Karl Stott was sweating big time. The small, cramped space had taken on an acrid, monkey-house smell.

Stott glanced at the floor, back up. It looked like he was going to disappoint these very scary cops, and that notion seemed to be making him ill. More sweat. "Well, we don't really keep detailed records, if you know what I mean. Ninety percent of the people who sign the register are named Smith, Jones, or Johnson."

"Is every rental on the books?" Byrne asked.

"What . . . what do you mean?"

"I mean, do you sometimes let friends or acquaintances use these rooms off the books?"

Stott looked shocked. The crime scene techs had examined the lock on the door to room ten and determined it had not recently been jimmied or picked. Anyone entering that room recently had used a key.

"Of course not," Stott said, indignant at the suggestion he might be guilty of petty larceny.

"We'll need to see your credit card receipts," Byrne said.

He nodded. "Sure. No problem. But as you might expect, this is mostly a cash business."

"Do you remember renting these rooms?" Byrne asked.

Stott ran a hand over his face. It was clearly Miller time for him. "They all kind of look alike to me. And I've got a bit of a, well, drinking problem, okay? I ain't proud of it, but there it is. By ten o'clock I'm in my cups."

"We'd like you to come down to the Roundhouse tomorrow," Jessica said. She handed Stott a card. Stott took it, his shoulders sagging.

Cops.

Out front, Jessica drew a time line on her notepad. "I think we've got the time frame down to a ten-day window. These shower rods were installed two weeks ago, which means that between the time Isaiah Crandall returned *Psycho* to The Reel Deal and Adam Kaslov rented it, our doer got the tape off the shelf, rented this motel room, committed the crime, and got it back on the shelf."

Byrne nodded in agreement.

In the next few days they would be able to narrow this down further, based on the results of the blood evidence. In the meantime, they would start with the missing-person database and see if there was someone matching the general description of the victim on the tape, someone who hadn't been seen in a week.

Before returning to the Roundhouse, Jessica turned and looked at the door to room ten.

A young woman had been murdered in this place, and a crime that might have gone undetected for weeks or maybe months was, if their calculations were correct, only a week or so old.

The madman who did this might have thought he had a pretty good lead on the dumb old cops.

He was wrong.

The chase was on.

THERE IS A MOMENT IN *DOUBLE INDEMNITY,* THE GREAT BILLY Wilder noir based on the novel by James M. Cain, when Phyllis, played by Barbara Stanwyck, looks at Walter, played by Fred MacMurray. The moment comes when Phyllis's husband unwittingly signs an insurance form, thereby sealing his fate. His untimely death, by certain means, would now produce an insurance settlement that was twice the normal payoff. A double indemnity.

There is no great music cue, no dialogue. Just a look. Phyllis looks at Walter with a secret knowledge—and no small measure of sexual tension—and they know they have just crossed a line. They have reached a point of no return, after which they will be murderers.

I am a murderer.

There is no denying or escaping that now. No matter how long I live, or what I do with the rest of my life, this will be my epitaph.

I am Francis Dolarhyde. I am Cody Jarrett. I am Michael Corleone.

And I have much to do.

Will any of them see me coming?

Perhaps.

Those who accept their guilt, yet refuse their penance, might feel me approach, like an icy breath on the nape of their necks. And it is for this reason I must be careful. It is for this reason I must move through the city like a ghost. The city might think that what I am doing is random. It is anything but.

"It's right here," she says.

I slow the car.

"It's kind of a mess inside," she adds.

"Oh, I wouldn't worry about that," I say, knowing full well that it will soon get messier. "You should see my place."

She smiles as we pull into her driveway. I glance around. No one is watching.

"Well, here we are," she says. "Ready?"

I smile back, turn off the engine, touch the bag on the seat. The camera is inside, batteries charged.

Ready.

"HEY, HANDSOME."

Byrne took a quick breath, braced himself before turning around. It had been awhile since he had seen her, and he wanted his face to reflect the warmth and affection he truly felt for her, not the shock and surprise most people revealed.

When Victoria Lindstrom arrived in Philadelphia from Meadville, a small town in northwestern Pennsylvania, she had been a vibrant seventeen-year-old beauty. Like a lot of pretty girls who made the journey, at that time her fantasy was to become a model, to live the American dream. Like many of these girls, the dream quickly turned sour, becoming instead the grim nightmare of urban street life. The street was Victoria's introduction to a violent man who would all but destroy her life. A man named Julian Matisse.

For a young woman like Victoria, Matisse had possessed a certain enameled charm. When she refused his repeated advances, he followed her home one night, to the two-room apartment on Market Street she shared with her cousin Irina. Matisse stalked her, on and off, for weeks.

And then one night he attacked.

Julian Matisse had cut Victoria's face with a box cutter, jigsawing her perfect flesh into a rough topography of gaping wounds. Byrne had seen the crime scene photographs. The amount of blood was staggering.

After nearly a month in the hospital, with her face still heavily bandaged, she had bravely testified against Julian Matisse. He received a sentence of ten to fifteen years.

The system being what it was, and still is, Matisse was released after forty months. His grim handiwork lasted much longer.

Byrne had first met her in her late teens, not long before she met Matisse; he had seen her literally stop traffic one day on Broad Street. With her silver eyes and raven hair and lucent skin, Victoria Lindstrom was once a stunningly beautiful young woman. She still was, if you could look past the horror. Kevin Byrne found that he could. Most men could not.

Byrne struggled to get to his feet, reaching for the cane halfway up, the pain shrieking through his body. Victoria put a gentle hand on his shoulder, leaned over, kissed him on the cheek. She eased him back down into the chair. He let her. For a brief moment, Victoria's perfume filled him with a potent mixture of desire and nostalgia. It brought him back to the first time they had met. They had both been so young then, and life had yet to sling its arrows.

Now they were on the second-floor food court of Liberty Place, the office and shopping complex at Fifteenth and Chestnut streets. Byrne's tour had officially ended at six o'clock. He had wanted to follow the Rivercrest Motel blood evidence for a few more hours, but Ike Buchanan had ordered him off duty.

Victoria sat down. She wore tight faded jeans and a fuchsia silk blouse. If time and tide had brought a few small crinkles to the corners of her eyes, they'd done nothing to her figure. She looked as trim and sexy as the first time they'd met.

"I read about you in the papers," she said, opening her coffee. "I was very sorry to hear of your troubles."

"Thank you," Byrne replied. In the past few months, he had heard this many times. He had stopped reacting to it. Everyone he knew—well meaning, all—had a different term for it. *Troubles, incident, accident, confrontation.* He had been shot in the head. That was the reality. He guessed most people had trouble saying *Hey, I heard you were shot in the head. You okay?*

"I wanted to . . . get in touch," she added.

Byrne had heard this many times, too. He understood. Life flowed. "How have you been, Tori?"

She butterflied her hands. Not bad, not good.

Byrne heard giggling nearby, derisive laughter. He turned to see a pair of teenaged boys sitting a few tables away, wannabe bangers, suburban white kids in the standard baggy hip-hop drag. They kept glancing over, mimicking horror-mask faces. Perhaps the presence of Byrne's cane meant they believed he was no threat. They were wrong.

"I'll be right back," Byrne said. He started to rise, but Victoria put a hand on his arm.

"It's okay," she said.

"No it isn't."

"Please," she said. "If I got upset every time . . . "

Byrne turned fully in his chair, glared at the punks. They held his gaze for a few seconds, but were no match for the cold green fire of his eyes. None but the hardest of the hard cases were. A few seconds later, they seemed to understand the wisdom of leaving. Byrne watched them walk the length of the food court, then get on the escalators. They didn't even have the balls to take one final shot. Byrne turned back to Victoria. He found her smiling at him. "What?"

"You haven't changed," she said. "Not one bit."

"Oh, I've changed." Byrne gestured to the cane. Even that simple movement brought a sword of agony.

"No. You are still gallant."

Byrne laughed. "I've been called many things in my life. Never gallant. Not once."

"It's true. Do you remember how we met?"

Like it was yesterday, Byrne thought. He was working vice out of Central when they got the call to raid a massage parlor in Center City.

When they rounded up the girls that night, Victoria had descended the steps into the front room of the row house wearing a blue silk kimono. She had taken his breath away, along with that of every other man in the room.

A detective—a weasel-faced little shit with bad teeth and worse breath—made a derogatory remark about Victoria. Although he would have been hard-pressed to explain why at the time, or even now, Byrne had braced the man against a wall so hard that the drywall had caved in.

Byrne didn't remember the detective's name, but he could easily recall the color of Victoria's eye shadow that day.

Now she counseled runaways. Now she talked to girls who had stood in her shoes fifteen years earlier.

Victoria stared out the window. The sunlight highlighted the bas-relief network of scars on her face. *My God,* Byrne thought. *The pain she must have endured.* A deep anger at the brutality of what Julian Matisse did to this woman began to rise within him. Again. He battled it back.

"I wish they could see it," Victoria said. Her tone was distant, now, thick with a familiar melancholy, a sadness she had lived with for many years.

"What do you mean?"

Victoria shrugged, sipped her coffee. "I wish they could see it from the inside."

Byrne had a feeling he knew what she was talking about. It appeared she wanted to tell him. He asked. "See what?"

"Everything." She took out a cigarette, paused, rolling it between her long, slender fingers. There was no smoking here. She needed the prop. "Every day I wake up, I'm in a hole, you know? A deep, black hole. If I have a really good day, I just about break even. Reach the surface. If I have a great day? I might even see a little sliver of sunlight. Smell a flower. Hear a baby's laugh.

"But if I have a bad day—which is most days—well, then. *That's* what I wish people could see."

Byrne didn't know what to say. He had flirted with bouts of depression in his life, but nothing like what Victoria had just described. He reached out, touched her hand. She looked out the window for a few moments, then continued.

"My mother was beautiful, you know," she said. "She still is to this day."

"So are you," Byrne said.

She looked back, frowned at him. Beneath the grimace, though, was the slightest blush. He could still bring the color to her face. That was good.

"You're full of shit. But I love you for it."

"I mean it."

She waved a hand at her face. "You don't know what it's like, Kevin."

"Yes, I do."

Victoria looked at him, giving him the floor. She lived in the world of group therapy, and in it everyone told their story.

Byrne tried to organize his thoughts. He really wasn't prepared for this. "After I was shot, all I could think about was one thing. Not about whether I was coming back to the job. Not about whether or not I could go out on the street again. Or even if I *wanted* to go out on the street again. All I could think about was Colleen."

"Your daughter?"

"Yes."

"What about her?"

"I just kept wondering if she was ever going to look at me the same way again. I mean, all her life, I've been the guy who's looked out for her, right? This big, strong guy. Daddy. Daddy the cop. It scared me to death that she would see me so small. That she would see me diminished.

"After I came out of my coma, she came to the hospital alone. My wife wasn't with her. I'm lying in the bed, most of my hair is shaved off, I'm twenty pounds down, fading in and out on the painkillers. I glance up and she's standing at the foot of my bed. I look at her face and I see it."

"See what?"

Byrne shrugged, searching for the word. He soon found it. "Pity," he said. "For the first time in her life, I saw *pity* in my little girl's eyes. I mean, there was love and respect there, too. But there was a look of pity and it broke my heart. It occurred to me that, at that moment, if she was in trouble, if she needed me, I wouldn't have been able to do a damn thing." Byrne glanced over at his cane. "I'm not in much better shape today."

"You will come back. Better than ever."

"No," Byrne said. "I don't think so."

"Men like you always come back."

Now it was Byrne's turn to color. He fought it. "Men like me?"

"Yes, you are a big man, but that's not what makes you strong. What makes you strong is inside."

"Yeah, well . . ." Byrne let the sentiment settle. He finished his coffee, realizing it was time. There was no way to sugarcoat what he had to tell her. He opened his mouth and just said it: "He's out."

Victoria held his gaze for a few moments. There was no need for Byrne to qualify his statement, nor say any more. No need to identify the *he*.

"Out," she said.

"Yes."

Victoria nodded, taking it in. "How?"

"His conviction is being appealed. The DA's office believes it may have evidence that he was framed for the murder of Marygrace Devlin." Byrne continued, telling her what he knew, about the allegedly planted evidence. Victoria remembered Jimmy Purify well.

She ran a hand through her hair, her hands betraying a slight shake. Within a second or two, she regained her composure. "It's funny. I'm not really afraid of him anymore. I mean, when he attacked me, I thought I had a lot to lose. My looks, my . . . life, such as it was. I had nightmares about him for a long time. But now . . ."

Victoria shrugged and began to spin her coffee cup in her hands. She looked exposed, vulnerable. But she was, in reality, tougher than he was. Could he walk down the street with his face segmented like hers, head held high? No. Probably not.

"He's going to do it again," Byrne said.

"How do you know?"

"I just do."

Victoria nodded.

Byrne said: "I want to stop him."

Somehow, the world did not cease spinning when he said these words, the sky did not turn an ominous gray, the clouds did not split.

Victoria knew what he was talking about. She leaned in, lowered her voice. "How?"

"Well, I have to find him first. He'll probably make contact with his old low-life crowd, the porno freaks and S-and-M types." Byrne realized that this might have sounded harsh. Victoria had come from this milieu. Perhaps she felt he was judging her. Luckily, she did not.

"I'll help you."

"I can't ask you to do that, Tori. That's not why—"

Victoria held up a hand, stopping him. "Back in Meadville, my Swedish grandmother had a saying. 'Eggs cannot teach a hen.' Okay? This is *my* world. I will help you."

Byrne's Irish grandmothers had their wisdom, too. There was no arguing with it. Still seated, he reached out, took Victoria in his arms. They hugged.

"We begin tonight," Victoria said. "I'll call you in an hour."

She slipped on her oversize sunglasses. The lenses covered a third of her face. She got up from the table, touched his cheek, and left.

He watched her walk away—the fluid, sexy metronome of her stride.

She turned and waved, blew a kiss, then disappeared down the escalator. She was still a knockout, Byrne thought. He wished for her a happiness he knew she would never find.

He got to his feet. The pain in his legs and back were shards of fire. He had parked more than a block away, and the distance now seemed enormous. He inched his way along the length of the food court, leaning on his cane, down the escalator and across the lobby.

Melanie Devlin. Victoria Lindstrom. Two women full of sadness and anger and fear, their once happy lives shipwrecked on the dark shoals of one monstrous man.

Julian Matisse.

Byrne now knew that what had begun as a mission to clear Jimmy Purify's name had become something else.

As he stood on the corner of Seventeenth and Chestnut, the maelstrom of a hot Philadelphia summer evening flowing around him, Byrne knew in his heart that, if he did nothing else with what was left of his life, if he found no higher purpose, he would make certain of one thing: Julian Matisse would not live to cause a single human being any more pain.

THE ITALIAN MARKET RAN THREE BLOCKS OR SO ALONG NINTH Street in South Philly, roughly between Wharton and Fitzwater streets, and was home to some of the best Italian food in the city, probably the country. Cheese, produce, shellfish, meats, coffee, pastries, bread—for more than a hundred years, the market had been the beating heart of Philly's large Italian American population.

As Jessica and Sophie walked up Ninth Street, Jessica thought about the scene in *Psycho*. She thought of the killer entering the bathroom, throwing back the curtain, raising the knife. She thought of the young woman's screams. She thought of the huge splatter of blood in that bathroom.

She held Sophie's hand a little tighter.

They were on their way to Ralph's, the landmark Italian restaurant. They had dinner once a week with Jessica's father, Peter.

"So how was school?" Jessica asked.

They walked in that lazy, no-place-to-be, not-a-care-in-the-world way that Jessica remembered from her childhood. Oh, to be three again.

"Preschool," Sophie corrected.

"Preschool," Jessica said.

"I had an awfully good time," Sophie said.

When Jessica had joined the force, she'd spent her first year patrolling this beat. She knew every crack in the sidewalk, every chipped brick, every doorway, every sewer grate—

"Bella ragazza!"

—and every voice. This one could only belong to Rocco Lancione, owner of Lancione & Sons, purveyors of fine meats and poultry.

Jessica and Sophie turned around to see Rocco standing in the doorway of his shop. He had to be in his midseventies now. He was a short, plump man with jet-black dyed hair and a blindingly white, spotlessly clean apron, courtesy of the fact that his sons and grandsons did all the work at their meat store these days. Rocco had tips missing from two fingers on his left hand. A hazard of the butcher's trade. To this day he kept his left hand in his pocket when he was outside the store.

"Hi, Mr. Lancione," Jessica said. No matter how old she got, he would always be *Mr.* Lancione.

With his right hand, Rocco reached behind Sophie's ear and magically produced a piece of Ferrara *torrone,* the individually boxed nougat candy Jessica had grown up with. Jessica remembered many a Christmas Day when she had wrestled her cousin Angela for the last piece of Ferrara *torrone.* Rocco Lancione had been finding the sweet, chewy confection behind little girls' ears for almost fifty years. He held it out in front of Sophie's widening eyes. Sophie glanced at Jessica before taking it. *That's my girl,* Jessica thought.

"It's okay, honey," Jessica said.

The candy was snatched and stashed in a blur.

"Say thank you to Mr. Lancione."

"Thank you."

Rocco wagged a warning finger. "Wait until after your dinner to eat that, okay, sweetie?"

Sophie nodded, clearly plotting a predinner strategy.

"How's your father?" Rocco asked.

"He's good," Jessica said.

"Is he happy in his retirement?"

If you called abject misery, mind-numbing boredom and spending sixteen hours a day bitching about the crime rate happy, he was ecstatic. "He's great. Taking it easy. We're off to meet him for dinner."

"Villa di Roma?"

"Ralph's."

Rocco nodded his approval. "Give him my best."

"I sure will."

Rocco hugged Jessica. Sophie offered a cheek to be kissed. Being an Italian male, and never passing the opportunity to kiss a pretty girl, Rocco bent down and happily complied.

What a little diva, Jessica thought.

Where does she get it?

PETER GIOVANNI STOOD on the Palumbo playground, impeccably turned out in cream linen slacks, a black cotton shirt, and sandals. With his ice-white hair and deep tan he could have passed for an escort working the Italian Riviera, waiting to charm some wealthy American widow.

They headed to Ralph's, with Sophie on point just a few feet ahead.

"She's getting big," Peter said.

Jessica looked at her daughter. She *was* getting bigger. Wasn't it just yesterday she took her first wobbly steps across the living room? Wasn't it just yesterday that her feet didn't reach the pedals of her tricycle?

Jessica was just about to respond when she glanced at her father. He had that wistful look he was starting to have with some regularity. Was it all retirees, or just retired cops? Jessica wondered. She asked, "What is it, Pa?"

Peter waved a hand. "Ah. Nothing."

"Pa."

Peter Giovanni knew when he had to answer. It had been this way with his late wife, Maria. It was this way with his daughter. One day, it would be this way with Sophie. "I just . . . I just don't want you to make the same mistakes I made, Jess."

"What are you talking about?"

"You know what I mean."

Jessica did, but if she didn't press the issue, it would give credence to what her father was saying. And she couldn't do that. She didn't *believe* that. "I really don't."

Peter looked up and down the street, gathering his thoughts. He waved to a man leaning out of the third-floor window of a trinity row house. "You can't make your life all about the job."

"It isn't."

Peter Giovanni labored under the yoke of guilt that he had neglected

his children when they were growing up. Nothing could have been far-
ther from the truth. When Jessica's mother, Maria, passed away from
breast cancer at the age of thirty-one, when Jessica was only five, Peter
Giovanni dedicated his life to raising his daughter and his son, Michael.
Maybe he wasn't there for every Little League game, and every dance
recital, but every birthday, every Christmas, every Easter was special. All
Jessica could remember were happy times growing up in the house on
Catharine Street.

"Okay," Peter began. "How many of your friends are not on the job?"

One, Jessica thought. Maybe two. "Plenty."

"Gonna make me ask you to name them?"

"Okay, Lieutenant," she said, surrendering to the truth. "But I like
the people I work with. I like cops."

"Me, too," Peter said.

For as long as she could remember, cops had been Jessica's extended
family. From the moment her mother died, she had been cocooned in a
family of blue. Her earliest memories were of a houseful of officers. She
remembered well a female officer who would come over and take her
shopping for school clothes. There were always patrol cars parked on the
street in front of their house.

"Look," Peter began again. "After your mother died, I had no idea
what to do. I had a young son and a younger daughter. I lived, breathed,
ate, and slept the job. I missed so much of your lives."

"That's not true, Dad."

Peter held up a hand, stopping her. "Jess. We don't have to pretend."

Jessica let her father have his moment, as misguided as it was.

"Then after Michael . . ." In the past fifteen or so years, that's about
as far as Peter Giovanni had ever gotten with that sentence.

Jessica's older brother, Michael, was killed in Kuwait in 1991. Her
father shut down that day, closing his heart to any and all feelings. It
wasn't until Sophie came along that he dared to reopen.

It wasn't long after Michael's death that Peter Giovanni entered a
reckless phase on the job. If you're a baker or a shoe salesman, being
reckless is not the worst thing in the world. For a cop, it *is* the worst
thing in the world. When Jessica got her gold shield, it was all the incen-
tive Peter needed. He turned in his papers the same day.

Peter reined in his emotions. "You've got, what, eight years on the
job now?"

Jessica knew that her father knew *exactly* how long she had been in blue. Probably to the week, day, and hour. "Yeah. About that."

Peter nodded. "Don't stay too long. That's all I'm saying."

"What's too long?"

Peter smiled. "Eight and a half years." He took her hand in his, squeezed. They stopped walking. He looked into her eyes. "You know I'm proud of you, right?"

"I know, Pa."

"I mean, you're thirty years old and you're working homicides. You're working real cases. You're making a difference in people's lives."

"I hope so," Jessica said.

"There just comes a time when . . . the cases start working *you*."

Jessica knew exactly what he meant.

"I just worry about you, honey." Peter trailed off, the emotion once again stealing his words for the moment.

They got their feelings in check, entered Ralph's, got a table. They ordered their usual cavatelli with meat sauce. They talked no more of the job or crime or the state of affairs of the City of Brotherly Love. Instead, Peter enjoyed the company of his two girls.

When they parted company, they hugged a little longer than usual.

"Why do you want me to put it on?"

She holds the white dress up in front of her. It is a scoop-neck white T-shirt dress, long-sleeved, flared at the hips, cut just below the knee. It took a little searching to locate one, but I finally found it at a Salvation Army thrift store in Upper Darby. The dress is inexpensive, but on her figure it will look fabulous. It is the kind of dress that was popular in the 1980s.

Tonight it is 1987.

"Because I think it would look good on you."

She turns her head and smiles slightly. Coy and demure. I hope this won't be a problem. "You're a kinky boy, aren't you?"

"Guilty as charged."

"Is there anything else?"

"I want to call you Alex."

She laughs. "Alex?"

"Yes."

"Why?"

"Let's just say it's a screen test of sorts."

She thinks about it for a few moments. She holds the dress up again, stares at herself in the full-length cheval glass. The idea seems to appeal to her. Finally.

"Oh, why not?" she says. "I'm a little drunk."

"I'll be right out here, Alex," I say.

She steps into the bathroom, sees that I have filled the tub. She shrugs, closes the door.

Her apartment is decorated in the funky, eclectic style, a décor comprising an amalgam of mismatched sofas, tables, bookcases, prints, and rugs that were probably donated by family members, with the occasional flourish of color and individuality purchased at Pier 1 or Crate & Barrel or Pottery Barn.

I flip through her CDs, looking for something from the 1980s. I find Celine Dion, Matchbox 20, Enrique Iglesias, Martina McBride. Nothing that really speaks to the era. Then I luck out. At the back of the drawer is a dusty boxed set of *Madame Butterfly*.

I put the CD in the player, forward to "Un bel di, vedremo." Soon the apartment is filled with longing.

I cross the living room and ease open the bathroom door. She spins around quickly, a little surprised to see me standing there. She sees the camera in my hand, hesitates for a moment, then smiles. "I look like such a slut." She turns to the right, then the left, smoothing the dress over her hips, striking a *Cosmo* cover pose.

"You say that like it's a bad thing."

She giggles. She really is adorable.

"Stand over here," I say, pointing to an area at the foot of the tub.

She obeys. She vamps for me. "What do you think?"

I look her up and down. "You look perfect. You look just like a movie star."

"Sweet talker."

I step forward, camera raised, and push her gently backward. She falls into the tub with a great splash. I need her dripping wet for the shot. She flails her arms and legs wildly, trying to get out of the tub.

She manages to rise to her feet, soaking wet, appropriately outraged. I cannot blame her. In my defense, I made sure the water in the tub was not too hot. She turns to face me, rage in her eyes.

I shoot her in the chest.

One quick shot, bringing the pistol up from my hip. The wound blossoms on the white dress, spreading outward like small red hands offering benediction.

She stands quite still for a moment, the reality of it all slowly dawning on her pretty face. There is that initial look of violation, followed quickly by the horror of what has just happened to her, this abrupt and violent punctuation of her young life. I look behind her to see the thick impasto of tissue and blood on the venetian blind.

She slides down the tile wall, slicking it crimson. She sinks into the tub.

With the camera in one hand and the gun in the other, I walk forward, as smoothly as I can. It is certainly not as smooth as it would be on a track, but I think it will lend a certain immediacy to the moment, a certain vérité.

Through the lens, the water runs red—scarlet fish struggling to the surface. The camera loves blood. The light is ideal.

I zoom in on her eyes—dead white orbs in the bathwater. I hold the shot for a moment, then—

CUT TO:

A few minutes later. I am ready to strike the set, as it were. I have everything packed and ready. I start *Madame Butterfly* at the beginning of *atto secondo.* It really is moving.

I wipe down the few things I have touched. I pause at the door, surveying the set. Perfect.

That's a wrap.

BYRNE CONSIDERED WEARING A SHIRT AND TIE, BUT DECIDED against it. The less attention he called to himself in the places he had to go, the better. On the other hand, he wasn't quite the imposing figure he once was. And maybe that was a good thing. Tonight he needed to be small. Tonight he needed to be one of *them*.

When you're a cop, there are only two types of people in the world. Knuckleheads and cops. Them and us.

The thought made him consider the question. Again.

Could he really retire? Could he *really* become one of them? In a few years, when the older cops he knew had retired, and he got pulled over, they really wouldn't know him. He'd be a just another knucklehead. He'd tell the scrub who he was, and where he'd worked, and some stupid story about the job; he'd flash his retirement ID and the kid would let him go.

But he wouldn't be inside. Being inside meant everything. Not just the respect, or the authority, but the juice. He thought he had made the decision. Obviously he wasn't ready.

He decided on a black dress shirt and black jeans. He was surprised to find that his black peg-legged Levi's fit him again. Perhaps there was an upside to being shot in the head. You lose weight. Maybe he'd write a book: *The Attempted Murder Diet*.

He had made it through most of the day without his cane—having steeled himself with pride and Vicodin—and he considered not bringing it with him now, but soon banished the thought. How was he supposed to get around without it? *Face it, Kevin. You need a cane to walk.* Besides, maybe he would appear weak, and that was probably a good thing.

On the other hand, a cane might make him more memorable, and that was something he didn't want. He had no idea what they might find this night.

Oh, yeah. I remember him. Big guy. Walked with a limp. That's the guy, Your Honor.

He took the cane.

He also took his weapon.

WITH SOPHIE BATHED AND DRIED—AND POWDERED, ANOTHER one of her new things—Jessica began to relax. And with the calm came the doubts. She considered her life as it was. She had just turned thirty. Her father was getting older, still vibrant and active, but aimless and alone in his retirement. She worried about him. Her little girl was growing up by the moment, and somehow the possibility loomed that she might grow up in a house in which her father did not live.

Hadn't Jessica just been a little girl herself, running up and down Catharine Street, a water ice in hand, not a care in the world?

When did all this happen?

WHILE SOPHIE COLORED a coloring book at the dining room table, and all was right with the world for the moment, Jessica put a videotape in the VCR.

She had taken a copy of *Psycho* out of the Free Library. It had been quite awhile since she had seen the movie start-to-finish. She doubted if she could ever watch it again without thinking about this case.

When she was in her teens she had been a fan of horror movies, the sort of fare that took her and her friends to the cineplex on Friday nights. She remembered renting movies while she babysat for Dr. Iacone and his two little boys—she and her cousin Angela watching *Friday the 13th*, *Nightmare on Elm Street,* the *Halloween* series.

Her interest faded the minute she became a cop, of course. She saw enough of the reality every day. She didn't need to call it entertainment at night.

Still, a movie like *Psycho* certainly transcended the slasher fare.

What was it about this film that made the killer want to reenact the scene? Beyond that, what made him want to share with an unsuspecting public in such a twisted way?

What was the mind-set?

She watched the scenes leading up to the shower sequence with a dark anticipation, although she really didn't know why. Did she really think that every copy of *Psycho* in the city had been altered? The shower scene passed without incident, but it was the scenes directly afterward that got her added attention.

She watched Norman clean up after the murder—spreading the shower curtain on the floor, dragging his victim's body onto it, mopping the tile and tub, backing Janet Leigh's car up to the motel room door.

Norman then carries the body to the open car trunk and places it inside. Afterward, he returns to the motel room and methodically collects all of Marion's belongings, including the newspaper containing the money she had stolen from her boss. He stuffs all of it into the trunk of the car and drives it to the edge of the lake nearby. Once there, he pushes it into the water.

The car begins to sink, slowly being consumed by the black water. Then it stops. Hitchcock cuts to a reaction shot of Norman, who glances around, nervously. After an excruciating few seconds, the car continues to descend, eventually disappearing from view.

Cut to the next day.

Jessica hit PAUSE, her mind racing.

The Rivercrest Motel was just a few blocks from the Schuylkill River. If their doer was as obsessed with re-creating the murder from *Psycho* as he appeared to be, maybe he took it all the way. Maybe he stuffed the body into the trunk of a car and submerged it in water, the way Anthony Perkins had done with Janet Leigh.

Jessica picked up the phone and called the Marine Unit.

2 0

THIRTEENTH STREET WAS THE LAST REMAINING SEEDY STRETCH of downtown, at least as far as adult entertainment was concerned. From Arch Street, where it was bounded by two adult bookstores and one strip joint, to about Locust Street, where there was another short belt of adult clubs and a larger, more upscale "gentleman's club," it was the one street the Philadelphia Convention and Visitors Bureau told visitors to avoid despite the fact it ran smack into the Convention Center.

By ten o'clock, the bars were starting to fill up with their strange smorgasbord of rough trade and out-of-town business types. What Philly lacked in quantity, it certainly made up for in breadth of depravity and innovation: from underwear lap dances to maraschino cherry dances. In the BYOB places, the law permitted customers to bring their own liquor, which allowed full nudity on the premises. In some of the places where alcohol *was* served, the girls wore a thin latex covering that made it *look* like they were nude. If necessity was the mother of invention in most areas of commerce, it was the lifeblood of the adult entertainment industry. One BYOB club, the Show and Tell, had lines around the block on weekends.

By midnight, Byrne and Victoria had visited half a dozen clubs. No one had seen Julian Matisse or, if they had, they were too afraid to acknowledge it. The possibility that Matisse had left town was becoming more and more likely.

At around one o'clock, they arrived at a club called Tick Tock. It was another licensed club that catered to that second-tier businessman, the guy from Dubuque who had concluded his business in Center City and found himself drunk and horny and diverted on his way back to the Hyatt Penn's Landing or the Sheraton Society Hill.

As they approached the front door of the freestanding building, they heard a loud discussion between a big man and a young woman. They were in the shadows at the far end of the parking lot. At one time, Byrne might have intervened, even off duty. Those days were behind him.

The Tick Tock was a typical urban strip club—a short runway bar with a pole, a handful of sad and sagging dancers, a two-watered-down-drink minimum. The air was dense with smoke, cheap cologne, and the primal smell of sexual desperation.

A tall, skinny black girl with a platinum wig was on the pole when they walked in, dancing to an old Prince song. Every so often she'd get down on her knees and crawl the area in front of the men at the bar. Some of the men waved money; most didn't. Every so often she'd pick up the bills and hook them on her G-string. If she stayed in the red and yellow lights she looked passable, at least for a downtown club. If she stepped into the white light, you could see the mileage. She avoided the white spotlights.

Byrne and Victoria stayed at the back bar. Victoria sat a few stools away from Byrne, giving him his play. The men were all very interested in her until they got a good look. They did their double takes, not entirely ruling her out. It was still early. It was clear they all felt they could do better. For the money. Occasionally a business type would stop, lean in, whisper something to her. Byrne wasn't worried. Victoria could handle herself.

Byrne was on his second Coke when a young woman approached, sidled up next to him. She wasn't a dancer; she was a pro, working the back of the room. She was on the tall side, brunette, wore a charcoal pin-striped business suit and black stiletto heels. The skirt was very short, and she wore nothing under the blazer. Byrne figured her routine was to fulfill the secretary fantasy a lot of these visiting businessmen had for their office mates back home. Byrne recognized her as the girl being pushed around in the parking lot earlier. She had the flushed, healthy complexion of a recently transplanted country girl, perhaps from Lancaster or Shamokin, someone who hadn't been at this long. That glow will certainly fade, Byrne thought.

"Hi."

"Hi," Byrne replied.

She looked him up and down, smiled. She was very pretty. "You are one big guy, fella."

"All my clothes are big. It works out well."

She smiled. "What's your name?" she asked, having to shout over the music. A new dancer was up, a chunky Latina in a strawberry-red teddy and maroon pumps. She danced to an old-school song by the Gap Band.

"Denny."

She nodded, as if he had just given her a tip on her taxes. "My name's Lucky. Nice to meet you, Denny."

She said *Denny* with an emphasis that told Byrne she knew it was not his real name and, at the same time, that she didn't care. Nobody at the Tick Tock had a real name.

"Nice to meet you," Byrne replied.

"Whatcha up to tonight?"

"Actually, I'm looking for an old friend of mine," Byrne said. "He used to come here all the time."

"Oh yeah? What's his name?"

"His name is Julian Matisse. Know him?"

"Julian? Yeah, I know him."

"Know where I can find him?"

"Yeah, sure," she said. "I can take you right to him."

"Right now?"

The girl looked around the room. "Gimme a minute."

"Sure."

Lucky made her way across the room, over to where Byrne figured the offices were. He caught Victoria's eye and gave her a nod. After a few minutes, Lucky returned. She had her purse over her shoulder.

"Ready to go?" she asked.

"Sure."

"I generally don't provide such services for free, ya know," she said with a wink. "Gal's gotta make a living."

Byrne reached into his pocket. He pulled out a hundred-dollar bill, tore it in half. He handed one half to Lucky. He didn't have to explain.

She grabbed the half, smiled and took him by the hand, said: "Told ya I was Lucky."

As they headed to the door, Byrne caught Victoria's eye again. He held up five fingers.

THEY WALKED A block to a crumbling corner building, the type of structure that was known in Philly as a Father, Son and Holy Ghost—a three-story row house. Some called it a trinity. Lights burned in a few of the windows. They walked down the side street and around back. They entered the row house and walked up the rickety stairs. The pain in Byrne's back and legs was excruciating.

At the top of the stairs, Lucky pushed open the door, entered. Byrne followed.

The apartment was crackhead-filthy. Stacks of newspapers and old magazines lined the corners. It smelled like rotting dog food. A broken pipe in the bathroom or kitchen had left a damp, briny odor throughout the space, warping the old linoleum, decaying the baseboards. There were half a dozen scented candles burning throughout, but they did little to mask the stench. From somewhere nearby a rap song played.

They walked to the front room.

"He's in the bedroom," Lucky said.

Byrne turned toward the door to which she was pointing. He glanced back, saw the infinitesimal tic on the girl's face, heard the creak of the floorboard, caught the flickering reflection in the window overlooking the street.

As far as he could tell, there was just one coming.

Byrne timed the impact, silently counting down as the heavy footsteps approached. He sidestepped at the last second. The guy was big, broad-shouldered, young. He slammed into the plaster. When he recovered, he turned, dazed, came at Byrne again. Byrne planted his feet and brought the cane up and out with all his strength. It caught the guy in the throat. A clot of blood and mucus flew out of his mouth. The guy tried to regain his balance. Byrne hit him again, this time low, just below the knee. He screamed once, then folded to the floor, scrambling to get something out of his waistband. It was a Buck knife in a canvas sheath. Byrne stepped on the man's hand with one foot, kicked the knife across the room with the other.

The man was not Julian Matisse. It had been a setup, a classic ambush. Byrne had all but known that it would be, but if word just happened to spread that a guy named Denny was looking for someone, and that you fucked with him at your own peril, it might make the rest of the night and the next few days move a little more smoothly.

Byrne looked at the man on the floor. He was clutching his throat, gasping for air. Byrne turned to the girl. She was shaking, backing slowly toward the door.

"He . . . he made me do it," she said. "He hurts me." She pushed up her sleeves, revealing black-and-blue bruises on her arms.

Byrne had been in this business a long time, and he knew who was telling the truth and who wasn't. Lucky was just a kid, not a day over twenty. Guys like this guy preyed on girls like her all the time. Byrne rolled the guy over, reached into his back pocket, pulled out his wallet, took his driver's license. His name was Gregory Wahl. Byrne rummaged his other pockets and found a thick roll of cash in a rubber band—maybe a grand. He peeled off a hundred, pocketed it, then tossed the money to the girl.

"You're . . . fuckin' . . . *dead,*" Wahl managed.

Byrne pulled up his own shirt, revealing the butt of the Glock. "We can end this right now if you like, Greg."

Wahl continued to stare at him, but the threat was gone from his face.

"No? Don't want to play anymore? Didn't think so. Look at the floor," Byrne said. The man complied. Byrne turned his attention to the girl. "Leave town. Tonight."

Lucky looked side-to-side, unable to move. She had noticed the gun, too. Byrne saw that the roll of cash had already been spirited away. "What?"

"Run."

Fear flashed in her eyes. "But if I do, how do I know you won't——"

"This is a one-time-only offer, Lucky. Good for another five seconds."

She ran. *Amazing what women can do in high heels when they have to,* Byrne thought. In a few seconds he heard her footsteps on the stairs. Then he heard the back door slam.

Byrne knelt down. For the moment, the adrenaline negated any pain he may have felt in his back and legs. He grabbed Wahl by the hair and pulled his head up. "If I ever see you again this will seem like a good time. In fact, if I even *hear* about a businessman getting rolled down here in the next few *years* I'm going to assume it was you." Byrne held the driver's license in front of his face. "I'm going to take this with me as a memento of our special time together."

He stood up, grabbed his cane. He drew his weapon. "I'm going to look around. You are not going to move an inch. Hear me?"

Wahl remained defiantly silent. Byrne took the Glock, put the barrel against the man's right knee. "You like hospital food, Greg?"

"Okay, *okay.*"

Byrne walked across the front room, edged open the doors to the bathroom and bedroom. The windows were wide open in the bedroom. Someone had been in there. A cigarette burned in an ashtray. But now the room was empty.

BYRNE RETURNED TO the Tick Tock. Victoria was standing near the ladies' room, chewing on a fingernail. He made his way over. The music was pounding.

"What happened?" Victoria asked.

"Nothing," Byrne said. "Let's go."

"Did you find him?"

"No," he said.

Victoria gave him the eye. "Something happened. Tell me, Kevin."

Byrne took her by the hand. He led her toward the door.

"Let's just say I hit the Wahl."

THE X BAR was in the basement of an old furniture depot on Erie Avenue. A tall black man in a yellowing white linen suit stood at the door. He wore a Panama hat and red patent-leather shoes, a dozen or so gold bangle bracelets on his right wrist. Two doorways west, partially shadowed, stood a shorter but far more muscular man—shaved head, sparrow tats on his massive arms.

The cover charge was twenty-five dollars each. They paid a pretty young woman in a pink leather fetish dress just inside the door. She slipped the money through a metal slot in the wall behind her.

They entered and went down a long, narrow staircase to an even longer hallway. The walls were painted a glossy raspberry enamel. The thumping rhythm of a disco song got louder as they neared the end of the corridor.

The X Bar was one of the few hard-core S&M clubs left in Philadelphia, a throwback to the hedonistic 1970s, a pre-AIDS world in which anything went.

Before they made the turn into the main room, they encountered a niche built into the wall, a deep alcove in which a woman sat on a chair. She was middle-aged, white. She wore a leather master mask. At first, Byrne wasn't sure if she was real or not. The skin on her arms and thighs looked waxen, and she sat absolutely still. When a pair of men approached, the woman stood up. One of the men wore a full-torso straitjacket and a dog collar attached to a leash. The other man roughly yanked him to the woman's feet. The woman took out a riding crop and lightly flailed the one in the straitjacket. Soon he began to cry.

As Byrne and Victoria made their way across the main room, Byrne saw that half the people were in S&M costumes: leather and chains, spikes, catsuits. The other half were the curious, the hangers-on, the parasites on the lifestyle. At the far end was a small stage with a lone spotlight on a wooden chair. No one was on the stage at the moment.

Byrne walked behind Victoria. He watched the reactions she aroused. The men immediately spotted her: her sexy figure, the smooth confident gait, that mane of black shiny hair. When they saw her face they did a double take.

But in this place, in this lighting, she was exotica. All styles were served here.

They made their way to the back bar, where a bartender was wiping down the mahogany. He wore a leather vest, no shirt, a studded collar. He had greasy brown hair, swept back from his forehead, a deep widow's peak. Each forearm held an elaborate spider tattoo. At the last second, the man looked up. He saw Victoria and smiled a mouthful of yellow teeth, topped by grayish gums.

"Hey, baby," he said.

"How are you?" Victoria replied. She slipped onto the last stool.

The man leaned over and kissed her hand. "Never better," he replied.

The bartender looked over her shoulder, saw Byrne, and his smile quickly faded. Byrne held his gaze until the man looked away. Byrne then glanced behind the bar. Next to the shelves of liquor were racks of books appealing to the BDSM culture—leather sex, fisting, tickling, slave training, spanking.

"The place is crowded," Victoria said.

"You should see it on Saturday nights," the man replied.

I'll pass, Byrne thought.

"This is a good friend of mine," Victoria said to the bartender. "Denny Riley."

The man was forced to officially acknowledge Byrne's presence. Byrne shook hands with him. They had met before, but the man at the bar didn't remember. His name was Darryl Porter. Byrne had been there the night Porter had been busted for procuring and contributing to the delinquency of a minor. The bust came at a party in Northern Liberties where a group of underaged girls were found partying with a pair of Nigerian businessmen. Some of the girls were as young as twelve. Porter, if Byrne remembered correctly, had done only a year or so on a plea bargain. Darryl Porter was a chicken hawk. For this and many other reasons, Byrne wanted to wash his hand.

"So what brings you to our little slice of heaven?" Porter asked. He poured a glass of white wine and set it in front of Victoria. He didn't even ask Byrne.

"I'm looking for an old friend," Victoria said.

"Who would that be?"

"Julian Matisse."

Darryl Porter furrowed his brow. Either he was a good actor or he didn't know, Byrne thought. He watched the man's eyes. Then—a flicker? Definitely.

"Julian's in jail. Greene, last I heard."

Victoria sipped her wine, shook her head. "He's out."

Darryl Porter mugged, wiped down the bar. "First I'm hearing of it. I thought he was pulling the whole train."

"He's out on some kind of technicality, I think."

"Julian's good people," Porter said. "We go back."

Byrne wanted to jump across the bar. Instead he glanced to his right. A short, bald man was sitting on the stool next to Victoria. The man was meekly giving Byrne the eye. He wore a Campfire Girl outfit.

Byrne turned his attention back to Darryl Porter. Porter filled a few drink orders, returned, leaned over the bar, whispered something in Victoria's ear, keeping eye contact with Byrne the whole time. Men and their fucking power trips, Byrne thought.

Victoria laughed, tossed her hair over a shoulder. It made Byrne's stomach flip to think she would in any way be flattered by the attentions of someone like Darryl Porter. She was so much more than that. Maybe she was just playing her part. Maybe it was jealousy on *his* part.

"We've got to run," Victoria said.

"Okay, babe. I'll ask around. If I hear anything, I'll call you," Porter said.

Victoria nodded. "Cool."

"Where can I reach you?" he asked.

"I'll call you tomorrow."

Victoria dropped a ten on the bar. Porter folded it up and handed it back to her. She smiled, slipped off her stool. Porter smiled back, went back to wiping down the bar. He didn't look at Byrne again.

On stage, a pair of women in blindfolds and gag ball trainers knelt before a huge black man in a leather mask.

The man held a thong whip.

BYRNE AND VICTORIA stepped out in the humid night air, no closer to finding Julian Matisse than they had been at the beginning of the night. After the madness of the X Bar, the city was shockingly still and quiet. It even smelled clean.

It was nearly four o'clock.

On the way to the car, they rounded a corner and saw two kids: young black boys, maybe eight and ten years old, patched jeans, ratty sneaks. They sat on a row house stoop behind a box full of mixed-breed puppies. Victoria looked over at Byrne, lower lip out, eyebrows aloft.

"No, no, no," Byrne said. "Unh-unh. No way."

"You should have a puppy, Kevin."

"Not me."

"Why not?"

"Tori," Byrne said. "I have enough trouble taking care of myself."

She gave him a puppy look of her own then knelt down next to the box and surveyed the small sea of furry faces. She grabbed one of the dogs, stood, and held him up in the streetlight, like a chalice.

Byrne leaned against the brick wall, propped his cane. He took the dog. The puppy's rear legs freewheeled in the air as it began to lick his face.

"He likes you, man," the younger kid said. He was obviously the Donald Trump of this organization.

As far as Byrne could tell, the puppy was a shepherd-collie mix, another child of the night. "If I were interested in buying this dog—and I'm not saying I am—how much would you want for it?" he asked.

"Fiddy dollars," the kid said.

Byrne looked at the handmade sign on the front of the cardboard box. "It says twenty dollars on the box."

"That's a five."

"That's a two."

The kid shook his head. He stepped in front of the box, obscuring Byrne's view. "Nunh-unh. These is thorobed dogs."

"Thorobeds?"

"Yeah."

"You sure?"

"Most def."

"What kind are they exactly?"

"They Philadelphia pit bulls."

Byrne had to smile. "Is that right?"

"No doubt," the kid said.

"I've never heard of that breed."

"They the best, man. They do they bidness outside, they guard the house, they don't eat that much." The kid smiled. Killer charm. He was headed all the way in one direction or the other.

Byrne glanced at Victoria. He was starting to soften. Slightly. He tried his best to conceal it.

Byrne slipped the puppy back into the box. He looked at the boys. "Isn't it a little late for you guys to be out?"

"Late? Nah, man. It's *early*. We up *early*. We businessmen."

"All right," Byrne said. "You guys stay out of trouble." Victoria took his arm as they turned and walked away.

"Don't you want the dog?" the kid asked.

"Not tonight," Byrne said.

"Forty for you," the kid said.

"I'll let you know tomorrow."

"They might be gone tomorrow."

"Me, too," Byrne said.

The kid shrugged. And why not?

He had a thousand years to go.

WHEN THEY REACHED Victoria's car on Thirteenth Street, they saw a van across the street being vandalized. Three teenaged boys broke the driver's window with a brick, setting off the alarm. One of them reached in, grabbed whatever was on the front seat. It looked like a pair of thirty-five-millimeter cameras. When the kids spotted Byrne and Victoria, they took off down the street. In a second they were gone.

Byrne and Victoria shared a glance, a shake of the head. "Hang on," Byrne said. "I'll be right back."

He crossed the street, turned 360, making sure he was not being observed, and, after wiping it down with his shirttail, dropped Gregory Wahl's driver's license into the burglarized vehicle.

VICTORIA LINDSTROM LIVED in a small apartment in the Fishtown section. It was decorated in a very feminine style: French provincial furniture, gauzy scarves on the lamps, floral wallpaper. Everywhere he looked he saw an afghan or a knitted throw. Byrne envisioned many a night when Victoria sat here alone, needles in hand, a glass of Chardonnay at her side. Byrne also noted that, with every light on, it was still dim. All the lamps had low-watt bulbs. He understood.

"Would you like a drink?" she asked.

"Sure."

She poured him three inches of bourbon, handed him the glass. He sat on the arm of her couch.

"We try again tomorrow night," Victoria said.

"I really appreciate this, Tori."

Victoria waved him off. Byrne read a lot in the wave. Victoria had a stake in getting Julian Matisse off the street again. Or, perhaps, off the world.

Byrne gulped half the bourbon. Almost instantly it met the Vicodin in his system and produced a warm glow inside. He had held off drinking alcohol all night for that very reason. He glanced at his watch. It was time to go. He had taken more than enough of Victoria's time.

Victoria walked him to the door.

At the door, she put her arms around his waist, her head on his chest. She had kicked off her shoes and, without them, she seemed small. Byrne had never really realized how petite she was. Her spirit always made her seem larger than life.

After a few moments, she looked up at him, her silver eyes nearly black in the dim light. What began as an affectionate hug and a kiss on the cheek, the parting of two old friends, suddenly became something else. Victoria pulled him close and kissed him deeply. Afterward, they pulled back and looked at each other, not so much out of lust as, perhaps, surprise. Had this always been in them? Had this feeling been simmering just below the surface for fifteen years? The look on Victoria's face told Byrne he wasn't going anywhere.

She smiled as she began to unbutton his shirt.

"What exactly are your intentions here, Miss Lindstrom?" Byrne asked.

"I'll never tell."

"Yes you will."

More buttons. "What makes you think so?"

"I happen to be a very skilled lawman," Byrne said.

"Is that right?"

"Oh yes."

"Will you take me into a small room?" She unbuttoned a few more buttons.

"Yes."

"Will you make me sweat?"

"I'll certainly do my best."

"Will you make me talk?"

"Oh, there's no question about that. I am a seasoned interrogator. KGB."

"I see," Victoria said. "And what is KGB?"

Byrne held up his cane. "Kevin Gimp Byrne."

Victoria laughed as she slid his shirt off, and led him to the bedroom.

AFTERWARD, AS THEY lay in the afterglow, Victoria took one of Byrne's hands in hers. The sun was just beginning to breach the horizon.

Victoria gently kissed his fingertips, one by one. She then took his right forefinger and slowly traced the scars on her face.

Byrne knew that, after all these years, after they had finally made love, what Victoria was doing right then was far more intimate than sex. He had never felt closer to a human being in his life.

He thought about all the stations of her life to which he had been present—the teenaged firebrand, the victim of a horrible attack, the strong, independent woman she had become. He realized that he had long harbored a great and mysterious well of feelings for her, a cache of emotion he had never been able to identify.

When he felt the tears on her face, he knew.

All this time, the feelings had been love.

THE MARINE UNIT OF THE PHILADELPHIA POLICE DEPARTMENT
had been in operation for more than 150 years, its charter having evolved
over time from one of assisting the commerce of marine traffic up and
down the Delaware and Schuylkill rivers to one of patrol, recovery, and
rescue. In the 1950s the unit added diving to its duty roster, and since
that time had become one of the elite aquatic divisions in the nation.

Essentially, the Marine Unit was an extension and supplement to the
PPD patrol force whose job it was to respond to any and all water-related
emergencies, as well as recoveries of persons, property, and evidence
from the water.

They had begun dragging the river at first light, starting at an area
just south of the Strawberry Mansion Bridge. The Schuylkill River was
murky, with no visibility from the surface. The process would be slow
and methodical, with divers working a grid along the banks in fifty-foot
segments.

By the time Jessica arrived on the scene at just after eight, they had
cleared a two-hundred-foot section. She found Byrne standing on the
bank, silhouetted against the dark water. He had his cane with him. Jes-

sica's heart nearly broke. She knew he was a proud man, and a concession to weakness—any weakness—was hard. She made her way down to the river, a pair of coffees in hand.

"Good morning," Jessica said, handing Byrne a cup.

"Hey," he said. He hoisted the cup. "Thanks."

"Anything?"

Byrne shook his head. He put his coffee on a bench, lit a cigarette, glanced at the bright red matchbook. It was from the Rivercrest Motel. He held it up. "If we don't find anything, I think we should take another run at this dump's manager."

Jessica thought about Karl Stott. She didn't like him for the murder, but she didn't think he was telling the full truth, either. "Think he's holding out?"

"I think he has a hard time remembering things," Byrne said. "On purpose."

Jessica looked out over the water. Here, on this gentle bend of the Schuylkill River, it was hard to reconcile what happened just a few blocks away at the Rivercrest Motel. If she was right about her hunch—and there was an overwhelming chance she was not—she wondered how such a beautiful place as this could host such horror. The trees were in full bloom; the water gently rocked the boats at the dock. She was just about to respond when her two-way radio crackled to life.

"Yeah."

"Detective Balzano?"

"I'm here."

"We found something."

THE CAR WAS a 1996 Saturn, submerged in the river a quarter mile from the Marine Unit's own mini station on Kelly Drive. The station was only manned during daywork so, under cover of darkness, no one would have seen someone driving or pushing the car into the Schuylkill. The car had no plates on it. They would run it off the VIN, the vehicle identification number, providing it was still in the car and intact.

When the car breached the surface of the water, all eyes on the riverbank turned to Jessica. Thumbs-up all around. She found Byrne's eyes. In them, she saw respect, and no small measure of admiration. It meant everything.

THE KEY WAS still in the ignition. After taking a number of photographs, a CSU officer removed it, opened the trunk. Terry Cahill and half a dozen detectives crowded around the car.

What they saw inside would live with them for a very long time.

The woman in the trunk had been destroyed. She had been stabbed repeatedly and, because of her time submerged in the water, most of the smaller wounds had puckered and closed. The larger wounds—a few in particular on the woman's stomach and thighs—oozed a brackish brown liquid.

Because she had been in the trunk of the car, and not fully exposed to the elements, her body was not covered with debris. This might make the medical examiner's job a little easier. Philadelphia was bounded by two large rivers; the ME's office had a good deal of experience with floaters.

The woman was nude, positioned on her back, her arms out to the sides, her head turned to the left. The stab wounds were too numerous to count at the scene. The cuts were clean, indicating that no animals or river life had been at her.

Jessica forced herself to look at the victim's face. Her eyes were open, shocked with red. Open, but totally void of expression. Not fear, not anger, not sorrow. Those were emotions for the living.

Jessica thought about the original scene in *Psycho,* the way the camera backed up from a close-up of Janet Leigh's face, how pretty and intact the actress's face had looked in that shot. She looked at the young woman in the trunk of this car and thought about what a difference reality makes. No makeup artist here. This was what death really looked like.

The two detectives gloved up.

"Look," Byrne said.

"What?"

Byrne pointed to the waterlogged newspaper on the right side of the trunk. It was a copy of the *Los Angeles Times.* He gently opened the paper with a pencil. Inside were wadded-up rectangles of paper.

"What is that, fake money?" Byrne asked. Bunched up inside the paper were a few stacks of what looked like photocopied hundred-dollar bills.

"Yeah," Jessica said.

"Oh, this is great," Byrne said.

Jessica leaned in, looked a little more closely. "How much do you want to bet there's forty thousand dollars in funny money in there?" she asked.

"I'm not following," Byrne said.

"In *Psycho*, Janet Leigh's character steals forty grand from her boss. She buys a Los Angeles newspaper and stashes the money inside. In the movie it's the *Los Angeles Tribune*, but that paper's defunct."

Byrne stared at her for a few seconds. "How the hell do you know this?"

"I looked it up on the Internet."

"The Internet," he said. He leaned over, poked at the phony money again, shook his head. "This guy's a real fucking piece of work."

At this point, Tom Weyrich, the deputy medical examiner, arrived with his photographer. The detectives stood back and let Dr. Weyrich in.

As Jessica pulled off her gloves and breathed in the fresh air of a new day, she felt pretty good about her hunch paying off. This was no longer about the gauzy specter of a murder committed in two dimensions on a television screen, the ethereal notion of a crime.

They had a body. They had a homicide.

They had a case.

LITTLE JAKE'S NEWSSTAND was a fixture on Filbert Street. Little Jake sold all the local papers and magazines, as well as the Pittsburgh, Harrisburg, Erie, and Allentown papers. In addition, he carried a selection of out-of-state dailies and a selection of adult magazines, discreetly displayed behind him, and covered with squares of cardboard. It was one of the few places in Philadelphia where the *Los Angeles Times* was for sale over the counter.

Nick Palladino went with the recovered Saturn and the CSU team. Jessica and Byrne interviewed Little Jake while Terry Cahill canvassed the immediate area up and down Filbert.

Little Jake Polivka had gotten his nickname due to the fact that he was somewhere in the neighborhood of six three and three hundred pounds. He was always slightly stooped over inside the kiosk. With his bushy beard, long hair, and hunched posture, he reminded Jessica of the Hagrid character in the Harry Potter movies. She had always wondered why Little Jake simply didn't buy or build a bigger kiosk, but had never asked.

"Do you have any regulars who buy the *Los Angeles Times?*" Jessica asked.

Little Jake thought for a few moments. "Not that I can think of. I only get the Sunday edition, and only four of them at that. Not a big seller."

"Do you get them on the day they're published?"

"No. I get them maybe two or three days late."

"The date we're interested in was from two weeks ago. Can you remember who you might have sold the paper to?"

Little Jake stroked his beard. Jessica noticed there were crumbs in it, remnants of this morning's breakfast. At least, she *assumed* it was this morning's. "Now that you mention it, a guy did come by and ask for it a few weeks ago. I was out of the paper at the time, but I'm pretty sure I told him when they were coming in. If he came back and bought one, I wasn't here. My brother runs the shop two days a week now."

"Do you remember what he looked like?" Byrne asked.

Little Jake shrugged. "Hard to remember. I see a lot of people here. And it's usually just this much." Little Jake squared his hands into a rectangular shape, like a movie director, framing the opening in his kiosk.

"Anything you can remember would be very helpful."

"Well, as I recall he was about as ordinary as you can get. Ball cap, sunglasses, maybe a dark blue jacket."

"What kind of cap?"

"Flyers, I think."

"Any markings on the jacket? Logos?"

"Not that I can remember."

"Do you remember his voice? Any accent?"

Little Jake shook his head. "Sorry."

Jessica made her notes. "Do you remember enough about him to talk to a sketch artist?"

"Sure!" Little Jake said, clearly animated over the prospect of being part of a real-life investigation.

"We'll arrange it." She handed Little Jake a card. "In the meantime, if you think of anything, or if you see this guy again, give us a call."

Little Jake handled the card with reverence, as if she had handed him a Larry Bowa rookie card. "Wow. Just like on *Law and Order.*"

Exactly, Jessica thought. Except on *Law & Order* they usually solved everything in about an hour. Less, when you cut out the commercials.

JESSICA, BYRNE, AND Terry Cahill sat in Interview A. The photocopied money and issue of the *Los Angeles Times* were at the lab. A sketch of the man Little Jake described was in the works. The car was on its way to the lab garage. It was that downtime between the discovery of the first concrete lead and the first forensic report.

Jessica looked at the floor, found the piece of cardboard Adam Kaslov had been nervously toying with. She picked it up, started twisting it and untwisting it, finding that it was indeed therapeutic.

Byrne took out a matchbook, turned it over and over in his hands. This was *his* therapy. You couldn't smoke anywhere in the Roundhouse. The three investigators considered the day's events in silence.

"Okay, who the hell are we looking for here?" Jessica finally asked, more as a rhetorical question, due to the anger that had begun to roil inside her, fueled by the image of the woman in the trunk of the car.

"You mean, why did he do it, right?" Byrne asked.

Jessica considered this. In their line of work, the who and the why were so closely linked. "Okay. I'll settle for why," she said. "I mean, is this just a case of someone trying to be famous? Is this an instance of a guy just trying to get on the news?"

Cahill shrugged. "Hard to say. But if you spend any time at all with the folks from Behavioral Science, you know that ninety-nine percent of cases like this go way deeper than that."

"What do you mean?" Jessica asked.

"I mean it takes a hell of a profound psychosis to do something like this. So deep that you could find yourself sitting next to the killer and never know it. This kind of stuff can be buried big time."

"When we ID the vic, we'll know a lot more," Byrne said. "Let's just hope it's personal."

"What do you mean?" Jessica asked again.

"If it's personal, it's going to end here."

Jessica knew that Kevin Byrne was of the shoe-leather school of investigation. You hit the street, you question, you intimidate the lowlifes, you get answers. He did not discount the academics. It just wasn't his style.

"You mentioned Behavioral Science," Jessica said to Cahill. "Don't tell my boss, but I'm not sure exactly what they do." She had gotten her degree in criminal justice, but it didn't encompass much from the field of criminal psychology.

"Well, primarily they study behavior and motivation, mostly in the area of training and research," Cahill said. "It's a far cry from the excitement of *The Silence of the Lambs,* though. Most of the time it's pretty dry, clinical stuff. They study gang violence, stress management, community policing, crime analysis."

"They must see the worst of the worst," Jessica said.

Cahill nodded. "When the headlines die down about a grisly case, these guys go to work. It may not look all that exciting to the average law enforcement professional, but a lot of cases get made down there. VICAP wouldn't be what it is without them."

Cahill's cell phone rang. He excused himself, stepped out of the room.

Jessica thought about what he had said. She replayed the *Psycho* shower scene in her mind. She tried to imagine the horror of that moment from the victim's point of view—the shadow on the shower curtain, the sound of the water, the rustle of the plastic as it was being whisked back, the gleam of the knife. She shivered. She twisted her piece of cardboard tighter.

"What's your gut on this?" Jessica asked. As sophisticated and high-tech as Behavioral Science and all the federally funded task forces might be, she would trade them all for the instincts of a detective like Kevin Byrne.

"My gut says that this is no thrill killing," Byrne said. "This is *about* something. And whoever he is, he wants our undivided attention."

"Well, he's got it." Jessica unrolled the piece of twisted cardboard in her hands, fully intending to twist it back up. She never got that far. "Kevin."

"What?"

"Look." Jessica carefully flattened the bright red rectangle on the battered table, avoiding putting her fingerprints on it. The look on Byrne's face said it all. He put his matchbook down next to the piece of cardboard. They were identical.

The Rivercrest Motel.

Adam Kaslov had been to the Rivercrest Motel.

HE CAME BACK TO THE ROUNDHOUSE VOLUNTARILY, AND THAT was a good thing. They certainly did not have enough to pick him up or hold him. They had told him that they simply needed to clear up a few loose ends. A classic ruse. If he caved during the interview, they had him.

Terry Cahill and ADA Paul DiCarlo observed the interview through the two-way mirror. Nick Palladino stuck with the car. The VIN was obscured, so identifying the owner was going to take a little while.

"So how long have you lived in North Philadelphia, Adam?" Byrne asked. He sat across from Kaslov. Jessica stood with her back to the closed door.

"About three years. Ever since I moved out of my folks' house."

"Where do they live?"

"Bala Cynwyd."

"Is that where you grew up?"

"Yes."

"What does your dad do, if I may ask?"

"He's in real estate."

"And your mom?"

"She's, you know, a housewife. Can I ask——"

"Do you like living in North Philly?"

Adam shrugged. "It's okay."

"Spend a lot of time in West Philly?"

"Some."

"How much would that be exactly?"

"Well, I work there."

"At the theater, right?"

"Yes."

"Cool job?" Byrne asked.

"I guess," Adam said. "Doesn't pay much."

"But at least the movies are free, right?"

"Well, the fifteenth time you have to sit through a Rob Schneider movie it doesn't seem like a bargain."

Byrne laughed, but it was clear to Jessica that he didn't know Rob Schneider from Rob Petrie. "That theater is on Walnut, isn't it?"

"Yes."

Byrne made a note, even though they knew all this. It made it look official. "Anything else?"

"What do you mean?"

"Is there any other reason you go to West Philly?"

"Not really."

"What about school, Adam? Last time I checked, Drexel was in that part of town."

"Well, yeah. I go there for school."

"Are you a full-time student?"

"Just part-time in summer."

"What are you studying?"

"English," Adam said. "I'm an English major."

"Any film classes?"

Adam shrugged. "A couple."

"What sort of things do you study in those classes?"

"Theory and criticism mostly. I just don't see what——"

"Are you a sports fan?"

"Sports? Like what?"

"Oh, I don't know. Hockey maybe. You like the Flyers?"

"They're okay."

"You have a Flyers cap by any chance?" Byrne asked.

This seemed to spook him, as if he thought the police might be following him. If he was going to shut down, it would begin now. Jessica noticed one of his shoes begin to tap the floor. "Yeah, why?"

"We just have to cover all bases."

This made no sense, of course, but the ugliness of this room, and the proximity of all these police officers, stayed Adam Kaslov's objections. For the moment.

"Ever been to a motel in West Philly?" Byrne asked.

They watched him closely, looking for the tic. He looked at the floor, the walls, the ceiling, anywhere but Kevin Byrne's jade eyes. Finally, he said, "Why would I go to a motel there?"

Bingo, Jessica thought.

"Sounds like you're answering a question with a question, Adam."

"Okay, then," he said. "No."

"You've never been to a place called the Rivercrest Motel on Dauphin Street?"

Adam Kaslov swallowed hard. Again, his eyes roamed the room. Jessica gave him something on which to focus his attention. She dropped the unrolled matchbook on the table. It was flattened in a small evidence bag. When Adam saw it, his face drained of all color. He asked: "Are you telling me that the . . . the incident on the *Psycho* tape was done at the . . . this Rivercrest Motel?"

"Yes."

"And you think that I—"

"Right now we're just trying to sort out what happened. That's what we do," Byrne said.

"But I've never been there."

"Never?"

"No. I . . . I found those matches."

"We have a witness who *puts* you there."

When Adam Kaslov had arrived at the Roundhouse, John Shepherd had taken a digital photograph of him, creating for him a visitor ID badge. Shepherd had then headed out to the Rivercrest, where he had shown the picture to Karl Stott. Shepherd called in and said that Stott recognized Adam as someone who had been to the motel at least twice in the past month.

"Who said I was there?" Adam asked.

"Not important, Adam," Byrne said. "What *is* important is that you just lied to the police. That's something we never recover from." He glanced at Jessica. "Isn't that right, Detective?"

"That's correct," Jessica said. "It hurts our feelings, and then we have a very hard time trusting you."

"She's right. We don't trust you now," Byrne added.

"But why . . . why would I bring the tape to you if I had anything to do with it?"

"Can you tell us why someone would kill somebody, videotape the murder, then insert the footage onto a prerecorded tape?"

"No," Adam said. "I can't."

"Neither can we. But if you can accept that someone actually did that, it's not much of a leap to think that the same person would bring the tape in just to taunt us. Crazy is crazy, right?"

Adam looked at the floor, remained silent.

"Tell us about the Rivercrest, Adam."

Adam rubbed his face, wrung his hands. When he looked up, the detectives were still there. He spilled. "Okay. I've been there."

"How many times?"

"Twice."

"Why do you go there?" Byrne asked.

"I just did."

"What, for a vacation or something? Did you book it through your travel agent?"

"No."

Byrne leaned forward, lowered his voice. "We're going to get to the bottom of this, Adam. With or without your help. Did you see all those people on the way up here?"

After a few seconds, Adam realized that an answer was expected. "Yes."

"See, those people never go home. They have no social or family lives whatsoever. They are on the job twenty-four hours a day, and nothing gets by them. Nothing. Take a moment to think about what you're doing. The very next thing you say may be the most important thing you ever say in your life."

Adam looked up. His eyes were shiny. "You can't tell anybody about this."

"That depends on what it is you have to tell us," Byrne said. "But if it doesn't figure into this crime, it won't leave this room."

Adam looked at Jessica, then quickly looked away. "I went there with somebody," he said. "A woman. She's a *woman*."

He said this emphatically, as if to say that suspecting him of murder was one thing. Suspecting him of being gay was far worse.

"Do you remember what room you stayed in?" Byrne asked.

"I don't know," Adam said.

"Try real hard."

"I . . . I think it was room ten."

"Both times?"

"I think so."

"What kind of car does this woman drive?"

"I really don't know. We never went in her car."

Byrne leaned back. No need to come at him hard for the moment. "Why didn't you just tell us this earlier?"

"Because," Adam began, "because she's married."

"We're going to need her name."

"I . . . can't tell you that," Adam said. He glanced from Byrne to Jessica, then at the floor.

"Look at me," Byrne said.

Slowly, reluctantly, Adam complied.

"Do I strike you as the kind of person who's going to accept that as an answer?" Byrne asked. "I mean, I know we don't know each other, but take a quick glance around this place. Do you think it looks this shitty by accident?"

"I . . . I don't know."

"Okay. Fair enough. Here's what we'll do," Byrne said. "If you don't tell us this woman's name, you're going to force us to poke around in your life. We're going to get the names of all the people in your classes, all your professors. We're going to drop in at the dean's office and ask them about you. We're going to talk to your friends, family, coworkers. Is that what you really want?"

Incredibly, instead of caving in, Adam Kaslov just looked at Jessica. For the first time since she'd met him she thought she saw something in his eyes, something sinister, something that said he was not just some scared kid in over his head. There might have even been the hint of a smile on his face. Adam asked: "I need a lawyer, don't I?"

"I'm afraid we really can't advise you on something like that, Adam," Jessica said. "But I will say that, if you have nothing to hide, you have nothing to worry about."

If Adam Kaslov was as big a film and TV buff as they suspected he was, he had probably seen enough scenes exactly like this one to know he had every right to stand up and walk out of the building without saying another word.

"Can I go now?" Adam asked.

Thanks again, Law & Order, Jessica thought.

JESSICA CONSIDERED LITTLE Jake's description: *Flyers cap, sunglasses, maybe a dark blue jacket.* A uniformed officer had looked through the windows of Adam Kaslov's car while Adam was being questioned. None of these items was in plain sight, nor was there a gray wig, a housedress, or a dark cardigan.

Adam Kaslov had a direct connection to the murder tape, he had been to the murder scene, and he had lied to the police. Was it enough for a search warrant?

"I don't think so," Paul DiCarlo said. When Adam had said his father was in real estate, he had neglected to mention that his father was Lawrence Kaslov. Lawrence Kaslov was one of the biggest developers in eastern Pennsylvania. If they moved too soon on this kid, there would be a wall of pin-striped suits up in a second.

"Maybe this will tip it," Cahill said, entering the room. He had a fax in hand.

"What is it?" Byrne asked.

"Young Mr. Kaslov has a record," Cahill replied.

Byrne and Jessica exchanged a glance. "I ran him," Byrne said. "He was clean."

"Not squeaky."

They all glanced at the fax. At fourteen, Adam Kaslov was arrested for videotaping his neighbor's teenaged daughter through her bedroom window. He received counseling and community service. He served no time in a juvenile facility.

"We can't use this," Jessica said.

Cahill shrugged. He knew as well as anyone else in the room that juvenile records are supposed to be sealed. "Just FYI."

"We're not even supposed to *know* this," Jessica added.

"Know *what*?" Cahill asked with a wink.

"Teen voyeurism is a long way from what was done to that woman," Buchanan said.

They all knew this was true. Still, every piece of information, regardless of how it was obtained, helped. They just had to be careful about the official path that took them to the next step. Any first-year law student could get a case thrown out based on illegally obtained records.

Paul DiCarlo, who was doing his best not to listen, on purpose, continued: "Right. So. When you ID the victim, and you put Adam within a mile of her, I'll be able to sell a search warrant to a judge. But not until then."

"Should we put a tail on him?" Jessica asked.

Adam was still sitting in Interview Room A. But not for long. He had already asked to leave, and every minute the door stayed locked nudged the department toward a problem.

"I can give it a few hours," Cahill said.

Buchanan looked encouraged by this. It meant the bureau would be picking up the tab for overtime on a detail that probably would not produce anything.

"You sure?" Buchanan asked.

"Not a problem."

A few minutes later, Cahill caught up to Jessica by the elevators. "Look, I really don't think this kid is going to amount to much. But I've got a few ideas about the case. How about after your tour I buy you a cup of coffee? We'll kick it around."

Jessica looked at Terry Cahill's eyes. There was always a moment with a stranger—an attractive stranger, she was loath to admit—when the innocent-sounding comment, the ingenuous offer had to be examined. Was he asking her out? Was he making a move? Or was he actually asking her for a cup of coffee to discuss a homicide investigation? She had scanned his left hand the moment she met him. He wasn't married. She, of course, was. However tenuously.

Jesus, Jess, she thought. *You've got a friggin' gun on your hip. You're probably safe.*

"Make it a scotch and you're on," she said.

FIFTEEN MINUTES AFTER Terry Cahill left, Byrne and Jessica met in the coffee room. Byrne read her mood.

"What's wrong?" he asked.

Jessica held up the evidence bag with the Rivercrest Motel matchbook. "I didn't read Adam Kaslov right the first time," Jessica said. "And it bugs the shit out of me."

"Don't worry about it. If he's our boy—and I'm not convinced he is—there are a hell of a lot of layers between the face he shows the world and the nutcase on that tape."

Jessica nodded. Byrne was right. Still, she prided herself on her ability to translate people. Every detective brought specials skill to the table. Hers were the ability to organize, and her acumen at reading people. Or so she thought. She was just about to say something when Byrne's phone rang.

"Byrne."

He listened, his intense green eyes shifting back and forth for a moment. "Thanks." He snapped shut his phone, the hint of a smile at the edges of his mouth, something Jessica had not seen in a while. She knew the look. Something was breaking.

"What's up?" she asked.

"That was CSU," he said, heading out the door. "We've got an ID."

THE *PSYCHO* VICTIM'S NAME WAS STEPHANIE CHANDLER. SHE was twenty-two years old, single, by all accounts a friendly, outgoing young woman. She lived with her mother on Fulton Street. She worked at a Center City public relations firm called Braceland Westcott McCall. They had identified her through the vehicle identification number on her car.

The preliminary report from the medical examiner's office was in. The manner of death, as expected, was ruled a homicide. Stephanie Chandler had been underwater approximately one week. The murder weapon was a large, nonserrated knife. She had been stabbed eleven times and, although he would not testify to it, at least at this point, because it was not his purview, Dr. Tom Weyrich believed that Stephanie Chandler was indeed killed on the videotape.

The tox screen revealed no evidence of illegal drugs in her system; a trace amount of alcohol. The ME had also run a rape kit. It was inconclusive.

What the reports could not say was why Stephanie Chandler was in a run-down motel in West Philly in the first place. Or, most important, who with.

A fourth detective, Eric Chavez, was now on the case, partnered with Nick Palladino. Eric was the fashion plate of the Homicide Unit, always turned out in an Italian suit. Single and available, if Eric wasn't talking about his new Zegna tie, he was talking about the newest Bordeaux in his wine rack.

As far as the detectives could piece together, the last day of Stephanie's life had gone like this:

Stephanie, a vibrant, petite young woman who favored tailored suits and Thai food and Johnny Depp movies, left for work, as always, at just after 7:00 AM, driving her champagne-colored Saturn from the Fulton Street address to her office building on South Broad Street, where she parked in an underground garage. That day she and a few of her co-workers had gone down to Penn's Landing at lunchtime to watch a film crew set up for a shot along the riverfront, hoping to catch a glimpse of a celebrity or two. At five thirty, she took the elevator down to the garage, drove out the Broad Street exit.

Jessica and Byrne would visit the Braceland Westcott McCall offices while Nick Palladino, Eric Chavez, and Terry Cahill headed down to Penn's Landing to canvass.

THE RECEPTION AREA of Braceland Westcott McCall was decorated in a modern Scandinavian style—straight lines, light cherry desks and bookcases, metal-edged mirrors, frosted-glass panels, and well-framed poster art that heralded the company's upscale clients: recording studios, advertising agencies, clothing designers.

Stephanie's boss was a woman named Andrea Cerrone. Jessica and Byrne met Andrea in Stephanie Chandler's cubicle on the top floor of the Broad Street office building.

Byrne took the lead in the questioning.

"Stephanie was pretty trusting," Andrea said, a bit unsteadily. "A little gullible, I guess." Andrea Cerrone was clearly shaken by the news of Stephanie's death.

"Was she seeing anyone?"

"Not that I know of. She got hurt pretty easily, so I think she was in shutdown mode for a while."

Andrea Cerrone was not yet thirty-five, a short, wide-hipped woman with silver-streaked hair and pastel blue eyes. Although she was somewhat overweight, her clothes were tailored with an architectural precision. She wore a dark olive linen suit and a honey-colored pashmina.

Byrne moved on. "How long did Stephanie work here?"

"About a year. She came here right out of college."

"Where did she go to school?"

"Temple."

"Did she have any problems with anyone here at work?"

"Stephanie? Hardly. Everybody liked her and she liked everyone. I don't remember a cross word ever coming out of her mouth."

"What did you think when she didn't show up for work last week?"

"Well, Stephanie had a lot of sick days coming. I thought she took the day off, even though it was unlike her not to call in. The next day I called her cell phone, left a few messages. She never got back to me."

Andrea reached for a tissue, dabbed her eyes, perhaps now realizing why her phone never rang.

Jessica made a few notes. No cell phone had been found in the Saturn or near the crime scene. "Did you call her house?"

Andrea shook her head, her lower lip beginning to tremble. Jessica knew that the dam was about to break.

"What can you tell me about her family?" Byrne asked.

"I think there's just her mother. I don't recall her ever talking about her father, or any brothers or sisters."

Jessica glanced at Stephanie's desk. In addition to the pen caddy and neatly stacked file folders, there was a silver-framed five-by-six photograph of Stephanie and an older woman. In this picture—smiling, standing in front of the Wilma Theater on Broad Street—Jessica thought the young woman looked happy. She found it hard to reconcile the photo with the image of the brutalized corpse she had seen in the trunk of the Saturn.

"This is Stephanie and her mother?" Byrne asked, pointing to the photo on the desk.

"Yes."

"Have you ever met her mother?"

"No," Andrea said. She reached for a tissue from Stephanie's desk. She dabbed at her eyes.

"Did Stephanie have a bar or a restaurant she liked to go to after work?" Byrne asked. "Anywhere she frequented?"

"Sometimes we'd go to the Friday's next to the Embassy Suites on the parkway. If we felt like dancing we'd go to Shampoo."

"I have to ask this," Byrne said. "Was Stephanie gay or bi?"

Andrea almost snorted. "Uh, no."

"Did you go down to Penn's Landing with Stephanie?"

"Yes."

"Did anything unusual happen?"

"I'm not sure what you mean."

"Was anybody bothering her? Following her?"

"I don't think so."

"Did you see her do anything out of the ordinary?" Byrne asked.

Andrea thought for a few moments. "No. We were just hanging around. Hoping maybe to see Will Parrish or Hayden Cole."

"Did you see Stephanie talking to anyone?"

"I wasn't really paying attention. But I think she did talk to a guy for a while. Men were always coming on to her."

"Can you describe the guy?"

"White guy. Flyers cap. Sunglasses."

Jessica and Byrne exchanged a glance. This fit with Little Jake's recollection. "How old?"

"No idea. I really didn't get that close."

Jessica showed her a picture of Adam Kaslov. "Could this be the guy?"

"I don't know. Maybe. I just remember thinking that the guy wasn't her type."

"What was her type?" Jessica asked, flashing back to Vincent's routine. She imagined everyone had a type.

"Well, she was pretty picky about the men she dated. She always went for the well-dressed guy. Chestnut Hill types."

"Was this guy she was talking to part of the crowd, or was he part of the production company?" Byrne asked.

Andrea shrugged. "I really don't know."

"Did she say she knew this guy? Or maybe that she gave him her number?"

"I don't think she knew him. And I'd be really surprised if she gave him her phone number. Like I said. Not her type. But then again, maybe he was just dressed down. I just didn't get a really close look at him."

Jessica made a few more notes. "We'll need the names and contact information for everyone who works here," she said.

"Sure."

"Would you mind if we looked through Stephanie's desk?"

"No," Andrea said. "It's okay."

While Andrea Cerrone drifted back into the reception area, afloat on her wave of shock and grief, Jessica snapped on a pair of latex gloves. She began her invasion of Stephanie Chandler's life.

The left-hand drawers held hanging files, mostly press releases and press clippings. A few folders were stuffed with proof sheets of black-and-white press photos. The photos were mostly of the stab-and-grab variety, the type of photo op where two people pose holding a check or a plaque or a citation of some sort.

The middle drawer held the nutrients of office life: paper clips, pushpins, mailing labels, rubber bands, brass brads, business cards, glue sticks.

In the top right-hand drawer was the urban survival kit of the young single workingwoman: a small tube of hand lotion, lip balm, a few samplers of perfume, mouthwash. There was also a spare pair of panty hose, a trio of books: *The Brethren* by John Grisham, *Windows XP for Dummies,* and a book titled *White Heat,* the unauthorized biography of Ian Whitestone, the Philadelphia-native director of *Dimensions*. Whitestone was directing the new Will Parrish movie, *The Palace.*

There were no notes, no threatening letters, nothing to tie Stephanie to the horror of what had happened to her on the videotape.

It was the picture on Stephanie's desk of her and her mother that had already begun to haunt Jessica. Not the fact that, in the picture, Stephanie was so vibrant and alive, but rather what the picture represented. A week earlier it was an artifact of a life, the proof of a living, breathing young woman, a human being with friends, ambition, sorrows, thoughts, and regrets. A human being with a future.

Now it was a document of the dead.

FAITH CHANDLER LIVED IN A PLAIN BUT WELL-MAINTAINED brick-front row house on Fulton Street. Jessica and Byrne met with the woman in her small living room overlooking the street. Outside the window, a pair of five-year-olds played hopscotch under the watchful eyes of their grandmothers. Jessica wondered what the laughing children sounded like to Faith Chandler on this, the darkest day of her life.

"I'm very sorry for your loss, Mrs. Chandler," Jessica said. Even though she had had occasion to say these words a number of times since joining the Homicide Unit in April, it appeared that it was not going to get any easier to say them.

Faith Chandler was in her early forties, a woman who had the creased look of late nights and early mornings, a working-class woman who suddenly found herself the statistic of another demographic, that of *victim of violent crime*. Old eyes in a middle-aged face. She was employed as a night waitress at the Melrose Diner. In her hands was a scratched plastic tumbler with an inch of whiskey. Next to her, on a TV tray, was a half-full bottle of Seagram's. Jessica wondered how far into the process the woman was.

Faith didn't respond to Jessica's offer of condolence. Perhaps the woman thought that, if she didn't respond, if she didn't acknowledge Jessica's offer of sympathy, it might not be true.

"When was the last time you saw Stephanie?" Jessica asked.

"Monday morning," Faith said. "Before she left for work."

"Was there anything unusual about her that morning? Anything different about her mood or her routine?"

"No. Nothing."

"Did she say that she had plans for after work?"

"No."

"When she didn't come home Monday night, what did you think?"

Faith just shrugged, dabbed at her eyes. She sipped her whiskey.

"Did you call the police?"

"Not right away."

"Why not?" Jessica asked.

Faith put her glass down, knitted her hands in her lap. "Sometimes Stephanie would stay with friends. She was a grown woman, independent. I work nights, you see. She works days. Sometimes we really didn't see each other for days on end."

"Did she have any brothers or sisters?"

"No."

"What about her father?"

Faith waved a hand, snapping back to the moment, by way of her past. They'd hit a nerve. "He hasn't been part of her life for years."

"Does he live in Philadelphia?"

"No."

"We learned from her coworkers that Stephanie had been dating someone until recently. What can you tell us about him?"

Faith studied her hands again for a few moments before answering. "You have to understand that Stephanie and I were never close that way. I knew she was seeing someone, but she never brought him around. She was a secretive girl in a lot of ways. Even when she was small."

"Is there anything else you can think of that might help?"

Faith Chandler looked at Jessica. In Faith's eyes was that burnished look Jessica had seen many times, a shell-shocked look of anger and pain and grief. "She was kind of a wild girl when she was a teenager," Faith said. "Right through college."

"Wild how?"

Faith shrugged again. "Willful. Ran with a pretty fast crowd. Lately she had settled down, gotten this good job." Pride battled sorrow in her voice. She sipped her whiskey.

Byrne caught Jessica's eye. He then quite deliberately directed his gaze at the entertainment center, and Jessica followed the line of sight. The unit, which stood in one corner of the living room, was one of those entertainment-center-*cum*-armoires. It looked like expensive wood— rosewood, perhaps. The doors were slightly ajar, and it was obvious from across the room that inside was a flat-screen TV; above it, a rack of expensive-looking audio and video equipment. Jessica glanced around the living room while Byrne continued to ask questions. What had struck Jessica as tidy and tasteful when she'd arrived was now clearly tidy and *expensive*: A Thomasville dining room set and living room suite, Stiffel lamps.

"May I use your bathroom?" Jessica asked. She had grown up in an almost identical row house, and knew that the bathroom was on the second floor. That was the point of her question.

Faith looked at her, her face a blank screen, as if she hadn't understood. She then nodded and pointed at the staircase.

Jessica walked up the narrow wooden stairs to the second floor. To her right was a small bedroom; straight ahead, the bathroom. Jessica glanced down the steps. Faith Chandler, entranced by her grief, was still sitting on the couch. Jessica slipped into the bedroom. The framed posters on the wall indicated that it was Stephanie's room. Jessica opened the closet. Inside were half a dozen pricey suits, as many pairs of good-quality shoes. She checked the labels. Ralph Lauren, Dana Buchman, Fendi. All full labels. It appeared that Stephanie wasn't an outlet shopper, where many times the tags were cut in half. On the top shelf were few pieces of Tumi luggage. It appeared that Stephanie Chandler had good taste and a budget to support it. But where was the money coming from?

Jessica gave a quick glance around the room. On one wall was a poster from *Dimensions,* the Will Parrish supernatural thriller. That, and the Ian Whitestone book in her desk at the office, proved that she was a fan of either Ian Whitestone or Will Parrish, or both.

On the dresser was a pair of framed photos. One was of a teenaged Stephanie with her arm around a pretty brunette, who was about the same age. *Friends forever* kind of pose. The other picture was a younger Faith Chandler sitting on a bench in Fairmount Park, holding an infant.

Jessica went quickly through Stephanie's drawers. In one she found an accordion file of paid bills. She found Stephanie's four most recent

Visa bills. She laid them out on the dresser, took out her digital camera, and took a photo of each. She did a quick scan of the list of posted charges, looking for high-end stores. Nothing. Nor were there charges to saksfifthavenue.com, nordstrom.com, or even any of the online discounters that sold high-end goods: bluefly.com, overstock.com, smart bargains.com. It was a good bet she wasn't buying these designer clothes herself. Jessica put her camera away, then slipped the Visa bills back into the file. If anything she discovered on the bills turned into a lead, she would be hard-pressed to say how she got the information. She'd worry about that later.

In another slot in the file, she found the documents Stephanie had signed when she signed up for her cell phone service. There were no monthly bills detailing minutes used and numbers called. Jessica copied down the cell phone number. She then took out her own cell phone, dialed Stephanie's number. It rang three times, then switched over to voice mail:

Hi . . . this is Steph . . . please leave your message at the beep and I'll get back to you.

Jessica clicked off. The call had established two things. Stephanie Chandler's cell phone was still active, and it wasn't located in her bedroom. Jessica called the number again, got the same result.

I'll get back to you.

Jessica thought about how, when Stephanie made that cheerful greeting, she'd had no idea what was coming her way.

Jessica put everything back where she had found it, padded back down the hallway, stepped into the bathroom, flushed the toilet, ran the water in the sink for a few moments. She descended the stairs.

". . . all her friends," Faith said.

"Can you think of anyone who might have wanted to hurt Stephanie?" Byrne asked. "Someone who may have had a grudge against her?"

Faith just shook her head. "She didn't have enemies. She was a good person."

Jessica met Byrne's eyes again. Faith was hiding something, but now was not the moment to press her. Jessica nodded slightly. They would take a run at her later.

"Again, we're terribly sorry for your loss," Byrne said.

Faith Chandler fixed them in a blank stare. "Why . . . why would someone do something like this?"

There were no answers. None that would suffice, or even begin to salve this woman's grief. "I'm afraid we can't answer that," Jessica said. "But I can promise you that we'll do everything we can to find who did this to your daughter."

Like her offer of condolences, this seemed to ring hollow in Jessica's mind. She hoped it sounded sincere to the grief-stricken woman sitting in the chair by the window.

THEY STOOD ON the corner. They looked in two directions, but were of one mind. "I've got to get back and brief the boss," Jessica finally said.

Byrne nodded. "I'm officially off for the next forty-eight, you know."

Jessica heard the sadness in that statement. "I know."

"Ike is going to tell you to keep me out of the loop."

"I know."

"Call me if you hear anything."

Jessica knew she couldn't do that. "Okay."

FAITH CHANDLER SAT ON HER DEAD DAUGHTER'S BED. WHERE had she been when Stephanie had smoothed the bedspread for the last time, creasing it beneath the pillow in her precise and dutiful way? What had she been doing when Stephanie had placed her menagerie of plush animals in a perfect row against the headboard?

She had been at work, as always, dogging the end of another shift, her daughter a constant, a given, an absolute.

Can you think of anyone who might have wanted hurt Stephanie?

She had known the moment she opened the door. The pretty young woman and the tall, confident-looking man in the dark suit. They had a look about them that said they did this often. Brought heartache to the door like carryout.

It was the young woman who told her. She had known it would be. Woman-to-woman. Eye-to-eye. It was the young woman who had cut her in two.

Faith Chandler glanced at the corkboard on her daughter's bedroom wall. Clear plastic pushpins prismed rainbows in the sun. Business cards, travel brochures, newspaper clippings. It was the calendar that hurt the most. Birthdays in blue. Anniversaries in red. Future past.

She had thought about slamming the door in their faces. Maybe that would have kept the pain from entering. Maybe that would have kept the heartache out there with the people in the papers, the people on the news, the people in the movies.

Police learned today that . . .

This just in . . .

An arrest has been made . . .

Always in the background as she made dinner. Always someone else. Flashing lights, white-sheeted gurneys, grim-faced spokesmen. Over at six thirty.

Oh, Stephie love.

She drained her glass, the whiskey in search of the sorrow within. She picked up the phone, waited.

They wanted her to come down to the morgue and identify the body. Would she know her own daughter in death? Wasn't it *life* that made her Stephanie?

Outside, the summer sun dazzled the sky. The flowers would never be brighter or more fragrant; the children, never happier. All the time in the world for hopscotch and grape drink and rubber pools.

She slipped the photograph out of the frame on the dresser, turned it over in her hands, the two girls in it forever frozen at life's threshold. What had been a secret all these years now demanded to be free.

She replaced the phone. She poured another drink.

There would be time, she thought. God willing.

There would be time.

PHIL KESSLER LOOKED LIKE A SKELETON. IN ALL THE TIME
Byrne had known him, Kessler had been a hard drinker, a two-fisted glut-
ton, at least twenty-five pounds overweight. Now his hands and face
were gaunt and pallid, his body a brittle husk.

Despite the flowers and bright get-well cards scattered around the
man's hospital room, despite the brisk activity of the crisply clad staff, a
team dedicated to preserving and prolonging life, the room smelled like
sadness.

While a nurse took Kessler's blood pressure, Byrne thought about
Victoria. He didn't know if this was the beginning of something real, if
he and Victoria would ever be intimate again, but waking up in her apartment made him feel as if something had been reborn within him, as if
something long dormant had poked through the soil of his heart.

It felt good.

Victoria had made him breakfast that morning. She had scrambled
two eggs, made him rye toast, and served it to him in bed. She had put a
carnation on his tray and a lipstick kiss on his folded napkin. Just the
presence of that flower and that kiss told Byrne how much was missing

from his life. Victoria had kissed him at the door and told him that she had a group meeting with the runaways she counseled later that evening. She said the group would be over by eight o'clock and that she would meet him at the Silk City Diner on Spring Garden at eight fifteen. She said she had a good feeling. Byrne shared it. She believed they would find Julian Matisse this night.

Now, sitting in a hospital room next to Phil Kessler, the good feeling was gone. Byrne and Kessler had gotten whatever pleasantries they had available to them out of the way, and had fallen into an uncomfortable silence. Both men knew why Byrne was there.

Byrne decided to get it over with. For any number of reasons he did not want to be in the same room with this man.

"Why, Phil?"

Kessler thought about his answer. Byrne didn't know if the long lag time between question and answer was pain medication or conscience.

"Because it's the right thing to do, Kevin."

"Right thing for who?"

"Right thing for me."

"But what about Jimmy? He can't even defend himself."

This seemed to reach Kessler. He may not have been much of a cop in his day, but he understood the process of due process. Every man had the right to face his accuser.

"The day we took Matisse down. You remember it?" Kessler asked.

Like yesterday, Byrne thought. There were so many cops on Jefferson Street that day, it looked like an FOP convention.

"I went into that building knowing that what I was doing was wrong," Kessler said. "I've lived with it ever since. Now I can't live with it anymore. I'm sure as hell not going to die with it."

"You're saying that Jimmy planted the evidence?"

Kessler nodded. "It was his idea."

"I don't fucking believe it."

"Why? You think Jimmy Purify was some kind of saint?"

"Jimmy was a great cop, Phil. Jimmy was stand-up. He wouldn't do it."

Kessler stared at him for a few moments, his eyes seeming to focus on a middle distance. He reached for his water glass, struggling to get the plastic cup off the tray and up to his mouth. Byrne's heart went out to the man at that moment. But he didn't help. After a while, Kessler got the cup back onto the tray.

"Where did you get the gloves, Phil?"

Nothing. Kessler just stared at him with those cold, light-fading eyes. "How many years you got left, Kevin?"

"What?"

"Time," he said. "How much time you got?"

"I have no idea." Byrne knew where this was going. He let it play.

"No, you don't. But I do, see? I got a month. Less, probably. I ain't gonna see the first leaf fall this year. No snow. I ain't gonna see the Phillies fuck up in the play-offs. By the time Labor Day rolls around I'm gonna be dealing with it."

"Dealing with it?"

"My life," Kessler said. "Defending my life."

Byrne got up. This was going nowhere, and even if it was, he couldn't bring himself to badger the man any longer. The bottom line was that Byrne could not believe it of Jimmy. Jimmy had been like his brother. He had never known a man to be more in tune with the right and wrong of a situation than Jimmy Purify. Jimmy was the cop who went back the next day and paid for the hoagies they got on the cuff. Jimmy Purify paid his fucking *parking* tickets.

"I was there, Kevin. I'm sorry. I know Jimmy was your partner. But this is the way it went down. I ain't saying Matisse didn't do it, but the way we got him was wrong."

"You know Matisse is on the street, right?"

Kessler didn't respond. He closed his eyes for a few moments. Byrne wasn't sure if he had fallen asleep or not. Soon he opened his eyes. They were wet with tears. "We didn't do right by that girl, Kevin."

"What girl? Gracie?"

Kessler shook his head. "No." He held up a thin, bony hand, offering it up like evidence. "My penance," he said. "How are *you* going to pay?"

Kessler turned his head, looked out the window again. The sunlight revealed the skull beneath the skin. Beneath that, the soul of a dying man.

As Byrne stood in the doorway he knew, the way he had known so many things over the years, that there was something else to this, something other than a man's reparation in the last moments of his life. Phil Kessler was hiding something.

We didn't do right by that girl.

BYRNE TOOK HIS hunch to the next level. On the promise of discretion, he called an old friend in the homicide division of the DA's office. He had trained Linda Kelly, and since that time she had risen steadily through the ranks. Discretion was certainly in her purview.

Linda ran Phil Kessler's financials, and one red flag flew high. Two weeks ago—the day Julian Matisse was released from prison—Kessler had made a ten-thousand-dollar deposit in a new account in an out-of-state bank.

THE BAR IS STRAIGHT OUT OF *FAT CITY*, A NORTH PHILLY DIVE with a broken air conditioner, a grimy tin ceiling, and a graveyard of dead plants in the window. It reeks of disinfectant and old pork fat. There are two of us at the bar, four more scattered at tables. The jukebox plays Waylon Jennings.

I glance at the guy on my right. He is one of those Blake Edwards drunks, an extra in *Days of Wine and Roses*. He looks like he could use another. I get the guy's attention.

"How's it going?" I ask.

It doesn't take long for him to summarize. "Been better."

"Who hasn't?" I reply. I point to his nearly empty glass. "One more?"

He looks at me a little more closely, perhaps searching for motive. He'll never find it. His eyes are glassy, veined with drink and fatigue. There is something beneath the exhaustion, though. Something that speaks of fear. "Why not?"

I motion to the bartender, swirl my finger over our empties. The bartender pours, grabs my check, retreats to the register.

"Tough day?" I ask.

He nods. "Tough day."

"Like the great George Bernard Shaw once said: 'Alcohol is the anesthesia by which we endure the operation of life.'"

"I'll drink to that," he says on the tail of a sad smile.

"There was a movie once," I say. "I think it was with Ray Milland." Of course, I *know* it was with Ray Milland. "He played an alcoholic."

The guy nods. *"Lost Weekend."*

"That's the one. There's one scene where he talks about the effect that alcohol has on him. It's a classic. An ode to the bottle." I stand straighter, square my shoulders. I do my best Don Birnam, quoting from the movie: "It tosses the sandbags overboard so the balloon can soar. Suddenly I'm above the ordinary. I'm competent. I'm walking a tightrope over Niagara Falls. I'm one of the great ones.'" I put my glass back down. "Or something like that."

The guy stares at me for a few moments, trying to focus his eyes. "That's pretty fucking good, man," he finally says. "You've got a great memory."

He is slurring his words.

I hoist my glass. "Better days."

"Couldn't be worse than this one."

Of course it could.

He downs his shot, drains his beer. I follow suit. He begins to fish around in his pocket for his keys.

"One more for the road?" I ask.

"No thanks," he says. "I'm good."

"You sure?"

"Yeah," he says. "I gotta get up early tomorrow." He slides off his stool, heads for the rear of the bar. "Thanks anyway."

I drop a twenty on the bar, glance around. Four dead drunks at the rickety tables. Myopic barkeep. We don't exist. We are background. I'm wearing a Flyers cap and tinted shades. Twenty extra foam pounds around my waist.

I follow him to the back door. We step into the wet kiln of the late afternoon, emerging into the small parking lot behind the bar. There are three cars.

"Hey, thanks for the drink," he says.

"You are more than welcome," I reply. "You okay to drive?"

He holds up a single key attached to a leather fob. A door key. "Walking home."

"Smart man." We are standing behind my car. I open the trunk. It is lined with clear plastic. He glances inside.

"Wow, that is one clean car you've got," he says.

"I have to keep it spotless for work."

He nods. "What do you do?"

"I'm an actor."

It takes a moment for the absurdity to register. He scans my face again. Soon recognition dawns. "We've met before, haven't we?" he asks.

"Yes."

He waits for me to say more. I do not offer more. The moment drags out. He shrugs. "Well, okay, good seeing you again. I'm gonna get going."

I put my hand on his forearm. In my other hand is a straight razor. Michael Caine in *Dressed to Kill*. I flick open the razor. The keened steel blade shimmers in the marmalade-colored sunlight.

He looks at the razor, then back up into my eyes. It is clear that he now recalls where we met. I knew he eventually would. He remembers me from the video store, standing at the rack of classic films. Fear blossoms on his face.

"I . . . I have to go," he says, suddenly sober.

I tighten my grip on his arm and say: "I'm afraid I can't allow that, Adam."

THE LAUREL HILL CEMETERY WAS NEARLY DESERTED AT THIS hour. Situated on seventy-four acres overlooking Kelly Drive and the Schuylkill River, it was home to Civil War generals as well as victims of the *Titanic*. Its once magnificent arboretum setting was rapidly deteriorating into a scar of overturned headstones, weed-choked fields, and crumbling mausoleums.

Byrne stood in the cool shade of a huge maple for a while, resting. *Lavender,* he thought. *Gracie Devlin's favorite color was lavender.*

When he regained his strength, he walked over to Gracie's grave site. He was surprised that he found the plot so quickly. It was a small, inexpensive marker, the kind for which you settle when the high-pressure sales tactics fail and the salesman needs to move on. He looked down at the stone.

Marygrace Devlin.

ETERNAL GRACE read the inscription above the carving.

Byrne did a little landscaping around the stone, pulling the overgrown grass and weeds, brushing the dirt from the face.

Had it really been two years since he stood here with Melanie and

Garrett Devlin? Had it really been two years since they gathered in the cold winter rain, black-clad silhouettes against the deep violet horizon? He had lived with his own family then, the coming sadness of his divorce not even on his radar. He had driven the Devlins home that day, helped at the reception in their small row house. He had stood in Gracie's room that afternoon. He remembered the smell of lilacs and floral perfume and moth cakes. He remembered the collection of ceramic figures from *Snow White and the Seven Dwarfs* on Gracie's bookshelf. Melanie had told him that the only figurine her daughter needed was Snow White to complete the set. She told him that Gracie intended to buy the final piece the day she was killed. Three times Byrne had returned to the theater where Gracie was murdered, looking for the figurine. He never found it.

Snow White.

Since that night, every time Byrne heard the name *Snow White* his heart ached a little more.

He eased himself to the ground. The relentless heat was warming on his back. After a few moments he reached out, touched the headstone and—

—the images slam into his mind with a brutal and untamed fury . . . Gracie on the rotted floorboards of the stage . . . Gracie's clear blue eyes clouded with terror . . . the eyes of menace in the darkness above her . . . the eyes of Julian Matisse . . . Gracie's screams blotting out all sound, all thought, all prayer—

Byrne was flung backward, gut-shot, his hand exploding off the cool granite. His heart raced to burst. The well of tears in his eyes brimmed.

So real. My God, so real.

He looked around the cemetery, soul-shaken, his pulse thrumming in his ears. There was no one near him, no one watching. He found a small measure of calm within him, gripped it, held on tight.

For a few unworldly moments he found it hard to reconcile the fury of his vision with the peace of the graveyard. He was soaked with sweat. He glanced at the headstone. It looked perfectly ordinary. It *was* perfectly ordinary. The brutal power was within *him*.

There was no doubt. The visions were back.

BYRNE SPENT THE early evening in physical therapy. As much as he hated to admit it, the therapy was helping. A little. He seemed to have a little more mobility in his legs, a little more flexibility in his lower back. Still, he would never concede this to the Wicked Witch of West Philadelphia.

A friend of his ran a gym in Northern Liberties. Instead of driving back to his apartment, Byrne grabbed a shower at the gym, then a light dinner at a neighborhood diner.

At about eight o'clock he pulled into the parking lot next to the Silk City Diner to wait for Victoria. He cut the engine, waited. He was early. He thought about the case. Adam Kaslov was no stone killer. Still, there was no such thing as coincidence, not in his experience. He thought about the young woman in the trunk of the car. He had never gotten used to the level of savagery available to the human heart.

He replaced the image of the young woman in the trunk of the car with the images of making love to Victoria. It had been such a long time since he had felt the swell of romantic love in his chest.

He recalled the first time, the only other time in his life he had felt that way. The time he met his wife. He recalled that summer day with a precious clarity, smoking pot next to the 7-Eleven with some of the Two-Street boys—Des Murtaugh, Tug Parnell, Timmy Hogan—listening to Thin Lizzy on Timmy's shitty boom box. It wasn't that anyone liked Thin Lizzy all that much, but they were Irish, damnit, and that *meant* something. "The Boys Are Back in Town," "Jailbreak," "Fighting My Way Back." Those were the days. The girls with their big hair and glitter makeup. The guys with the skinny ties, gradient shades, and sleeves pushed up.

But there was never a Two-Street girl with more attitude than Donna Sullivan. Donna had on a white pin-dot sundress that day, the kind with the thin straps on the shoulders, the kind that swayed with every step. She was tall and noble and confident in her bearing; her strawberry-blond hair was back in a ponytail, luminous like summer sunshine on Jersey sand. She was walking her dog, a little Yorkie she called Brando.

When Donna got up to the store, Tug was already down on all fours, panting like a dog, asking to be walked on a chain. That was Tug. Donna rolled her eyes, but she smiled. It was a girlish smile, a playful grin that said she could go along with the clowns of the world. Tug rolled onto his back, working the gag for all it was worth.

When Donna looked at Byrne, she gave him a different smile, a woman's smile, one that offered everything and revealed nothing, one that found its way deep into Kevin Byrne's tough-guy chest. A smile that said: *If you are the man in this group of boys, you will be with me.*

Gimme the puzzle, God, Byrne had thought at that moment, looking at that beautiful face, those aquamarine eyes that seemed to bore right through him. *Gimme the puzzle to this girl, God, and I'll solve it.*

Tug noticed that Donna had noticed the big guy. Like always. He got up and, if it had been anyone but Tug Parnell, would've felt foolish. "This side of beef is Kevin Byrne. Kevin Byrne, Donna Sullivan."

"You're the one they call Riff Raff, right?" she asked.

Byrne reddened in a flash, embarrassed at the handle for the very first time. The nickname had always given Byrne a certain sense of ethnic bad-boy pride, but coming from Donna Sullivan's lips that day, it sounded, well, stupid. "Uh, yeah," he said, feeling even dumber.

"Want to walk with me awhile?" she asked.

It was like asking him if he had any interest in breathing. "Sure," he said.

And thus she had him.

They walked down to the river, their hands brushing, never quite reaching out, fully sensing each other's nearness. When they returned to the neighborhood at just after dusk, Donna Sullivan kissed him on the cheek.

"You're not so tough, you know," Donna said.

"I'm not?"

"No. I think you may even be sweet."

Byrne grabbed his heart in mock cardiac arrest. "Sweet?"

Donna laughed. "Don't worry," she said. She lowered her voice to a honey whisper. "Your secret is safe with me."

He watched her walk up to the house. She turned, silhouetted in the doorway, and blew him another kiss.

He fell in love that day, and he thought it would never end.

The cancer got Tug in '99. Timmy was running a plumbing crew in Camden. Six kids, last he heard. Des was killed by a drunk driver in '02. Himself.

And now Kevin Francis Byrne again felt that rush of romantic love, for only the second time in his life. He had been adrift for so long. Victoria had the power to change all that.

He decided to call off this crusade to find Julian Matisse. Let the system run its game. He was too old and too tired. When Victoria showed, he would tell her, they would have a few cocktails, call it a night.

The one good thing that came out of all this was that he had found her again.

He looked at his watch. Nine ten.

He got out of his car, walked into the diner, thinking he had missed Victoria, thinking maybe she had not seen his car and had gone inside. She was not inside. He took out his cell phone, called her number, got her voice mail. He called the runaway shelter where she counseled, and was told that she had left awhile ago.

When Byrne got back to the car, he had to look twice to make sure it *was* his car. For some reason, his car now had a hood ornament. He glanced around the lot, a little disoriented. He looked back. It *was* his car.

As he got closer, he felt the hair rise on the back of his neck, and the skin begin to dimple on his arms.

It wasn't a hood ornament. Someone had put something on the hood of his car while he was inside the diner, a small ceramic figure sitting on an oaken keg. A figurine from a Disney movie.

It was Snow White.

"NAME FIVE HISTORICAL ROLES PLAYED BY GARY OLDMAN," SETH said.

Ian's face lit up. He had been reading the first of a short stack of scripts. No one read or absorbed a screenplay faster than Ian Whitestone.

But even a mind as quick and encyclopedic as Ian's should have taken more than a few seconds on this one. Not a chance. Seth had barely mouthed the question before Ian was spitting out the answer.

"Sid Vicious, Pontius Pilate, Joe Orton, Lee Harvey Oswald, and Albert Milo."

Gotcha, Seth thought. *Le Bec-Fin here we come.* "Albert Milo was fictional."

"Yes, but everyone knows he was really supposed to be Julian Schnabel in *Basquiat.*"

Seth glared at Ian for a moment. Ian knew the rules. No fictionalization of real-life characters. They were sitting in Little Pete's Restaurant on Seventeenth Street, across from the Radisson hotel. As wealthy as Ian Whitestone was, he lived on diner food. "Okay, then," Ian said. "Ludwig van Beethoven."

Shit, Seth thought. He really thought he'd had him this time.

Seth finished his coffee, wondering if he'd ever stump the man. He looked out the window, saw the first flashbulb pop across the street, saw the crowd swell toward the entrance to the hotel, watched the adoring fans gather around Will Parrish. He then glanced back at Ian Whitestone, his nose once more stuck in a script, the food still untouched on his plate.

What a paradox, Seth thought. Although it was a paradox suffused with a strange sort of logic.

Granted, Will Parrish was a bankable movie star. He had been responsible for well over a billion dollars in worldwide ticket sales over the past two decades, and was one of only half a dozen or so American actors over the age of thirty-five who could "open" a movie. On the other hand, Ian Whitestone could pick up the phone and get any of the five major studio heads on the line within minutes. These were the only people in the world who could green-light a film budgeted at nine figures. And they were all on Ian's speed dial. Even Will Parrish couldn't say that.

In the film trade, at least at the creative level, the real power was with men like Ian Whitestone, not Will Parrish. If he was so inclined—and he quite often was—Ian Whitestone could pluck that heart-stoppingly beautiful yet thoroughly untalented nineteen-year-old girl from the crowd and drop her right into the middle of her wildest dreams. With a brief layover in his bed, of course. All without lifting a finger. All without causing a stir.

Yet in just about any city other than Hollywood, it was Ian Whitestone, not Will Parrish, who could sit unmolested and virtually unobserved in a diner and eat his meal in peace. No one would know that the creative force behind *Dimensions* liked to put tartar sauce on his hamburgers. No one would know that the man once referred to as the second coming of Luis Buñuel liked to put a tablespoon of sugar into his Diet Coke.

But Seth Goldman knew.

He knew these things and so much more. Ian Whitestone was a man with appetites. If no one knew about his culinary peculiarities, only one other man knew that, when the sun dropped below the lowest roofline, when people dressed in their nighttime masks, Ian Whitestone saw the city as his own twisted and dangerous buffet.

Seth looked across the street, spotted a young, stately redhead at the back of the crowd. She had not gotten anywhere near the movie star before he had been whisked away in his stretch limo. She looked crestfallen. Seth glanced around. No one was watching.

He rose from the booth, exited the restaurant, spritzed his breath, crossed the street. When he reached the other curb he thought about what he and Ian Whitestone were about to do. He thought about how his connection to the Oscar-nominated director ran much deeper than that of the average executive assistant, about how the tissue that bound them snaked through a darker place, a place that sunshine never graced, a place where the screams of the innocent were never heard.

THE CROWD AT FINNIGAN'S WAKE WAS STARTING TO THICKEN. The raucous, multilevel Irish pub on Spring Garden Street was a venerated cop hangout that drew its clientele from all of Philly's police districts. Everyone from the top brass to the rookie patrolman stopped here from time to time. The food was decent, the beer was cold, and the atmosphere was pure Philly blue.

But you had to count your drinks at Finnigan's. You could *literally* bump into the commissioner here.

Above the bar was a banner proclaiming: BEST WISHES SERGEANT O'BRIEN! Jessica stopped upstairs, got her pleasantries out of the way. She came back down to the first floor. It was noisier down there, but right now she wanted the quiet anonymity of a boisterous cop bar. She had just turned the corner into the main room when her cell phone rang. It was Terry Cahill. Although it was hard to hear, she did pick up that he was taking a rain check on their drink. He said he had tailed Adam Kaslov to a bar in North Philly, and had then gotten a call from his ASAC. There was a bank robbery in Lower Merion, and they needed him at the scene. He had to shut down the surveillance.

Stood up by a fed, Jessica thought.

She needed new perfume.

Jessica made her way to the bar. The place was wall-to-wall blue. Officer Mark Underwood was sitting at the front bar with two young guys, early twenties, both of whom had the buzz cuts and bad-boy posture that fairly screamed *rookie cop.* Probies even *sat* tough. You could smell the testosterone.

Underwood waved her over. "Hey, you made it." He gestured to the two guys next to him. "Two of my charges. Officers Dave Nihiser and Jacob Martinez."

Jessica let it sink in. A cop she had helped train was already training new officers. Where had the time gone? She shook hands with the two young men. When they found out she was in Homicide, they looked at her with a great deal of respect.

"Tell 'em who your partner is," Underwood said to Jessica.

"Kevin Byrne," she replied.

Now the young men looked at her with awe. Byrne's street rep was that big.

"I secured a crime scene for him and his partner in South Philly a couple of years ago," Underwood said with a chest full of pride.

The two probies mugged and nodded, as if Underwood had said he once caught for Steve Carlton.

The bartender brought Underwood's drink. He and Jessica clinked glasses, sipped, settled in. It was a different surrounding for the two of them, far from the days when she was his mentor on the streets of South Philly. The big-screen TV in the front of the bar was showing a Phillies game. Somebody got a hit. The bar roared. Finnigan's was nothing if it wasn't loud.

"You know, I grew up not too far from here," he said. "My grandparents had a candy store."

"A candy store?"

Underwood smiled. "Yeah. You know the phrase 'like a kid in a candy store'? I was that kid."

"That must have been fun."

Underwood sipped his drink, shook his head. "It was until I OD'd on circus peanuts. Remember circus peanuts?"

"*Oh* yeah," Jessica said, recalling well the spongy, sickeningly sweet, peanut-shaped candies.

"I got sent to my room once, right?"

"You were a bad boy?"

"Believe it or not. So just to get back at my grandmother I stole a huge bag of banana-flavored circus peanuts—and by huge I mean *wholesale* huge. Maybe twenty pounds. We used to put them in the glass canisters up front and sell them individually."

"Don't tell me you ate the whole thing."

Underwood nodded. "Just about. Ended up getting my stomach pumped. I haven't been able to look at a circus peanut since. Or a banana for that matter."

Jessica glanced across the bar. A pair of pretty college girls in halter tops were eyeing Mark, whispering, giggling. He was a good-looking young man. "So how come you're not married, Mark?" Jessica vaguely remembered a moon-faced girl hanging around back in the day.

"Got close once," he said.

"What happened?"

He shrugged, sipped his drink, hesitated. Maybe she shouldn't have asked. "Life happened," he finally said. "The job happened."

Jessica knew what he meant. She'd had a few semi-serious relationships before becoming a cop. All of them fell by the wayside when she entered the academy. Afterward, she found that the only people who understood what she did every day were other cops.

Officer Nihiser tapped his watch, drained his drink, stood.

"We've got to run," Mark said. "We're on last out and we've got to get some food in us."

"And this was just getting good," Jessica said.

Underwood stood, took out his wallet, pulled out a few bills, handed them to the barmaid. He put his wallet down on the bar. It fell open. Jessica glanced at his ID.

VANDEMARK E. UNDERWOOD.

He caught her looking, scooped up his wallet. But it was too late.

"Vandemark?" Jessica asked.

Underwood looked around quickly. He pocketed his billfold in a flash. "Name your price," he said.

Jessica laughed. She watched Mark Underwood leave. He held the door for an older couple on his way out.

As she toyed with the ice cubes in her glass, she observed the ebb and flow of the pub. She watched cops stroll in, stroll out. She waved to Angelo Turco from the Third. Angelo had a beautiful tenor voice, sang at all the police benefit functions, many of the officers' weddings. With a little training he could have been Philadelphia's answer to Andrea Bocelli. He even opened a Phillies game once.

She saw Cass James, a secretary and all-around sister confessor from Central. Jessica could only imagine how many secrets Cass James held, and what kind of Christmas presents she must get. Jessica had never seen Cass actually pay for a drink.

Cops.

Her father was right. All her friends were on the force. So what was she supposed to do about it? Join the Y? Take a macramé class? Learn to ski?

She finished her drink and was just about to gather her things to leave when she sensed someone sitting down next to her, on the very next stool to her right. Seeing as there were three stools open on either side of her, it could only mean one thing. She felt herself tense up. But why? She knew why. She'd been out of the dating pool for so long, the mere thought of fielding an advance, fueled by a few scotches, scared the hell out of her, as much for what she might not do as for what she might. She'd gotten married for many reasons, and this was one of them. The bar scene, and all its attendant games, never appealed to her much. And now that she was thirty—and the possibility of divorce loomed on the horizon—it terrified her more than it ever had before.

The figure next to her lurked closer, closer. She could feel warm breath on her face. The nearness demanded her attention.

"Can I buy you a drink?" the shadow asked.

She looked over. Caramel eyes, dark wavy hair, a two-day scruff. He had broad shoulders, a small cleft in his chin, long eyelashes. He wore a tight black T-shirt and faded Levi's. Just to make matters worse, he was wearing Acqua di Gio by Armani.

Shit.

Just her type.

"I was just about to leave," she said. "Thanks anyway."

"One drink. I promise."

She almost laughed. "I don't think so."

"Why not?"

"Because with guys like you it's never one drink."

He feigned heartbreak. It made him even cuter. "Guys like me?"

Now she did laugh. "Oh, and now you're going to tell me I've never met anyone quite like you, right?"

He didn't answer her right away. Instead, he looked from her eyes, down to her lips, back to her eyes.

Stop it.

"Oh, I'll bet you've met a lot of guys like me," he said with a sly grin. It was the kind of smile that said he was in complete control.

"Why do you say that?"

He sipped his drink, paused, played the moment out. "Well, for one thing, you're a very beautiful woman."

Here we go, Jessica thought. *Bartender, get me a long-handled shovel.* "And two?"

"Well, two should be obvious."

"Not to me."

"Two is that you are clearly out of my league."

Ah, Jessica thought. The humility pitch. Self-deprecating, handsome, polite. Bedroom eyes. She was absolutely certain that this combo had gotten scads of women into the sack. "And yet you still came over and sat next to me."

"Life is short," he said with a shrug. He crossed his arms, flexing his muscular forearms. Not that Jessica was looking or anything. "When that guy left, I figured it was now or never. I figured that, if I didn't at least try, I would never be able to live with myself."

"How do you know he's not my boyfriend?"

He shook his head. "Not your type."

Cocky bastard. "And I'll bet you know exactly what my type is, right?"

"Absolutely," he said. "Have a drink with me. I'll explain it to you."

Jessica cruised his shoulders, his broad chest. The gold crucifix on the chain around his neck winked in the bar lights.

Go home, Jess.

"Maybe some other time."

"There is no time like now," he said. The sincerity in his voice dripped. "Life is so unpredictable. Anything could happen."

"For instance," she said, wondering why she was prolonging this, deep in denial about the fact that she already *knew* why.

"Well, for instance, you could walk out of here and a stranger with far more nefarious intentions could do you terrible bodily harm."

"I see."

"Or you might step into the middle of an armed robbery in progress and be taken hostage."

Jessica wanted to take out her Glock, lay it on the bar, and tell him she could probably deal with that scenario. Instead, she just said: "Uh-huh."

"Or a bus might jump the curb, or a grand piano might fall from the sky, or you might—"

"—get buried under an avalanche of bullshit?"

He smiled. "Exactly."

He *was* cute. She had to give him that. "Look, I'm really flattered, but I'm a married woman."

He drained his drink, spread his hands in surrender. "He's a very lucky man."

Jessica smiled, dropped a twenty on the bar. "I'll tell him."

She slid off her stool, walked to the door, using all the determination in her arsenal not to turn around and look. Her undercover training paid off sometimes. But that didn't mean she didn't work her walk for all it was worth.

She pushed open the heavy front door. The city was a blast furnace. She walked out of Finnigan's, around the corner, down Third Street, keys in hand. The temperature hadn't dropped more than a degree or two in the last few hours. Her blouse stuck to her back like a damp washcloth.

By the time she reached her car she heard the footsteps behind her and knew who it was. She turned. She was right. His swagger was as brash as his routine.

Nefarious stranger, indeed.

She stood, her back to her car, waiting for the next clever line, the next macho come-on designed to knock down her walls.

Instead, he did not say a word. Before she knew it he had her pinned against the car, his tongue in her mouth. His body was hard; his hands strong. She dropped her purse, her keys, her defenses. She kissed him back as he lifted her into the air. She wrapped her legs around his lean hips. He made her weak. He took her will.

She let him.

It was one of the reasons she married him in the first place.

THE SUPER LET HIM IN JUST BEFORE MIDNIGHT. THE APART-
ment was stifling and oppressive and quiet. The walls still held the echoes
of their passion.

Byrne had driven Center City looking for Victoria, visiting all the
places he thought she might be, all the places she might not, coming up
empty. On the other hand, he didn't really expect to find her sitting in
some bar, totally unaware of the time, a graveyard of empties in front of
her. It was unlike Victoria not to call him if she couldn't make their appointment.

The apartment was just as he had left it earlier that morning: their
breakfast dishes still in the sink, the bedclothes still in the shape of their
bodies.

Although he felt like a prowler, Byrne stepped into the bedroom,
opened the top drawer in Victoria's dresser. The brochure of her life
stared back: a small box of earrings, a clear plastic envelope with ticket
stubs of touring Broadway shows, a selection of drugstore reading glasses
in a variety of frames. There was also an assortment of greeting cards. He
took one out of the envelope. It was a birthday card of the sentimental

stripe, this one with a glossy fall harvest scene at dusk on the cover. Was Victoria's birthday in autumn? Byrne wondered. There was so much he didn't know about her. He opened the card to find a long message scrawled on the left-hand side, a long message written in Swedish. A few bits of glitter fell to the floor.

He slipped the card back into the envelope, glanced at the postmark. BROOKLYN, NY. Did Victoria have family in New York? He felt like a stranger. He had shared her bed, and felt like an onlooker into her life.

He opened her lingerie drawer. The scent of lavender sachet floated up, filling him with both dread and desire. The drawer was full of what looked like very expensive-looking camisoles and slips and hosiery. He knew that Victoria was very sensitive about her outward appearance, despite the tough-girl posturing. Beneath her clothes, though, it seemed she spared no expense to make herself feel beautiful.

He closed the drawer, feeling a little ashamed. He really did not know what he was looking for. Perhaps he wanted to see another segment of her life, a piece of the riddle that might immediately explain why she had not come to meet him. Perhaps he was waiting for a flash of prescience, a vision that might point him in the right direction. But there was none. There was no violent memory in the folds of these fabrics.

Besides, even if he were able to mine this area, it would not explain the Snow White figurine. He knew where that had come from. In his heart he knew what had happened to her.

Another drawer, this one filled with socks and sweatshirts and T-shirts. No clues there. He closed all the drawers, gave a hurried glance through her nightstands.

Nothing.

He left a note on Victoria's dining room table, then drove home, wrestling with the idea of calling in a missing-person report. But what would he say? A woman in her thirties didn't show up for a date? No one had seen her in four or five hours?

When he arrived in South Philly, he found a parking spot about a block from his apartment. The walk seemed endless. He stopped, tried calling Victoria's number again. He got her voice mail. He didn't leave a message. He struggled up the stairs, feeling every moment of his age, each facet of his fear. He'd grab a few hours' sleep and then start looking for Victoria again.

He fell into bed at just after two. Within minutes he was asleep, and the nightmares began.

THE WOMAN WAS TIED TO THE BED, FACEDOWN. SHE WAS NAKED, her skin streaked with shallow scarlet welts from the whipping. The light from the camera highlighted the smooth planes of her back, the sweat-slicked curves of her hips.

The man entered from the bathroom. He was not imposing in a physical sense, but rather carried about him a cinematic villainy. He wore a leather mask. His eyes were dark and menacing behind the slits; his hands held an electric prod.

As the camera rolled, he stepped forward slowly, fully erect. At the foot of the bed he hesitated, the hammer of a heart between strikes.

Then took her again.

THE PASSAGE HOUSE WAS A SAFE HAVEN AND SHELTER ON LOM-bard Street. It provided counsel and protection to teenaged runaways; since its founding nearly a decade earlier, more than two thousand girls had passed through its doors.

The storefront building was whitewashed and clean, recently painted. The insides of the windows were webbed with ivy and flowering clema-tis and other climbing plants, woven through white wooden latticework. Byrne imagined that the purpose of the greenery was twofold. To mask the street—where all the temptations and dangers lurk—and to indicate to the girls who were considering just passing by that inside there was life.

As he approached the front doors, Byrne knew it might be a mistake to identify himself as a police officer—this was anything but an official visit—but if he came in like a civilian, asking questions, he could be some-one's father, boyfriend, dirty uncle. At a place like the Passage House, he could be the problem.

Out front, a woman was washing the windows. Her name was Shakti Reynolds. Victoria had mentioned her many times, always in glowing terms. Shakti Reynolds was one of the founders of the center. She had devoted her life to the cause after losing a daughter to street violence years earlier. Byrne badged her, hoping the move would not come back to haunt him.

"What can I do for you, Detective?"

"I'm looking for Victoria Lindstrom."

"She's not here, I'm afraid."

"Was she supposed to be in today?"

Shakti nodded. She was a tall, broad-shouldered woman of about forty-five, with close-cropped gray hair. Her toffee skin was smooth and wan. Byrne noticed the patches of scalp showing through the woman's hair and wondered if she had recently gone through chemotherapy. He was once again reminded that the city was made up of people who fought their own dragons each day, and it wasn't always about him.

"Yes, she's usually here by now," Shakti said.

"She hasn't called?"

"No."

"Are you at all concerned about that?"

At this, Byrne saw the woman's jawline tighten slightly, as if she thought he was challenging her personal commitment to her employees. In a moment she relaxed. "No, Detective. Victoria is very dedicated to the center, but she is also a woman. And a single woman at that. We're fairly loose here."

Byrne continued, relieved he hadn't insulted or alienated her. "Has anyone been asking for her lately?"

"Well, she's quite popular with the girls. They see her more as an older sister than an adult."

"I mean someone from outside the group."

She dropped her squeegee into the bucket, thought for a few moments. "Well, now that you mention it a guy stopped by the other day asking for her."

"What did he want?"

"He wanted to see her, but she was on a sandwich run."

"What did you tell him?"

"I didn't tell him anything. Just that she wasn't in. He asked a few more questions. Nosy-type questions. I called Mitch over and the guy took one look at him and left."

Shakti gestured to a man sitting at a table inside, playing solitaire. *Man* was a relative term. *Mountain* was more accurate. Mitch went about 350.

"What did this guy look like?"

"White, average height. Snaky looking, I thought. Didn't like him from the get-go."

If anyone's antennae were tuned to snaky men, it was Shakti Reynolds, Byrne thought. "If Victoria stops by, or this guy comes back, please give me a call." He handed her a card. "My cell phone number is on the back. That's the best way to get hold of me in the next few days."

"Sure," she said. She slipped the card into the pocket of her worn flannel shirt. "Can I ask you something?"

"Please."

"Should I be worried about Tori?"

Absolutely, Byrne thought. About as worried as a person could or should be for another. He looked into the woman's shrewd eyes, wanted to tell her *no,* but she was probably as attuned to street bullshit as he was. Probably more so. Instead of crafting a story for her, he simply said: "I don't know."

She held up the card. "I'll call if I hear anything."

"I'd appreciate it."

"And if there's anything I can do on this end, please let me know."

"I will," Byrne said. "Thanks again."

Byrne turned to walk to his car. Across the street from the shelter a pair of teenaged girls watched and waited and paced and smoked, perhaps summoning the courage to cross the street. Byrne slipped into his car thinking that, like a lot of journeys in life, the last few feet were the hardest.

SETH GOLDMAN AWOKE IN A SWEAT. HE LOOKED AT HIS HANDS. Clean. He sprang to his feet, naked and disoriented, his heart pounding in his chest. He looked around. He experienced that enervating feeling where you have no idea where you are—not which city, not which country, not which planet.

One thing was certain.

This ain't the Park Hyatt. The wallpaper was peeling in long, brittle scabs. There were deep brown water stains on the ceiling.

He found his watch. It was after *ten.*

Fuck.

The call sheet. He found it and discovered he had less than an hour to be on set. He also discovered that he had the thick binder containing the director's copy of the script. Of all the tasks a director's assistant had— and these ran the gamut from secretary, to psychologist, to caterer, to chauffeur, to drug runner—the most important was as guardian of the shooting script. There were no duplicates of this version of the script, and outside the egos of the leading man and lady, it was the most fragile and delicate item in the entire rarefied world of the production.

If the script was here, and Ian was not, Seth Goldman was fucked.
He picked up his cell phone—

She had green eyes.
She had cried.
She had wanted to stop.

—and called the production office, made his excuses. Ian was in a rage. Erin Halliwell was out sick. Plus, the public relations person from the Thirtieth Street station had not gotten back to them on the final arrangements for the shoot. The set piece of *The Palace* was going to be filmed in the huge train station at Thirtieth and Market streets in less than seventy-two hours. It was a sequence three months in the planning, by far the most expensive shot in the entire film. Three hundred extras, an elaborate track, a number of in-camera special effects. Erin had been on point for the negotiations and now it was up to Seth to finalize the details, on top of everything else he had to do.

He looked around. The room was trashed.

When had they left?

As he gathered his clothes, he straightened up the room, bagging everything that needed to be thrown out in the plastic bag from the wastebasket in the motel room's small bathroom, knowing that he was going to miss something. He would take the trash with him, as always.

Before he left the room he examined the bedsheets. Good. At least something was going right.

No blood.

JESSICA BRIEFED ADA PAUL DICARLO ON WHAT THEY HAD
learned the previous afternoon. Eric Chavez, Terry Cahill, and Ike Buchanan sat in. Chavez had spent the early morning sitting outside Adam
Kaslov's apartment. Adam had not gone to work, and a pair of phone
calls went unanswered. Chavez spent the past two hours digging up background on the Chandler family.

"Pretty expensive furnishings for a woman working for minimum
and tips," Jessica said. "Especially one who drinks."

"She drinks?" Buchanan asked.

"She drinks," Jessica replied. "Stephanie's closet was full of designer
clothes, too." They had printouts of the Visa bills she had photographed.
They had gone over them. Nothing out of the ordinary.

"Where's the money coming from? Inheritance? Child support? Ali-
mony?" Buchanan asked.

"Her husband took a powder almost ten years ago. Never gave them
a dime that I can find," Chavez said.

"Rich relative?"

"Maybe," Chavez said. "But they've lived at that address for twenty years. And dig this. Three years ago Faith paid off her mortgage in one lump sum."

"How big of a lump?" Cahill asked.

"Fifty-two thousand."

"Cash?"

"Cash."

They all let this sink in.

"Let's get that sketch from the news vendor and Stephanie's boss," Buchanan said. "And let's get on her cell phone records."

AT TEN THIRTY, Jessica faxed a request for a search warrant to the district attorney's office. Within an hour they got it. Eric Chavez then ran Stephanie Chandler's financials. She had little more than three thousand dollars in her bank account. According to Andrea Cerrone, Stephanie made thirty-one thousand dollars per year. This was not a Prada budget.

As uncaring as it may have sounded to anyone outside the department, the good news was that they had evidence now. A body. Scientific evidence with which they could work. They could now begin to piece together what had happened to this woman, and perhaps *why* it happened.

BY ELEVEN THIRTY, they had phone records. Within the past month Stephanie had made only nine calls on her cell phone. Nothing stood out. But the record from the landline at the Chandler house was a little more interesting.

"Yesterday, after you and Kevin left, there were twenty calls to a single number from the Chandler home phone," Chavez said.

"Twenty to the same number?" Jessica asked.

"Yeah."

"Do we know whose number?"

Chavez shook his head. "No. It's registered to a disposable cell phone. The longest call lasted fifteen seconds. The rest were just a few seconds long."

"Local number?" Jessica asked.

"Yeah. Two-one-five exchange. The number was one of a block of ten cell phones that were purchased last month at a wireless store on Passyunk. All prepaids."

"The ten phones were purchased together?" Cahill asked.

"Yeah."

"Why would someone buy ten phones?"

"According to the manager of the store, small companies will buy a block of phones like this if they have a project where a number of employees are going to be in the field at the same time. She said it keeps a cap on time spent on the phone. Also, if an out-of-town firm sends a number of employees to another city, they'll buy ten consecutive numbers just to keep things tidy."

"Do we know who bought the phones?"

Chavez consulted his notes. "The phones were purchased by a company called Alhambra LLC."

"Philly company?" Jessica asked.

"Don't know yet," Chavez said. "The address they gave is a mail drop on South. Nick and I are taking a ride up to the wireless store and see if we can shake anything else loose. If not, we'll stake the mail drop for a few hours, see if anyone picks up mail."

"What's the number?" Jessica asked. Chavez gave it to her.

Jessica put the desk phone on speakerphone, dialed the number. It rang four times, then clicked over to the standard *user not available* recording. She redialed. Same result. She hung up.

"I ran a Google search on Alhambra," Chavez added. "Got a lot of hits, nothing local."

"Stay with the phone number," Buchanan said.

"We're on it," Chavez said.

Chavez left the room as a uniformed officer poked his head in. "Sergeant Buchanan?"

Buchanan spoke briefly with the uniformed officer, then followed him out of the Homicide Unit.

Jessica processed the new information. "Faith Chandler placed twenty calls to a disposable cell. What do you think that was all about?" she asked.

"No idea," Cahill said. "You call a friend, you call a business, you leave a message, right?"

"Right."

"I'll get back in touch with Stephanie's boss," Cahill said. "See if this Alhambra LLC rings a bell."

They assembled in the duty room and drew a straight line on a city map from the Rivercrest Motel to the offices of Braceland Westcott McCall. They would begin a canvass of the people, shops, and businesses on that line.

Someone had to have seen Stephanie on the day she disappeared.

As they began to divide up the canvass, Ike Buchanan returned. He walked toward them, his face grim, a familiar object in his hand. When the boss had that look on his face it usually meant two things. More work, and a *lot* more work.

"What's up?" Jessica asked.

Buchanan held the object up, a formerly benign, now ominous item made of black plastic, and said: "We've got another tape."

BY THE TIME SETH REACHED THE HOTEL, HE HAD MADE HIS calls. Somehow, he had created a fragile symmetry to his day. Providing there were no disasters, he would survive it. If Seth Goldman was anything, he was a survivor.

Then disaster presented itself in a cheap rayon dress.

Standing outside the front entrance to the hotel, she looked a thousand years old. Even from ten feet away he could smell the alcohol.

In low-budget horror movies, there was a surefire way to tell that the monster lurked nearby. There was always a musical cue. The threatening cellos before the bright brass of the attack.

For Seth Goldman, no music was needed. The end—his end—was a silent indictment in a woman's puffy red eyes.

He couldn't let it happen. *Couldn't*. He had worked too hard, too long. Everything was riding on *The Palace* and he would not let anything get in the way.

How far would he go to stanch the flow? He would soon find out.

Before anyone saw them, he took her by the arm and led her to a waiting cab.

"I THINK I CAN MANAGE," THE OLD WOMAN SAID.

"I wouldn't hear of it," Byrne replied.

They were in the parking lot of the Aldi on Market Street. Aldi was the no-frills supermarket chain that sold limited brands at discount prices. The woman was in her late seventies or early eighties, spindly and gaunt. She had fine features and translucent powdered skin. Despite the heat, and the fact that no rain was in the forecast for at least three days, she wore a double-breasted wool coat and bright blue galoshes. She was trying to load half a dozen grocery bags into her car, a twenty-year-old Chevy.

"But look at you," she said. She gestured toward his cane. "*I* should be helping *you*."

Byrne laughed. "I'm fine, ma'am," he said. "Just twisted my ankle."

"Of course, you're still a young man," she said. "At my age, if I twisted an ankle, they might put me down."

"You look pretty spry to me," Byrne said.

The woman smiled beneath the veil of a schoolgirl blush. "Oh, now."

Byrne grabbed the bags and started loading them into the backseat of the Chevy. Inside, he noticed a few rolls of paper towels, a few boxes of Kleenex. There were also a pair of mittens, an afghan, a knit cap, and a soiled quilted ski vest. Seeing as this woman probably didn't frequent the slopes of Camelback Mountain, Byrne figured she carted around this wardrobe on the off chance that the temperature might dip down to a frigid seventy-five degrees.

Before Byrne could load the last bag into the car his cell phone chirped. He took it out, snapped it open. It was a text message from Colleen. In it, she told him that she was not leaving for camp until Tuesday, and wondered if they could have dinner Monday night. Byrne messaged her back that he would love to have dinner. On her end, the phone would vibrate and she could read the message. She replied immediately:

KEWL! LUL CBOAO :)

"What is *that?*" the woman asked, pointing to his phone.

"It's a cell phone."

The woman looked at him for a moment, as if he had just told her it was a spaceship built for very, very small aliens. "That's a *telephone?*" she asked.

"Yes, ma'am," Byrne said. He held it up for her to see. "It has a camera built in, a calendar, an address book."

"My, my," she said, shaking her head side to side. "I believe the world has passed me by, young man."

"It's all moving too fast, isn't it?"

"Praise His name."

"Amen," Byrne said.

She began to slowly make her way toward the driver's door. Once inside she reached into her purse, produced a pair of quarters. "For your troubles," she said. She tried to hand them to Byrne. Byrne raised both hands in protest, more than a little moved by the gesture.

"That's okay," Byrne said. "You take that and buy yourself a cup of coffee." Without protest, the woman slipped the two coins back into her purse.

"Time was when you could get a cup of coffee for a nickel," she said.

Byrne reached over to close the door for her. With a movement he would have thought was too quick for a woman of her age she took his hand in hers. Her papery skin felt cool and dry to the touch. Instantly, the images ripped through his mind—

—a damp, dark room . . . the sounds of a TV in the background . . . Welcome Back, Kotter *. . . the flicker of votive candles . . . a woman's anguished sobs . . . the sound of bone on flesh . . . screams in the blackness . . .* Don't make me go up to the attic *. . .*

—as he tore back his hand. He wanted to move slowly, not wanting to alarm or insult the woman, but the images were terrifyingly clear, heart-breakingly real.

"Thank you, young man," the woman said.

Byrne took a step back, trying to compose himself.

The woman started her car. After a few moments she waved a thin, blue-veined hand, and angled across the lot.

Two things stayed with Kevin Byrne as the old woman drove away. The image of the young woman who still lived in her clear, ancient eyes.

And the sound of that terrified voice in his head.

Don't make me go up to the attic . . .

HE STOOD ACROSS the street from the building. It looked different in daylight, a squalid relic of his city, a scar on a moldering urban block. Every so often a passerby would stop, try to look through the grimy glass-block squares that checkerboarded the front.

Byrne took an item out of his coat pocket. It was the napkin that Victoria had given him when she had brought him breakfast in bed, the white linen square with the imprint of her lips in deep red lipstick. He turned it over and over in his hands as he drew the layout of the street in his mind. To the right of the building across the street was a small parking lot. Next to that, a used-furniture mart. In front of the furniture store was an array of bright plastic bar stools in the shape of tulips. To the left of the building was an alleyway. He watched a man exit the front of the building, around the corner to the left, down the alley, then down a set of iron stairs to an access door beneath the structure. A few minutes later, the man emerged carrying a pair of cardboard boxes.

It was a storage cellar.

That's where he would do it, Byrne thought. In the cellar. He would meet the man later that night in the cellar.

No one would hear them down there.

THE WOMAN IN THE WHITE DRESS ASKED: *WHAT ARE YOU DOING here? Why are you here?*

The knife in her hand appeared extremely sharp and, as she began to absently dig at the outside of her right thigh, it sliced through the material of her dress, splotching it with a Rorschach of blood. Thick steam filled the white bathroom, slicking the tiled walls, misting the mirror. Scarlet streaked and dripped from the razor-keened blade.

Do you know how it is when you meet somebody for the first time? the woman in white asked. Her tone was casual, almost conversational, as if she were having a cup of coffee or a cocktail with an old friend.

The other woman, the bruised and damaged woman in the terry-cloth robe, just stared, the terror building behind her eyes. The bathtub began to overflow, rippling over the side. Blood dappled the floor, pooling in a glossy, ever-widening circle. Downstairs, water began to seep through the ceiling. The big dog lapped at it on the hardwood floor.

Upstairs, the woman with the knife screamed: *You're a stupid, selfish bitch!*

Then she attacked.

Glenn Close hacked at Anne Archer in a life-and-death struggle as the tub began to overflow, flooding the bathroom floor. Downstairs, Michael Douglas's character—Dan Gallagher—took the kettle off the boil. Instantly he heard the screams. He bolted upstairs, ran into the bathroom, and slammed Glenn Close into the mirror, smashing it. They fought tooth and nail. She slashed him across the chest with the knife. They plunged into the tub. Soon Dan got the best of her, choking the life out of her. She finally stopped thrashing. She was dead.

Or was she?

And that's where the edit was.

Individually, simultaneously, the investigators watching the video tensed their muscles in anticipation of what they might see next.

The video jerked and rolled. The new image was a different bathroom, much dimmer, the light source coming from the left side of the frame. Ahead was a beige wall, a white slatted window treatment. There was no sound.

Suddenly a young woman rises to midframe. She is wearing a white, scoop-neck T-shirt dress, long-sleeved. It is not an exact duplicate of that worn by Glenn Close's character—Alex Forrest—in the film, but it is similar.

As the tape rolls, the woman steadies herself, centered in the frame. She is soaking wet. She is furious. She appears outraged, ready to pounce.

She stops.

Her expression suddenly turns from rage to fear, her eyes widening in horror. Someone, probably whoever was holding the camera, raises a small-caliber gun into the right side of the frame and pulls the trigger. The bullet slams into the woman's chest. The woman reels but doesn't instantly fall. She looks down at the widening intaglio of red.

She then slides down the wall, her blood painting the tile in bright crimson swaths. She slips slowly into the tub. The camera moves toward the young woman's face beneath the reddening bathwater.

The video shudders, rolls, then returns to the original film, to the scene where Michael Douglas shakes hands with a detective in front of his formerly idyllic home. In the movie, the nightmare is over.

Buchanan shut off the tape. As with the showing of the first tape, the occupants of the small room were stunned into silence. Every high they had felt in the past twenty-four hours or so—catching the break on the *Psycho* tape, finding the plumbing supply house, finding the motel room where Stephanie Chandler had been killed, finding the Saturn submerged along the banks of the Delaware—went out the window.

"This is one very bad actor," Cahill finally said.

The word floated for a moment before settling into the image bank. *The Actor.*

There was never any sort of official ritual when criminals got a nickname. It just happened. Whenever a person committed a series of crimes, instead of calling him the doer, or their unsub—short for *unknown subject*—it was sometimes easier to give him a nickname. This time it stuck.

They were looking for the Actor.

And it looked like he was far from taking his final bow.

WHENEVER THERE WERE two homicide victims, apparently killed by the same person—and there was no doubt that what they had witnessed on the *Fatal Attraction* tape was indeed a homicide, and little doubt it was the same killer as the *Psycho* tape—the first thing detectives look for is a connection between the victims. As obvious as it sounds, it was still true, yet not necessarily an easy link to establish.

Were they acquaintances, relatives, co-workers, lovers, former lovers? Did they attend the same church, health club, encounter group? Did they shop at the same stores, bank at the same bank? Did they share a dentist, doctor, lawyer?

Until they could identify the second victim, finding the connection would be unlikely. The first thing they would do is print an image of the second victim from the tape and recanvass everywhere they'd been for Stephanie Chandler. If they could establish that Stephanie Chandler knew the second victim, it might be a short leap to identifying the second woman, and finding the link. The prevailing theory was that there was a ferocious level of passion to these two homicides, which indicated some sort of intimacy between victims and killer, a level of familiarity that could not be achieved through casual acquaintance, or fuel such viciousness.

Someone had killed two young women and saw fit—through the prism of whatever dementia colored his daily life—to record the murders on tape. Not to taunt the police, necessarily. But rather to first horrify an unsuspecting public. It was certainly an MO that no one in the Homicide Unit could ever recall encountering before.

Something connected these people. Find the connection, find the common ground, find the parallels between these two lives, and they would find their killer.

Mateo Fuentes provided them with a fairly clear photographic image of the young woman on the *Fatal Attraction* tape. Eric Chavez was off to check on missing persons. If this victim was killed more than seventy-two hours earlier, there was a chance her disappearance had been called in. The other investigators assembled in Ike Buchanan's office.

"How did we get this?" Jessica asked.

"Courier," Buchanan said.

"Courier?" Jessica asked. "Is our doer changing his MO on us?"

"Not sure. But there was a partial rental sticker on it."

"Do we know where it was from?"

"Not yet," Buchanan said. "Most of the label was scraped off. But some of the bar code remained intact. The digital imaging lab is looking at it."

"Which courier service brought it?"

"Small company on Market called Blazing Wheels. Bike messengers."

"Do we know who sent it?"

Buchanan shook his head. "According to the kid who delivered it, he met with a guy at the Starbucks on Fourth and South. The guy paid cash."

"Don't you have to fill out a form?"

"All false. Name, address, phone. Dead ends."

"Can the messenger describe the guy?"

"He's with a sketch artist now."

Buchanan held up the tape.

"This is a wanted man, people," he said. Everyone knew what he meant. Until this psychopath was shut down, you ate standing up, and you didn't even think about sleeping. "Find this son of a bitch."

39

THE LITTLE GIRL IN THE LIVING ROOM WAS BARELY TALL ENOUGH to see over the coffee table. On television, the cartoon figures bounced and gamboled and zoomed, their manic movement a loud and colorful display. The little girl giggled.

Faith Chandler tried to focus. She was so tired.

In that space between memories, the bullet train of years, the little girl became twelve, about to enter junior high school. She stood tall and straight, the last moment before the boredom and utter misery of adolescence took over her mind; the furious hormones, her body. Still her little girl. Ribbons and smiles.

Faith knew she had to do something, but she could not think. She had made a phone call before she left for Center City. Now she was back. She was supposed to call again. But who? What had she meant to say?

There were three full bottles on the table, a full tumbler in front of her. Too much. Not enough. Never enough.

God, grant me the serenity . . .

There is no serenity.

She looked to her left once more, into the living room. The little girl was gone. The little girl was a dead woman now, cold in some gray marble room downtown.

Faith lifted the glass to her lips. She spilled some whiskey on her lap. She tried again. She swallowed. The fires of sorrow and guilt and regret flared within her.

"Stephie," she said.

She lifted the glass again. This time he helped her bring it to her lips. In a little while he would help her drink straight from the bottle.

40

As Jessica walked up Broad Street, she considered the nature of these crimes. She knew that, generally speaking, serial killers go to great lengths—or at least *some* lengths—to conceal their deeds. They find out-of-the-way dump sites, remote burial grounds. But the Actor was putting his victims on display in the most public and private of arenas: people's living rooms.

They all knew that the case had just become much bigger. The grip of passion needed to do what was done on the *Psycho* tape had become something else. Something cold. Something infinitely more calculating.

As much as Jessica wanted to call Kevin, to update him and get his take, she was ordered—ordered in no uncertain terms—to keep him out of the loop for the time being. He was on limited duty and the city was currently fighting two multimillion-dollar civil suits regarding officers who, even though cleared by doctors to return to work, had come back too soon. One had swallowed his barrel. The other had been gunned down in a drug raid when he could not run. There were enough detectives available, and Jessica was told to work with the team on duty.

She thought about the look on the young woman's face in the *Fatal*

Attraction video, the change from anger to fear to paralyzing horror. She thought about the gun rising into the frame.

For some reason, she thought mostly about the T-shirt dress. She hadn't seen one of them in years. She'd had a few when she was a teenager, of course, as did all of her friends. They were all the rage when she was starting junior high. She thought about the way it made her look shapely in those gangly scarecrow years, the way it gave her hips, something she was willing to give back now.

But mostly she thought about the blood blossoming on the front of the woman's dress. There was something unholy about that stigmata of bright red, the way it spread on the wet white fabric.

As Jessica neared city hall she noticed something that unnerved her even further, something that cloistered her hopes for any sort of rapid solution to this horror.

It was a hot summer day in Philly.

Almost all the women wore white.

JESSICA BROWSED THE racks of mystery fiction, thumbing through some of the new releases. She hadn't read a good crime novel in a while although, ever since she joined the Homicide Unit, she hadn't had much tolerance for crime as entertainment.

She was in the huge, multilevel Borders on South Broad Street, right near city hall. She had decided to walk instead of eating lunch today. Any day now, Uncle Vittorio would close a deal for her to be on ESPN2, which would mean she would have a bout set up, which would mean she'd have to go into training—no more cheesesteaks, no more scones, no more tiramisu. She hadn't run in nearly five days, and she was pretty pissed at herself about that. If for no other reason, running was a great way to relieve the stress of the job.

For all cops, the specter of weight gain loomed large, due to the hours, the pressure, the ease of living a fast-food life. Not to mention the booze. For women cops, it was worse. She had known many fellow female officers who had entered the force a size four and left a twelve or fourteen. It was one of the reasons she had gotten into boxing in the first place. The steel mesh of discipline.

Of course, as soon as these thoughts crossed her mind, she caught the aroma of warm pastries wafting down the escalator from the café on the second floor. Time to go.

She had to meet up with Terry Cahill in a few minutes. They were going to canvass the coffee shops and lunch counters near Stephanie Chandler's office building. Pending identification of the Actor's second victim, it was all they had going.

Near the checkout counters on the main floor of the bookstore she saw a tall, freestanding rack of books labeled LOCAL INTEREST. Displayed were a number of volumes about Philadelphia, mostly small-press editions covering the city's history, attractions, colorful citizens. There was one title that jumped out at her:

Gods of Mayhem: A History of Murder in Cinema.

The book was about crime film and its various motifs and themes, from black comedies like *Fargo* to classic noir movies such as *Double Indemnity* to bizarre fare like *Man Bites Dog.*

Aside from the title, what caught Jessica's eye was the short blurb about the author. A man named Nigel Butler, PhD, professor of film studies at Drexel University.

By the time she reached the door she was on her cell phone.

FOUNDED IN 1891, Drexel University was located on Chestnut Street in West Philadelphia. Among its eight colleges and three schools was the highly respected College of Media Arts and Design, which also included a screenwriting program.

According to the brief biography on the back of the book, Nigel Butler was forty-two, but he looked much younger in person. The man in the author photo had a salt-and-pepper beard. The man in the black suede blazer in front of her was clean-shaven, and that seemed to take a decade off his appearance.

They met in his small, book-filled office. The walls were lined with well-framed movie posters from the 1930s and '40s, mostly noir: *Criss Cross, Phantom Lady, This Gun for Hire.* There were also a number of eight-by-ten head shots of Nigel Butler as Tevye, Willy Loman, King Lear, Ricky Roma.

Jessica introduced herself and Terry Cahill. She took the lead in the questioning.

"This is about the video killer case, isn't it?" Butler asked.

They had kept most of the details of the *Psycho* killing from the press, but a story had run in the *Inquirer* that the police were investigating a bizarre homicide that someone had filmed.

"Yes, sir," Jessica said. "I'd like to ask you a few questions, but I want your assurance that I can count on your discretion."

"Absolutely," Butler said.

"I'd appreciate it, Mr. Butler."

"Actually, it's *Dr.* Butler, but please call me Nigel."

Jessica gave him a basic background on the case, including the discovery of the second tape, leaving out the more gruesome details, as well as anything that might compromise the investigation. Butler listened the whole time, his face impassive. When she was finished, he asked: "What can I do to help?"

"Well, we're trying to get a handle on why he is doing this, and where this might be going."

"Of course."

Jessica had been wrestling with a notion since she had first seen the *Psycho* tape. She decided to just ask. "Is someone making snuff movies here?"

Butler smiled, sighed, shook his head.

"Did I say something funny?" Jessica asked.

"I'm sorry," Butler said. "It's just that, of all the urban legends, the legend of the snuff movie is probably the most stubborn."

"What do you mean?"

"I mean they don't exist. Or at least, I've never seen one. Nor has any of my colleagues."

"Are you saying that this is something you would watch if given the opportunity?" Jessica asked, hoping her tone wasn't as judgmental as she felt.

Butler seemed to think about this for a few moments before answering. He sat on the edge of the desk. "I've written four books on film, Detective. I've been a film buff my whole life, ever since my mother dropped me off at the movies in 1974 to see *Benji*."

Jessica was appropriately surprised. "You're saying that *Benji* started a lifelong scholarly interest in film?"

Butler laughed. "Well, I saw *Chinatown* instead. I've never been the same." He pulled a pipe out of a rack on the desk, started the pipe smoker's ritual: cleaning, filling, tamping. He filled it, got a coal going. The aroma was sweet. "I was an alternative-press film critic for years, seeing five to ten movies a week, from the sublime artistry of Jacques Tati, to the indescribable banality of Pauly Shore. I own sixteen-millimeter prints of thirteen of what I consider to be the best fifty films ever made, and I'm nearing the purchase of number fourteen—Jean-Luc Godard's *Weekend,* in case you were wondering. I'm a big fan of French New Wave and a hopeless Francophile." Butler puffed his pipe, continued. "I once sat through all fifteen hours of *Berlin Alexanderplatz,* and the director's cut of *JFK,* which just *seemed* like fifteen hours. I have a daughter studying acting. If you were to ask me if there was a short film I would not watch, based on its subject matter, just for the experience, I would have to say no."

"Regardless of the subject matter," Jessica said, glancing at the photo on Butler's desk. In it, Butler stood at the foot of a stage with a smiling teenaged girl.

"Regardless of the subject matter," Butler echoed. "To me, and if I may speak for my colleagues, it is not necessarily about the subject of the film or the style or motif or theme, it is basically about the committing of light to celluloid. The fact that it was done and it remains. I don't think too many film scholars would call John Waters' *Pink Flamingos* art, but it remains an important arti*fact.*"

Jessica tried to absorb this. She wasn't sure she was ready to accept the possibilities of such a philosophy. "So you're saying there's no such thing as a snuff film."

"No," he said. "But every so often a mainstream Hollywood film will come along, stoking the fire, and the legend is reborn."

"Which Hollywood films are you talking about?"

"Well, *8MM* for one," Nigel said. "And then there was that silly exploitation film *Snuff* from the midseventies. I think the main difference between the concept of a snuff film and what you're describing to me is that what you're describing to me could hardly be classified as erotic."

Jessica was incredulous. "And a snuff movie *is?*"

"Well, according to legend—or at least in the simulated brand of snuff film that has actually been produced and released—there *are* certain adult-film conventions."

"For instance."

"For instance, there is usually a teenaged girl or boy and a character that dominates them. There is generally a rough sexual element, a good deal of hard S and M. What you're talking about seems to be a different pathology altogether."

"Meaning?"

Butler smiled again. "I teach film studies, not abnormal psych."

"Can you glean anything from the choice of films?" Jessica asked.

"Well, *Psycho* would seem an obvious choice. Too obvious, in my opinion. Every time there is a top one hundred horror film list compiled, it always places near the top, if not *the* top. I believe it shows a lack of imagination on this . . . madman's part."

"And what about *Fatal Attraction*?"

"An interesting leap. The films are twenty-seven years apart. One is considered horror, the other is a rather mainstream thriller."

"What would you choose?"

"You mean, if I were advising him?"

"Yes."

Butler sat on the edge of the desk. Academics loved academic exercise. "*Great* question," he said. "Off the top of my head I would say, if you really wanted to get creative about all this—staying in the horror genre, although *Psycho* is forever misrepresented as a horror film when it is not—to go with something by Dario Argento or Lucio Fulci. Maybe Herschell Gordon Lewis or even early George Romero."

"Who are these people?"

"The first two were pioneers of seventies Italian splatter cinema," Terry Cahill said. "The latter two were their American counterparts. George Romero is most noted for his zombie series: *Night of the Living Dead, Dawn of the Dead,* et cetera."

Everybody seems to know about this stuff but me, Jessica thought. *Now would be a good time brush up on this subject.*

"If you want to talk pre-Tarantino crime cinema, I would go with Peckinpah," Butler added. "But all of this is moot."

"Why do you say that?"

"There doesn't seem to be an obvious progression insofar as style or motif at work here. I would say that the person you are looking for is not particularly cerebral about horror or crime cinema."

"Any idea what his next choice might be?"

"You want me to extrapolate the mind-set of a killer?"

"Let's call it an academic exercise."

Nigel Butler smiled. Touché. "I should think he might choose something recent. Something released in the past fifteen years. Something that someone might actually rent."

Jessica made a few final notes. "Again, I would appreciate you keeping this all to yourself for the time being." She handed him a card. "If you think of anything else that might be helpful, please don't hesitate to call."

"*D'accord,*" Nigel Butler replied. As they walked to the door, he added: "I don't mean to be forward, but has anyone ever told you that you look like a movie star?"

Here we go, Jessica thought. Was he coming on to her? In the middle of all this? She shot a glance at Cahill. He was clearly fighting a smile. "Excuse me?"

"Ava Gardner," Butler said. "A *young* Ava Gardner. Maybe around the time of *East Side, West Side.*"

"Uh, no," Jessica said, brushing the bangs from her forehead. Was she primping? *Stop it.* "But thanks for the compliment. We'll be in touch."

Ava Gardner, she thought, walking to the elevators. *Please.*

ON THE WAY back to the Roundhouse, they swung by Adam Kaslov's apartment. Jessica rang the buzzer and knocked. No answer. She called his two places of employment. No one had seen him in the past thirty-six hours. These facts, added to the others, were probably enough to get a warrant. They couldn't use his juvenile record, but maybe they wouldn't need it. She dropped Cahill off at the Barnes & Noble on Rittenhouse Square. He said he wanted further peruse books on crime cinema, buying whatever he thought might be relevant. Nice to have Uncle Sam's credit card, Jessica thought.

When Jessica returned to the Roundhouse, she wrote up a request for a search warrant and faxed it to the DA's office. She didn't expect much, but it never hurt to ask. As to phone messages, there was only one. It was from Faith Chandler. It was marked URGENT.

Jessica dialed the number, got the woman's answering machine. She tried a second time, this time leaving a message, including her cell phone number.

She hung up the phone, wondering.

Urgent.

I WALK THE BUSTLING STREET, BLOCKING THE NEXT SCENE, body-to-body in this sea of cold strangers. Joe Buck in *Midnight Cowboy*. Extras greet me. Some smile, some look away. Most will never remember me. When the final draft is written, there will be reaction shots, and throwaway dialogue:

He was there?

I was there that day!

I think I saw him!

CUT TO:

A coffee shop, one of the cookie-cutter chains on Walnut Street, just around the corner from Rittenhouse Square. Coffee-cult figures hover over alternative weeklies.

"What can I get for ya?"

She is no more than nineteen, with fair skin, a thin intriguing face, frizzy hair pulled back into a ponytail.

"Tall latte," I say. Ben Johnson in *The Last Picture Show*. "And I'll have one of them there bis-cottis." Them there? I almost laugh. I don't, of course. I've never broken character and I'm not going to start now. "I'm new to this city," I add. "I haven't seen a friendly face in weeks."

She makes my coffee, bags the biscotti, caps my cup, taps the touch screen. "Where are you from?"

"West Texas," I say with a broad smile. "El Paso. Big Bend country."

"Wow," she replies, as if I had told her I was from Neptune. "You're a long way from home."

"Aren't we all?" I hand her a five.

She stops, frozen for a moment, as if I have said something profound. I step out onto Walnut Street, feeling tall and fit. Gary Cooper in *The Fountainhead*. Tall is a method, like weakness.

I finish my latte, breeze into a men's clothing store. I fashion up, vogue briefly near the door, gather my suitors. One of them steps forward.

"Hi," the salesman says. He is thirty. His hair is cropped short. He is suited and booted, wearing a wrinkled gray T-shirt beneath a navy-blue three-button number at least one size too small. This seems to be a fashion statement of some sort.

"Hello," I say. I wink at him and he colors slightly.

"What can I show you today?"

Your blood on my Bokhara? I think, channeling Patrick Bateman. I give him my toothy Christian Bale. "Just looking."

"Well, I'm here to offer assistance, and I hope you'll allow me the privilege of doing so. My name is Trinian."

Of course it is.

I think of those great St. Trinian's British comedies from the 1950s and '60s, and consider making a reference. I notice he has a bright orange Skechers watch on his wrist, and realize that I would be wasting my breath.

Instead, I frown—bored and beleaguered by my excessive wealth and station. He is even more interested now. In this setting, abuse and intrigue are lovers.

Twenty minutes later it hits me. Perhaps I have known it all along. It really is all about the skin. Skin is where you stop, and the world starts. Everything you are—your mind, your personality, your soul—is contained and constrained by your skin. In here, in my skin, I am God.

I slip into my car. I have just a few hours to get into character.

I'm thinking Gene Hackman in *Extreme Measures*.

Or maybe even Gregory Peck in *The Boys from Brazil*.

MATEO FUENTES FREEZE-FRAMED THE IMAGE AT THE POINT IN the *Fatal Attraction* tape when the gun was fired. He toggled back, forward, back, forward. He ran the tape in slow motion, each field rolling top-to-bottom on the frame. On the screen, a hand came up on the right side of the frame and stopped. The shooter wore a surgical glove, but it wasn't his hand they were interested in, although they had already narrowed down the make and model of the pistol. The Firearms Unit was still working on it.

The star of the movie, at this point, was the jacket. It looked like a satin jacket, the type of jacket that baseball teams or roadies at rock concerts wear—dark, shiny, and with a ribbed band at the wrist.

Mateo printed off a hard copy of the image. It was impossible to tell what color the jacket was—black or navy blue. This jibed with Little Jake's recollection of a man in a dark blue jacket inquiring about the *Los Angeles Times*. It wasn't much. There had to be thousands of jackets like that in Philly. Still, they would have a composite suspect sketch that afternoon.

Eric Chavez entered the room, extremely animated, a computer printout in hand. "We've got a location on where the *Fatal Attraction* tape is from."

"Where?"

"It's a dump called Flickz on Frankford," Chavez said. "Independent store. Guess who owns it."

Jessica and Palladino said the name at the same time.

"Eugene Kilbane."

"One and the same."

"Son of a bitch." Jessica found herself subconsciously clenching her fists.

Jessica filled Buchanan in on their interview with Kilbane, leaving out the part about the assault and battery. If they brought Kilbane in, he was sure to bring it up anyway.

"You like him for this?" Buchanan asked.

"No," Jessica said. "But what are the chances that this is coincidence? He knows something."

Everyone looked at Buchanan with the anticipation of pit bulls circling the fight ring.

Buchanan said: "Bring him in."

"I DIDN'T WANT to get involved," Kilbane said.

For the moment, Eugene Kilbane was sitting at one of the desks in the duty room of the Homicide Unit. If they didn't like any of his answers, he would soon be moving to one of the interrogation rooms.

Chavez and Palladino had found him at The White Bull Tavern.

"Did you think we wouldn't be able to trace the tape back to you?" Jessica asked.

Kilbane looked at the tape, which was on the desk in front of him in a clear evidence bag. It appeared as if he thought scraping the label off the side might have been enough to fool seven thousand cops. Not to mention the FBI.

"Come on. You know my record," he said. "Shit has a way of sticking to me."

Jessica and Palladino looked at each other as if to say: *Don't give us this kind of opening, Eugene. The fucking jokes will start writing themselves and we'll be here all day.* They restrained themselves. For the moment.

"Two tapes, both of them containing evidence in murder investigations, both rented at stores you own," Jessica said.

"I know," Kilbane said. "It looks bad."

"Gee, ya think?"

"I . . . I don't know what to say."

"How did the tape get here?" Jessica asked.

"I have no idea," Kilbane said.

Palladino held up the artist's sketch of the man who'd hired the bicycle messenger to deliver the tape. It was an extraordinarily good likeness of one Eugene Kilbane.

Kilbane hung his head for a few moments, then looked around the room, meeting the eyes of everyone there. "Do I need a lawyer here?"

"You tell *us*," Palladino said. "You got something to hide, Eugene?"

"Man," he said. "You try to do the right thing, see what it gets you."

"Why did you send the tape to us?"

"Hey," he said. "I got a conscience, you know."

This time, Palladino held up Kilbane's rap sheet, turned it to Kilbane's face. "Since when?" he asked.

"Since always. I was raised a Catholic."

"This from a pornographer," Jessica said. They all knew why Kilbane had come forward, and it had nothing to do with conscience. He had violated his parole by having an illegal weapon on him the day before, and he was trying to buy them off. With one phone call he could be back in prison tonight. "Spare us the homily."

"Yeah, okay. I'm in the adult entertainment business. So what? It's legal. Where's the harm?"

Jessica didn't know where to start. She started anyway. "Let's see. AIDS? Chlamydia? Gonorrhea? Syphilis? Herpes? HIV? Ruined lives? Destroyed families? Drugs? Violence? Let me know when you want me stop."

Kilbane just stared, a little overwhelmed. Jessica stared him down. She wanted to go on, but what was the point? She wasn't in the mood, and it wasn't the time or the place to debate the sociological ramifications of pornography with someone like Eugene Kilbane. There were two dead people to think about.

Bested before he even began, Kilbane reached into his briefcase, a tattered faux-alligator attaché. He pulled out another tape. "You'll change your tune when you see this."

———

THEY SAT IN a small room in the AV Unit. Kilbane's second tape was surveillance footage from Flickz, the store where the *Fatal Attraction* tape had been rented. Apparently, the security cameras were real at that location.

"Why are the cameras active at this store and not at The Reel Deal?" Jessica asked.

Kilbane looked dope-slapped. "Who told you *that?*"

Jessica didn't want to get Lenny Puskas or Juliet Rausch, the two employees at The Reel Deal, in any trouble. "Nobody, Eugene. We checked it out ourselves. You really think it's a big secret? Those camera heads at The Reel Deal are from, what, the late seventies? They look like shoe boxes."

Kilbane sighed. "I got more of a theft problem at Flickz, okay? Fucking kids rob you blind."

"What exactly is on this tape?" Jessica asked.

"I maybe got a lead for you."

"A lead?"

Kilbane looked around the room. "Yeah, you know. A *lead.*"

"Watch much *CSI*, Eugene?"

"Some. Why?"

"No reason. So what is this lead?"

Kilbane put his hands out to his sides, palms up. He smiled, destroying whatever was remotely likable about his face, and said: "That's entertainment."

A FEW MINUTES later, Jessica, Terry Cahill, and Eric Chavez crowded around the editing bay in the AV Unit. Cahill had returned from his bookstore project empty-handed. Kilbane sat in the chair next to Mateo Fuentes. Mateo looked disgusted. He cocked his body at about a forty-five-degree angle away from Kilbane, as if the man smelled like a compost heap. In fact, he smelled like Vidalia onions and Aqua Velva. Jessica had the feeling that Mateo was ready to spray Kilbane with Lysol if he touched anything.

Jessica studied Kilbane's body language. Kilbane seemed both nervous and excited. *Nervous* the detectives could understand. *Excited,* not so much. Something was up here.

Mateo hit the PLAY button on the surveillance tape VCR. Immediately the image rolled to life on the monitor. It was a high-angle shot of a long, narrow video store, similar in layout to The Reel Deal. Five or six people milled about.

"This is from yesterday," Kilbane said. There was no date or time code readout on the tape.

"What time?" Cahill asked.

"I don't know," Kilbane said. "Sometime after eight. We change the tapes around eight and we're open until midnight at that location."

A small corner of the front window of the store revealed that it was dark outside. If it became important, they'd check the sunset stats from the day before to pin down a more precise time.

On the tape, a pair of black teenaged girls cruised the racks of new releases, keenly observed by a pair of black teenaged boys who acted out, playing the fools, trying to get their attention. The boys failed miserably and, after a minute or two, skulked off.

At the bottom of the frame, a serious-looking older man with a white goatee and black Kangol cap read every word on the back of a pair of tapes in the documentary section. He moved his lips as he read. The man soon left, and for a few minutes there were no customers visible.

Then a new figure walked into the frame from the left side, into the middle section of the store. He approached the center rack that held older VHS releases.

"There he is," Kilbane said.

"There *who* is?" Cahill asked.

"You'll see. That rack goes from *f* to *h*," Kilbane said.

On the tape, it was impossible to gauge the man's height from such a high angle. He was taller than the top rack, which probably put him over five nine or so, but beyond that he looked exceedingly average in all ways. He stood still, back to the camera, perusing the rack. So far, there had been no profile shot, no glimpse of his face, just a vantage from behind as he entered the frame. He wore a dark bomber jacket, dark ball cap, and dark trousers. Over his right shoulder was a slim leather shoulder bag.

The man picked up a few tapes, flipped them over, read the credits, put them back on the rack. He stepped back, hands on hips, surveyed the titles.

Then a middle-aged, quite rotund white woman approached from the right side of the frame. She wore a flower-print shift and had her thinning hair in hot rollers. It appeared as if she said something to the man. Staring straight ahead, still denying the camera his profile—as if he knew the security camera position—the man answered her, gesturing to his left. The woman, nodded, smiled, smoothed the dress over her abundant hips, as if waiting for the man to continue the conversation. He did not. She then huffed out of the frame. The man did not watch her go.

A few more moments passed. The man looked at a few more tapes, then quite casually took a videotape out of the bag and put it on the shelf. Mateo rewound the tape, replayed the section, then froze the tape and slowly zoomed in, sharpening the image as much as possible while he did so. The graphic on the front of the videotape box became clearer. The image was a black-and-white photograph of a man on the left and a woman with curly blond hair on the right. Down the center, splitting the photo in two, was a ragged red triangle.

The tape was *Fatal Attraction.*

The sense of excitement was palpable in the room.

"Now, see, the employees are supposed to make customers leave bags like that at the front counter," Kilbane said. "Fucking *idiots.*"

Mateo rewound the tape to the point where the figure entered the frame, played it back in slow motion, froze the image, enlarged it. It was very grainy, but it was clear that there was elaborate embroidery on the back of the man's satin jacket.

"Can you get closer?" Jessica asked.

"*Oh,* yeah," Mateo said, firmly center stage. This was his wheelhouse.

He began to work his magic, tapping keys, adjusting levers and knobs, bringing the image up and in. The embroidered picture on the back of the jacket appeared to be a green dragon, its narrow head breathing a thin crimson flame. Jessica made a note to look into tailors who specialized in embroidery.

Mateo worked the image to the right and down, centering it on the man's right hand. It was clear that he was wearing a surgical glove.

"*Jesus,*" Kilbane said, shaking his head, running a hand over his jaw. "Fucking guy comes in the store wearing latex gloves and there's no red flag with my employees. They are *so* fucking yesterday, man."

Mateo flipped on a second monitor. On it was the freeze-frame of the killer's hand holding the weapon in the *Fatal Attraction* killing tape. The gunman's right sleeve had a ribbing similar to the jacket in the surveillance video. Although not concrete evidence, the jackets were definitely similar.

Mateo hit a few keys and began printing off hard copies of both images.

"When was the *Fatal Attraction* tape rented?" Jessica asked.

"Last night," Kilbane said. "Late."

"When?"

"I don't know. After eleven. I could look it up."

"And you're saying that whoever rented it watched the tape and brought it back to you?"

"Yeah."

"When?"

"This morning."

"When?"

"I don't know. Ten, maybe?"

"Did they drop it in the bin or did they bring it inside?"

"They brought it right to me."

"What did they say when they brought the tape back?"

"Just that there was something wrong with it. They wanted their money back."

"That's it?"

"Well, *yeah.*"

"They didn't happen to mention that someone had spliced in an actual homicide?"

"You gotta understand who comes into that store. I mean, at that store, people brought back that movie *Memento* saying that there was something wrong with the tape. They said the movie was on the tape backward. You believe *that?*"

Jessica continued to stare at Kilbane for a few moments, then turned to Terry Cahill.

"*Memento* was a story told in reverse," Cahill said.

"Uh, okay," Jessica replied. "Whatever." She turned her attention back to Kilbane. "Who rented the *Fatal Attraction* tape?"

"Just a regular," Kilbane said.

"We'll need the name."

Kilbane shook his head. "He's just a regular schmuck. He ain't got nothing to do with this."

"We'll need the name," Jessica repeated.

Kilbane stared at her. You'd think a two-time loser like Kilbane would know better than to try to finesse the cops. On the other hand, if he was smarter, he wouldn't be a two-time loser. Kilbane was just about to object when he glanced at Jessica. Perhaps a phantom pain in his side flared momentarily, recalling Jessica's wicked body shot. He acquiesced and gave them the name of the customer.

"Do you know the woman on the surveillance tape?" Palladino asked. "The woman who talked to that man?"

"What, that heifer?" Kilbane screwed up his face, as if *GQ* gigolo studs like him would never associate with an overweight middle-aged woman who went out in public wearing hot rollers. "Uh, no."

"Have you seen her in the store before?"

"Not that I remember."

"Did you watch the whole tape before you sent it to us?" Jessica asked, knowing the answer, knowing that someone like Eugene Kilbane could not resist.

Kilbane looked at the floor for a moment. Obviously, he had. "Yeah."

"Why didn't you bring it in yourself?"

"I thought we went over this."

"Tell us again."

"Look, you might want to be a little nicer to me."

"And why is that?"

"Because I can break this case wide open for you."

Everyone just stared at him. Kilbane cleared his throat. It sounded like a farm tractor backing out of a muddy culvert. "I want assurances that you're going to overlook my little, uh, indiscretion of the other day." At this he lifted up his shirt. The game zipper he'd had on his belt—the weapons violation that would have put him back in prison—was gone.

"We'll want to hear what you have to say first."

Kilbane seemed to think about the offer. It wasn't what he wanted, but it appeared as if it was all he was going to get. He cleared his throat again, looked around the room, perhaps expecting everyone to hold their breath in anticipation of his earth-shattering revelation. It didn't happen. He plowed ahead anyway.

"The guy on the tape?" Kilbane said. "The guy who put the *Fatal Attraction* tape back on the shelf?"

"What about him?" Jessica asked.

Kilbane leaned forward, playing the moment for all that it was worth, and said: "I know who he is."

"SMELLS LIKE A SLAUGHTERHOUSE."

He was rake-handle-skinny, and looked like a man unstuck in time, unencumbered by history. There was good reason for that. Sammy Du-Puis was trapped in 1962. Today Sammy wore a black alpaca cardigan, blue-on-blue point-collar dress shirt, gray iridescent sharkskin pants, and pointy cap-toe oxfords. His hair was slicked back, fused with enough hair tonic to grease a Chrysler. He smoked an unfiltered Camel.

They met on Germantown Avenue, near Broad Street. The aroma of simmering barbecue and hickory smoke from Dwight's Southern permeated the air with its fatty sweet tang. It made Kevin Byrne salivate. It made Sammy DuPuis nauseous.

"What, not a big fan of soul food?" Byrne asked.

Sammy shook his head, hit his Camel hard. "How do people eat that shit? It's all fuckin' fat and gristle. You might as well just put it into a needle and shoot it into your heart."

Byrne glanced down. The gun was laid out on a black velvet cloth between them. There was something about the scent of oil on steel, Byrne thought. There was a terrible power in that smell.

Byrne picked it up, checked the action, sighted the barrel, mindful of the fact that they were in a public place. Sammy generally worked out of his house in East Camden, but Byrne didn't have time to cross the river today.

"I can do it for six fifty," Sammy said. "And that is a bargain for such a *beauty*-full weapon."

"Sammy," Byrne said.

Sammy was silent for a few moments, conveying poverty, oppression, destitution. It didn't work. "Okay, six," he said. "And I'm losing money."

Sammy DuPuis was a gun dealer who never dealt to drug dealers or anyone in a gang. If there was a backroom small-arms dealer with scruples, it was Sammy DuPuis.

The item for sale was a SIG-Sauer P-226. It may not have been the prettiest handgun ever made—far from it—but it was accurate, reliable, and rugged. And Sammy DuPuis was a man of deep discretion. On this day, these were Kevin Byrne's main concerns.

"This better be cold, Sammy." Byrne put the weapon in his coat pocket.

Sammy wrapped the other guns in the cloth, said: "Like my first wife's ass."

Byrne pulled his roll, peeled off six hundred-dollar bills. He handed them to Sammy. "You bring the bag?" Byrne asked.

Sammy looked up immediately. His forehead was corrugated with thought. As a rule, getting Sammy DuPuis to stop counting money was no small feat, but Byrne's question stopped him cold. If what they were doing was outside the law—and it broke at least half a dozen laws that Byrne could think of, both state and federal—what Byrne was suggesting broke just about every other.

But Sammy DuPuis did not judge. If he did, he wouldn't be in the business he was in. And he wouldn't cart around the silver case he carried in the trunk of his car, the valise that held instruments of such dark purpose that Sammy only spoke of their existence in hushed tones.

"You sure?"

Byrne just stared.

"Okay, okay," Sammy said. "Sorry I asked."

They got out of the car, walked to the trunk. Sammy looked up and down the street. He hesitated, fumbling with his keys.

"Checking for the cops?" Byrne asked.

Sammy laughed a nervous little twitter. He opened the trunk. Inside was a group of canvas bags, attaché cases, duffels. Sammy moved a few of the leatherette cases to the side. He opened one. Inside was an array of cell phones. "Sure you don't want a clean cell instead? A PDA, maybe?" he asked. "I can put you in a BlackBerry 7290 for seventy-five bucks."

"Sammy."

Sammy hesitated again, then zipped up the leatherette satchel. He cracked another case. This one was ringed with dozens of amber vials. "How about pills?"

Byrne thought about it. He knew Sammy had amphetamines. He was exhausted, but the uppers would just make things worse.

"No pills."

"Fireworks? Porno? I can get you a Lexus for ten G's."

"You *do* remember I have a loaded weapon in my pocket, don't you?" Byrne asked.

"You're the boss," Sammy said. He pulled out a sleek Zero Halliburton suitcase, dialed the three digits, subconsciously shielding the operation from Byrne. He opened the case, then stepped away, lit another Camel. Even for Sammy DuPuis, the contents of this case were hard to look at.

GENERALLY THERE WERE NO MORE THAN A FEW OFFICERS IN
the AV Unit in the basement of the Roundhouse at any given time. This
afternoon there were half a dozen detectives crowded around the monitor in the small editing bay next to the control room. Jessica was certain
that the fact that a hard-core porno movie was running had nothing to do
with it.

Jessica and Cahill had driven Kilbane back to Flickz, where he had
gone into the adult section and retrieved an X-rated title called *Philadelphia Skin*. He had emerged from the back room like a covert government
operative retrieving secret enemy files.

The movie opened with a stock footage view of the skyline of
Philadelphia. The production values seemed fairly high for an adult title.
Then the film cut to the inside of an apartment. This footage looked
standard—bright light, slightly overexposed digital video. Within seconds there was a knock at the door.

A woman entered the frame, answered the door. She was young and
delicate, a gaminelike body in a pale yellow teddy. Barely legal by all ap-
pearances. When she opened the door fully, a man stood there. He was

of average height and build. He wore a blue satin bomber jacket and leather face mask.

"You call for a master plumber?" the man asked.

A few of the detectives laughed, then quickly stowed it. The possibility existed that the man asking the question was their killer. When he turned away from the camera, they saw that he was wearing the same jacket as the man in the surveillance video: dark blue with an embroidered green dragon.

"I'm new to this city," the girl said. "I haven't seen a friendly face in weeks."

As the camera moved closer to her, Jessica could see that the young woman wore a delicate pink feathered mask, but Jessica could see her eyes—haunted, scared eyes, portals to a deeply damaged soul.

The camera then panned to the right, following the man down a short hallway. At this point, Mateo freeze-framed it, made a Sony print of the image. Although the freeze-frame from the surveillance tape, at this size and resolution, was quite fuzzy, when the two images were put side by side the results were all but conclusive.

The man in the X-rated movie and the man putting the tape back on the shelf at Flickz appeared to be wearing the same jacket.

"Anyone recognize this design?" Buchanan asked.

No one did.

"Let's check it against gang symbols, tattoos," he added. "Let's find tailors who do embroidery."

They watched the rest of the video. Another man in a mask was in the film also, along with a second girl in a feather mask. The movie was of the S&M, rough-sex vintage. It was hard for Jessica to believe that the S&M aspects of the film were not causing the young women severe pain or injury. It looked like they were being seriously beaten.

When it was over, they watched the meager "credits." The film was directed by someone named Edmundo Nobile. The actor in the blue jacket's name was Bruno Steele.

"What's the actor's real name?" Jessica asked.

"I don't know," Kilbane said. "But I know the people who distributed the film. If anyone can find him, they can."

PHILADELPHIA SKIN WAS distributed by a Camden, New Jersey, company called Inferno Films. Inferno Films had been in business since 1981, and in that time had released more than four hundred films, mostly hard-core adult titles. They sold their product wholesale to adult bookstores, as well as retail through their websites.

The detectives decided that a full-on approach to the company—search warrant, raid, interrogations—might not yield the desired results. If they went in with badges flashing, the chances of the company circling the wagons, or suddenly getting amnesia about one of their "actors," were high, as were the chances that they might tip the actor and therefore put him in the wind.

They decided that the best way to handle this was through a sting operation. When all eyes turned to Jessica, she knew what it meant.

She would be going undercover.

And her guide into the netherworld of Philadelphia porn would be none other than Eugene Kilbane.

ON THE WAY out of the Roundhouse, Jessica crossed the parking lot and nearly ran into someone. She looked up. It was Nigel Butler.

"Hello, Detective," Butler said. "I was just coming up to see you."

"Hi," she said.

He held up a plastic bag. "I put together a few books for you. They might help."

"You didn't have to bring them down," Jessica said.

"It wasn't a problem."

Butler opened the bag and took out three books, all oversize paper-back editions. *Shots in the Mirror: Crime Films and Society, Gods of Death,* and *Masters of Mise en Scene.*

"This is very generous. Thanks very much."

Butler glanced at the Roundhouse, looked back at Jessica. The moment drew out.

"Is there anything else?" Jessica asked.

Butler grinned. "I was kind of hoping for a tour."

Jessica glanced at her watch. "Any other day it would be no problem."

"Oh, I'm sorry."

"Look. You've got my card. Give me a call tomorrow and we'll set something up."

"I'll be out of town for a few days, but I'll call when I return."

"That will be great," Jessica said. She held up the bag of books. "And thanks again for these."

"*Bonne chance,* Detective."

Jessica walked to her car, thinking about Nigel Butler in his ivory tower, surrounded by well-framed posters from movies where the guns all had blanks, the stuntmen fell onto air mattresses, and the blood was fake.

The world she was about to enter was about as far from academia as she could imagine.

JESSICA MADE A pair of Lean Cuisine dinners for her and Sophie. They sat on the couch and ate off TV trays, one of Sophie's favorite things. Jessica flipped on the TV, cruised the channels, and settled on a movie. Mid-1990s fare with clever dialogue and sizzling action. Background noise. As they ate their dinner, Sophie detailed her day in preschool. In honor of the upcoming birthday of Beatrix Potter, Sophie told Jessica, her class had made rabbit hand puppets out of lunch bags. The afternoon was devoted to a climate study via the learning of a new song called "Drippy the Raindrop." Jessica had the feeling she'd know all the words to "Drippy the Raindrop" in short order, whether she wanted to or not.

Just as she was about to clear their plates, Jessica heard a voice. A *familiar* voice. The recognition brought her attention back to the movie. The film was *Kill Game 2,* the second in the popular series of Will Parrish action movies. This one was about a South African drug lord.

But it wasn't Will Parrish's voice that caught Jessica's attention—indeed, Parrish's gravelly drawl was as recognizable as that of just about any actor working. Instead, it was the voice of the beat cop who was covering the back of the building.

"We've got officers at all the exits," the beat cop said. "These scumbags are *ours.*"

"No one gets in or out," Parrish replied, his formerly white dress shirt covered in Hollywood blood, his feet bare.

"Yes, sir," the officer said. He was a little taller than Parrish, had a strong jawline, ice-blue eyes, slender build.

Jessica had to look twice, then twice more, just to be sure she wasn't hallucinating. She was not. There could be no question about it. As hard as it was to believe, it was true.

The man playing the beat cop in *Kill Game 2* was Special Agent Terry Cahill.

JESSICA GOT ON her computer, onto the Internet.

What was the database with all the movie information? She tried a few acronyms and came up with IMDb in short order. She entered *Kill Game 2* and clicked on "Full Cast and Crew." She scrolled down and there, near the bottom, playing "Young Cop," was his name. Terrence Cahill.

Before closing the page she scrolled through the rest of the credits. Next to "Technical Adviser" was his name again.

Incredible.

Terry Cahill was in the movies.

AT SEVEN O'CLOCK, Jessica dropped Sophie off at Paula's, then hit the shower. She dried her hair, put on lipstick and perfume, slipped into a pair of black leather pants and a red silk blouse. A pair of sterling-silver drop earrings completed the look. She had to admit, she didn't look too bad. A little slutty perhaps. But after all, that was the point, wasn't it?

She locked the house, walked over to the Jeep. She had parked in the driveway. Before she could slip behind the wheel, a carload of teenaged boys drove by the house. They honked the horn and whistled.

I've still got it, she thought with a smile. At least in Northeast Philly. Besides, while she was on IMDb, she had looked up *East Side, West Side.* Ava Gardner was only twenty-seven in that movie.

Twenty-*seven.*

She got into the Jeep and headed into the city.

DETECTIVE NICOLETTE MALONE was petite, tanned, and toned. Her hair was an almost silver blond, and she wore it in a ponytail. She wore tight, faded Levi's, a white T-shirt, and a black leather jacket. On loan from Narcotics, around Jessica's age, she had followed a path to a gold badge that was strikingly similar to Jessica's: She came from a cop family, had spent four years in uniform, three years as a divisional detective.

Although they had never met, they were aware of each other by reputation. More so on Jessica's part. For a brief period, earlier in the year, Jessica had been convinced that Nicci Malone was having an affair with Vincent. She wasn't. It was Jessica's hope that Nicci had heard nothing about her schoolgirl suspicions.

They met in Ike Buchanan's office. ADA Paul DiCarlo was present.

"Jessica Balzano, Nicci Malone," Buchanan said.

"How ya doin'?" Nicci said, extending a hand. Jessica took it.

"Nice to meet you," Jessica said. "I've heard a lot about you."

"I never touched him. I swear to God." Nicci winked, smiled. "Just kidding."

Shit, Jessica thought. Nicci knew all about it.

Ike Buchanan looked appropriately confused. He went on. "Inferno Films is essentially a one-man outfit. The owner is a guy named Dante Diamond."

"What's the play?" Nicci asked.

"You are casting a new hard-core movie and you want this Bruno Steele to be in it."

"How are we going in?" Nicci asked.

"Lightweight body microphones, wireless, remote taping capability."

"Armed?"

"That will be your choice," DiCarlo said. "But there's a good chance you will be searched or go through metal detectors at some point."

When Nicci met Jessica's eyes, they silently agreed. They would go in unarmed.

AFTER JESSICA and Nicci were briefed by a pair of veterans from the vice squad—including names to float, terms to use, along with a variety of tells—Jessica waited in the duty room of the Homicide Unit. Before long Terry Cahill entered. When she was sure that he had noticed her, she struck a tough-guy pose, hands on hips.

"We've got officers at all the exits," Jessica said, mimicking the line from *Kill Game 2.*

Cahill looked at her for moment, questioningly; then it registered. "Uh-oh," he said. He was dressed casually. He was not going to be on this detail.

"How come you didn't tell me that you've been in the movies?" Jessica asked.

"Well, there've only been two, and I like to keep my two lives separate. For one thing, the FBI isn't crazy about it."

"How did you get started?"

"It started when the producers of *Kill Game 2* called the bureau asking for some technical assistance. Somehow the ASAC knew I was a movie nut and recommended me for the job. As much as the bureau is secretive about its agents, it's also desperate to have itself portrayed in an accurate light."

The PPD wasn't much different, Jessica thought. A number of television shows had been produced that focused on the department. It was rare when they got things right. "What was it like working with Will Parrish?"

"He's a great guy," Cahill said. "Very generous and down to earth."

"Are you in the movie he's making now?"

Cahill looked around, lowered his voice. "Just a walk-on. But don't tell anyone around here. Everybody wants to be in showbiz, right?"

Jessica zipped her lips.

"In fact, we're shooting my little part tonight," Cahill said.

"And for that you're giving up the glamour of a stakeout?"

Cahill smiled. "It's dirty work." He stood, glanced at his watch. "Have you ever done any acting?"

Jessica almost laughed. Her one brush with the legitimate stage had come when she was in second grade at St. Paul's. She had been a co-star in a lavish production of the nativity scene. She played a sheep. "Uh, not that you'd notice."

"It's a lot harder than it looks."

"What do you mean?"

"You know those lines I had in *Kill Game 2*?" Cahill asked.

"What about them?"

"I think we did thirty takes."

"How come?"

"You have any idea how hard it is to say 'these scumbags are ours' with a straight face?"

Jessica tried it. He was right.

AT NINE O'CLOCK, Nicci walked into the Homicide Unit, turning the head of every male detective on duty. She had changed into a sweet little black cocktail dress.

One at a time she and Jessica went into one of the interview rooms, where they were fitted with wireless body microphones.

EUGENE KILBANE PACED nervously around the parking lot of the Roundhouse. He wore a powder-blue suit and white patent-leather loafers, the kind with the silver chain across the upper. He lit each cigarette with the previous one.

"I'm not sure I can do this," Kilbane said.

"You can do this," Jessica said.

"You don't understand. These people can be dangerous."

Jessica glared at Kilbane. "Um, that's pretty much the *point,* Eugene."

Kilbane looked from Jessica to Nicci to Nick Palladino to Eric Chavez. Sweat gathered on his upper lip. He wasn't getting out of this.

"Shit," he said. "Let's just go."

KEVIN BYRNE UNDERSTOOD THE RUSH OF CRIME. HE KNEW WELL the adrenaline surge of larcenous or violent or antisocial behavior. He had arrested many a suspect still in the flush of the moment and knew that, in the grip of that rarefied feeling, criminals seldom considered what they had done, its consequence to the victim, its consequence to themselves. There was, instead, a bitter glow of accomplishment, a feeling that society had prohibited this behavior and they had done it anyway.

As Byrne prepared to leave his apartment—the ember of this feeling igniting inside him, against his better instincts—he had no idea how this evening would conclude, whether he would end up with Victoria safe in his arms, or with Julian Matisse at the end of his pistol sight.

Or, he was afraid to admit, neither.

Byrne pulled a pair of workman's overalls from his closet, a grimy jumpsuit belonging to the Philadelphia Water Department. His uncle Frank had recently retired from the PWD, and Byrne had gotten the overalls from him once when he needed to go undercover a few years earlier. Nobody looks at the guy working on the street. City workers, like street vendors, panhandlers, and the elderly, are part of the urban curtain. Human scenery. Tonight Byrne needed to be invisible.

He looked at the figurine of Snow White on his dresser. He had handled it carefully when he removed it from the hood of his car, placing it in an evidence bag as soon as he slipped back behind the wheel. He didn't know if it ever would be needed as evidence, or if Julian Matisse's fingerprints would be on it.

Nor did he know which side of the legal process he would come down on by the time this long night was over. He put the jumpsuit on, grabbed his toolbox, and left.

HIS CAR WAS bathed in darkness.

A group of teenagers—all about seventeen or eighteen, four boys and two girls—stood half a block away, watching the world go by, waiting for their shot at it. They smoked, shared a blunt, sipped from a pair of brown-paper-clad forties, snapped the dozens on each other, or whatever they called it these days. The boys competed for the girls' favors; the girls primped and preened, above it all, missing nothing. It was every urban summertime corner. Always had been.

Why was Phil Kessler doing this to Jimmy? Byrne wondered. He had stopped at Darlene Purify's house that afternoon. Jimmy's widow was a woman not yet beyond the reach of the tendrils of grief. She and Jimmy had divorced more than a year before Jimmy's death, but she had not stopped caring. They had shared a life. They shared the lives of three children.

Byrne tried to remember what Jimmy's face looked like when he was telling one of his stupid jokes, or when he got really serious at four in the morning, back in his drinking days, or when he was interrogating some asshole, or that time when he dried the tears of a little Chinese kid on the playground who had run right out of his shoes getting chased by some bigger kid. Jimmy took that kid over to Payless that day and hooked him up with a new pair of sneaks, out of his own pocket.

Byrne couldn't remember.

But how could this be?

He remembered every punk he had ever arrested. Every single one.

He remembered the day his father bought him a slice of watermelon from a vendor on Ninth Street. He was about seven years old; the day was hot and humid; the watermelon was ice cold. His old man had on a red-striped shirt and white shorts. His old man told a joke to the vendor—a dirty joke, because he whispered it out of Kevin's earshot. The vendor laughed high and loud. He had gold teeth.

He remembered every fold in the bottom of his daughter's tiny feet on the day she was born.

He remembered Donna's face when he had asked her to marry him, the way she cocked her head at that slight angle, as if skewing the world might give her some sort of insight into his true intentions.

But Kevin Byrne couldn't remember Jimmy Purify's face, the face of a man he had loved, a man who had taught him just about everything he knew about the city, the job.

God help him, he couldn't remember.

He looked up and down the avenue, scanning his three car mirrors. The teenagers had moved on. It was time. He got out, grabbed the toolbox and a clipboard. He felt as if he were swimming in the overalls, due to the weight he had lost. He pulled the ball cap down as low as he could.

If Jimmy were with him, this would be the moment he would flip up his collar, shoot his cuffs, and declare that it was *showtime y'all*.

Byrne crossed the avenue and stepped into the darkness of the alley.

THE MORPHINE WAS A WHITE SNOWBIRD BENEATH HIM. To-
gether they soared. They visited his grandmother's row house on Parrish
Street. His father's Buick LeSabre rattled gray-blue exhaust at the curb.

Time toggled on, off. The pain reached for him again. For a moment
he was a young man. He could bob, weave, counter. The cancer was a big
middleweight, though. Fast. A hook to his stomach flared—red and blaz-
ingly hot. He pressed the button. Soon the cool white hand gently ca-
ressed his forehead . . .

He sensed a presence in the room. He looked up. A figure stood at
the foot of the bed. Without his glasses—and even they did not help
much anymore—he could not recognize the man. He had for a long time
imagined what might be the first thing to go, but he had not counted on
it being memory. In his job, in his life, memory had been everything.
Memory was the thing that haunted you. Memory was the thing that
saved you. His long-term memory seemed intact. His mother's voice.
The way his father smelled of tobacco and 3-IN-ONE Oil. These were his
senses and now his senses were betraying him.

What had he done?

What was her name?

He couldn't remember. He couldn't remember much of anything now.

The figure drew closer. The white lab coat glowed in a celestial light. Had he passed? No. He felt his limbs, heavy and thick. The pain stabbed at his lower abdomen. The pain meant he was still alive. He pressed the pain button, closed his eyes. The girl's eyes stared at him out of the darkness.

"How are you, Doctor?" he finally managed.

"I'm fine," the man replied. "Are you in much pain?"

Are you in much pain?

The voice was familiar. A voice from his past.

The man was no doctor.

He heard a snap, then a hiss. The hiss became a roar in his ears, a terrifying sound. And there was good reason. It was the sound of his own death.

But soon the sound seemed to come from a place in North Philadelphia, a vile and ugly place that had haunted his dreams for more than three years, a terrible place where a young girl had died, a young girl he knew he would soon meet again.

And that thought, more than the thought of his own death, scared Detective Phillip Kessler to the bottom of his soul.

THE TRESONNE SUPPER CLUB WAS A DARK, SMOKY RESTAURANT on Sansom Street in Center City. It was formerly the Coach House, and in its day—somewhere in the early 1970s—it was considered a destination, one of the tonier steak houses in town, frequented by members of the Sixers and Eagles, along with politicos of varying degree of stature. Jessica recalled when she, her brother, and their father had come here for dinner when she was seven or eight years old. It had seemed like the most elegant place in the world.

Now it had become a third-tier eatery, its clientele an amalgam of shadowy figures from the worlds of adult entertainment and the fringe publishing industry. The deep burgundy drapes, at one time heralding a New York City chophouse ambience, were now mildewed and grimed with a decade of nicotine and grease.

Dante Diamond was a Tresonne regular, usually holding court at the large, semicircular booth at the back of the restaurant. They had run his rap sheet and learned that, of his three trips to the Roundhouse in the past twenty years, he had been charged with nothing more than two counts of pandering and a misdemeanor drug possession.

His most recent photograph was ten years old, but Eugene Kilbane was certain he would know him on sight. Besides, in a club like Tresonne, Dante Diamond was royalty.

The restaurant was half full. There was a long bar to the right, booths to the left, a dozen or so tables in the center. The bar was separated from the dining room by a partition made of colored plastic panels and plastic ivy. Jessica noticed that the ivy had a thin layer of dust on it.

As they made their way toward the end of the bar, all heads turned toward Nicci and Jessica. The men scoped Kilbane, sizing him immediately, cataloging his position on the food chain of power and masculine impact. It was immediately clear that in this place, he was perceived as neither a rival nor a threat. His weak chin, destroyed upper lip, and cheap suit pigeonholed him as a loser. It was the two pretty young women with him who gave him, at least temporarily, the cachet he needed to work the room.

There were two stools open at the end of the bar. Nicci and Jessica sat down. Kilbane stood. Within a few moments, the bartender approached.

"Good evening," the bartender said.

"Yeah. How ya doin'?" Kilbane replied.

"Quite well, sir."

Kilbane leaned forward. "Dante around?"

The bartender gave him a stony look. "Who?"

"Mr. Diamond."

The bartender half-smiled, as if to say: *Better.* He was in his late fifties, trim and savvy, manicured nails. He wore a royal blue satin vest and crisp white shirt. He had the look of many years behind the mahogany. He placed a trio of napkins on the bar. "Mr. Diamond isn't in tonight."

"Do you expect him?"

"Impossible to say," the bartender said. "I'm not his social secretary." The man locked eyes with Kilbane, communicating that this line of questioning was over. "What can I get for you and the young ladies?"

They ordered. A coffee for Jessica, a Diet Coke for Nicci, and a double bourbon for Kilbane. If Kilbane thought he was going to drink all night on the city's dime, he was mistaken. The drinks arrived. Kilbane turned to face the dining room. "This place has really hit the fucking skids," he said.

Jessica wondered by what criteria a lowlife like Eugene Kilbane judged something like that.

"I see a few people I know. I'm gonna ask around," Kilbane added. He drained his bourbon in one gulp, straightened his tie, and walked into the dining room.

Jessica looked around the room. There were a few middle-aged couples in the dining room whom she had a hard time believing had anything to do with the business. The Tresonne did, after all, advertise in *City Paper, Metro, The Report,* and other venues. But for the most part, the clientele was hard-looking men in their fifties and sixties—pinkie rings, collar bars, monogrammed cuffs. It looked like a waste-management convention.

Jessica glanced to her left. One of the men at the bar had been ogling her and Nicci since they sat down. Out of the corner of her eye, she saw him smooth his hair and spritz his breath. He ambled over.

"Hi," he said to Jessica, smiling.

Jessica turned to look at the man, giving him the obligatory twice-over. He was about sixty. Sea-foam rayon shirt, beige polyester sport coat, tinted steel-rimmed aviator glasses. "Hi," she said.

"I understand you and your friend are actresses."

"Where did you hear that?" Jessica asked.

"You have that look."

"What look is that?" Nicci asked, smiling.

"Theatrical," he said. "And very beautiful."

"It just so happens we are." Nicci laughed, tossed her hair. "Why do you ask?"

"I'm a film producer." Seemingly out of nowhere, he produced a pair of business cards. Werner Schmidt. Lux Productions. New Haven, Connecticut. "I'm casting a new full-length feature. High-def digital. Woman on woman."

"Sounds interesting," Nicci said.

"Hell of a script. The writer went to USC film school for a semester." Nicci nodded, feigning deep attention.

"But before I say anything else, I have to ask you something," Werner added.

"What?" Jessica asked.

"Are you police officers?"

Jessica flicked a glance at Nicci. She looked back. "Yes," she said. "Both of us. We're detectives on an undercover sting."

Werner looked slapped for a second, like he'd had the wind knocked out of him. Then he burst into laughter. Jessica and Nicci laughed with him. "That was good," he said. "That was really fucking good. I like that."

Nicci couldn't leave it alone. She was a pistol. Full mag. "We've met before, right?" she asked.

Werner looked even more encouraged now. He pulled in his stomach, stood a little straighter. "I was thinking the same thing."

"You ever work with Dante?"

"Dante Diamond?" he asked with hushed reverence, as if uttering the name *Hitchcock* or *Fellini*. "Not yet, but Dante is a class act. Great organization." He turned and pointed to a woman sitting at the end of the bar. "Paulette has made a number of films with him. Do you know Paulette?"

It sounded like a test. Nicci played it cool. "Never had the pleasure," she said. "Please invite her over for a drink."

Werner was off like a shot. The prospect of standing around the bar with three women was a dream come true. In a moment he was back with Paulette, a bottle brunette around forty. Kitten heels, leopard dress. Thirty-eight DD.

"Paulette St. John, this is . . ."

"Gina and Daniela," Jessica said.

"Pleased, I'm sure," Paulette said. Jersey City. Maybe Hoboken.

"What are you drinking?" Jessica asked.

"Cosmo."

Jessica ordered for her.

"We're trying to locate a guy named Bruno Steele," Nicci said.

Paulette smiled. "I know Bruno. Big dick, can't spell *ignorant*."

"That's him."

"Haven't seen him in years," she said. Her drink arrived. She sipped it delicately, like a lady. "Why are you looking for Bruno?"

"A friend is casting a film," Jessica said.

"There are lots of guys around. Younger guys. Why him?"

Jessica noticed that Paulette was weaving a bit, slurring her words. Still, she had to be careful with her response. One wrong word and they could be shut out. "Well, for one thing, he's got the right look. Plus, the film is hard S and M, and Bruno knows when to pull back."

Paulette nodded. Been there, felt that.

"Loved his work in *Philadelphia Skin*," Nicci said.

At the mention of the movie, Werner and Paulette looked at each other. Werner opened his mouth, as if to stop a Paulette from saying anything further, but Paulette continued. "I remember that crew," she said. "Of course, after the *incident,* nobody really wanted to work together again."

"What do you mean?" Jessica asked.

Paulette looked at her as if she were crazy. "You don't know about what happened on that shoot?"

Jessica flashed on the scene in *Philadelphia Skin* where the girl opened the door. *Those sad, haunted eyes.* She took a chance, asked. "Oh, you mean with that little blonde?"

Paulette nodded, sipped her drink. "Yeah. That was fucked *up.*"

Jessica was just about to press her when Kilbane returned from the men's room, pink with purpose. He got in between them, leaned into the bar. He turned to Werner and Paulette. "Could you excuse us for a sec?"

Paulette nodded. Werner held up both hands. He wasn't going to take anyone's play. They both retreated to the end of the bar. Kilbane turned back to Nicci and Jessica.

"I've got something," he said.

When someone like Eugene Kilbane comes rushing out of a men's room with a statement like that, the possibilities are endless, and all unsavory. Instead of speculating, Jessica asked: "What?"

He leaned closer. It was clear he had just splashed on more cologne. A *lot* more cologne. Jessica nearly gagged. Kilbane whispered: "The crew that made *Philadelphia Skin* is still in town."

"And?"

Kilbane raised his glass, rattled the cubes. The bartender poured him a double. If the city was paying, he was drinking. Or so he thought. Jessica would cut him off after this one.

"They're shooting a new movie tonight," he finally said. "Dante Diamond is directing it." He gulped his drink, put the glass down. "And we're invited."

AT JUST AFTER TEN O'CLOCK, THE MAN FOR WHOM BYRNE WAS waiting rounded the corner, a thick ring of keys in his hand.

"Hey, how ya doin'?" Byrne asked, cap brim pulled low, eyes hidden.

The man found him in the dim light, a little startled. He saw the PDW jumpsuit and relaxed. A little. "What's up, chief?"

"Same crap, different diaper."

The man snorted. "Tell me about it."

"You guys got any problems with the water pressure up there?" Byrne asked.

The man glanced at the bar, then back. "Not that I know of."

"Well, we got the call and they sent me," Byrne said. He glanced at the clipboard. "Yeah, this is the right place. Mind if I take a look at the pipes?"

The man shrugged, glanced down the steps to the access door that led to the cellar underneath the building. "Ain't my pipes, ain't my problem. Help yourself, bro."

The man walked down the rusting iron steps, unlocked the door. Byrne glanced up and down the alley, then followed.

The man flipped on the light—a bare 150-watt bulb in a metal mesh cage. In addition to the dozens of stacked upholstered bar stools, disassembled tables, and stage props were maybe a hundred cases of liquor.

"Holy *crap*," Byrne said. "I could stay down here for a while."

"Between you and me, this is all shit. The good stuff is locked in my boss's office upstairs."

The man pulled a pair of boxes off a stack, set them down by the door. He consulted a computer readout in his hand. He began to count some of the boxes that were left. He made a few notes.

Byrne put the toolbox down, quietly shut the door behind him. He assessed the man in front of him. The man was a little bit younger, without question faster. But Byrne had something he didn't. The element of surprise.

Byrne flicked the baton out, stepped from the shadow. The *snick* of the baton reaching its full length caught the man's attention. He turned to Byrne, a questioning look on his face. It was too late. Byrne swung the twenty-one-inch tactical steel rod as hard as he could. It caught the man perfectly, just below the right knee. Byrne heard the cartilage rip. The man barked once, then crumbled to the floor.

"What the . . . *Jesus!*"

"Shut up."

"Fuck . . . you." The man began to rock, holding his knee. "Mother-*fucker.*"

Byrne pulled the SIG. He dropped onto Darryl Porter with all his weight. Both knees on the man's chest, two-hundred-plus pounds. The blow knocked the air out of Porter. Byrne pulled off his ball cap. Recognition alit on Porter's face.

"*You,*" Porter said between gasps. "I fuckin' . . . *knew* I knew you from somewhere."

Byrne held up the SIG. "I've got eight rounds in here. Nice even number, am I right?"

Darryl Porter just glared.

"Now, I want you to think about how many things you have on your body that comes in pairs, Darryl. I'm going to start with your ankles, and every time you fail to answer my question, another pair is mine. And you *know* where I'm heading with this."

Porter gasped for air. Byrne's weight on his chest didn't help.

"Here we go, Darryl. These are the most important moments of your rotten, pointless life. No second chances. No makeup exams. Ready?"

Silence.

"Question one: Did you tell Julian Matisse I was looking for him?"

Cold defiance. This guy was way too tough for his own good. Byrne put the barrel against the Porter's right ankle. Upstairs, the music pounded.

Porter squirmed, but the weight on his chest was too much. He couldn't move. "You're not gonna fucking *shoot* me," Porter yelled. "You know why? You know how I know that? I'm gonna *tell* you how I know that, motherfucker." His voice was high and crazy. "You're not gonna shoot me because—"

Byrne shot him. The blast was deafening in this small confined space. Byrne hoped the music covered it. Either way, he knew he had to wrap this up fast. The bullet had only grazed Porter's ankle, but Porter was way too jazzed to know that. He was sure Byrne had blown his foot off. He screamed again. Byrne put the barrel of the weapon against Porter's temple.

"Know what? I've changed my mind, shitbag. I *am* going to kill you after all."

"Wait!"

"I'm listening.

"I tuh-told him."

"Where is he?"

Porter gave him an address.

"He's there now?" Byrne asked.

"Yeah."

"Give me a reason not to kill you."

"I . . . didn't *do* anything."

"What, you mean *today*? You think that matters to someone like me? You're a pedophile, Darryl. A white slaver. A pimp and a pornographer. I think the city can survive without you."

"Don't!"

"Who's going to miss you, Darryl?"

Byrne pulled the trigger. Porter screamed, then fainted. The chamber was empty. Byrne had emptied the rest of the magazine before coming down into the cellar. He didn't trust himself.

As Byrne mounted the steps, the mixture of smells nearly made him dry-heave. The reek of just-burned gunpowder mixed with that of mold and wood rot and the sugar of cheap booze. Beneath that, the smell of fresh urine. Darryl Porter had pissed in his pants.

IT WAS FIVE minutes after Kevin Byrne left that Darryl Porter was able to get to his feet. Partially because the pain was off the charts. Partially because he was certain that Byrne was waiting for him just outside the door, ready to finish what he had started. Porter really thought that the man had taken his foot off. He steadied himself for a moment or two, hobbled to the exit, and meekly poked out his head. He looked both ways. The alley was empty.

"Hey!" he yelled.

Nothing.

"Yeah," he said. "You *better* run, bitch."

He jerked his way up the stairs, one tread at a time. The pain was mind-scrambling. He finally reached the top step thinking that he *knew* people. Oh, he knew *lots* of people. People that made him look like a goddamn Boy Scout. Because, cop or no cop, this fucker was going *down*. You don't pull this shit on Darryl Lee Porter and get away with it. Hell no. Who *said* you can't kill a detective?

As soon as he got upstairs he would drop a dime. He glanced out onto the street. A police sector car sat on the corner, probably having responded to some bar disturbance. He didn't see an officer. Never around when you need them.

For a fleeting moment Darryl thought about going to the hospital, but how was he going to pay for it? There wasn't exactly a benefits package working at the X Bar. No, he'd patch himself up the best he could, check it in the morning.

He dragged himself behind the building then up the wobbly wrought-iron stairs, stopping twice to catch his breath. Most of the time, living in two cramped, shitty rooms above the X Bar was a pain in the ass. The smell, the noise, the clientele. Now it was a blessing, because it took all his strength just to make it to his front door. He unlocked the door, stepped inside, made his way to the bathroom, flipped on the fluorescent light. He poked around his medicine chest. Flexeril. Klonopin. Ibuprofen. He took two of each, then started to fill the tub. The pipes rattled and clanked, spewing forth a gallon or so of rusty, briny-smelling water into the scum-ringed tub. When it ran as clear as it was going to run, he put the stopper in, turned the hot water on full blast. He sat on the edge of the tub, checked his foot. The blood had stopped flowing. Barely. His foot was starting to turn blue. Hell, it was turning *black*. He touched the area with a forefinger. The pain shot to his brain in a fiery comet.

"You are *so* fuckin' dead." He'd make the call as soon as he'd soaked his foot.

A few minutes later, after having eased his foot into the hot water, after the various drugs had started their magic, he thought he heard someone outside his door. Or did he? He turned the water off for a moment, listened, cocking his head toward the back of the apartment. Had that fucker followed him up? He glanced around the immediate area for a weapon. A crusty Bic disposable razor and a stack of porno mags.

Great. The closest knife was in the kitchen and that was ten agonizing steps away.

The music from the bar downstairs rumbled and thundered again. Had he locked the door? He thought so. Although, in the past, he had left it open a few drunken nights only to have a few of the fucking head cases who frequented the X Bar come waltzing in, looking for a place to rut. Fucking lowlifes. He had to get a new job. At least in the strip clubs, the spill wasn't bad. The only thing he could hope to pick up at closing time at the X was a dose of herpes or a pair of Ben Wa balls up the ass.

He turned off the water, which was already running cold. He eased himself to his feet, slowly extricated his foot from the tub, spun around, and was more than a little shocked to see another man standing in his bathroom. A man who seemed to have no footsteps.

This man had a question for him, too.

When he answered, the man said something Darryl did not understand. It sounded like a foreign language. It sounded like it might be French.

Then, in a motion almost too fast to detect, the man grabbed him by the neck. His hands were terribly strong. In a blur the man pushed his head beneath the surface of the filthy water. One of Darryl Porter's last sights was the corona of a tiny red light, burning in the dim radiance of his dying.

The tiny red light of a video camera.

THE WAREHOUSE WAS HUGE AND SOLID AND SPRAWLING. IT seemed to take up most of a block. It was formerly a ball-bearing manufacturing company, and after that it had served as a warehouse for some of the Mummers' floats.

A chain-link fence surrounded the enormous parking lot. The lot was cracked and strangled with weeds, scattered with debris and discarded tires. A smaller, private lot hugged the building's north side, near the main entrance. In that lot were a pair of vans and a handful of late-model cars.

Jessica, Nicci, and Eugene Kilbane drove in a rented Lincoln Town Car. Nick Palladino and Eric Chavez followed in a surveillance van on loan from Narcotics. The van was state of the art, fitted with antennae disguised as a roof rack, and a periscope camera. Both Nicci and Jessica were outfitted with wireless body units that had the ability to transmit up to three hundred feet. Palladino and Chavez parked the van on a side street, with a straight line of sight to the windows on the north side of the building.

KILBANE, JESSICA, AND Nicci stood near the front door. The tall windows on the first floor were covered, on the inside, with a black opaque material. To the right of the door were a speaker and a button. Kilbane rang the intercom. After three rings, a voice came on.

"Yeah."

The voice was deep, nicotine-ravaged, menacing. Backwater-crazy. As a friendly greeting, it meant *go the fuck away*.

"I have an appointment with Mr. Diamond," Kilbane said. Despite his best effort to sound as if he still carried some juice at this level, he sounded scared shitless. Jessica almost—almost—felt sorry for him.

From the speaker: "There's nobody here by that name."

Jessica looked up. The surveillance camera above them scanned left, then right. Jessica winked at the lens. She wasn't sure if there was enough light for the camera to see it, but it was worth a shot.

"Jackie Boris sent me," Kilbane said. It sounded like a question. Kilbane looked at Jessica and shrugged. After nearly a full minute, the buzzer buzzed. Kilbane opened the door. They all stepped inside.

Inside the main entrance, to the right, was a tired, paneled reception area, probably last remodeled in the 1970s. Along the window wall were a pair of stained cranberry velveteen couches. A pair of upholstered chairs sat opposite. Between them was a square chrome-and-smoked-glass coffee table in the Parsons style, covered with ten-year-old *Hustler* magazines.

The only thing that looked like it had been created in the past twenty or so years was the door into the main warehouse. This was steel and had both a dead bolt and an electronic lock.

In front of it sat a very large human.

He was broad-shouldered and solid, like a bouncer at the gates of hell. He had a shaved head, a creased scalp, a huge rhinestone earring. He wore a black mesh T-shirt and charcoal dress slacks. He sat in an uncomfortable-looking plastic chair, reading a copy of *Motocross Action*. He looked up, bored and put out by these new visitors to his little fiefdom. As they approached, he stood, extended a hand, palm out, stopping them.

"My name is Cedric. Know this. If you are, in any way, wrong, you will deal with me."

He let that sentiment settle in, then picked up an electronic wand, ran it over them. When he was satisfied, he punched in a code on the door, turned a key, and opened it.

Cedric led them down a long, stiflingly hot corridor. On either side were eight-foot sections of cheap paneling, obviously erected to partition off the rest of the warehouse. Jessica couldn't help but wonder what was on the other side.

At the end of the maze, they emerged into the body of the first floor. The enormous room was so large that the lights from the movie set in the corner seemed to reach into the darkness fifty or so feet, then to be swallowed by the gloom. Jessica noticed a few fifty-gallon drums in the murkiness; a forklift loomed like a prehistoric beast.

"Wait here," Cedric said.

Jessica watched Cedric and Kilbane walk toward the set. Cedric's hands were out to his sides, prevented from closer contact with his body by his huge upper arms. He had that odd, bodybuilder duck waddle.

The set was brightly lit, and from where they stood looked to be a young girl's bedroom. On the walls were posters of boy bands; on the bed, a collection of pink stuffed animals and satin pillows. At the moment, there were no actors on the set.

After a few minutes, Kilbane and another man returned.

"Ladies, this is Dante Diamond," Kilbane said.

Dante Diamond was surprisingly normal looking, considering his profession. A youthful sixty, he had formerly blond hair, now touched with silver, the de rigueur goatee, a small hoop earring. He had a UV tan and veneered teeth.

"Mr. Diamond, this is Gina Marino and Daniela Rose."

Eugene Kilbane was playing his role well, Jessica thought. She was somewhat impressed with the man. However, she was still glad she'd punched him.

"Charmed." Diamond shook their hands. Very professional and warm, soft-spoken. Like a bank manager. "You are both extraordinary-looking young ladies."

"Thank you," Nicci said.

"Where might I have seen your work?"

"We did a few films for Jerry Stein last year," Nicci said. The two vice detectives with whom Jessica and Nicci had talked before the detail had given them all the names they would need. Or so Jessica hoped.

"Jerry is an old friend," Diamond said. "Does he still drive that gold 911?"

Another test, Jessica thought. Nicci looked over at her, shrugged. Jessica shrugged back. "Never went on a picnic with the man," Nicci replied, smiling. When Nicci Malone smiled at a man, it was game, set, and match.

Diamond returned the smile, a twinkle in his eye, bested. "Of course," he said. He gestured toward the set. "We're getting ready to shoot. Please join us on the set. There's a full bar and buffet. Make yourselves at home."

Diamond walked back over to the set, chatting softly with a young woman smartly dressed in a white linen pantsuit. She made notes on a clipboard.

If Jessica didn't know what these people were doing, she would have a hard time differentiating between a porno movie shoot and wedding planners setting up for a reception.

Then, in a nauseating instant, she was reminded where she was when a man walked out of the darkness, and onto the set. He was big, and wore a sleeveless rubber vest and a leather master mask.

In his hand was a switchblade.

BYRNE PARKED A BLOCK AWAY FROM THE ADDRESS DARRYL Porter had given him. It was a busy street in North Philly. Almost every house on the street was occupied and had the lights on. The house that Porter had directed him to was dark, but it was attached to a hoagie shop that was doing a brisk business. Half a dozen teenagers lounged on cars out front, eating their sandwiches. Byrne was sure he would be seen. He waited as long as he could, got out of the car, slipped behind the house, picked the lock. He stepped inside, drew the SIG.

Inside, the air was dense and hot, clogged with the smell of rotting fruit. Flies buzzed. He stepped into the small kitchen. Stove and fridge to the right, sink to the left. A kettle sat on one of the burners. Byrne felt it. Cold. He reached behind the fridge, unplugged it. He didn't want the light carrying into the living room. He eased open the door. Empty, save for a pair of moldering pieces of bread and a box of baking soda.

He cocked his head, listened. The jukebox was playing in the hoagie shop next door. The house was silent.

He thought about his years on the force, about how many times he had entered a row house, never knowing what to expect. Domestic disturbances, breaking and entering, home invasions. Most row houses had a similar layout, and if you knew where to look, you would rarely be surprised. Byrne knew where to look. As he moved throughout the house, he checked the likely niches. No Matisse. No signs of life. He walked up the stairs, weapon out front. He searched the two small bedrooms and closets on the second floor. He descended the two flights to the basement. An abandoned washer, a long-rusted brass bed frame. Mice scurried in the beam of his Maglite.

Empty.

Back to the first floor.

Darryl Porter had lied to him. There was no food trash, no mattress, no human sounds or smells. If Matisse had ever been here, he was gone now. The house was vacant. Byrne holstered the SIG.

Had he really cleared the basement? He'd look again. He turned to descend the steps. And that's when he felt the shift in the atmosphere, the unmistakable presence of another human being. He felt the tip of the blade at the small of his back, felt a slight trickle of blood, and heard the familiar voice say:

"We meet again, Detective Byrne."

MATISSE PULLED THE SIG from the holster on Byrne's hip. He held it up in the streetlight streaming through the window. "Sweet," he said. Byrne had reloaded the weapon after leaving Darryl Porter. It had a full magazine. "Doesn't look like department issue, Detective. Naughty, naughty." Matisse put the knife on the floor, keeping the SIG at the small of Byrne's back. He continued to pat him down.

"I kind of expected you a little earlier," Matisse said. "Darryl doesn't really strike me as the sort to stand up to too much punishment." Matisse frisked Byrne's left side. He took a small roll of bills out his pant pocket. "Did you have to hurt him, Detective?"

Byrne remained silent. Matisse checked his left jacket pocket.

"And what have we here?"

Julian Matisse removed the small metal box from Byrne's left coat pocket, keeping the weapon to Byrne's spine. In the dark, Matisse did not see the thin wire running up Byrne's sleeve, around the back of his jacket, then down the right sleeve to the button in his hand.

When Matisse stepped to the side to get a better look at the object in his hand, Byrne pressed the button, sending sixty thousand volts of electricity into Julian Matisse's body. The Taser, one of two he had purchased from Sammy DuPuis, was a state-of-the-art device, fully charged. As the Taser sparked and bucked, Matisse shrieked, reflexively discharging the handgun. The slug missed Byrne's back by only a few inches, slamming into the dry wood floor. Byrne pivoted, threw a hook toward Matisse's midsection. But Matisse was already on the floor, the effects of the Taser making his body spasm and jerk. His face was locked in a silent scream. The smell of singed flesh drifted up.

When Matisse settled down, docile and spent, his eyes blinking rapidly, the reek of fear and defeat coming off him in waves, Byrne knelt next to him, removed the weapon from his limp hand, got very close to his ear, and said:

"Yes, Julian. We meet again."

MATISSE SAT IN the chair in the center of the basement. There had been no response to the sound of the gunshot, no one banging on the door. This was, after all, North Philly. Matisse's hands were duct-taped behind him; his feet, to the legs of the wooden chair. When he came around, he didn't struggle against the tape, didn't flail about. Perhaps he did not have the strength. He calmly assessed Byrne with his predator's eyes.

Byrne looked at the man. In the two years since he had seen him last, Julian Matisse had put on some prison bulk, but there was something about him that seemed diminished. His hair was a little longer. His skin was pitted and greasy, his cheeks sunken. Byrne wondered if he had the first stages of the virus.

Byrne had stuffed the second Taser unit down the front of Matisse's jeans.

When Matisse regained some of his strength, he said: "Looks like your partner—or should I say, your dead *ex*-partner—was dirty, Detective. Imagine that. A dirty Philly cop."

"Where is she?" Byrne asked.

Matisse twisted his face into a parody of innocence. "Where is *who*?"

"Where is she?"

Matisse just glared at him. Byrne placed the nylon gym bag on the floor. The bulk and shape and heft of the bag was not lost on Matisse. Byrne then removed his belt, slowly wrapped it around his knuckles.

"Where is she?" he repeated.

Nothing.

Byrne stepped forward and punched Matisse in the face. Hard. After a moment, Matisse laughed, then spit the blood out of his mouth, along with a pair of teeth.

"Where is she?" Byrne asked.

"I don't know what the fuck you're talking about."

Byrne feinted another punch. Matisse flinched.

Tough guy.

Byrne crossed the room, unwrapped his hand, unzipped the gym bag, then began to lay the contents on the floor, in the wedge of street-light drawn by the window. Matisse's eyes widened for a second, then narrowed. He was going to play hard. Byrne wasn't surprised.

"You think you can hurt me?" Matisse asked. He spit some more blood. "I've been through things that would make you cry like a fucking baby."

"I'm not here to hurt you, Julian. I just want some information. The power is in your hands."

Matisse snorted at this. But deep down he knew what Byrne meant. This is the nature of the sadist. Put the onus of the pain on the subject.

"Now," Byrne said. "Where is she?"

Silence.

Byrne planted his feet again, threw a hard hook. This time to the body. The blow caught Matisse right behind his left kidney. Byrne stepped away. Matisse vomited.

When Matisse caught his breath, he managed: "Thin line between justice and hatred, isn't there?" He spit on the floor again. A putrescent stench filled the room.

"I want you to think about your life, Julian," Byrne said, ignoring him. He stepped around the puddle, got close. "I want you to think about all the things you've done, the decisions you've made, the steps you've taken to lead you to this moment. Your lawyer isn't here to protect you. There's no judge to make me stop." Byrne got to within a few inches of Matisse's face. The smell was stomach churning. He took the switch of the Taser in hand. "I'm going to ask you again. If you don't answer me, we ratchet all this up a notch, and we never return to the good old days of right now. Understand?"

Matisse did not say a word.

"Where is she?"

Nothing.

Byrne pressed the button, sending sixty thousand volts into Julian Matisse's testicles. Matisse screamed, loud and long. He upended the chair, falling backward, cracking his head on the floor. But that pain paled in comparison with the fire raging through his lower body. Byrne knelt down next to him, covered the man's mouth, and in that instant the images smashed together behind his eyes—

—*Victoria crying . . . pleading for her life . . . struggling against nylon ropes . . . the knife slicing her skin . . . the glossy blood in the moonlight . . . her screams a long shrill siren in the blackness . . . screams that join a dark chorus of pain . . .*

—as he grabbed Matisse's hair. He yanked the chair upright and brought his face close once more. Matisse's face was now spiderwebbed with blood and bile and vomit. "Listen to me. You are going to tell me where she is. If she's dead, if she's suffering in any way whatsoever, I'll be back. You think you understand pain but you do not. I will teach you."

"Fuck . . . you," Matisse whispered. His head lolled to the side. He faded in and out of consciousness. Byrne took an ammonia cap out of his pocket, cracked it under the man's nose. He came to. Byrne gave him a moment to reorient himself.

"Where is she?" Byrne asked.

Matisse looked up, tried to focus. He smiled through the blood in his mouth. His top two front teeth were missing. The rest were slicked pink. "I did her. Just like Snow White. You'll never find her."

Byrne cracked another ammonia cap. He needed Matisse lucid. He put it beneath the man's nose. Matisse jerked his head backward. From a cup he had brought with him, Byrne took a handful of ice, held it against Matisse's eyes.

Byrne then took out his cell phone, opened it. He navigated through the menu until he got to the pictures folder. He opened the most recent picture he had taken, one he had snapped that morning. He turned the LCD screen toward Matisse.

Matisse's eyes widened in horror. He began to shake.

"No . . ."

Of all the things Matisse had expected to see, a photograph of Edwina Matisse standing in front of the Aldi supermarket on Market Street, where she always shopped, was not one of them. Seeing a picture of his mother, in this context, clearly chilled him to the bottom of his being.

"You can't . . . ," Matisse said.

"If Victoria is dead, I'm going to stop by and pick up your mother on the way back, Julian."

"No . . ."

"*Oh* yes. And I will bring her to you in a fucking jar. So help me God."

Byrne closed his phone. Matisse's eyes began to fill with tears. Soon his body was racked with sobs. Byrne had seen it all before. He thought of Gracie Devlin's sweet smile. He felt no sympathy for this man.

"Still think you know me?" Byrne asked.

Byrne dropped a piece of paper into Matisse's lap. It was the grocery list he had taken from the floor of the backseat of Edwina Matisse's car. Seeing his mother's delicate handwriting broke Matisse's will.

"Where is Victoria?"

Matisse struggled against the duct tape. When he'd exhausted himself he fell limp and spent. "No more."

"Answer me," Byrne said.

"She's . . . she's in Fairmount Park."

"Where?" Byrne asked. Fairmount Park was the largest urban park in the country. It covered four thousand acres. *"Where?"*

"Belmont Plateau. By the softball field."

"Is she dead?"

Matisse didn't answer. Byrne cracked another ammonia cap, then picked up the small butane blowtorch. He positioned it an inch from Matisse's right eye. He poised his lighter.

"Is she dead?"

"I don't know!"

Byrne backed off, wrapped Matisse's mouth tightly in duct tape. He checked the man's hands and legs. Secure.

Byrne gathered his tools, put them in the bag. He exited the house. Heat shimmered the asphalt, ringing the sodium streetlamps with a carbon-blue aura. North Philly raged with a manic energy this night, and Kevin Byrne was its soul.

He slipped into his car and headed to Fairmount Park.

NICCI MALONE WAS ONE HELL OF AN ACTRESS. OF THE FEW
times Jessica had gone undercover, she had always been a little concerned
about getting made as a cop. Now, seeing Nicci work the room, Jessica
was almost envious. The woman had a certain confidence, an air that said
she knew who she was and what she was doing. She got inside the skin of
the role she was playing in a way that Jessica never could.

Jessica watched the crew adjust the lighting between takes. She didn't
know much about film production, but this entire operation looked like
a high-budget undertaking.

It was the subject matter that she found troubling. The story appeared to be about a pair of teenaged girls being dominated by a sadistic
grandfather type. At first, Jessica had thought the two young actresses
were about fifteen years old, but as she milled around the set, drawing
closer, she saw that they were probably twenty.

Jessica imagined the girl in the *Philadelphia Skin* video. That had been
set in a room not unlike this one.

What had happened to that girl?

Why did she look familiar?

Watching the filming of a three-minute scene turned Jessica's stomach. In the scene, the man in the master mask verbally humiliated the two girls. They wore filmy, soiled negligees. He tied them back-to-back on the bed, circling them like a giant vulture.

He struck them repeatedly as he interrogated them, always with an open hand. It took everything in Jessica's being to stop herself from stepping in. It was clear that the man was making contact. The girls were reacting with what sounded like real screams and looked like real tears, but when Jessica saw the girls laughing between takes, she realized that the blows were not hard enough to cause injury. Maybe they even enjoyed it. In any event, for Detective Jessica Balzano, it was hard to believe that crimes were not being committed here.

The toughest part to watch came at the scene's end. The man in the mask left one of the girls tied, spread-eagle, on the bed, while the other was on her knees before him. Looking down at her, he took out his switchblade, flicked it open. He cut her negligee off in shreds. He spat on her. He made her lick his boots. Then he put the knife to the girl's throat. Jessica and Nicci looked at each other, both ready to rush in. It was here, mercifully, that Dante Diamond had yelled: "Cut."

Fortunately, the man in the mask did not take this directive literally.

Ten minutes later, Nicci and Jessica stood by the small, makeshift buffet table. Dante Diamond may have been a lot of things, but he wasn't cheap. The table held a number of pricey tidbits: crudités, shrimp toast, scallops in bacon, mini quiche Lorraine.

Nicci grabbed some food and took a walk up to the set just as one of the older actresses approached the buffet table. She was in her forties, in great shape. Henna-red hair, elaborate eye makeup, painfully high stilettos. She was dressed like a strict schoolmaster. The woman had not been in the earlier scene.

"Hi," she said to Jessica. "My name's Bebe."

"Gina."

"Are you in the production?"

"No," Jessica said. "I'm here as Mr. Diamond's guest."

She nodded, popped a pair of shrimp into her mouth.

"Ever work with Bruno Steele?" Jessica asked.

Bebe picked a few items from the buffet table, put them onto a Styrofoam plate. "Bruno? Oh, yeah. Bruno's a doll."

"My director really would like to hire him for a film we're putting together. Hard S and M. We just can't seem to find him."

"I know where Bruno is. We were just partying with him."

"Tonight?"

"Yeah," she said. She grabbed a bottle of Aquafina. "Like, a couple of hours ago."

"No shit."

"He told us to stop back around midnight. I'm sure he wouldn't mind you coming with."

"Cool," Jessica said.

"I've got one more scene, then we'll get out of here." She adjusted her outfit, grimaced. "This corset is fucking killing me."

"Is there a ladies' room?" Jessica asked.

"I'll show you."

Jessica followed Bebe across part of the warehouse floor. They went down a service hallway to a pair of doors. The ladies' room was huge, built to accommodate a full shift of women when the building had been a manufacturing plant. A dozen stalls and sinks.

Jessica stood at the mirrors with Bebe.

"How long have you been in the business?" Bebe asked.

"About five years," Jessica said.

"Just a baby," she said. "Don't stay too long," she added, echoing Jessica's father's words about the department. Bebe put her lipstick back into her clutch. "Give me half an hour."

"Sure thing."

Bebe left the bathroom. Jessica waited a full minute, poked her head out into the hallway, walked back into the bathroom. She checked all the stalls, stepped into the last cubicle. She spoke directly into her body microphone, hoping she wasn't so deep into the brick building that the surveillance team didn't pick up a signal. She was not equipped with an earpiece or receiver of any sort. Her communication, if any, was one-way.

"I don't know if you heard all that, but we've got a lead. A woman said she was partying with our suspect and she's going to take us there in about thirty minutes. That's three-oh minutes. We may not be going out the front entrance. Heads up."

She thought about repeating what she said, but if the surveillance team didn't hear her the first time, they wouldn't hear her the second. She didn't want to take any unnecessary chances. She adjusted her clothes, stepped out of the stall, and was just about to turn and leave when she heard the click of the hammer. Then she felt the steel of the barrel against the back of her head. The shadow on the wall was huge. It was the gorilla from the front door. Cedric.

He had heard every word.

"You're not going anywhere," he said.

5 2

THERE IS A MOMENT IN EVERY FILM WHERE THE MAIN CHARAC-
ter finds himself unable to return to his former life, that part of his con-
tinuum that existed before the opening of the narrative. Generally, this
point of no return occurs at the midway point of the story, but not always.

I have passed that point.

Tonight it is 1980. Miami Beach. I close my eyes, find my center, hear
the salsa music, smell the salt air.

My costar is handcuffed over a steel rod.

"What are you doing?" he asks.

I could tell him but—as all the books on screenwriting say—it is
much more effective to show than tell. I check the camera. It is on a mini
tripod, poised on a milk crate.

Perfect.

I put on the yellow rain slicker, hook it closed.

"Do you know who I am?" he asks, his voice beginning to ascend with
fear.

"Let me guess," I say. "You're the guy who usually plays the second heavy, am I right?"

His face looks appropriately mystified. I don't expect him to get it. "What?"

"You're the guy who stands behind the villain of the piece and tries to look menacing. The guy who never gets the girl. Well, sometimes, but it's never the beautiful girl, is it? If at all, you get that hard-looking blonde, the one who drinks her bottom-shelf whiskey neat, the one who's going a bit thick around the middle. Kind of the Dorothy Malone type. And only after the villain gets his."

"You're crazy."

"You have no idea."

I step in front of him, examine his face. He tries to struggle away but I take his face in my hands.

"You really ought to take better care of your skin."

He stares at me, speechless. That won't last long.

I cross the room, take the chain saw from the case. It is heavy in my hands. All the best weaponry is. I smell the scent of oil. It is a well-maintained piece of equipment. It is going to be a shame to lose it.

I pull the cord. It starts immediately. The roar is loud, impressive. The chain saw blade rumbles and belches and smokes.

"Jesus Christ, no!" he screams.

I face him, feeling the terrible power of the moment.

"*Mira!*" I yell.

When I touch the blade to the left side of his head, his eyes seem to register the truth of the scene. There is no look quite like the look people get at this moment.

The blade descends. Great chunks of bone and brain tissue fly. The blade is very sharp and in no time at all I have cut all the way down to his neck. My raincoat and face mask are covered in blood and skull fragments and hair.

"Now the leg, eh?" I scream.

But he can no longer hear me.

The chain saw rumbles in my hands. I shake the flesh and gristle from the blade.

And go back to work.

BYRNE PARKED ON MONTGOMERY DRIVE AND BEGAN TO MAKE his way across the plateau. The city skyline winked and sparkled in the distance. Ordinarily, he would have stopped and marveled at the view from Belmont Plateau. Even as a lifelong Philadelphian, he never tired of it. But tonight his heart was laden with sadness and fear.

Byrne trained his Maglite on the ground, looking for a blood trail, footprints. He found neither.

He approached the softball field, checking for any sign of a struggle. He searched the area behind the backstop. No blood, no Victoria.

He circled the field. Twice. Victoria was not there.

Had she been found?

No. There would still be a police presence if this was a crime scene. It would be taped off, and there would be a sector car protecting the site. CSU would not process this scene in darkness. They would wait until morning.

He retraced his steps, finding nothing. He crossed the plateau again, passing through a copse of trees. He looked beneath the benches. Nothing. He was just about to call in a search team—knowing that what he had done to Matisse would mean the end of his career, his freedom, his life—when he saw her. Victoria was on the ground, behind a small clump of bushes, covered in filthy rags and newspaper. And there was a lot of blood. Byrne's heart shattered into a thousand pieces.

"My God. Tori. *No.*"

He knelt next to her. He pulled the rags away. Tears obscured his vision. He wiped them away with the back of his hand. "Ah, *Christ*. What did I do to you?"

She had been cut across the stomach. The wound was deep and gaping. She had lost a lot of blood. Byrne dry-heaved. He had seen oceans of blood in his time on the job. But this. *This . . .*

He felt for a pulse. It was faint, but it was *there*.

She was alive.

"Hang on, Tori. Please. God. Hang on."

His hands shaking, he took out his cell phone and called 911.

BYRNE STAYED WITH her until the very last second. When EMS rescue pulled up, he hid among the trees. There was nothing more he could do for her.

Except pray.

BYRNE DID HIS best to maintain calm. It was difficult. The wrath inside him, at this moment, was bright and brass and savage.

He had to calm down. Had to think.

Now was the moment when all crimes went bad, when the science went on the record, the moment when the smartest of the criminals screwed up, the moment that investigators live for.

Investigators like himself.

He thought of the items in the bag in the trunk of his car, the artifacts of dark purpose he had purchased from Sammy DuPuis. He would take all night with Julian Matisse. There were many things, Byrne knew, that were worse than death. He intended to explore each and every one of them before the night was out. For Victoria. For Gracie Devlin. For everyone Julian Matisse had ever hurt.

There was no way back from this. For the rest of his life, no matter where he lived, no matter what he did, he would wait for the knock on the door; he would suspect the man in the dark suit who approached him with grim determination, the car that slowly pulled to the curb as he walked up Broad Street.

Surprisingly, his hands were steady, his pulse even. For now. But he knew that there was a world of distance and difference in that hairbreadth between pulling the trigger and staying your finger.

Could he pull the trigger?

Would he?

As he watched the taillights of the EMS rescue disappear up Montgomery Drive, he felt the weight of the SIG-Sauer in his hand, and had his answer.

"THIS HAS NOTHING TO DO WITH MR. DIAMOND OR HIS BUSI-ness. I'm a homicide detective."

Cedric had hesitated after finding the wire. He had patted her down roughly, torn it off. It was clear what was coming next. He had put the gun to her forehead, and made her get down on her knees.

"You're pretty fucking hot for a cop, you know that?"

Jessica just stared. Watched his eyes. His hands. "You're going to kill a gold-badge detective where you work?" she asked, hoping her voice didn't betray her fear.

Cedric smiled. Incredibly, he wore a retainer. "Who says we'd leave your body here, bitch?"

Jessica considered her options. If she could get to her feet, she could land one shot. It would have to be well placed—the throat or the nose—and even then might only give her a few seconds to get out of the room. She did not take her eyes off the gun.

Cedric stepped forward. He unbuttoned his pants. "You know, I never fucked a cop before."

As he did this, the barrel of the gun pointed away from her momentarily. If he took his pants off, it would be the last opportunity to make her move. "You might want to think this through, Cedric."

"Oh, I'm thinking about it, baby." He began to unzip his zipper. "I been thinking about it since you walked in."

Before he got his zipper all the way down, a shadow crossed the floor.

"Drop the gun, Sasquatch."

It was Nicci Malone.

From the look on Cedric's face, Nicci had a gun to the back of his head. His face drained of all color, his attitude of all menace. He slowly put the weapon on the floor. Jessica picked it up. She trained it on him. It was a .38 Smith & Wesson revolver.

"Very good," Nicci said. "Now put your hands on top of your head, and interlace your fingers."

The man shook his head slowly, side-to-side. But he didn't comply. "You ain't gonna make it out of here."

"No? And why is that?" Nicci asked.

"They're gonna miss me any minute now."

"Why, because you're so lovable? Shut the fuck up. And put your hands on top of your head. Last time I'm going to tell you."

Slowly, reluctantly, he put his hands on his head.

Jessica got to her feet, keeping the .38 pointed at the man, wondering where Nicci got *her* weapon. They had been searched with the metal detector on the way in.

"Now on your knees," Nicci said. "Pretend you're on a date."

With no small effort, the big man got down on his knees.

Jessica got behind him and saw that it wasn't a gun in Nicci's hand. It was a steel towel rack. This girl was *good.*

"How many other security guards are here?" Nicci asked.

Cedric remained silent. Perhaps it was because he fancied himself as so much more than a security guard. Nicci whacked him on the side of the head with the pipe.

"*Ow.* Jesus."

"I don't think you're focusing here, Moose."

"*Damn,* bitch. There's just me."

"I'm sorry, what did you call me?" Nicci asked.

Cedric began to sweat. "I'm . . . I didn't mean—"

Nicci nudged him with the rod. "Shut up." She turned to Jessica. "You okay?"

"Yeah," Jessica said.

Nicci nodded toward the door. Jessica crossed the room, looked into the hallway. Empty. She walked back to where Nicci and Cedric were. "Let's do it."

"Okay," Nicci said. "You can put your hands down now."

Cedric thought that she was letting him go. He smirked.

But Nicci wasn't letting him off the hook. What she really wanted was a clean shot. When he dropped his hands, Nicci wound up and cracked the rod into the back of his head. Hard. The impact echoed off the grimy tile walls. Jessica wasn't sure it was hard enough, but after a second she saw the man's eyes roll up in his head. He folded. Within a minute they had him facedown inside a stall, with a fistful of paper towels in his mouth and his hands bound behind him. It was like dragging an elk.

"I can't believe I'm leaving a Jil Sander belt in this fucking shithole," Nicci said.

Jessica almost laughed. Nicolette Malone was her new role model.

"Ready?" Jessica asked.

Nicci gave the gorilla one more shot with the club for good measure and said: "Let's bounce."

LIKE ALL STAKEOUTS, after the first few minutes or so the adrenaline eased off.

They had left the warehouse and driven across town in the Lincoln Town Car, Bebe and Nicci in the backseat. Bebe had given them directions. When they arrived at the address, they identified themselves to Bebe as law enforcement. She was surprised but not shocked. Bebe and Kilbane were now in temporary custody at the Roundhouse, where they would remain until the operation was over.

The target house was on a dark street. They did not have a search warrant for the premises, so they could not enter. Not yet. If Bruno Steele had told a group of porno actresses to meet him here at midnight, chances were good he'd be back.

Nick Palladino and Eric Chavez were in the van, half a block away. In addition, two sector cars with two uniformed officers each were nearby.

While they waited for Bruno Steele, Nicci and Jessica changed back into street clothes. Jeans and T-shirts and running shoes and Kevlar vests. Jessica felt an enormous sense of relief having her Glock back on her hip.

"Ever partner with a woman before?" Nicci asked. They were alone in the lead car, a few hundred feet from the target house.

"No," Jessica said. In all her time on the street, from her training officer to the veteran cop who had showed the ropes of walking the beat in South Philly, she had always been paired with a man. When she was in the Auto Unit, she was one of two women, and the other had worked the desk. It was a new experience, and—she had to admit—a good one.

"Same here," Nicci said. "You'd think more women would be drawn to Narcotics, but after a while the glamour sort of wears off."

Jessica couldn't tell if Nicci was kidding or not. Glamour? She could understand a man wanting to go cowboy on such a detail. Hell, she was married to one of them. She was just about to answer when headlights washed the rearview.

From the radio: "Jess."

"I see it," Jessica said.

They watched the car slowly approach in the side mirrors. Jessica could not immediately tell the make or model of the car from that distance and in that light. It looked to be a midsize.

The car passed them. It had a single occupant. It rolled slowly to the corner, turned, and was gone.

Had they been made? No. It didn't seem likely. They waited. The car didn't double back.

They stood down. And waited.

IT IS LATE, I AM TIRED. I NEVER WOULD HAVE THOUGHT THAT this sort of work was so physically and spiritually draining. Think of all the film monsters over the years, how hard they must have labored. Think of Freddy, of Michael Myers. Think of Norman Bates, Tom Ripley, Patrick Bateman, Christian Szell.

I have much to do in the next few days. And then I will be done.

I gather my belongings from the backseat, my plastic bag full of bloody clothes. I will burn them first thing in the morning. For now I will take a hot bath, make a cup of chamomile tea, then probably be asleep before my head hits the pillow.

"A hard day's work makes a soft bed," my grandfather used to say.

I get out of the car, lock it. I breathe deeply the midsummer night air. The city smells clean and fresh, charged with promise.

Weapon in hand, I begin to make my way to the house.

At just after midnight, they saw their man. Bruno Steele was walking across the vacant lot behind the target house.

"I've got a visual," came the radio.

"I see him," Jessica said.

Steele hesitated near the door, looking both ways up and down the street. Jessica and Nicci slid slowly down in the seat, just in case another car rolled up the street and silhouetted them in the headlights.

Jessica picked up her two-way radio, keyed it, whispered: "Are we good?"

"Yeah," Palladino said. "We are good."

"Uniforms ready?"

"Ready."

We've got him, Jessica thought.

We've fucking got him.

Jessica and Nicci drew their weapons, slipped quietly out of the car. As they neared their subject, Jessica made eye contact with Nicci. It was a moment for which all police officers live. The excitement of an arrest, tempered by the fear of the unknown. If Bruno Steele was the Actor, he had brutally killed two women that they knew of, both in cold blood. If he was their unsub, he was capable of anything.

They closed the distance in shadow. Fifty feet. Thirty feet. Twenty. Jessica was just about to draw down on the subject when she stopped.

Something was wrong.

In that moment, reality came crashing down around her. It was one of those times—unsettling enough in life in general, potentially fatal on the job—when you realize that what you thought you had in front of you, what you assumed to be one thing, was not only something else, but something wholly other.

The man in the doorway was not Bruno Steele.

The man was Kevin Byrne.

THEY STEPPED ACROSS THE STREET, INTO THE SHADOWS. JESSICA didn't ask Byrne what he was doing there. That would come later. She was just about to head back to the surveillance vehicle when Eric Chavez raised her on channel.

"Jess."

"Yeah."

"There's music coming from the house."

Bruno Steele was already inside.

BYRNE WATCHED THE team prepare to take the house. Jessica had quickly briefed him on the events of the day. With each word she said, Byrne saw his life and career spiral. It all fell into place. Julian Matisse was the Actor. Byrne had been so close, he had not seen it. The system was now going to do to what it did best. And Kevin Byrne was right under its wheels.

A few minutes, Byrne thought. If he had gotten there a few minutes before the strike team, this would have been over. Now, when they found

Matisse tied up in that chair, bloodied and beaten, they would trace it all back to him. Regardless what Matisse had done to Victoria, Byrne had kidnapped and tortured the man.

Conrad Sanchez would find cause for a police brutality charge at the very least, maybe even federal charges. There was a very real possibility that Byrne might be sharing a holding cell, right next to Julian Matisse, this very night.

NICK PALLADINO and Eric Chavez took the lead into the row house; Jessica and Nicci, the rear. The four detectives searched the first and second floors. They were clear.

They began to make their way down the narrow stairs.

It was a damp, vile heat that permeated the house, redolent of sewage and human salt. Beneath it, something primal. Palladino reached the bottom tread first. Jessica followed. They ran their Maglites over the cramped room.

And saw the very heart of evil.

It was a slaughter. Blood and viscera everywhere. Flesh clung to the walls. At first, the source of the blood was not apparent. But soon it dawned on them what they were looking at, that the thing draped over the metal rod was once a human being.

Although it would be more than three hours before fingerprint tests would confirm it, at that moment what the detectives knew for certain was that the man known to adult-film aficionados as Bruno Steele—but better known to the police and the courts and the penal system, and to his mother, Edwina, as Julian Matisse—had been cut in half.

The bloody chain saw at his feet was still warm.

58

THEY SAT IN A BOOTH AT THE BACK OF A SMALL BAR ON VINE Street. The image of what was found in the cellar of the row house in North Philly pulsed between them, unyielding in its profanity. They had both seen a lot in their time on the force. They had rarely seen the brutality of what was done in that room.

CSU was processing the scene. It was going to take all night and most of the next day. Somehow, the media was already all over the story. Three television stations were camped across the street.

While they waited, Byrne told Jessica his story, starting from the moment he had received the call from Paul DiCarlo and ending at the moment she had surprised him outside the row house in North Philly. Jessica had the feeling he had not told her everything.

When he exhausted his tale, there were a few moments of silence. The silence spoke volumes about them—about who they were as police officers, as people, but especially as partners.

"You okay?" Byrne finally asked.

"Yeah," Jessica said. "It's you I'm worried about. I mean, two days back, and all of this."

Byrne waved her concern away. His eyes told another story. He downed his shot, called for another. When the barmaid brought his drink and left, he settled back. The booze softened his posture, eased the tension in his shoulders. It appeared to Jessica that he wanted to tell her something. She was right.

"What is it?" she prodded.

"I was just thinking about something. About Easter Sunday."

"What about it?" She had never talked to him in any kind of depth about his ordeal getting shot. She had wanted to ask, but she figured he would tell her when he was ready. Maybe now was that time.

"When it all happened," he began, "there was this split second, right when the bullet hit me, when I saw it all happening. Like it was happening to someone else."

"You saw it?"

"Not exactly. I don't mean in any New Age out-of-body way. I mean I saw it in my mind. I watched myself fall to the floor. Blood everywhere. *My* blood. And the only thing that kept running through my head, was this . . . this picture."

"What picture?"

Byrne stared into the shot glass on the table. Jessica could tell that this was not easy for him. She had all the time in the world. "A picture of my mother and father. An old black-and-white snapshot. The kind with that rough edge. Remember those?"

"Sure," Jessica said. "Got a shoe box full at home."

"The picture is of them on their honeymoon in Miami Beach, standing in front of the Eden Roc, caught in what might have been the happiest moment of their lives. Now, everyone knew that they couldn't afford the Eden Roc, right? But that's what you did in those days. You stayed at some place called the Aqua Breeze or the Sea Dunes and you took a picture in front of the Eden Roc or the Fontainebleau, and pretended you were rich. My old man in this ugly purple-and-green Hawaiian shirt, big tanned forearms, bony white knees, grinning like the Cheshire cat. It was like he was saying to the world: *Can you believe my dumb mick luck here? What the hell did I do right to deserve this woman?*"

Jessica listened. Byrne had never before revealed much about his family.

"And my mother. Ah, what a beauty. A real Irish rose. She just stood there in this white sundress with little yellow flowers on it, this half smile on her face, like she had you all figured out, like she was saying, *Watch your step, Padraig Francis Byrne, because you're gonna be on thin ice the rest of your life.*"

Jessica nodded, sipped her drink. She had the same snapshot somewhere. Her parents had honeymooned on Cape Cod.

"They hadn't even thought of me when that picture was taken," Byrne said. "But I was in their plans, right? And as I fell to the floor on Easter Sunday, my blood all over the place, all I could think about was someone saying to them, on that bright sunny day in Miami Beach: *You know that kid? That chubby little bundle you're going to have? Someone's gonna put a bullet in his head one day and he's going to die the most undignified death imaginable.* Then, in the picture, I saw their expressions change. I saw my mother start to cry. I saw my old man clench and unclench his fists, which is the way he handles all emotion, even to this day. I saw my old man standing in the ME's office, standing at my grave. I knew I couldn't let go. I knew there was something left for me to do. I knew that I had to survive to do it."

Jessica tried to absorb this, to ferret out the subtext of what he was telling her. "Do you still feel that way?" she asked.

Byrne's eyes cut more deeply into her than anyone ever had. For a second, it felt like he turned her arms and legs into cement. It appeared he might not answer. Then he said, simply: "Yes."

An hour later they stopped by St. Joseph's Hospital. Victoria Lindstrom was out of surgery and in ICU. Her condition was critical but stable.

A few minutes later they stood in the parking lot, in the hush of the predawn city. The sun was coming up soon, but Philly still slept. Somewhere out there, beneath the watchful eye of William Penn, between the peaceful flow of the rivers, amid the drifting souls of the night, the Actor was planning his next horror.

Jessica drove home to catch a few hours' sleep, thinking about what Byrne had been through in the past forty-eight hours. She tried not to judge him. As far as she was concerned, up until the time Kevin Byrne left that cellar in North Philly for Fairmount Park, what had happened down there was between him and Julian Matisse. There had been no witnesses, and there would be no investigation into Byrne's conduct. Jessica was relatively certain that Byrne had not told her every detail, but that was all right. The Actor was still loose in their city.

They had work to do.

THE *SCARFACE* TAPE WAS RENTED AT AN INDEPENDENT VIDEO outlet in University City. For once, Eugene Kilbane did not own the store. The man who rented the tape was Elian Quintana, who worked as a night security guard at the Wachovia Center. He had watched the doctored video with his daughter, a sophomore at Villanova, who had fainted at the sight of the real murder. She was currently sedated under doctor's orders.

In the edited version of the film, a bruised and battered and screaming Julian Matisse is seen handcuffed over a metal rod in the makeshift shower stall in the corner of the basement. A figure in a yellow rain slicker steps into the frame, takes a chain saw, and cuts the man virtually in half. It is spliced into the film at the moment when Al Pacino visits the Colombian drug dealer at the second-floor motel room in Miami. The young man who brought in the tape, an employee of the video store, had been questioned and released, as had Elian Quintana.

There were no other fingerprints on the tape. There were no fingerprints on the chain saw. There was no surveillance video of the tape being placed on the rack at the video store. There were no suspects.

WITHIN A FEW hours of the discovery of Julian Matisse's body in the row house in North Philly, a total of ten detectives were assigned to the case.

Sales of camcorders had skyrocketed in the city, and the possibility of copycat crimes was very real. The task force had dispatched an undercover plainclothes detective to every independently owned video store in the city, the theory being that the Actor was choosing them because of the ease with which he could bypass the older security systems.

For the PPD, and the Philadelphia field office of the FBI, the Actor was now Priority One. The story had received international attention, and crime nuts, film nuts, and nuts of all trees were coming into the city.

From the moment the story broke, a near hysteria had taken place at video stores, both independent and chain, overrun with people renting graphically violent films. Channel 6 Action News set up crews to interview people coming out with armloads of VHS tapes.

"Of all the *Nightmare on Elm Street* tapes, I hope the Actor kills someone like Freddy does in Part Three—"

"I rented *Se7en*, but when I got to the part where the lawyer gets the pound of flesh removed, it was the same scene as in the original . . . bummer—"

"I've got *The Untouchables* . . . Maybe the Actor goes Louisville Slugger on some guy's head in it like De Niro does."

"I hope I see some of the murders like they have in—"

"*Carlito's Way*—"

"*Taxi Driver*—"

"*The Public Enemy*—"

"*The Getaway*—"

"*M*—"

"*Reservoir Dogs*—"

To the department, the possibility of someone not coming forward with a tape—opting to keep it or sell it on eBay—was as disturbing as it was possible.

Jessica had three hours until the task force meeting. Word was she might be heading the task force, and the notion was more than a little daunting. There was an average of ten years' experience in the unit for every detective assigned to the task force, and she would be directing them.

She began to gather her files and notes when she saw the pink WHILE YOU WERE OUT slip. Faith Chandler. She had not yet returned the woman's phone call. She had forgotten all about her. The woman's life was tattered by grief and pain and loss and Jessica had neglected to follow up. She picked up the phone, dialed. After a few rings, a woman answered.

"Hello?"

"Mrs. Chandler, this is Detective Balzano. I'm sorry I haven't been able to get back to you."

Silence. Then: "This is . . . I'm Faith's sister."

"Oh, I'm sorry," Jessica said. "Is Faith in?"

More silence. Something was wrong. "Faith isn't . . . Faith is in the hospital."

Jessica felt the floor drop away. "What happened?"

She heard the woman sniffle. After a moment, "They don't know. They say it might be acute alcohol poisoning. There were a lot of . . . well, that's what they said. She's in a coma. They say she probably won't make it."

Jessica recalled the bottle on the TV table when they had visited Faith Chandler. "When did this happen?"

"After Stephanie . . . well, Faith has a bit of a problem with alcohol. I guess she just couldn't stop. I found her early this morning."

"Was she home at the time?"

"Yes."

"Was she alone?"

"I guess so . . . I mean, I don't know. She was when I found her. Before that, I just don't know."

"Did you or anyone call the police?"

"No. I called nine-one-one."

Jessica glanced at her watch. "Stay right there. We'll be there in ten minutes."

FAITH'S SISTER SONYA was an older, heavier version of Faith. But where Faith's eyes were soul-weary, threaded with sorrow and exhaustion, Sonya's were clear and alert. Jessica and Byrne talked to her in the small kitchen at the back of the row house. There was a single glass in the strainer by the sink, rinsed and already dry.

———

THE MAN SAT on a stoop two doors down from Faith Chandler's row house. He was in his seventies. He had wild gray hair down to his shoulders, a five-day stubble, and sat in what looked like a motorized wheelchair from the 1970s—bulky, jury-rigged with cup holders, bumper stickers, radio antennae, and reflectors, but very well maintained. His name was Atkins Pace. He spoke with a deep Louisiana drawl.

"Do you sit out here a lot, Mr. Pace?" Jessica asked.

"Just about every day when it's nice, *chère*. I got my radio, I got my iced tea. What more could a man want? 'Cept maybe a pair a legs to chase pretty girls with."

The twinkle in his eyes said he was just making light of his situation, something he had probably done for years.

"Were you sitting out here yesterday?" Byrne asked.

"Yessir."

"What time?"

Pace looked at the two detectives, summing up the situation. "This is about Faith, isn't it?"

"Why do you ask that?"

"Because I seen the paramedics take her away this morning."

"Faith Chandler is in the hospital, yes," Byrne replied.

Pace nodded, then made the sign of the cross. He was nearing an age where folks fit into one of three categories. *Already, just about,* and *not quite yet.* "Can you tell me what happened to her?" he asked.

"We're not sure," Jessica replied. "Did you see her at all yesterday?"

"Oh yeah," he said. "I seen her."

"When?"

He looked skyward, as if gauging the time by the position of the sun. "Well, I'll bet it was in the afternoon. Yes'm. I'd say that was most accurate. After twelve noon."

"Was she coming or going?"

"Coming home."

"Was she alone?" Jessica asked.

He shook his head. "No, ma'am. She was with a fella. Nice looking. Looked like a schoolteacher maybe."

"Have you ever seen him before?"

Back up to the sky. Jessica was starting to think this man used the heavens as his own private PDA. "Nope. New one to me."

"Did you notice anything out of the ordinary?"

"The ordinary?"

"Were they arguing, anything like that?"

"No," Pace said. "It was pretty much business as usual, if you know what I mean."

"I don't. Tell me."

Pace looked left, then right. Stoop gossip coming. He leaned forward. "Well, she looked to be in her cups. Plus, they was carrying a few more bottles. I don't like to tell tales, but you asked, and there you have it."

"Would you be able to describe the man who was with her?"

"*Oh* yeah," Pace said. "Right down to his shoelaces if you want."

"Why is that?" Jessica asked.

The man fixed her with a knowing smile. It erased a few years from his furrowed face. "Young lady, I've been in this chair over thirty years. Watching people is what I *do*."

He then closed his eyes and rattled off everything Jessica was wearing, right down to her earrings and the color of the pen in her hand. He opened his eyes, winked.

"Very impressive," she said.

"It's a gift," Pace replied. "Not one I asked for, but I most definitely have it, and I try to use it for the good of humankind."

"We'll be right back," Jessica said.

"I'll be right here, *chère*."

Back inside the row house, Jessica and Byrne stood in the center of Stephanie's bedroom. At first they'd believed that the answer to what had happened to Stephanie was contained in these four walls—her life as it stood on the day she left it. They had examined every item of clothing, every letter, every book, every trinket.

As Jessica looked at the room now, she noticed that everything was exactly the same as it had been a few days earlier. Except for one thing. The picture frame on the dresser—the one that had held a photograph of Stephanie and her friend—was now empty.

IAN WHITESTONE WAS A MAN OF HIGHLY CULTIVATED HABIT, A creature of such detail and precision and economy of thought that those around him were often treated like items on an agenda. In all the time he'd known Ian, Seth Goldman had never seen the man exhibit a single emotion that seemed to come to him naturally. Seth had never known a man with a more icily clinical approach to personal relationships. Seth wondered how he would take the news.

The climactic sequence of *The Palace* was to be filmed in a virtuoso, three-minute shot, filmed at the Thirtieth Street train station. It would be the final shot of the film. It was the shot that would secure the nomination for best director, if not best picture.

The wrap party was going to be held at a fashionable nightclub on Second Street called 32 Degrees, a Euro bar named for its fashion of serving shots in glasses made of solid ice.

Seth stood in the hotel bathroom. He found he could not look at himself. He held the photograph by the edge, flicked his lighter. In seconds, the picture caught the flame. He dropped it into the hotel bathroom's sink. In an instant, it was gone.

Two more days, he thought. It was all he needed. Two more days and they could leave the sickness behind.

Until it all began again.

Jessica headed the task force, her first. Her number one priority was to coordinate resources and manpower with the FBI. Second, she would liaison with the brass, give status reports, prepare a profile.

A sketch of the man who was seen walking down the street with Faith Chandler was in the works. Two detectives were following the chain saw used to kill Julian Matisse. Two detectives were following the embroidered jacket worn by Matisse in *Philadelphia Skin*.

The first task force meeting was scheduled for 4:00 PM.

The victim photographs were taped to a whiteboard: Stephanie Chandler, Julian Matisse, and a photograph taken from the *Fatal Attraction* video of the still-unidentified female victim. There had not yet been a missing-person report matching the woman's description. The medical examiner's preliminary report on the death of Julian Matisse was due any minute.

The request for a search warrant for Adam Kaslov's apartment had been denied. Jessica and Byrne were certain it had a lot more to do with the fact that Lawrence Kaslov was plugged in at some pretty high levels than a lack of circumstantial evidence. On the other hand, the fact that no one had seen Adam Kaslov for days seemed to indicate that his family had whisked him out of town, or even out of the country.

The question was: Why?

JESSICA RECAPPED THE case from the moment Adam Kaslov had brought the *Psycho* tape to the police. Except for the tapes themselves, they had little to go on. Three bloody, arrogant, nearly public executions, and they had nothing.

"It's pretty clear that the Actor is fixated on the bathroom as a crime scene," Jessica said. "*Psycho, Fatal Attraction,* and *Scarface* all have murders committed in the bathroom. We're cross-referencing murders that have taken place in the bathroom in the past five years right now." Jessica pointed to the collage of crime scene photographs. "The victims are Stephanie Chandler, twenty-two; Julian Matisse, forty; and an as-yet-unidentified female, who appears to be in her late twenties or early thirties.

"Two days ago we thought we had him. We thought Julian Matisse, who also went by the name of Bruno Steele, was our doer. Matisse, instead, was responsible for the kidnapping and attempted murder of a woman named Victoria Lindstrom. Ms. Lindstrom is in critical condition at St. Joseph's."

"What did Matisse have to do with the Actor?" Palladino asked.

"We don't know," Jessica said. "But whatever the motive is for the murder of these two women, we have to assume it applies to Julian Matisse. Connect Matisse to these two women, we'll have our motive. If we can't tie these people together, we have no way of knowing where he's going to strike next."

There was no disagreement about the fact that the Actor would strike again.

"There is usually a depression phase in the cycle of a killer like this," Jessica said. "We're not seeing it here. This is a spree, and according to all the research, he is not going to stop until he fulfills his plan."

"What's the link that put Matisse in this?" Chavez asked.

"Matisse was in an adult film called *Philadelphia Skin,*" Jessica said. "And it's clear that something happened on the set of that movie."

"What do you mean?" Chavez asked.

"*Philadelphia Skin* seems to be the center of everything. Matisse was the actor in the blue jacket. The man returning the tape to Flickz wore the same or a similar jacket."

"Do we have anything on the jacket?"

Jessica shook her head. "It wasn't found where we found Matisse's body. We're still canvassing tailor shops."

"How does Stephanie Chandler figure into it?" Chavez asked.

"Not known."

"Could she have been an actress in the film?"

"It's possible," Jessica said. "Her mother said she had been a little wild in college. She didn't elaborate. The time frame would match up. Unfortunately, everyone in that movie wears a mask."

"What were the actresses' stage names?" Chavez asked.

Jessica consulted her notes. "One name is listed as Angel Blue. The other is Tracy Love. Again, we've run the names, no hits. But we might be able to get more of what happened on that shoot from the woman we met at Tresonne."

"What was her name?"

"Paulette St. John."

"Who is *that*?" Chavez asked, seemingly concerned that the task force was interviewing porno actresses and he had been left out of the loop.

"An adult-film actress. It's a long shot, but it's worth a try," Jessica said.

Buchanan said: "Get her in here."

HER REAL NAME was Roberta Stoneking. In the daytime, she looked like a hausfrau, a plain, albeit busty, thirty-eight-year-old thrice-divorced New Jersey mother of three with more than a nodding acquaintance with Botox. Which is precisely who she was. Today, instead of a low-cut leopard-print dress, she wore a hot pink velour tracksuit and new cherry-red running shoes. They met in Interview A. For some reason, there were a lot of male detectives observing this particular interview.

"It may be a big city, but the adult-film business is a small community," she said. "Everybody knows everybody, and everybody knows everybody else's business."

"Like we said, this has nothing to do with anybody's livelihood, okay? We're not concerned with the adult-film business per se," Jessica said.

Roberta turned an unlit cigarette over and over. It appeared that she was deciding how much to say, and how to say it, probably to place herself as far away from any culpability as possible. "I understand."

On the table was a printout close-up of the young blond girl from *Philadelphia Skin. Those eyes,* Jessica thought. "You mentioned that something happened during the shoot of this film."

Roberta took a deep breath. "I don't know much, okay?"

"Whatever you can tell us will be helpful."

"All I heard was that a girl died on the set," she said. "Even that might have been half the story. Who knows?"

"This was Angel Blue?"

"I think so."

"Died how?"

"I don't know."

"What was her real name?"

"I have no idea. There are people I've made ten movies with, I don't know their names. It's that kind of business."

"And you never heard any specifics about the girl's death?"

"Not that I can recall."

She was playing them, Jessica thought. She sat on the edge of the table. Woman-to-woman now. "Come on, Paulette," she said, using the woman's stage name. Maybe it would help them bond. "People talk. There had to be scuttlebutt about what happened."

Roberta looked up. In the harsh fluorescence she looked every one of her years and then some. "Well, I heard she was using."

"Using what?"

Roberta shrugged. "Not sure. Smack, probably."

"How do you know?"

Roberta frowned at Jessica. "Despite my youthful appearance, I've been around the block, Detective."

"Was there a lot of drug use on the set?"

"There's a lot of drug use in the whole business. Depends on the person. Everybody's got their disease, everybody's got their cure."

"Besides Bruno Steele, do you know the other guy who was in *Philadelphia Skin?*"

"I'd have to see it again."

"Well, unfortunately, he wears a mask the whole time."

Roberta laughed.

"Did I say something funny?" Jessica asked.

"Sweetie, there's other ways of recognizing guys in my business."

Chavez poked his head in. "Jess?"

Jessica instructed Nick Palladino to take Roberta down to AV and show her the film. Nick straightened his tie, smoothed his hair. There would be no hazard pay requested for this duty.

Jessica and Byrne stepped out of the room. "What's up?"

"Lauria and Campos caught a case in Overbrook. It looks like it might dovetail with the Actor."

"Why?" Jessica asked.

"First off, the vic is a white female, late twenties, early thirties. Shot once in the chest. Found at the bottom of her bathtub. Just like the *Fatal Attraction* killing."

"Who found her?" Byrne asked.

"Landlord," Chavez said. "She lives in a twin. Her neighbor came home after being out of town for a week, heard the same music playing over and over and over. Some kind of opera. Knocked on her door, got no answer, called the landlord."

"How long has she been dead?"

"No idea. ME's on the way there now," Buchanan said. "But here's the kicker. Ted Campos started going through her desk. Found her pay stubs. She works for a company called Alhambra LLC."

Jessica felt her pulse quicken. "What's her name?"

Chavez looked at his notes. "Her name is Erin Halliwell."

ERIN HALLIWELL'S APARTMENT was a funky collection of mismatched furniture, faux-Tiffany lamps, film books, and posters, along with an impressive array of healthy houseplants.

It smelled of death.

As soon as Jessica poked her head into the bathroom, she recognized the setting. It was the same wall, the same window treatment as the *Fatal Attraction* tape.

The woman's body had been taken from the tub and was on the bathroom floor, on a rubber sheet. Her skin was puckered and gray, the wound in her chest had tightened to a small hole.

They were getting closer, and the feeling was energizing the detectives, all of whom had been averaging four or five hours' sleep a night.

The CSU team was dusting the apartment for prints. A pair of task force detectives were following up on the pay stubs, visiting the bank from which the funds were drawn. The full force of the PPD was bearing down on this case, and it was starting to bear fruit.

BYRNE STOOD IN the doorway. Evil had crossed this threshold.

He watched the buzz of activity in the living room, listened to the sound of the camera's motor drive, smelled the chalky scent of the print powder. He had missed the chase these past months. The CSU officers were looking for minute traces of the killer, inaudible whispers of this woman's violent end. Byrne put his hands on the doorjambs. He was looking for something much deeper, much more ethereal.

He stepped into the room, snapped on a pair of latex gloves. He walked the scene, feeling that—

—she thinks they are going to have sex. He knows they are not. He is here to fulfill his dark purpose. They sit on the couch for a while. He toys with her long enough to get her interested. Had the dress been hers? No. He bought the dress for her. Why had she put it on? She wanted to please him. The Actor is fixated on Fatal Attraction. *Why? What is it about the movie he needs to re-create? Earlier they stood beneath huge lights. The man touches her skin. He wears many looks, many disguises. A doctor. A minister. A man with a badge . . .*

Byrne stepped over to the small desk and began the ritual of sifting through the dead woman's belongings. Her desk had been gone over by the primary detectives, but not with an eye toward the Actor.

In a large drawer he found a portfolio of photographs. Most were of the "soft touch" card variety: Erin Halliwell at sixteen, eighteen, twenty years old, sitting on the beach, standing on the boardwalk in Atlantic City, sitting at a picnic table at a family function. The last folder he looked in spoke to him in a voice the others had not. He called Jessica over.

"Look," he said. He held forth the eight-by-ten picture.

The photograph was taken in front of the art museum. It was a black-and-white group shot of maybe forty or fifty people. In the second row was a smiling Erin Halliwell. Next to her was the unmistakable face of Will Parrish.

Inscribed on the bottom, in a flourish of blue ink, was the following:

ONE DOWN, MANY MORE TO COME.
YOURS, IAN.

THE READING TERMINAL MARKET WAS A HUGE, BUSTLING MAR-
ket located at Twelfth and Market streets in Center City, just a block or
so from city hall. Opened in 1892, it was home to more than eighty vendors and covered nearly two acres.

The task force had learned that Alhambra LLC was a company established exclusively for the production of *The Palace*. The Alhambra was a
famous palace in Spain. Quite often, production companies form a separate enterprise to handle payroll, permits, and liability insurance for the
duration of the shoot. Quite often they take a name or a phrase from the
film and name the company office for it. It allows the production office to
open without a lot of hassles from would-be actors and paparazzi.

By the time Byrne and Jessica reached the corner of Twelfth and
Market, a number of large semitrucks had already parked there. The film
crew was setting up to shoot a second-unit sequence inside. The detectives were only there for a few seconds when a man approached them.
They were expected.

"Are you Detective Balzano?"

"Yes," Jessica said. She held up her badge. "This is my partner, Detective Byrne."

The man was in his late thirties. He wore a stylish navy blazer, white shirt, khakis. He had an air of competence about him, if not secretiveness. Narrow-set eyes, light brown hair, eastern European features. He carried a black leather binder and two-way radio.

"Nice to meet you," the man said. "Welcome to the set of *The Palace*." He extended his hand. "My name is Seth Goldman."

THEY SAT AT a coffee bar inside the market. The myriad aromas wreaked havoc with Jessica's willpower. Chinese food, Indian food, Italian food, seafood, Termini's bakery. She had eaten a peach yogurt and banana for lunch. *Yum.* It was supposed to last her until dinner.

"What can I say?" Seth said. "We're all terribly shaken by the news."

"What was Ms. Halliwell's position?"

"She was production manager."

"Were you very close to her?" Jessica asked.

"Not in the social sense," Seth said. "But we were working on our second film together, and during a shoot you work very closely, sometimes spending sixteen, eighteen hours a day together. You eat meals together, you travel in cars and on planes."

"Were you ever romantically involved with her?" Byrne asked.

Seth smiled, sadly. Apropos of the tragic occasion, Jessica thought. "No," he said. "Nothing like that."

"Ian Whitestone is your employer?"

"That's correct."

"Was there ever any kind of romantic involvement between Ms. Halliwell and Mr. Whitestone?"

Jessica saw the slightest tic. It was quickly covered, but it was a tell. Whatever Seth Goldman was about to say wasn't going to be the complete truth.

"Mr. Whitestone is a happily married man."

Hardly answers the question, Jessica thought. "Now, we may be nearly three thousand miles from Hollywood, Mr. Goldman, but we've heard that sometimes folks from that town *have* been known to sleep with folks other than their spouse. Hell, it's probably even happened out here in Amish country once or twice."

Seth smiled. "If Erin and Ian ever had a relationship other than professional, I was not aware of it."

I'll take that as a yes, Jessica thought. "When was the last time you saw Erin?"

"Let's see. I believe it was three or four days ago."

"On the set?"

"At the hotel."

"Which hotel?"

"The Park Hyatt."

"She was staying at the hotel?"

"No," Seth said. "Ian maintains a suite there when he's shooting in town."

Jessica made a few notes. One of them was to remind herself to chat with some of the hotel personnel about whether or not they had seen Erin Halliwell and Ian Whitestone in a compromising position.

"Do you recall what time that was?"

Seth thought about this for a few moments. "We had a shot in South Philly that afternoon. I left the hotel at maybe four o'clock. So it was probably right around that time."

"Did you see her with anybody?" Jessica asked.

"No."

"And you haven't seen her since?"

"No."

"Did she take a few days off?"

"It was my understanding she called in sick."

"You spoke with her?"

"No," Seth said. "I believe she sent a text message to Mr. Whitestone."

Jessica wondered if it was Erin Halliwell or her killer who sent the text message. She made a note to have Ms. Halliwell's cell phone dusted.

"What is your exact position in this company?" Byrne asked.

"I'm Mr. Whitestone's personal assistant."

"What sort of things does a personal assistant do?"

"Well, my job is everything from keeping Ian on schedule, to helping him with creative decisions, to scheduling his day, to driving him to and from the set. It can entail just about anything."

"How does a person get a job like this?" Byrne asked.

"I'm not sure what you mean."

"I mean, do you have an agent? Do you apply through industry want ads?"

"Mr. Whitestone and I met a number of years ago. We share a passion for film. He asked me to join his team and I was thrilled to do so. I love my job, Detective."

"Do you know a woman named Faith Chandler?" Byrne asked.

It was a planned shift, an abrupt change. It clearly caught the man off guard. He recovered quickly. "No," Seth said. "The name doesn't ring a bell."

"How about Stephanie Chandler?"

"No. I can't say I know her, either."

Jessica took out a nine-by-twelve envelope, extracted a photograph, pushed it along the counter. It was an enlargement of the photograph from Stephanie Chandler's desk at work, the picture of Stephanie and Faith in front of the Wilma Theater. Stephanie's crime scene photo would come next, if needed. "This is Stephanie on the left; her mother, Faith, on the right," Jessica said. "Does it help?"

Seth picked up the photograph, studied it. "No," he repeated. "Sorry."

"Stephanie Chandler was also murdered," Jessica said. "Faith Chandler is clinging to life in the hospital."

"Oh my." Seth put his hand to his heart momentarily. Jessica didn't buy the gesture. From the look on Byrne's face, neither did he. Hollywood shock.

"And you are absolutely certain you've never met either of them?" Byrne asked.

Seth looked at the photo again. He feigned deeper scrutiny. "No. We've never met."

"Could you excuse me for a second?" Jessica asked.

"Of course," Seth said.

Jessica slid off her stool, took out her cell phone. She took a few steps away from the counter. She dialed a number. In an instant, Seth Goldman's phone rang.

"I've got to take this," he said. He took out his phone, looked at the caller ID. And knew. He slowly raised his eyes and met Jessica's eyes. Jessica clicked off.

"Mr. Goldman," Byrne began. "Can you explain why Faith Chandler—a woman you've never met, a woman who just happens to be the mother of a homicide victim, a homicide victim who just happened to visit the set of a film your company is producing—called your cell phone twenty times the other day?"

Seth took a moment to compose his answer. "You must understand, in the film business there are a lot people who will do just about anything to get into the movies."

"You're not exactly a receptionist, Mr. Goldman," Byrne said. "I would think there would be a number of layers between you and the front door."

"There are," Seth said. "But there are some very determined, very clever people out there. Consider this. A call went out for extras on the set piece we're shooting soon. Huge, very complicated shot at the Thirtieth Street train station. The call was for one hundred fifty extras. We had more than two thousand people show up. Besides, we have a dozen phones allocated for this shoot. I don't always have this particular number."

"And you're saying that you do not recall ever having spoken to this woman?" Byrne asked.

"No."

"We'll need a list of the names of the people who may have had this particular phone."

"Yes, of course," Seth said. "But I hope you don't think anyone connected with the production company had anything to do with these . . . these . . ."

"When can we expect the list?" Byrne asked.

Seth's jaw muscles began to work. It was clear that this man was used to giving orders, not taking them. "I'll try and get it to you later today."

"That would be fine," Byrne said. "And we'll also need to talk to Mr. Whitestone."

"When?"

"Today."

Seth reacted as if he were a cardinal and they had requested an impromptu audience with the pope. "I'm afraid that's not possible."

Byrne leaned forward. He got to within a foot or so of Seth Goldman's face. Seth Goldman began to fidget.

"Have Mr. Whitestone call us," Byrne said. "Today."

THE CANVASS NEAR THE ROW HOUSE WHERE JULIAN MATISSE was killed produced nothing. Nothing was really expected. In that North Philly neighborhood amnesia, blindness, and deafness were the rule, especially when it came to talking to the police. The hoagie shop attached to the house had closed at eleven, and no one had seen Matisse that night, nor had anyone seen a man carrying a chain saw case. The property had been foreclosed upon, and if Matisse had been living there—and there was no evidence that he had—he had been squatting.

Two detectives from SIU had been tracking down the chain saw found at the scene. It had been purchased in Camden, New Jersey, by a Philadelphia tree service company, and reported stolen a week earlier. It was a dead end. There were still no leads on the embroidered jacket.

AS OF FIVE o'clock, Ian Whitestone had not called. There was no denying the fact that Whitestone was a celebrity, and handling celebrities in a police matter was a delicate thing. Still, the reasons for talking to him were strong. Every detective on the case wanted to just pick him up for questioning, but it was not that simple. Jessica was just about to call Paul DiCarlo back to press him on the protocol when Eric Chavez got her attention, waving the handset of his phone in the air.

"Call for you, Jess."

Jessica picked up her phone, punched the button. "Homicide. Balzano."

"Detective, this is Jake Martinez."

The name walked the edge of her recent memory. She couldn't immediately place it. "I'm sorry?"

"Officer Jacob Martinez. I'm Mark Underwood's partner. We met at Finnigan's Wake."

"Oh, right," she said. "What can I do for you, Officer?"

"Well, I'm not sure what to make of this, but we're over in Point Breeze. We were working traffic while they tore down the set for the movie they're making, and the owner of one of the stores on Twenty-third flagged us. She said that there was a guy hanging around her store who matched the description of your suspect."

Jessica waved Byrne over. "How long ago was this?"

"Just a few minutes," Martinez said. "She's a little hard to understand. I think she might be Haitian or Jamaican or something. But she had the suspect sketch that was in the *Inquirer* in her hand, and she kept pointing at it, saying that the guy had just been in her store. I think she said her grandson might have mixed it up with the guy a little."

The composite sketch of the Actor had run in that morning's paper. "Have you cleared the location?"

"Yes. But there's no one in the store now."

"Secured it?"

"Front and back."

"Give me the address," Jessica said.

Martinez did.

"What kind of store is it?" Jessica asked.

"A bodega," he said. "Hoagies, chips, sodas. Kinda run-down."

"Why does she think this guy was our suspect? Why would he be hanging around a bodega?"

"I asked her the same thing," Martinez said. "Then she pointed to the back of the store."

"What about it?"

"They have a video section."

Jessica hung up, briefed the other detectives. They had received

more than fifty calls already that day, calls from people who c.
have spotted the Actor on their block, in their yards, in the pai
should this one be any different?

"Because there's a video section in the store," Buchanan said. "You
and Kevin check it out."

Jessica got her weapon from her drawer, handed a copy of the street
address to Eric Chavez. "Find Agent Cahill," she said. "Ask him to meet
us at this address."

THE DETECTIVES STOOD in front of the location, a crumbling storefront deli called Cap-Haitien. Officers Underwood and Martinez, having secured the scene, had returned to their duties. The façade of the
market was a patchwork of plywood panels of bright red, blue, and yellow enamel, topped by bright orange metal bars. Skewed, handmade
signs in the window hawked fried plantains, grio, Creole fried chicken,
along with a Haitian beer called Prestige. There was also a sign proclaiming VIDEO AU LOYER.

About twenty minutes had passed since the owner of the store—an
elderly Haitian woman named Idelle Barbereau—had said the man had
been in her market. It was unlikely that the suspect, if it was their suspect, was still in the area. The woman described the man just as he
appeared in the sketch: white, medium build, wearing large tinted sunglasses, Flyers cap, dark blue jacket. She said he had come in the store,
milled around the racks in the center, then drifted into the small video
section at the back. He stayed there for a minute, then headed for the
door. She said he came in with something in his hands, but was leaving
without it. He didn't purchase anything. She'd had the Inquirer open to
the page displaying the sketch.

While the man was in the back of the store, she had called her grandson up from the cellar—a strapping nineteen-year-old named Fabrice.
Fabrice had blocked the door and gotten into a pushing match with the
subject. When Jessica and Byrne talked to Fabrice, he looked a little
shaken.

"Did the man say anything?" Byrne asked.

"No," Fabrice replied. "Nothing."

"Tell us what happened."

Fabrice said he had blocked the doorway in the hope that his grandmother would have time to call the police. When the man tried to step

around him, Fabrice grabbed the man by the arm, and within a second the man had him spun around, his own right arm pinned behind him. In another second, Fabrice said, he was on his way to the floor. He added that, on the way down, he lashed out with his left hand, striking the man, connecting with bone.

"Where did you hit him?" Byrne asked, glancing at the young man's left hand. Fabrice's knuckles were slightly swollen.

"Right over there," Fabrice said, pointing to the doorway.

"No. I mean on his *body.*"

"I don't know," he said. "I had my eyes closed."

"What happened then?"

"The next thing I knew, I was on the floor, facedown. It knocked the wind out of me." Fabrice took a deep breath, either to prove to the police he was all right, or to prove to himself. "He was strong."

Fabrice went on to say that the man then ran out of the store. By the time his grandmother was able to get out from behind the counter, and onto the street, the man was gone. Idelle then saw Officer Martinez directing traffic and told him about the incident.

Jessica glanced around the store, at the ceilings, at the corners.

There were no surveillance cameras.

JESSICA AND BYRNE searched the market. The air was dense with the pungent aromas of chilies and coconut milk, the racks were filled with standard bodega items—soups, canned meats, snacks, along with cleaning products and a variety of cosmetic sundries. In addition, there was a large display of candles and dream books and other assorted products associated with Santería, the Afro-Caribbean religion.

At the rear of the store was a small alcove bearing a few wire racks of videotapes. Above the racks were a pair of faded film posters—*L'Homme sur les Quais* and *The Golden Mistress.* In addition, smaller images of French and Caribbean movie stars, mostly magazine cutouts, were attached to the wall with yellowing tape.

Jessica and Byrne stepped into the niche. There were about one hundred videotapes in all. Jessica scanned the spines. Foreign titles, kids' titles, a few six-month-old major releases. Mostly French-language films.

Nothing spoke to her. Did any of these films have a murder committed in a bathroom? she wondered. Where was Terry Cahill? He might know. Jessica was starting to think the old woman was imagining things, and that her grandson had gotten body-slammed for nothing, when she saw it. There, on the bottom rack on the left, was a VHS tape with a rubber band doubled-banded around the center.

"Kevin," she said. Byrne walked over.

Jessica pulled on a latex glove and picked up the tape without thinking. Although there was no reason to think that there might be an explosive device attached to it, there was no telling where this murderous crime spree was headed. She chastised herself immediately after picking up the tape. This time she had dodged the bullet. But there *was* something attached.

A pink Nokia cell phone.

Jessica carefully turned the box over. The cell phone was turned on, but there was nothing visible on the small LCD screen. Byrne held open a large evidence bag. Jessica slipped the videocassette box in. Their eyes met.

They both had a pretty good idea whose phone it was.

A FEW MINUTES later they stood in front of the secured store, waiting for CSU. They looked up and down the street. The film crew were still gathering the tools and detritus of their craft—spooling cables, storing lights, breaking down craft service tables. Jessica scanned the workers. Was she looking at the Actor? Could one of these people walking up and down the street be responsible for these horrible crimes? She glanced back at Byrne. He was locked on the façade of the market. She got his attention.

"Why here?" Jessica asked.

Byrne shrugged. "Probably because he knows we're watching the chain stores and the independents," Byrne said. "If he wants to get a tape back on the shelf, he's got to come somewhere like this."

Jessica considered this. It was probably the case. "Should we be watching the libraries?"

Byrne nodded. "Probably."

Before Jessica could respond, she received a transmission on her two-way radio. It was garbled, unintelligible. She pulled it off her belt, adjusted the volume. "Say again."

A few seconds of static, then: "Goddamn FBI don't respect nothin'."

It sounded like Terry Cahill. No, it couldn't be. Could it? If it was, she *had* to have heard him wrong. She exchanged a glance with Byrne. "Say *again?*"

More static. Then: "Goddamn FBI don't respect nothin'."

Jessica's stomach dropped. The line was familiar to her. It was a phrase that Sonny Corleone says in *The Godfather.* She had seen the movie a thousand times. Terry Cahill wasn't kidding around. Not at a time like this.

Terry Cahill was in *trouble.*

"Where are you?" Jessica asked.

Silence.

"Agent Cahill," Jessica said. "What is your twenty?"

Nothing. Dead, icy silence.

Then they heard the gunshot.

"Shots fired!" Jessica yelled into her two-way radio. Instantly she and Byrne had their weapons drawn. They looked up and down the street. No sign of Cahill. The rovers had a limited range. He couldn't be far.

Within seconds an *officer needs assistance* call went out on the radio dispatch, and by the time Jessica and Byrne got to the corner of Twenty-third and Moore there were four sector cars already there, parked at all angles. The uniformed officers were out of their cars in a flash. They all looked to Jessica. She directed the perimeter as she and Byrne began to make their way down the alley that cut behind the stores, weapons drawn. There was no further communication from Cahill's two-way.

When did he get here? Jessica wondered. *Why didn't he checked in with us?*

They moved slowly down the alley. On either side of the passageway were windows, doorways, niches, alcoves. The Actor might have been in any one of them. Suddenly a window flew open. A pair of Hispanic boys, six or seven years old, probably drawn by the sound of the sirens, popped out their heads. They saw the weapons, and their expressions changed from surprise to fear to excitement.

"Please get back inside," Byrne said. They immediately shut the window, drew the curtains.

Jessica and Byrne continued down the alley, every sound drawing their attention. Jessica fingered the volume on the rover with her free hand. Up. Down. Back up. Nothing.

They turned a corner, into a short lane that led to Point Breeze Avenue. And they saw him. Terry Cahill was sitting on the ground, his back to the brick wall. He was holding his right shoulder. He had been shot. There was blood beneath his fingers, scarlet spreading onto the sleeve of his white shirt. Jessica rushed over. Byrne called in their location, kept an eye out, scanning the windows and rooftops above them. The danger had not necessarily passed. Within a few seconds, four uniformed officers arrived, Underwood and Martinez among them. Byrne directed them.

"Talk to me, Terry," Jessica said.

"I'm good," he said through gritted teeth. "It's a flesh wound." A slight amount of fresh blood tipped his fingers. The right side of Cahill's face was starting to swell.

"Did you see his face?" Byrne asked.

Cahill shook his head. He was clearly in a world of pain.

Jessica communicated the information that the suspect was still at large into her two-way. She heard at least four or five more sirens approaching. You sent out an *officer needs assistance* call in this department, and everyone and his mother came.

But even with twenty cops combing the area, it became clear, after five minutes or so, that their suspect had slipped away. Again.

The Actor was in the wind.

BY THE TIME Jessica and Byrne returned to the alley behind the market, Ike Buchanan and half a dozen detectives were on the scene. Paramedics were attending to Terry Cahill. One of the EMS techs found Jessica's eyes, nodded. Cahill would be okay.

"There goes my shot at the PGA tour," Cahill said as they loaded him onto a stretcher. "Want my statement now?"

"We'll get it at the hospital," Jessica said. "Don't worry about it."

Cahill nodded, winced in pain as they lifted the gurney. He looked at Jessica and Byrne. "Do me a favor, will you guys?"

"Name it, Terry," Jessica said.

"Take this fucker down," he said. "Hard."

THE DETECTIVES MILLED around the perimeter of the crime scene where Cahill had been shot. Although no one said it, they all felt like rookies, like a group of green recruits fresh out the academy. CSU had set up a perimeter of yellow tape and, as always, a crowd was gathering. Four CSU officers began to comb the area. Jessica and Byrne stood against the wall, lost in their thoughts.

Granted, Terry Cahill was a federal agent, and quite often there was an intense rivalry between agencies, but he was nonetheless a law enforcement officer working a case in Philadelphia. The grim faces and steely looks on all concerned spoke to the outrage. You don't shoot a cop in Philadelphia.

After a few minutes, Jocelyn Post, a veteran of CSU, held up a pair of tongs, smiling from ear to ear. Between the tips was a spent bullet.

"*Oh* yes," she said. "Come to Mama J."

Although they had found the discharged slug that had hit Terry Cahill in the shoulder, it was not always easy to determine the caliber and type of bullet when it had been fired, especially if the lead had struck a brick wall, which it had in this case.

Nonetheless, this was very good news. Anytime a piece of physical evidence was found—something that could be tested, analyzed, photographed, dusted, traced—it was a step forward.

"We've got the slug," Jessica said, knowing that this was a baby step in the investigation, happy to have the lead nonetheless. "It's a start."

"I think we can do better than that," Byrne said.

"What do you mean?"

"Look."

Byrne crouched down, picked up a metal rib from a broken umbrella lying in a pile of trash. He lifted the edge of plastic garbage bag. There, next to the Dumpster, partially hidden, was a small-caliber handgun. A banged-up, cheap black .25. It looked like the same weapon they had seen in the *Fatal Attraction* video.

This was no baby step.

They had the Actor's gun.

THE VIDEOTAPE FOUND IN CAP-HAITIEN WAS A FRENCH FILM, released in 1955. The title was *Les Diaboliques*. In it, Simone Signoret and Vera Clouzot—who portray the wife and former mistress of a thoroughly rotten man played by Paul Meurisse—murder Meurisse by drowning him in a bathtub. Like the rest of the Actor's masterpieces, this tape had a re-created murder replacing the original crime.

In this version of *Les Diaboliques,* a barely glimpsed man in a dark satin jacket with a dragon embroidered on the back pushes a man beneath the surface of the water in a grungy bathroom. Again, a bathroom.

Victim number four.

THERE WAS A clean print on the gun, a .25 ACP Raven manufactured by Phoenix Arms, a popular junk gun on the streets. You could pick up a Raven .25 anywhere in the city for under a hundred dollars. If the shooter was in the system, they would soon have a match.

There had been no slug recovered at the Erin Halliwell scene, so they would not know for certain if this weapon was used to kill her, even though the ME's office had presumptively concluded that her single wound was consistent with a small-caliber weapon.

Firearms had already determined that the Raven .25 was the gun used to shoot Terry Cahill.

As they had thought, the cell phone attached to the videocassette belonged to Stephanie Chandler. Although the SIM card was still active, everything else had been erased. There were no calendar entries, no address book listings, no text or e-mail messages, no logs of calls made or received. There were no fingerprints.

CAHILL GAVE HIS statement while getting patched up at Jefferson. The wound was a flesh wound, and he was expected to be released within a few hours. In the ER waiting room, half a dozen FBI agents congregated, giving a visiting Jessica Balzano and Kevin Byrne their backs. Nobody could have prevented what happened to Cahill, but tightly knit squads never looked at it that way. According the suits, the PPD had fucked up, and one of their own was now in the hospital.

In his official statement, Cahill said that he had been in South Philly when he had received the call from Eric Chavez. He had then monitored the channel and heard that the suspect was perhaps in the area of Twenty-third and McClellan. He had begun a search of the alleyways behind the storefronts when his assailant had come up behind him, put the gun to the back of his head, and forced him to say the lines from *The Godfather* into the two-way radio. When the suspect reached for Cahill's weapon, Cahill knew he had to make his move. They struggled, and the assailant punched him twice—once in the small of the back, once on the right side of his face—then the suspect's gun discharged. The suspect then fled down the alley, leaving his weapon behind.

A brief canvass of the area near the shooting yielded little. No one had seen or heard a thing. But now the police had a firearm, and that opened up a broad avenue of investigation to them. Guns, like people, had a history.

WHEN THE TAPE of *Les Diaboliques* was ready to be screened, ten detectives assembled in the studio room of the AV unit. The French-language film ran 122 minutes. At the point where Simone Signoret and Vera Clouzot drown Paul Meurisse, there is a crash edit. When the film changes over to the new footage, the new scene is a filthy bathroom—

grimy ceiling, peeling plaster, filthy rags on the floor, stacked magazines next to dirty toilet. A bare-bulb fixture next to the sink casts a dim, sickly light. A large figure on the right side of the screen holds the thrashing victim underwater with clearly powerful hands.

The camera shot is stationary, meaning that the camera was most likely on a tripod, or perched on something. To date there had been no evidence of a second suspect.

When the victim stops thrashing, his body floats to the surface of the dirty water. The camera is then picked up and moved in for a close-up. It was there that Mateo Fuentes froze the image.

"Jesus Christ," Byrne said.

All eyes turned to him. "What, you know him?" Jessica asked.

"Yeah," Byrne said. "I know him."

DARRYL PORTER'S APARTMENT above the X Bar was as sleazy and ugly as the man. All the windows were painted shut, and the hot sun on the glass gave the cramped space a cloying, dog-kennel smell.

There was an old avocado-colored sleeper couch covered with a filthy bedspread, a pair of stained armchairs. The floor, tables, and shelves were covered with water-stained magazines and newspapers. The sink offered a month of dirty dishes and at least five species of scavenging insects.

On one of the bookshelves over the TV were three sealed DVD copies of *Philadelphia Skin*.

Darryl Porter was in his bathtub, fully clothed, fully dead. The filthy bathwater had shriveled and leached Porter's skin a cement-gray color. His bowels had released into the water, and the stench in the confines of the small bathroom was overpowering. A pair of rats had already begun to seek out the gas-bloated corpse.

The Actor had now claimed four lives, or at least four of which they were aware. He was getting bolder. It was a classic escalation, and no one could predict what was coming next.

As the CSU set up to process yet another crime scene, Jessica and Byrne stood in front of the X Bar. They both looked shell-shocked. It was a moment where the horrors were flying fast and fleet and words were hard to come by. *Psycho, Fatal Attraction, Scarface, Les Diaboliques*—what the hell was coming next?

Jessica's cell phone rang, bringing with it the answer.

"This is Detective Balzano."

The call was from Sergeant Nate Rice, head of the Firearms Unit. He had two pieces of news for the task force. One was that the gun recovered from the scene behind the Haitian market was very likely the same make and model as the gun on the *Fatal Attraction* videotape. The second piece of news was a lot harder to digest. Sergeant Rice had just spoken to the fingerprint lab. They had a match. He gave Jessica the name.

"What?" Jessica asked. She knew she had heard Rice correctly, but her brain was not prepared to process the data.

"I said the same thing," Rice replied. "But it's a ten-point match."

A ten-point match, police were fond of saying, was name, address, Social Security number, and high school picture. If you had a ten-point, you had your man.

"And?" Jessica asked.

"And there's no doubt about it. The print on the gun belongs to Julian Matisse."

When Faith Chandler had shown up at the hotel, he knew it was the beginning of the end.

It was Faith who had called him. Called to tell him the news. Called to ask for more money. It was now only a matter of time until all the pieces began to fall into place for the police, and everything would be exposed.

He stood, naked, considering himself in the mirror. His mother stared back, her sad, liquid eyes judging the man he'd become. He brushed his hair, gently, using the beautiful brush Ian had bought for him at Fortnum & Mason, the exclusive British department store.

Don't make me give you the brush.

He heard activity outside the door to his hotel room. It sounded like the man who came around each day at this time to replenish the mini-bar. Seth looked at the dozen empty bottles scattered around the small table near the window. He was barely drunk. He had two bottles left. He could use more.

He pulled the tape out of the cassette housing, allowing it to pool on the floor at his feet. Next to the bed were already a dozen empty cassettes, their plastic hulls stacked like crystalline bones.

He looked next to the television. There were only a few more to go. He would destroy them all, then, perhaps, himself.

There came a knock at his door. Seth closed his eyes. "Yes?"

"Mini bar, sir?"

"Yeah," Seth said. He was relieved. But he knew it was only temporary. He cleared his throat. Had he been crying? "Hang on."

He slipped on his robe, unlocked the door. He stepped into the bathroom. He really didn't want to see anyone. He heard the young man enter, replace the bottles and snacks in the mini bar.

"Enjoying your stay in Philadelphia, sir?" the young man called from the other room.

Seth almost laughed. He thought about the past week, about how it had all come apart. "Very much," Seth lied.

"We hope you'll return."

Seth took a deep breath, scrambled his courage. "Take two dollars from the dresser," he called out. For the moment, his volume masked his emotions.

"Thank you, sir," the young man said.

A few moments later Seth heard the door close.

Seth sat on the edge of the tub for a full minute, his head in his hands. What *had* he become? He knew the answer, but he just could not admit it, even to himself. He thought about the moment that Ian Whitestone had walked into the car dealership so long ago, how they had talked well into the night. About film. About art. About women. About things so personal that Seth had never shared the thoughts with anyone else.

He ran the tub. After five minutes or so he toed the water. He cracked one of the two remaining little bottles of bourbon, poured it into a water glass, drank it in one gulp. He stepped out of his robe, slipped into the hot water. He had thought about a Roman death, but had quickly ruled it out. Frankie Pentangeli in *The Godfather: Part II*. He didn't have the courage for such a thing, if courage was indeed what it took.

He closed his eyes, just for a minute. Just for a minute, then he would call the police and start talking.

When had it begun? He wanted to examine his life in terms of grand themes, but he knew the simple answer. It began with the girl. She had never shot heroin before. She had been scared, but willing. So willing. As they all had been. He remembered her eyes, her cold dead eyes. He remembered loading her into the car. The terrifying ride into North Philly. The filthy gas station. The guilt. Had he slept through the night even *once* since that terrible evening?

Soon, Seth knew, there would be another knock at the door. The police would want to talk to him in earnest. But not just yet. Just a few minutes.

Just a few.

Then, faintly, he heard . . . moaning? Yes. It sounded like one of the porno tapes. Was it in the adjoining hotel room? No. It took a moment, but Seth soon realized that the sound was coming from his hotel room. From *his television*.

He sat up in the tub, his heart racing. The water was warm, not hot. He had been out for a while.

Someone was in the hotel room.

Seth craned his neck, trying to look around the bathroom door. It was ajar, but the angle was such that could not see more than a few feet into the room. He looked up. There was a lock on the bathroom door. Could he get out of the tub quietly, slam shut the door and lock it? Maybe. But then what? What would he do then? He had no cell phone in the bathroom.

Then, from right outside the bathroom door, just inches away, he heard a voice.

Seth thought of T. S. Eliot's line from "The Love Song of J. Alfred Prufrock."

Till human voices wake us . . .

"I'm new to this city," the voice outside his door said. "I haven't seen a friendly face in weeks."

And we drown.

JESSICA AND BYRNE DROVE TO THE OFFICES OF ALHAMBRA LLC. They had called the main number, and also Seth Goldman's cell phone. Both offered voice mail. They had called Ian Whitestone's hotel room at the Park Hyatt. They were told that Mr. Whitestone was not in, and he could not be reached.

They parked across the street from the small, nondescript building on Race Street. They sat in silence for a while.

"How the hell could Matisse's print be on the gun?" Jessica asked. The weapon had been reported stolen six years earlier. It could have passed though a hundred hands in the meantime.

"The Actor had to have taken it when he killed Matisse," Byrne said.

Jessica had a lot of questions to ask about that night, about Byrne's actions in that basement. She wasn't sure how to ask. Like a lot of things in her life, she just bulled ahead. "So when you were down in that basement with Matisse, did you search him? Did you search the house?"

"I patted him down, yeah," Byrne said. "But I didn't clear the whole house. Matisse could have had that .25 stashed anywhere."

Jessica considered this. "I think he got it another way. I have no idea why, but it's a gut feeling I have."

He just nodded. He was a man who ran on gut feelings. The two of them fell silent again. Not an uncommon thing on stakeouts.

Finally, Jessica asked, "How is Victoria?"

Byrne shrugged. "Still critical."

Jessica didn't know what to say. She suspected there mght be more than friendship between Byrne and Victoria, but even if she was just a friend, what had happened to her was horrifying. And it was clear that Kevin Byrne blamed himself. "I'm so sorry, Kevin."

Byrne looked out the side window, his emotions rushing him.

Jessica studied him. She recalled how he had looked in the hospital, months earlier. He looked so much better now, physically, almost as robust and strong as the day she'd met him. But she knew that what made a man like Kevin Byrne strong was on the inside, and she could not penetrate that shell. Not yet.

"And Colleen?" Jessica asked, hoping the talk didn't sound as small as it seemed. "How is she?"

"Tall. Independent. Becoming her mother. Other than that, nearly opaque."

He turned, looked at her, smiled. Jessica was glad for that. She'd just been getting to know him when he had been shot, but what she had learned in that short time was that he loved his daughter more than anything else in this world. She hoped that he wasn't growing distant from Colleen.

Jessica had begun a relationship with Colleen and Donna Byrne after Byrne had been attacked. They had seen each other at the hospital every day for more than a month, and had bonded through the tragedy. She had meant to get in touch with both of them but life, as it will, had intervened. Jessica had even learned a little sign language in that time. She vowed to rekindle the relationships.

"Was Porter the other man in *Philadelphia Skin?*" Jessica asked. They had run a check on a list of Julian Matisse's known associates. Matisse and Darryl Porter had known each other for at least a decade. The connection was there.

"Certainly possible," Byrne said. "Why else would Porter have three copies of the movie?"

Porter was, at that moment, on the ME's table. They would compare any distinguishing body marks to the masked actor in the film. Roberta Stoneking's viewing of the film was inconclusive, despite her claim.

"How do Stephanie Chandler and Erin Halliwell fit in?" Jessica asked. So far, they had not been able to establish a solid link between the women.

"The million-dollar question."

Suddenly a shadow darkened Jessica's window. It was a uniformed officer. Female, twenties, eager. A little *too* eager, maybe. Jessica nearly came out of her skin. She rolled down the window.

"Detective Balzano?" the officer asked, looking a little shamefaced at having scared the crap out of a detective.

"Yes."

"This is for you." It was a nine-by-twelve manila envelope.

"Thanks."

The young officer all but ran away. Jessica rolled the window back up. The few seconds it had been down had let out all the cool air from the AC. The city was a sauna.

"Getting jumpy in your old age?" Byrne asked, trying to sip his coffee and smile at the same time.

"Still younger than you, Pops."

Jessica tore open the envelope. It was the sketch of the man seen with Faith Chandler, courtesy of Atkins Pace. Pace had been right. His powers of observation and recall were stunning. She showed the sketch to Byrne.

"Son of a *bitch*," Byrne said. He decked a blue light on the dashboard of the Taurus.

The man in the sketch was Seth Goldman.

THE HEAD OF hotel security let them into the room. They had phoned the room from the hallway, knocked three times. From the hallway they could hear the unmistakable sounds of an adult film coming from inside the room.

When the door was open, Byrne and Jessica drew their weapons. The security man, a former PPD officer in his sixties, looked eager and willing and ready to take part, but he knew his job was complete. He backed off.

Byrne was first in. The sound of the porno tape was louder. It was coming from the hotel TV. The immediate room was empty. Byrne checked the beds and beneath; Jessica, the closet. Both clear. They edged open the bathroom door. They holstered their weapons.

"Ah, *shit,*" Byrne said.

Seth Goldman was floating in the red tub. It appeared that he had been shot twice in the chest. The feathers scattered about the room like so much fallen snow said that the shooter had used one of the hotel pillows to muffle the blast. The water was tepid, but not cold.

Byrne met Jessica's eyes. They were of one mind. This was all escalating so quickly, so violently, that it threatened to get well away from their abilities to investigate. It meant that the FBI would probably be taking over, bringing to bear the full force of its massive manpower and forensic capabilities.

Jessica began to sift through Seth Goldman's toiletries and other personal items in the bathroom. Byrne worked the closets, the dresser drawers. In the back of one of the drawers was a box of eight-millimeter videocassettes. Byrne called Jessica over to the television, slipped one of the tapes into the attached camcorder, hit PLAY.

It was a homemade S&M porno tape.

The image was of a dreary room with a queen-size mattress on the floor. A harsh light came from overhead. After a few seconds a young woman walked into the frame, sat down on the bed. She was about twenty-five or so, dark-haired, slender and plain. She wore a man's V-neck T-shirt, nothing else.

The woman lit a cigarette. A few seconds later, a man entered the frame. The man was naked, except for a leather mask. He carried a small bullwhip. He was white, in fairly toned shape, probably between thirty and forty. He began to whip the woman on the bed. Not hard, not at first.

Byrne glanced at Jessica. They had both seen a lot in their time on the force. It was never a surprise when they ran across the ugliness of what one person could do to another, but that knowledge never made it easier.

Jessica walked out of the room, her exhaustion a palpable thing inside her, her revulsion a bright red ember in her chest, her rage a gathering gale.

HE HAD MISSED HER. YOU DON'T ALWAYS GET TO CHOOSE YOUR partners on this job, but from the moment he met her, he knew she was the real thing. The sky was the limit for a woman like Jessica Balzano, and although he was only ten or twelve years older than she, he felt ancient in her company. She was the future of the unit, he was the past.

Byrne sat at one of the plastic booths in the Roundhouse lunchroom, sipped his cold coffee, thought about being back. How it felt. What it meant. He watched the younger detectives breeze through the room, their eyes so bright and clear, their loafers polished, their suits pressed. He envied them their energy. Had he looked like that at one point? Had he walked through this room twenty years earlier, a chest full of confidence, observed by some damaged cop?

He had just called the hospital for the tenth time that day. Victoria was listed in serious but stable condition. No change. He'd call again in an hour.

He had seen the crime scene photos of Julian Matisse. Although there was nothing human left, Byrne gazed upon the raw tissue as if he were looking at a shattered talisman of evil. The world was cleaner without him. He felt nothing.

It still did not answer the question of whether or not Jimmy Purify had planted the evidence in the Gracie Devlin case.

Nick Palladino entered the room, looking as tired as Byrne felt. "Did Jess go home?"

"Yeah," Byrne said. "She's been burning both ends."

Palladino nodded. "You hear about Phil Kessler?" he asked.

"What about him?"

"He died."

Byrne was neither shocked nor surprised. Kessler had looked bad the last time he had seen him, a man resolved to his fate, a man seemingly without the will or doggedness to fight.

We didn't do right by that girl.

If Kessler had not meant Gracie Devlin, it could only be one other person. Byrne struggled to his feet, downed his coffee, and headed off to Records. The answer, if there *was* an answer, would be there.

TRY AS HE might, he could not remember the girl's name. Obviously, he couldn't ask Kessler. Or Jimmy. He tried to zero in on the exact date. Nothing came back. There had been so many cases, so many names. Every time he seemed to get close, within a few months, something occurred to him to change his mind. He put together a brief list of notes about the case as he remembered them, then handed it off to an officer in Records. Sergeant Bobby Powell, a lifer like himself, and far better with computers, told Byrne he would get to the bottom of it, and get the file to him as soon as possible.

BYRNE PILED THE photocopies of the Actor's case files in the middle of his living room floor. Next to it he placed a six-pack of Yuengling. He took off his tie, his shoes. He found some cold Chinese food in the fridge. The old air conditioner barely cooled the room, even though it was rattling on high. He flipped on the TV.

He cracked a beer, picked up the remote. It was nearly midnight. He had not yet heard from Records.

As he cruised the cable channels, the images melted into each other. Jay Leno, Edward G. Robinson, Don Knotts, Bart Simpson, each face a—

—blur, linking to the next. Drama, comedy, musical, farce. I settle on an old noir, maybe from the 1940s. It isn't one of the major noir films, but it looks as if it was shot fairly well. In this scene, the femme fatale is trying to get something out of the heavy's raincoat while he talks on a pay phone.

Eyes, hands, lips, fingers.

Why do people watch movies? What do they see? Do they see who they want to be? Or do they see who they fear becoming? They sit in the darkness, next to total strangers, and for two hours they are the villains, the victims, the heroes, the forsaken. Then they get up, walk into the light and live their lives of despair.

I should rest, but I cannot sleep. Tomorrow is a very big day. I look back at the screen, turn the channel. A love story, now. Black-and-white emotions storm my heart as—

—JESSICA FLIPPED THROUGH THE CHANNELS. SHE WAS HAVING A hard time staying awake. She had wanted to sift through the time line of the case one more time before going to bed, but everything was fog.

She glanced at the clock. Midnight.

She turned off the TV, sat at her dining room table. She spread the evidence out in front of her. To the right was the pile of three books on crime cinema she had gotten from Nigel Butler. She picked up one of them. In it, Ian Whitestone was briefly mentioned. She learned that his idol was a Spanish director named Luis Buñuel.

As with every homicide, there was a wire. A wire that plugged into every aspect of the crime, ran through every person. Like the old-style Christmas lights, the string did not light up until all the bulbs were snapped into place.

She wrote the names down on a legal pad.

Faith Chandler. Stephanie Chandler. Erin Halliwell. Julian Matisse. Ian Whitestone. Seth Goldman. Darryl Porter.

What was the wire that ran through all these people?

She looked at the notes on Julian Matisse. How did his print get on that gun? There had been a break-in at the home of Edwina Matisse a year earlier. Maybe that was it. Maybe that was when their doer had obtained Matisse's gun *and* the blue jacket. Matisse had been in prison, and he might very likely have stored these items at his mother's house. Jessica got on the phone and had the police report faxed over to her. When she read it, nothing out of the ordinary popped out at her. She knew the uniformed officers who took the initial call. She knew the detectives who caught the case. Edwina Matisse reported that the only thing that was stolen was a pair of candlesticks.

Jessica looked at the clock. It was still a reasonable hour. She called one of the detectives on that case, a longtime veteran named Dennis Lassar. They got their pleasantries out of the way quickly, in deference to the hour. Jessica got to the point.

"Do you remember a break-in at a row house on Nineteenth? A woman named Edwina Matisse?"

"When was it?"

Jessica gave him the date.

"Yeah, yeah. Older woman. Kinda nuts. Had a grown son doing time."

"That's her."

Lassar detailed the case as he remembered it.

"So the woman reported that the only thing stolen was a pair of candlesticks? That sound right?" Jessica asked.

"If you say so. Lotta assholes under the bridge since then."

"I hear you," Jessica said. "Do you remember if the place was really ransacked? I mean, a lot more roughed up than a pair of candlesticks would have warranted?"

"Now that you mention it, it was. The son's room was torn apart," Lassar said. "But hey, if the vic says nothing's missing, then nothing's missing. I remember being in a hurry to get the hell out of there. Smelled like chicken broth and cat piss."

"Okay," Jessica said. "Do you remember anything else about the case?"

"I seem to recall there was something else about the son."

"What about him?"

"I think the FBI had been watching him before he went up."

The FBI had been watching a lowlife like Matisse? "Do you remember what that was about?"

"I think it was some Mann Act violation. Interstate transport of underaged girls. Don't quote me on it, though."

"Did an agent show up at the crime scene?"

"Yeah," Lassar said. "Funny how this shit comes back to you. Young guy."

"Do you remember the agent's name?"

"Now, *that* part's lost to the Wild Turkey forever. Sorry."

"No problem. Thanks."

She hung up, thought about calling Terry Cahill. He had been released from the hospital and was back working a desk. Still, it was probably a little late for a choirboy like Terry to be up. She'd talk to him tomorrow.

She put *Philadelphia Skin* into her laptop's DVD drive, forwarded it. She freeze-framed the scene near the beginning. The young woman in the feather mask stared out at her, her wide eyes vacant and pleading. She ran a check on the name *Angel Blue,* even though she knew it was false. Even Eugene Kilbane had no idea who the girl was. He said he'd never seen her before or after *Philadelphia Skin.*

But why do I know those eyes?

Suddenly Jessica heard a sound at the dining room window. It sounded as if it might be the laughter of a young woman. Both of Jessica's neighbors had children, but they were boys. She heard it again. A girl's giggle.

Close.

Very close.

She turned and looked at the window. There was a face staring at her. It was the girl from the video, the girl in the teal feather mask. Except now the girl was skeletal, her pale skin stretched tight over her skull, her mouth a ragged grin, a red slash in her pallid smear of features.

Then, in an instant, the girl was gone. Jessica soon sensed a presence right behind her. The girl was *right behind her.* Someone flipped on the lights.

Someone is in my house. How did—

No, the light was coming from the windows.

Huh?

Jessica picked her head off the table.

Oh my God, she thought. She'd fallen asleep at the dining room table. It was light out. *Bright* light out. Morning. She looked at her watch. No watch.

Sophie.

She shot to her feet, looked around, frantic for the moment, her heart racing to burst. Sophie was sitting in front of the TV, pajamas still on, a box of cereal in her lap, the TV showing cartoons.

"G'morning, Mom," Sophie said through a mouthful of Cheerios.

"What time is it?" Jessica asked, even though she knew it was rhetorical.

"I can't tell time," her daughter replied.

Jessica darted into the kitchen, looked at the clock. Nine thirty. In her entire life, she had never slept past nine. Ever. What a day to set the record, she thought. Some task force leader.

Shower, breakfast, coffee, dressed, more coffee. All in twenty minutes. A world record. A personal best, at least. She gathered the photos and files together. The photo on top was a still of the girl from *Philadelphia Skin.*

And that's when she saw it. Sometimes extreme fatigue coupled with extreme pressure can open the floodgates.

The first time Jessica had watched the film, she thought she had seen those eyes before.

Now she knew where.

BYRNE WOKE UP ON THE COUCH. HE HAD DREAMED OF Jimmy Purify. Jimmy and his pretzel logic. He had dreamed about a conversation they had once had, late one night in the unit, maybe a year before Jimmy's bypass. They had just brought down a very bad man, wanted on a triple. The mood was smooth and easy. Jimmy was working his way though a huge bag of barbecued potato chips, feet up, tie and belt undone. Someone brought up the fact that Jimmy's doctor had told him he had to cut down on fatty, greasy, sugary foods. These were three of Jimmy's four basic food groups, the other being single-malt.

Jimmy sat up. He assumed his Buddha pose. Everyone knew a pearl was forthcoming.

"This happens to be health food," he said. "And I can prove it."

Everyone just stared, meaning, *Let's have it*.

"Okay," he began, "Potatoes are a vegetable, am I right?" Jimmy's lips and tongue were a bright orange.

"Right," someone said. "Potatoes are a vegetable."

"And *barbecuing* is just another term for *grilling*, am I also right?"

"Can't argue with that," someone testified.

"Therefore, I am eating grilled vegetables. This is health food, baby."
Straight-faced, perfectly serious. Nobody did deadpan better.

Fucking Jimmy, Byrne thought.

God, he missed him.

Byrne got up, splashed some water on his face in the kitchen, put the
kettle on. When he walked back into the living room, the case was still
there, still open.

He circled the evidence. The epicenter of the case was right before
him, and the door was maddeningly closed.

We didn't do right by that girl, Kevin.

Why couldn't he stop thinking about this? He remembered the night
as if it were yesterday. Jimmy was having surgery to have bunions removed. Byrne had been partnered with Phil Kessler. The call came in
around 10:00 PM. A body was found in the bathroom of a Sunoco station
in North Philly. When they arrived on the scene Kessler, as always, found
something to do that had nothing to do with being in the same room as
the victim. He started a canvass.

Byrne had pushed open the door to the ladies' room. He was immediately accosted with the scents of disinfectant and human waste. On the
floor, wedged between the toilet and the grimy tiled wall, was a young
woman. She was slender and fair, no more than twenty years old. There
were a few track marks on her arm. She was clearly a user, but not
habitual. Byrne had felt for a pulse, found none. She was pronounced
dead at the scene.

He recalled looking at her, so unnaturally posed on the floor. He recalled thinking that this was not who she was supposed to be. She was
supposed to be a nurse, a lawyer, a scientist, a ballerina. She was supposed to be somebody other than a drug statistic.

There had been some signs of a struggle—contusions on her wrists,
some bruising on her back—but the amount of heroin in her system,
coupled with the fresh needle marks on her arms, indicated that she had
recently shot up, and it had been far too pure for her system. The official
cause of death was ruled an overdose.

But hadn't he suspected more?

There was a knock at his door, bringing Byrne back from the memory.
He answered. It was an officer with an envelope.

"Sergeant Powell said it was misfiled," the officer said. "He sends his
apologies."

"Thanks," Byrne said.

He closed the door, opened the envelope. The girl's picture was clipped to the front of the folder. He had forgotten how young she looked. Byrne purposely avoided looking at the name on the folder for the moment.

As he stared at her photograph, he tried to recall her first name. How could he have forgotten? He knew how. She was a junkie. A middle-class kid gone bad. In his arrogance, in his ambition, she had been a nobody to him. Had she been a lawyer at some white-shoe firm, or a doctor at HUP, or an architect at the city planning board, he would have treated the case differently. As much as he hated to admit it, in those days, it was true.

He opened the file, saw her name. And everything made sense.

Angelika. Her name was Angelika.

She was Angel Blue.

He flipped through the file. He soon found what he was looking for. She was not just another stiff. She was, of course, somebody's daughter.

As he reached for the phone, it rang, the sound echoing in tandem with the question caroming off the walls of his heart:

How will you pay?

NIGEL BUTLER'S HOME WAS A TIDY ROW HOUSE ON FORTY-second Street, near Locust. The outside was as ordinary as any well-kept brick row house in Philadelphia—a pair of flower boxes beneath the two front windows, a cheerful red door, a brass mailbox. If the detectives were correct in their assumptions, a full litany of horrors had been planned inside.

Angel Blue's real name was Angelika Butler. Angelika had been twenty years old when she was found in a North Philly gas station bathroom, dead from a heroin overdose. Or so the medical examiner's office had officially ruled.

"I have a daughter studying acting," Nigel Butler had said.

True statement, wrong verb tense.

Byrne told Jessica about the night he and Phil Kessler had gotten the call to investigate a dead girl in that North Philly gas station. Jessica told Byrne in detail of her two meetings with Butler. One, when she had met him at his office at Drexel. The other when Butler had stopped by the Roundhouse with books. She told Byrne of the series of eight-by-ten head shots of Butler in his many stage characters. Nigel Butler was an accomplished actor.

But Nigel Butler's real life was a much darker piece of drama. Before leaving the Roundhouse, Byrne had run a PDCH on the man. A police department criminal history was a basic criminal history report. Nigel Butler had twice been investigated for sexually abusing his daughter: once when she was ten; once when she was twelve. Both times the investigation had hit a dead end when Angelika had recanted her story.

When Angelika had entered the adult-film world, and met an unseemly end, it had probably sent Butler over the edge—jealousy, rage, paternal concern, sexual obsession. Who knew? The point was, Nigel Butler was now at the center of their investigation.

Yet even with all this circumstantial evidence, they still did not have enough for a search warrant of Nigel Butler's house. At that moment, Paul DiCarlo was going down a list of judges trying to change that.

Nick Palladino and Eric Chavez were staking out Butler's office at Drexel. The university had told them that Professor Butler was out of town for three days, and could not be reached. Eric Chavez had used his charm to find out that Butler had allegedly gone camping in the Poconos. Ike Buchanan had already put in a call to the Monroe County sheriff's office.

As they approached the door, Byrne and Jessica caught each other's eye. If their suspicions were correct, they were standing in front of the Actor's door. How would it play out? Hard? Easy? No door ever gave a clue. They drew their weapons, held them at their sides, glanced up and down the block.

Now was the time.

Byrne knocked on the door. Waited. No answer. He rang the bell, knocked again. Again, nothing.

They took a few steps back, looked at the house. Two windows upstairs. Both had white curtains drawn. The window to what was certainly the living room had matching curtains, slightly parted. Not enough to see in. The row house was in the middle of the block. If they wanted to go around back, they would have to walk all the way around. Byrne decided to knock again. Louder. He stepped back to the door.

That's when they heard the shots. They came from inside the house. A large-caliber weapon. Three quick blasts that rattled the windows.

They would not need a search warrant after all.

Kevin Byrne slammed a shoulder into the door. Once, twice, three times. It splintered open on the fourth attempt. "Police!" he yelled. He rolled into the house, gun raised. Jessica called for backup on her two-way, then followed, Glock poised, ready.

To the left, a small living room and dining room. Mid-day dark. Empty. Ahead, a hallway to what was probably the kitchen. Stairs up and down to the left. Byrne met Jessica's eyes. She would take the upstairs. Jessica let her eyes adjust. She scanned the floor in the living room and hallway. No blood. Outside, two sector cars screeched to a halt.

For the moment, the house was deathly quiet.

Then there was music. A piano. Heavy footsteps. Byrne and Jessica leveled their weapons toward the stairs. Sounds were coming from the basement. Two uniformed officers arrived at the door. Jessica instructed them to check upstairs. They drew their weapons, made their way up the steps. Jessica and Byrne began to descend the stairs into the basement.

The music became louder. Strings. The sound of waves on a beach.

Then came a voice.

"Is that the house?" a boy asked.

"That's it," a man answered.

A few moments of silence. A dog barked.

"Hey. I knew *there was a dog,"* the boy said.

Before Jessica and Byrne could round the corner into the basement, they looked at each other. And understood. There had been no gunshots. It had been a movie. When they stepped into the dim basement, they saw that the film was *Road to Perdition*. The film was playing on a large plasma screen, running through a 5.1 Dolby system, the volume cranked very high. The gunfire was from the film. The windows had rattled courtesy of a very large subwoofer. On the screen, Tom Hanks and Tyler Hoechlin stood on a beach.

Butler had known they were coming. Butler had set this all up for their benefit. The Actor was not ready for his final curtain.

"Clear!" one of the uniforms shouted above them.

But the two detectives already knew that. Nigel Butler was gone.

The house was empty.

BYRNE REWOUND THE tape to the scene where Tom Hanks's character—Michael Sullivan—kills the man he believes to be responsible for the murder of his wife and one of his sons. In the film, Sullivan shoots the man in a bathtub at a hotel.

The scene had been replaced with the murder of Seth Goldman.

SIX DETECTIVES SCOURED every inch of Nigel Butler's row house. On the basement walls were even more head shots of Butler's various stage roles: Shylock, Harold Hill, Jean Valjean.

They had issued a nationwide APB on Nigel Butler. State, county, local, and federal law enforcement agencies all had a photograph of the man, as well as a description and license plate of his car. Another six detectives fanned out across the Drexel campus.

In the basement was a wall of prerecorded videotapes, DVDs, and reels of sixteen-millimeter film. What they did not find were any video editing decks. No camcorder, no homemade videotapes, no evidence that Butler had spliced footage of the homicides into prerecorded tapes. Within an hour they would, with any luck, have a warrant to search the film department and all its offices at Drexel. Jessica was searching the basement when Byrne called her from the first floor. When she got upstairs and into the living room, she found Byrne by the bookshelf.

"You're not to going to believe this," Byrne said. In his hand was a large, leatherette-bound photo album. He flipped to a page about halfway through the book.

Jessica took the photo album from him. What she saw nearly took her breath away. There were a dozen pages of photographs of the teenage Angelika Butler. In some she was standing alone: at a birthday party, at a park. In some she was with a young man. A boyfriend perhaps.

In almost all of the pictures, Angelika's head had been replaced with a cutout photograph of a movie star—Bette Davis, Emily Watson, Jean Arthur, Ingrid Bergman, Grace Kelly. The young man's face had been defaced with what might have been a knife or an ice pick. Page after page, Angelika Butler—in the guise of Elizabeth Taylor, Jeanne Crain, Rhonda Fleming—stood next to a man whose face had been obliterated in a terrible rage. In some instances, there were rips in the page where the young man's face once was.

"Kevin." Jessica pointed to one picture, a picture where Angelika Butler wore the mask of a very young Joan Crawford, a picture where her defaced companion sat on a bench next to her.

In this picture, the man was wearing a shoulder holster.

HOW LONG HAS IT BEEN? I KNOW TO THE HOUR. THREE YEARS, two weeks, one day, twenty-one hours. The landscape has changed. The topography of my heart has not. I think of the thousands and thousands of people who have passed by this place in the past three years, the thousands of dramas unfolding. Despite all our claims to the contrary, we really do not care about each other. I see it every day. We are all simply extras in the movie, not even worthy of a credit. If we have a line, perhaps, we will be remembered. If not, we take our meager pay and strive to be the lead in someone's life.

Mostly, we fail. Remember your fifth kiss? The third time you made love? Of course not. Just the first. Just the last.

I glance at my watch. I pour the gasoline.

Act III.

I light the match.

I think of *Backdraft. Firestarter. Frequency. Ladder 49.*

I think of Angelika.

BY ONE O'CLOCK THEY HAD SET UP A SITUATION ROOM AT THE Roundhouse. Every piece of paper found in Nigel Butler's house had been boxed and tagged and was currently being sifted through for an address, a telephone number, or anything else that might provide a lead as to where he might have gone. If there really was a cabin in the Poconos, there was no rental receipt found, no deed located, no pictures taken.

The lab had the photo albums and had reported that the glue used to affix the photographs of movie stars to the face of Angelika Butler was standard white craft glue, but what was surprising was that it was fresh. In some instances, according to the lab, the glue was still wet. Whoever had glued those pictures into the album had done so in the past forty-eight hours.

AT ONE TEN, the call for which they were both hoping and dreading came in. It was Nick Palladino. Jessica took the call, put him on the speakerphone.

"What's up, Nick?"

"I think we found Nigel Butler."

"Where is he?"

"He's parked in his car. North Philly."

"Where?"

"In the parking lot of an old gas station on Girard."

Jessica glanced at Byrne. It was clear that he didn't need to be told which gas station. He had been there once. He knew.

"Is he in custody?" Byrne asked.

"Not exactly."

"What do you mean?"

Palladino took a deep breath, exhaled slowly. It seemed like a full minute passed before he answered. "He's sitting behind the wheel of his car," Palladino said.

A few more excruciating seconds passed. "Yeah? And?" Byrne asked.

"And the car is on fire."

BY THE TIME THEY ARRIVED, THE PFD HAD EXTINGUISHED the fire. The acrid smell of burning vinyl and immolated flesh hung upon the already humid summer air, steaming the entire block with a thick redolence of unnatural death. The car was a blackened husk; the front tires were melted into the asphalt.

As they got closer, Jessica and Byrne could see that the figure behind the wheel was charred beyond recognition, its flesh still smoldering. The corpse's hands were fused to the steering wheel. The blackened skull offered two empty caves where eyes once were. Smoke and greasy vapor rose from seared bone.

Four sector cars ringed the crime scene. A handful of uniformed officers directed traffic, kept the growing crowd away.

The arson unit would tell them exactly what happened here eventually, at least in the physical sense. When the fire started. *How* the fire started. Whether an accelerant was used. The psychological canvas on which this had all been painted was going to take a lot longer to profile and analyze.

Byrne considered the boarded-up structure before him. He recalled the last time he had come here, the night they had found Angelika Butler's body in the ladies' room. He had been a different man then. He recalled how he and Phil Kessler had pulled into the lot, parking just about where Nigel Butler's ruined shell of a car stood now. The man who had found the body—a homeless man who had teetered between running, in case he would be implicated, and staying, in case there was some sort of reward—had nervously pointed to the ladies' room. Within minutes they had determined that this was probably just another overdose, another young life thrown to the wind.

Although he couldn't swear to it, Byrne would bet that he had slept well that night. The thought made him sick to his stomach.

Angelika Butler had deserved every bit of his attention, just like Gracie Devlin. He had let Angelika down.

7 5

THE MOOD WAS MIXED AT THE ROUNDHOUSE. FOR WHAT IT WAS worth, the media was prepared to run with the story as a tale of a father's revenge. Those in the Homicide Unit, however, knew they had not exactly triumphed in the closing of this case. This was not a shining moment in the 255-year history of the department.

But life, and death, went on.

Since the discovery of the car, there had been two new, unrelated homicides.

AT SIX O'CLOCK Jocelyn Post entered the duty room, six CSU evidence bags in hand. "We found something in the trash at that gas station you should see. These were in a plastic portfolio, stuffed into a Dumpster."

Jocelyn arrayed the six bags on the table. In the bags were eleven-by-fourteens. They were the lobby cards—miniature movie posters originally designed for display in a movie theater's lobby—to *Psycho, Fatal Attraction, Scarface, Les Diaboliques,* and *Road to Perdition.* In addition, there was the torn corner from what might have been a sixth card.

"Do you know what movie this one is from?" Jessica asked, holding up the sixth bag. The piece of glossy cardboard had a partial bar code on it.

"No idea," Jocelyn said. "But I made a digital image and sent it to the lab."

It was probably a movie that Nigel Butler never got to, Jessica thought. It was *hopefully* a movie that Nigel Butler never got to.

"Well, let's follow up on it anyway," Jessica said.

"You got it, Detective."

BY SEVEN O'CLOCK, preliminary reports had been written, detectives were filing out. There was none of the joy or elation at having brought a bad man to justice usually prevalent at a time like this. Everyone felt relief that this bizarre and ugly chapter was closed. Everyone just wanted a long, hot shower, and a long, cold drink. The six o'clock news had broadcast video footage of the burned and smoldering shell of the car at the North Philly gas station. THE ACTOR'S FINAL PERFORMANCE? the crawl asked.

Jessica got up, stretched. She felt as if she hadn't slept in days. She probably hadn't. She was so tired, she couldn't remember. She walked over to Byrne's desk.

"Buy you dinner?"

"Sure," Byrne said. "What do you have a taste for?"

"I want something big and greasy and unhealthy," Jessica said. "Something with a lot of breading and a carb count that has a comma."

"Sounds good to me."

Before they could gather their belongings and leave the room they heard a sound. A rapid, beeping sound. At first, no one paid much attention. This was the Roundhouse, after all, a building full of beepers, pagers, cell phones, PDAs. Something was always beeping, pinging, clicking, faxing, ringing.

Whatever it was, it beeped again.

"Where the hell is that coming from?" Jessica asked.

All the detectives in the room rechecked their cell phones, their pagers. No one had received a message.

Then, three more times in quick succession. *Beep-beep. Beep-beep. Beep-beep.*

It was coming from inside a box of files on a desk. Jessica looked into the box. There, in an evidence bag on top, was Stephanie Chandler's cell phone. The bottom of the LCD screen was flashing. At some point during the day, Stephanie had received a call.

Jessica opened the bag, retrieved the phone. It had already been processed by CSU, so there was no reason to wear gloves.

1 MISSED CALL the readout proclaimed.

Jessica clicked the SHOW MESSAGE key. The LCD displayed a new screen. She showed the phone to Byrne. "Look."

There was a new message. The readout declared that a private number had sent the file.

To a dead woman.

They ran it down to the AV unit.

"IT'S A MULTIMEDIA message," Mateo said. "A video file."

"When was it sent?" Byrne asked.

Mateo checked the readout, then his watch. "A little over four hours ago."

"And it just came in now?"

"Sometimes that happens with really big files."

"Any way to tell where it was sent from?"

Mateo shook his head. "Not from the phone."

"If we play the video, it's not going to delete itself or anything, will it?" Jessica asked.

"Hang on," Mateo said.

He went into a drawer, retrieved a thin cable. He tried to plug it into the bottom of the phone. No fit. He tried another cable, failed again. The third one slipped into a small port. He plugged the other into a port on the front of a laptop. In a few moments, a program started on the laptop. Mateo tapped a few keys, and a progress bar appeared, apparently transferring the file from the phone to the computer. Byrne and Jessica looked at each other, once again in awe of Mateo Fuentes's capabilities.

A minute later, he put a fresh CD-ROM in the drive, dragged and dropped an icon.

"Done," he said. "We've got the file on the phone, on the hard drive, and on disc. No matter what happens, we're backed up."

"Okay," Jessica said. She was a little surprised to find that her pulse was racing. She had no idea why. Maybe the file was nothing at all. She wanted to believe that with all her heart.

"You want to watch it now?" Mateo asked.

"Yes and no," Jessica said. It was a video file, sent to the phone of a woman who had been dead for more than a week—a phone they had recently gotten courtesy of a sadistic serial killer who had just burned himself to death.

Or maybe that was all an illusion.

"I hear you," Mateo said. "Here we go." He clicked the PLAY arrow on the small button bar at the bottom of his video software screen. A few seconds later, the video rolled. The first few seconds of footage were a blur, as if the person holding the camera was whipping it right to left, then down, attempting to point it at the ground. When the image stabilized, and was brought into focus, they saw the subject of the video.

It was a baby.

A baby in a small pine coffin.

"*Madre de Dios,*" Mateo said. He made the sign of a cross.

As Byrne and Jessica stared in horror at the image, two things were clear. One was that the baby was very much alive. Two, that the video had a time code in the lower right-hand corner.

"This tape wasn't made with a camera phone, was it?" Byrne asked.

"No," Mateo said. "It looks like it was made with a basic camcorder. Probably an eight-millimeter tape camcorder, not a digital video model."

"How can you tell?" Byrne asked.

"Quality of image, for one thing."

On screen, a hand entered the frame, placing a lid on the wood coffin.

"Jesus Christ, no," Byrne said.

And that was when the first shovel full of dirt landed on the box. Within seconds the box was completely covered.

"Oh my God." Jessica felt nauseous. She turned away at the moment the screen went black.

"That's the whole file," Mateo said.

Byrne remained silent. He walked out of the room, immediately back in. "Run it again," he said.

Mateo clicked PLAY again. The image went from a blurry moving image to clarity as it came to focus on the baby. Jessica forced herself to watch. She noticed that the time code on the tape was from ten o'clock that morning. It was already past eight o'clock. She took out her cell phone. Within in a few seconds she had Dr. Tom Weyrich on the phone. She explained her reason for calling. She didn't know if her question fell

THE SKIN GODS 329

within the area of expertise of a medical examiner, but she didn't know who else to call.

"How big is the box?" Weyrich asked.

Jessica looked at the screen. The video was running for a third time. "Not sure," she said. "Maybe twenty-four by thirty inches."

"How deep?"

"I don't know. It looks to be about sixteen inches or so."

"Are there any holes in the top or sides?"

"Not in the top. Can't see the sides."

"How old is the baby?"

This part was easy. The baby looked to be about six months old. "Six months."

Weyrich was silent for a few moments. "Well, I'm no expert at this. I'll track someone down who is, though."

"How much air does he have, Tom?"

"Hard to say," Weyrich replied. "It's just over five cubic feet inside the box. Even with that small of a lung capacity, I'd say no more than ten to twelve hours."

Jessica looked at her watch again, even though she knew exactly what time it was. "Thanks, Tom. Call me if you talk to someone who can give this kid more time."

Tom Weyrich knew what she meant. "I'm on it."

Jessica hung up. She looked back at the screen. The video was at the beginning again. The baby smiled and moved his arms. At the outside, they had less than two hours to save his life. And he could be anywhere in the city.

MATEO MADE A second digital copy of the tape. The tape ran for a total of twenty-five seconds. When it was over, it cut to black. They watched it again and again, looking for something, anything, to give them a clue to where the baby might be. There were no other images on the recording. Mateo started it up again. The camera whipped downward. Mateo stopped it.

"The camera is on a tripod, and a fairly good one at that. At least for the home enthusiast. It's a smooth tilt, which tells me that the neck on the tripod is a ball head.

"But look here," Mateo continued. He started the recording again. As soon as he hit PLAY, he stopped it. On screen was an unrecognizable image. A thick vertical smudge of white against a reddish brown background.

"What is that?" Byrne asked.

"Not sure yet," Mateo said. "Let me run it through the dTective unit. I'll get a much clearer image. It will take a little time, though."

"How long?

"Give me ten minutes."

In an ordinary investigation, ten minutes would pass in a snap. To the baby in the coffin, it might be a lifetime.

Byrne and Jessica stood outside the AV Unit. Ike Buchanan walked into the room. "What's up, Sarge?" Byrne asked.

"Ian Whitestone is here."

Finally, Jessica thought. "Is he here to make a formal statement?"

"No," Buchanan said. "Someone kidnapped his son this morning."

WHITESTONE LOOKED AT the movie of the baby. They had transferred the clip to a VHS cassette. They watched it in the small snack room in the unit.

Whitestone was smaller than Jessica had expected. He had delicate hands. He wore two watches. He had come with a personal physician and someone who was probably a bodyguard. Whitestone identified the baby in the video as his son, Declan. He looked gut-shot.

"Why . . . why would someone do such a thing?" Whitestone asked.

"We were hoping you might be able to shed some light on that," Byrne said.

According to Whitestone's nanny, Aileen Scott, she had been taking Declan for a walk in his stroller at about nine thirty that morning. She had been struck from behind. When she awoke, hours later, she was in the back of an EMS rescue, on her way to Jefferson Hospital, and the baby was gone. The time frame told the detectives that, if the time code on the tape had not been manipulated, Declan Whitestone was buried within a thirty-minute drive of Center City. Probably closer.

"The FBI has been contacted," Jessica said. A patched and back-on-the-job Terry Cahill was at that moment assembling a team. "We're doing everything possible to find your son."

They walked back into the common room, over to a desk. They put the crime scene photographs of Erin Halliwell, Seth Goldman, and

Stephanie Chandler on the table. When Whitestone looked down, his knees buckled. He held on to the edge of the desk.

"What . . . what is *this*?" he asked.

"Both of these women were murdered. As was Mr. Goldman. We believe the man who kidnapped your son is responsible." There was no need to tell Whitestone about Nigel Butler's apparent suicide at this time.

"What are you saying? Are you saying that all of them are *dead*?"

"I'm afraid so, sir. Yes."

Whitestone weaved. His face turned the color of dried bones. Jessica had seen it many times. He sat down hard.

"What was your relationship to Stephanie Chandler?" Byrne asked.

Whitestone hesitated. His hands were shaking. He opened his mouth, but no sound emerged, just a parched, clicking noise. He looked like a man at risk of a coronary.

"Mr. Whitestone?" Byrne asked.

Ian Whitestone took a deep breath. Through trembling lips he said, "I think I should talk to my lawyer."

THEY HAD GOTTEN THE WHOLE STORY FROM IAN WHITESTONE. Or at least the part his attorney would allow him to tell. Suddenly the past ten days or so made sense.

Three years earlier—before all his meteoric success—Ian Whitestone made a film called *Philadelphia Skin,* directing under the name Edmundo Nobile, a character in one of Spanish director Luis Buñuel's films. Whitestone had used two young women from Temple University for the pornographic film, paying them each five thousand dollars for two nights' work. The two young women were Stephanie Chandler and Angelika Butler. The two men were Darryl Porter and Julian Matisse.

On the second night of filming, what happened to Stephanie Chandler was more than a little fuzzy, according to Whitestone's convenient memory. Whitestone said that Stephanie was shooting drugs. He said he didn't allow it on the set. He said that Stephanie left in the middle of the shoot and never returned.

Nobody in the room believed a word of it. But what was crystal clear was that everybody involved in the making of the film had paid dearly for it. Whether Ian Whitestone's son would pay for the crimes of his father was yet to be seen.

MATEO CALLED THEM down to the AV Unit. He had digitized the first ten seconds of the video field by field. He had also separated the audio track and cleaned it up. He played the audio first. There was only five seconds of sound.

First there was a loud hiss, then a rapid decrease in intensity, followed by silence. It was clear that whoever was operating the camera had turned down the microphone as he began to roll the tape.

"Run that back," Byrne said.

Mateo did. The sound was one of a quick burst of air, which began to fade immediately. Then the white noise of electronic silence.

"One more time."

Byrne seemed transfixed by the sound. Mateo looked to him before continuing with the video portion. "Okay," Byrne finally said.

"I think we have something here," Mateo said. He clicked through a number of still images. He stopped on one, enlarged it. "This is just over two seconds in. It's an image right before the camera tilts downward." Mateo tightened the focus slightly. The image was all but indecipherable. A splash of white against a reddish brown background. Rounded geometric shapes. Low contrast.

"I don't see anything," Jessica said.

"Hang on." Mateo ran the image through the digital enhancer. On screen, the image moved closer. After a few seconds, it became slightly clearer, but not clear enough to read. He zoomed and clarified one more time. Now the image was unmistakable.

Six block letters. All white. Three on top, three on the bottom. The image appeared to be:

ADI
ION

"What does it mean?" Jessica asked.

"I don't know," Mateo replied.

"Kevin?"

Byrne shook his head, stared at the screen.

"Guys?" Jessica asked the other detectives in the room. Shrugs all around.

Nick Palladino and Eric Chavez each got on a terminal and began to search for possibilities. Soon they both had hits. They found something called the ADI 2018 Process Ion Analyzer. It rang no bells.

"Keep looking," Jessica said.

BYRNE STARED AT the letters. They meant something to him, but he had no idea what. Not yet. Then, suddenly, the images touched the edge of his memory. ADI. ION. The vision came back on a long ribbon of re-membrance, a vague recollection of his youth. He closed his eyes and—

—heard the sound of steel on steel . . . eight years old now . . . running with Joey Principe from Reed Street . . . Joey was fast . . . hard to keep up . . . felt the rush of wind, spiked with diesel fumes . . . ADI . . . breathed the dust of a July afternoon . . . ION . . . heard the compressors fill the main reservoirs with high-pressure air—

He opened his eyes.

"Play the audio again," Byrne said.

Mateo brought the file up, clicked PLAY. The sound of the hissing air filled the small room. All eyes turned to Kevin Byrne.

"I know where he is," Byrne said.

THE SOUTH PHILADELPHIA train yards were a huge, foreboding par-cel of land at the southeastern end of the city, bounded by the Delaware River and I-95, along with the navy shipyards to the west and League Is-land to the south. The yards handled the bulk of the city's freight and cargo, while Amtrak and SEPTA handled the commuter lines out of the Thirtieth Street station across town.

Byrne knew the South Philly yards well. When he was growing up, he and his buddies would meet at the Greenwich Playground and ride their bikes down to the yards, usually sneaking onto League Island along Kitty Hawk Avenue, then onto the yards. They'd spend the day there, watching the trains come and go, counting boxcars, throwing things into the river. In his youth, the South Philly rail yards were Kevin Byrne's Omaha Beach, his Martian landscape, his Dodge City, a place he believed to be magic, a place he believed to be inhabited by Wyatt Earp, Sergeant Rock, Tom Sawyer, Eliot Ness.

Today he believed it to be a burial ground.

THE K-9 UNIT of the Philadelphia Police Department worked out of the training academy on State Road, and had more than three dozen dogs under its command. The dogs—all male, all German shepherds—were trained in three disciplines, that being the detection of cadavers, narcotics, and explosives. At one time there were well over one hundred animals in the unit, but a shifting of jurisdictions had reduced the force to a tightly knit, highly trained squad of fewer than forty men and dogs.

Officer Bryant Paulson was a twenty-year veteran of the unit. His dog, a seven-year-old shepherd named Clarence, was trained as a cadaver dog, but also worked patrol. Cadaver dogs were attuned to any and all human smells, not just that of the deceased. Like all police dogs, Clarence was a specialist. If you put a pound of marijuana in the middle of a field, Clarence would walk right by it. If the quarry was human— dead or alive—he would work all day and all night to find it.

At nine o'clock, a dozen detectives and more than twenty uniformed officers gathered at the western end of the rail yard, near the corner of Broad Street and League Island Boulevard.

Jessica gave Officer Paulson the nod. Clarence began to work the area. Paulson kept him on a fifteen-foot lead. The detectives hung back, in order to not disturb the animal. Air scenting is different from tracking, a method by which a dog follows a trail, head close to the ground, searching for human smells. It was also more difficult. Any shift in the wind could redirect a dog's effort, and any ground covered might have to be re-covered. The K-9 Unit of the PPD trained its dogs in what was called the "disturbed earth theory." In addition to any human smells, the dogs were trained to respond to any recently turned soil.

If the baby was buried here, the earth would be disturbed. There was no dog better at this than Clarence.

For now, all that the detectives could do was watch.

And wait.

BYRNE SURVEYED THE huge parcel of land. He was wrong. The baby wasn't here. A second dog and officer had joined the search, and together they had nearly covered the entire plot with no results. Byrne glanced at his watch. If Tom Weyrich's assessment had been accurate, the baby was already dead. Byrne walked alone toward the eastern end of the yard, toward the river. His heart was heavy with the image of that baby in the pine box, his memory now alive with the thousand adventures he had played out on these grounds. He stepped down into a shallow culvert, and up the other side, an incline that was—

—Pork Chop Hill . . . the last few meters to the summit of Everest . . . the mound at Veterans Stadium . . . the Canadian border, protected by—

Mounties.

He *knew*. ADI. ION.

"Over here!" Byrne yelled into his two-way.

He ran toward the tracks near Pattison Avenue. Within moments his lungs were on fire, his back and legs a network of raw nerve endings and searing pain. He scanned the ground as he ran, running the beam of the Maglite a few feet ahead. Nothing looked fresh. Nothing overturned.

He stopped, his lungs now spent, hands on his knees. He couldn't run anymore. He was going to let the baby down like he had let Angelika Butler down.

He opened his eyes.

And saw it.

At his feet was a square of recently overturned gravel. Even in the gathered dusk, he could see that it was darker than the surrounding earth. He glanced up to see a dozen cops racing his way, led by Bryant Paulson and Clarence. By the time the dog came within twenty feet, he began to bark and paw the ground, indicating that he had located his quarry.

Byrne fell to his knees, tearing the dirt and gravel away with his hands. Within seconds he came across loose, damp soil. Soil that had recently been turned over.

"Kevin." Jessica came over, helped him to his feet. Byrne backed off, breathing heavily, his fingers already raw from the sharp stones.

Three uniformed officers stepped in with shovels. They began to dig. A few seconds later they were joined by a pair of detectives. Suddenly they hit something solid.

Jessica looked up. There, less than thirty feet away, in the dim light thrown from the sodium lamps on I-95, she saw a rusted freight car. The two words were stacked, one atop the other, broken into three segments, separated by the battens on the steel boxcar.

CANADIAN
NATIONAL

On the center of the three sections were the letters ADI over the letters ION.

THE PARAMEDICS RUSHED over to the hole. They pulled out the small casket and began to pry it open. All eyes were on them. Except Kevin Byrne's. He couldn't bring himself to look. He closed his eyes, waited. It seemed like minutes. All he could hear was the sound of the nearby freight train, its drone a somnolent hum in the evening air.

In that moment between life and death Byrne recalled the day Colleen was born. She was about a week early, even then a force of nature. He recalled her tiny pink fingers curled against the white of Donna's hospital gown. So small . . .

When Kevin Byrne was absolutely certain they had been too late, that they had failed Declan Whitestone, he opened his eyes and heard the most beautiful noise. A little cough, then a thin cry that soon grew to a loud throaty wail.

The baby was alive.

The paramedics rushed Declan Whitestone to the EMS rescue. Byrne looked over at Jessica. They had won. They had trumped evil this time. But they both knew that this lead came from somewhere other than databases and spreadsheets, or psychological profiles, or even the highly attuned senses of the dogs. This came from a place about which they would never speak.

THEY SPENT THE rest of the night investigating the crime scene, writing out their reports, catching a few minutes' sleep as they could. As of 10:00 AM, the detectives had been on for twenty-six hours straight.

Jessica sat at a desk, wrapping up her report. As primary detective on the case, it was her responsibility. She had never been so exhausted in her life. She looked forward to a long bath and a full day and night's sleep. She hoped that sleep would not be invaded by dreams of a small baby buried in a pine box. She had called Paula Farinacci, her babysitter, twice. Sophie was fine. Both times.

Stephanie Chandler, Erin Halliwell, Julian Matisse, Darryl Porter, Seth Goldman, Nigel Butler.

And then there was Angelika.

Would they ever get to the bottom of what happened on the set of *Philadelphia Skin*? There was one man who could tell them, and there was a very good chance that Ian Whitestone would take that knowledge to his grave.

At ten thirty, while Byrne was in the bathroom, someone put a small box of Milk-Bones on his desk. When he returned, he saw it and began to laugh.

No one in this room had heard Kevin Byrne laugh in a long time.

LOGAN CIRCLE IS ONE OF WILLIAM PENN'S ORIGINAL FIVE squares. Situated on Benjamin Franklin Parkway, it is surrounded by some of the city's most impressive institutions: the Franklin Institute, the Academy of Natural Sciences, the Free Library, the art museum.

The three figures of Swann Fountain, at the center of the circle, represent the main waterways of Philadelphia: the Delaware, the Schuylkill, and the Wissahickon rivers. The area beneath the square was once a burial ground.

Talk about your subtext.

Today the area around the fountain is packed with summertime revelers and cyclists and tourists. The water sparkles: diamonds against a cerulean sky. Children chase each other in lazy figure eights. Vendors hawk their wares. Students read their textbooks, listen to their MP3 players.

I come upon the young woman. She is sitting on a bench, reading a book by Nora Roberts. She looks up. Recognition dawns on her pretty face.

"Oh, hi," she says.

"Hi."

"Nice to see you again."

"Mind if I sit down?" I ask, wondering if I've expressed myself correctly.

She brightens. She understood me after all. "Not at all," she replies. She bookmarks her book, closes it, slips it into her bag. She smooths the hem of her dress. She is a very precise and proper young lady. Well mannered and raised.

"I promise I won't talk about the heat," I say.

She smiles, looked at me quizzically. "The what?"

"Heat?"

She smiles. The fact that the two of us are speaking another language draws the attention of people nearby.

I study her for a moment, sifting her features, her soft hair, her demeanor. She notices.

"What?" she asks.

"Has anyone ever told you that you look like a movie star?"

There is a momentary flicker of concern on her face, but when I smile at her the apprehension dissipates.

"A movie star? I don't think so."

"Oh, I don't mean a current movie star. I'm thinking of an older star."

She screws up her face.

"Oh, that's not what I meant!" I say, laughing. She laughs with me. "I didn't mean old. What I meant was, there is a certain . . . understated glamour about you that reminds me of a movie star from the forties. Jennifer Jones. Do you know Jennifer Jones?" I ask.

She shakes her head.

"That's okay," I say. "I'm sorry. I've embarrassed you."

"Not at all," she says. But I can tell that she is just being polite. She glances at her watch. "I'm afraid I have to get going."

She stands, looks at all the items she had to carry. She glances toward the Market Street subway station.

"I'm going that way," I say. "I'd be happy to give you a hand."

She scrutinizes me again. It seems at first she is going to decline, but when I smile again, she asks: "Are you sure it wouldn't be out of your way?"

"Not at all."

I pick up her two large shopping bags, and slip her canvas tote over my shoulder. "I'm an actor myself," I say.

She nods. "I'm not surprised."

When we reach the crosswalk, we stop. I place my hand on her forearm, just for a moment. Her skin is pale and smooth and soft.

"You know, you've gotten a lot better." When she signs, she makes her handshapes slowly, deliberately, just for my benefit.

I sign back: "I've had inspiration."

The girl blushes. She is an Angel.

From some angles, in certain lights, she looks just like her father.

AT JUST AFTER NOON A UNIFORMED OFFICER WALKED INTO THE
duty room of the Homicide Unit, a FedEx envelope in hand. Kevin Byrne
was at a desk, feet up, eyes closed. In his mind, he found himself at the
train yards of his youth, garbed in a strange hybrid costume of pearl-
handled six-guns, army helmet liner, and silver space suit. He smelled
the deep brine of the river, the lush redolence of axle grease. The smell
of safety. In this world there were no serial killers, no psychopaths who
would cut a man in half with a chain saw or bury a baby alive. The only
danger that lurked was your old man's belt if you showed up late for dinner.

"Detective Byrne?" the uniformed officer asked, shattering the
dream.

Byrne opened his eyes. "Yes?"

"This just came for you."

Byrne took the envelope, looked at the return address. It was from a
Center City law firm. He opened it. Inside was another envelope. Attached was a letter from the law firm explaining that the sealed envelope
was from the estate of Phillip Kessler, to be sent on the occasion of his

death. Byrne opened the inner envelope. As he read the letter, a whole new set of questions was asked, the answers to which were lying in the morgue.

"I don't fucking believe this," he said, drawing the attention of the handful of detectives in the room. Jessica walked over.

"What is it?" she asked.

Byrne read aloud the contents of the letter from Kessler's lawyer. No one knew what to make of it.

"Are you telling me that Phil Kessler was *paid* to get Julian Matisse out of prison?" Jessica asked.

"That's what the letter says. Phil wanted me to know it, but not until after his death."

"What are you talking about? Who paid him?" Palladino asked.

"The letter doesn't say. But what it does say is that Phil received ten grand to bring the charge against Jimmy Purify to get Julian Matisse out of prison pending his appeal."

Everyone in the room was appropriately stunned.

"You think it was Butler?" Jessica asked.

"Good question."

The good news was that Jimmy Purify could rest in peace. His name would be cleared. But now that Kessler and Matisse and Butler were all dead, it didn't seem likely that they would ever get to the bottom of this.

Eric Chavez, who had been on the phone the whole time, finally hung up. "For what it's worth, the lab figured out what movie that sixth lobby card is from."

"What's the movie?" Byrne asked.

"*Witness.* The Harrison Ford movie."

Byrne glanced at the television. Channel 6 now had a live shot of the corner of Thirtieth and Market streets. They were interviewing people about how exciting it was that Will Parrish was making a movie at the train station.

"My God," Byrne said.

"What?" Jessica asked.

"This isn't over."

"What do you mean?"

Byrne quickly scanned the letter from Phil Kessler's lawyer. "Think about it. Why would Butler take himself out before the big finale?"

"With all due respect to the dead," Palladino began, "who gives a shit? The psycho is dead and that's that."

"We don't know if that was Nigel Butler in the car."

It was true. Neither the DNA nor dental report was back yet. There had simply been no good reason to think it was anyone *other* than Butler in that car.

Byrne was on his feet. "Maybe that fire was just a diversion. Maybe he did it because he needed more time."

"So who was in the car?" Jessica asked.

"No idea," Byrne said. "But why would he send us that movie of the baby being buried if he didn't want us to find him in time? If he really wanted to punish Ian Whitestone that way, why not just let the baby die? Why not just leave his dead son on his doorstep?"

No one had a good answer to this.

"All the film murders were in bathrooms, right?" Byrne continued.

"Right. What about it?" Jessica asked.

"In *Witness,* the little Amish kid witnesses a murder," Byrne replied.

"I'm not following," Jessica said.

On the television monitor, Ian Whitestone was shown entering the train station. Byrne took out his weapon, checked the action. On the way to the door he said: "The victim in that movie has his throat cut in the bathroom of the Thirtieth Street station."

THE THIRTIETH STREET STATION WAS ON THE NATIONAL REG-
ister of Historic Places. The eight-story, concrete-framed structure was
built in 1934, and covered two full city blocks.

On this day, it was even more crowded than usual. More than three
hundred extras, in full makeup and costume, milled around the main
room, waiting for the sequence that would be shot in the North Waiting
Room. In addition, another seventy-five crew members were there, including sound recordists, lighting technicians, cameramen, gaffers, and
various production assistants.

Although the train schedules had not been interrupted, the production did have the main terminal for two hours. Passengers were being
routed along a narrow rope corridor along the south wall.

When the police arrived, the camera was on a large crane, blocking
out the intricate shot, tracking through the crowd of extras in the main
room, then through the huge archway into the North Waiting Room,
where it would find Will Parrish, standing beneath the large Karl Bitter
bas-relief *Spirit of Transportation*. Maddeningly, for the detectives, all the
extras were dressed the same. It was some sort of dream sequence that

had them wearing long red monks' robes and black face masks. When Jessica made her way to the North Waiting Room, she saw a stand-in for Will Parrish who wore a yellow rain slicker.

The detectives searched the men's and ladies' rooms, trying not to cause any undue alarm. They did not find Ian Whitestone. They did not find Nigel Butler.

Jessica called Terry Cahill on his cell phone, hoping he might be able to run interference with the production company. She got his voice mail.

BYRNE AND JESSICA stood in the center of the enormous main room of the train station, near the information booth, in the shadow of the bronze angel sculpture.

"What the hell do we do?" Jessica asked, knowing the question was rhetorical. Byrne deferred to her judgment. From the moment they first met, he had treated her as an equal, and now that she was heading this task force, he did not pull the rank of experience. It was her call, and the look in his eyes said that he was behind her decision, whatever it may be.

There was only one choice. She might catch hell from the mayor, from the Department of Transportation, from Amtrak, SEPTA, and everyone else, but she had to do it. She spoke into her two-way radio. "Shut it down," she said. "No one in or out."

Before they could make a move, Byrne's cell phone rang. It was Nick Palladino.

"What's up, Nick?"

"We heard from the ME's office. We've got dental on the body in the burning car."

"What do we have?" Byrne asked.

"Well, the dental records didn't match Nigel Butler's," Palladino said. "So Eric and I took a chance and rode up to Bala Cynwyd."

Byrne took this in, one domino striking the next. "Are you saying what I think you're saying?"

"Yeah," Palladino said. "The body in the car was Adam Kaslov."

THE ASSISTANT DIRECTOR of the film was a woman named Joanna Young. Jessica found her near the food court, a cell phone in her hand, another cell phone to her ear, a crackling two-way clipped to her belt, and a long line of anxious people waiting to speak with her. She was not a happy camper.

"What is this all about?" Young demanded.

"I'm not at liberty to discuss it at this time," Jessica said. "But we really need to speak with Mr. Whitestone."

"I'm afraid he left the set."

"When?"

"He walked out about ten minutes ago."

"Alone?"

"He left with one of the extras, and I really wish—"

"Which door?" Jessica asked.

"The Twenty-ninth Street entrance."

"And you haven't seen him since?"

"No," she said. "But I hope he gets back soon. We're losing about a thousand dollars a minute here."

Byrne came over the two-way. "Jess?"

"Yes?"

"I think you should see this."

THE BIGGER OF the two men's rooms at the train station was a warren of large white-tiled rooms off the North Waiting Room. The sinks were in one room, the toilet stalls in another—a long row of stainless-steel doors with stalls on either side. What Byrne wanted Jessica to see was in the last stall on the left, inside the door. Scrawled at the bottom of the door was a series of numbers, separated by decimal points. And it looked to be written in blood.

"Did we get pictures of it?" Jessica asked.

"Yeah," Byrne said.

Jessica snapped on a glove. The blood was still tacky. "This is recent."

"CSU already has a sample on the way to the lab."

"What are these numbers?" Byrne asked.

"It looks like an IP address," Jessica answered.

"An IP address?" Byrne asked. "As in—"

"A website," Jessica said. "He wants us to go to a website."

8 0

IN ANY FILM OF MERIT, ANY FILM MADE WITH PRIDE, THERE IS a moment, always in the third act, when the hero must act. In this moment, not long before the climax of the film, the story takes a turn.

I open the door, light the set. All but one of my actors is in place. I position the camera. Light floods Angelika's face. She looks just like she used to. Young. Untouched by time.

Beautiful.

THE SCREEN WAS BLACK, BLANK, CHILLINGLY VOID OF CONTENT.

"Are you sure we're on the right website?" Byrne asked.

Mateo retyped the IP address into the address line of the web browser. The screen refreshed. Still black. "Nothing yet."

Byrne and Jessica walked from the editing bay into the studio room at the AV Unit. In the 1980s, the large, high-ceilinged room in the basement of the Roundhouse was home to the taping of a local-access show called *Police Perspectives*. The ceiling still held a number of large spotlights.

The lab had rushed preliminary tests on the blood found at the train station. They had typed it A negative. A call to Ian Whitestone's physician confirmed that A negative was Whitestone's type. Although it was unlikely that Whitestone had suffered the same fate as the victim in *Witness*—had his jugular been cut, there would have been pools of blood—that he was injured was almost a certainty.

"*Detectives*," Mateo said.

Byrne and Jessica ran back into the editing bay. The screen now had three words on it. A title. White letters centered on black. Somehow, the image was even more unsettling than the blank screen. The screen read:

THE SKIN GODS

"What does it mean?" Jessica asked.

"I don't know," Mateo said. He turned to his laptop. He typed the words into the Google text box. Only a few hits. Nothing promising or revealing. Again, at imdb.com. Nothing.

"Do we know where it's coming from?" Byrne asked.

"Working on it."

Mateo got on the phone, trying to track down the ISP, the Internet service provider to which the website was registered.

Suddenly the image changed. Now they were looking at a blank wall. White plaster. Brightly lit. The floor was dusty, made of hardwood planks. There was no clue within the frame as to where this might be. There was no sound.

The camera then panned slightly to the right to reveal a young girl in a yellow teddy. She wore a hood. She was slight, pale, delicate. She stood close to the wall, not moving. Her posture spoke of fear. It was impossible to tell her age, but she appeared to be a young teenager.

"What is this?" Byrne asked.

"It looks like a live webcam shot," Mateo said. "Not a high-resolution camera, though."

A man walked onto the set, approaching the girl. He wore the costume of one of the extras of *The Palace*—a red monk's robe and a full-face mask. He handed the girl something. It looked shiny, metallic. The girl held it for a few moments. The light was harsh, saturating the figures, bathing them in an eerie silver glow, so it was hard to see exactly what she was doing. She handed the item back to the man.

Within a few seconds, Kevin Byrne's cell phone beeped. Everyone looked at him. It was the sound his phone made when he received a text message, not a phone call. His heart began to slam in his chest. Hands trembling, he took out his phone, navigated to the text message screen. Before he read it, he looked up, at the laptop. The man on the screen pulled the hood off the young girl.

"Oh my God," Jessica said.

Byrne looked at his phone. Everything he had ever feared in life was contained in those five letters:

CBOAO.

SHE HAD KNOWN SILENCE ALL HER LIFE. THE NOTION, THE VERY concept of sound, was an abstract to her, but one she imagined fully. Sound was color.

To a lot of deaf people, silence was black.

To her, silence was white. An endless sheet of cloud white, rippling toward infinity. Sound, as she imagined it, was a beautiful rainbow against a pure white background.

When she first saw him, at the bus stop near Rittenhouse Square, she had thought he was pleasant looking, a little goofy, perhaps. He was reading from the *Handshape Dictionary,* trying to form the alphabet. She had wondered why he was trying to learn ASL—he either had a deaf relative or was trying to romance a deaf girl—but she hadn't asked.

When she had seen him again at Logan Circle, he had been helpful, carrying her packages toward the SEPTA station.

And then he had pushed her into the trunk of his car.

What this man had not counted on was her discipline. Without discipline, those who work with fewer than five senses would go mad. She knew that. All her deaf friends knew that. It was discipline that helped her overcome her fear of rejection from the hearing world. It was discipline that helped her live up to the high expectations her parents had for her. It was discipline that would get her through this. If this man thought she had never experienced anything as frightening as his strange and ugly game, he clearly didn't know any deaf girls.

Her father would be coming for her. He had never let her down. Ever.

So she waited. In discipline. In hope.

In silence.

THE BROADCAST WAS COMING FROM A CELL PHONE DATA TRANS-fer. Mateo brought a laptop up to the duty room, jacked into the Internet. He believed the setup was a web camera linked to a laptop, then routed out through a cell phone. It made it much harder to trace, because—unlike a landline, which was tied to a permanent address—the cell phone signal needed to be triangulated between cell phone towers.

Within minutes a request for a court order to trace the cell phone was faxed to the district attorney's office. Ordinarily, something like this would take hours. Not today. Paul DiCarlo personally ran it from his office at 1421 Arch Street to the top floor of the Criminal Justice Center, where Judge Liam McManus signed it. Ten minutes after that the Homicide Unit was on the phone with the cell phone company's security division.

Detective Tony Park was the go-to man in the unit when it came to things digital, things cellular. One of the few Korean American detectives on the force, a family man in his late forties, Tony Park was a calming influence on all those around him. Today that aspect of his personality, as much as his electronic expertise, was crucial. The unit was about to blow.

Park spoke on a landline and conveyed the progress of the trace to the roomful of anxious detectives. "They're running it through a tracing matrix now," Park said.

"Have they got a lock yet?" Jessica asked.

"Not yet."

Byrne paced the room like a caged animal. A dozen detectives lingered in or near the duty room, waiting for the word, waiting for a direction. There was no comforting or appeasing Byrne. All these men and women had families. It could just as easily be them.

"We have movement," Mateo said, pointing to the laptop screen. The detectives crowded around him.

On screen, the man in the monk's robe dragged another person into the frame. It was Ian Whitestone. He was wearing the blue jacket. He looked drugged. His head lolled on his shoulders. There was no visible blood on his face or hands.

Whitestone fell against the wall next to Colleen. The tableau was sickening in the harsh white light. Jessica wondered who else might be watching this, if this madman had disseminated the web address to the media, to the Internet at large.

The figure in the monk's robe then walked toward the camera and turned the lens. The image was choppy, grained by the lack of resolution and quick movement. When the image settled, it was on a double bed, surrounded by two cheap nightstands and table lamps.

"It's the movie," Byrne said, his voice cracking. "He's re-creating the movie."

With sickening clarity, Jessica recognized the setup. It was a re-creation of the motel room in *Philadelphia Skin*. The Actor was going to reshoot *Philadelphia Skin* with Colleen Byrne in the role of Angelika Butler.

They had to find him.

"They've got the tower," Park said. "It covers part of North Philly."

"Where in North Philly?" Byrne asked. He was in the doorway, nearly vibrating with anticipation. He slammed his fist three times into the doorjamb. *"Where?"*

"They're working on it," Park said. He pointed to a map on one of the monitors. "It's down to these two square blocks. Get on the street. I'll guide you."

Byrne was gone before he had finished the sentence.

IN ALL HER YEARS, SHE HAD ONLY WISHED ONCE THAT SHE COULD hear. Just once. And it hadn't been so long ago. Two of her hearing friends had gotten tickets to see John Mayer. John Mayer was to die. Her hearing friend Lula had played John Mayer's album *Heavier Things* for her, and she had touched the speakers, felt the bass and vocals. She knew his music. She knew it in her heart.

She wished she could hear now. There were two people in the room with her, and if she could hear them, she might be able to figure a way out of this.

If she could hear . . .

Her father had explained to her many times what he did. She knew that what he did was dangerous, and the people he arrested were the worst people in the world.

She stood with her back to the wall. The man had taken off her hood, and that was a good thing. She was terrifyingly claustrophobic. But now the light in her eyes was blinding. If she couldn't see, she couldn't fight.

And she was ready to fight.

THE AREA OF GERMANTOWN AVENUE NEAR INDIANA WAS A proud but long-struggling community of row houses and brick store-fronts, deep in the Badlands, a five-square-mile section of North Phila-delphia that ran from Erie Avenue south to Spring Garden; Ridge Avenue to Front Street.

At least a quarter of the buildings on the block were retail space, some occupied, most not; a clenched fist of three-story structures brac-ing each other, cavities between. The task of searching them all was going to be daunting, almost impossible. Generally, when the department chased a cell phone trace, they had some earlier intelligence with which to work: a suspect with a tie to the area, a known associate, a possible address. This time they had nothing. They had already run every check imaginable on Nigel Butler—previous addresses, rental properties he might have owned, addresses of family members. Nothing linked him to this area. They would have to search every square inch of this block, and search it blindly.

As crucial as the element of time was, they were walking a thin line, constitutionally speaking. Although there was enough leeway for them to storm a house if probable cause existed that someone was being harmed on the premises, that PC better be open and obvious.

By one o'clock, nearly twenty detectives and uniformed officers had descended on this enclave. They moved like a wall of blue through the neighborhood, holding up a photograph of Colleen Byrne, asking the same questions over and over. But this time, for the detectives, it was different. This time, they had to read the person on the other side of the threshold in an instant—kidnapper, killer, maniac, innocent.

This time, it was one of their own.

Byrne held back, behind Jessica, as she rang the doorbells, knocked on the doors. Each time, he would scan the face of the citizen, plugging in his radar, every sense on high alert. In his ear was an earpiece patched directly to an open phone line to both Tony Park and Mateo Fuentes. Jessica had tried to talk him out of the live updates, but she had failed.

Byrne's heart was ablaze. If anything happened to Colleen, he would take out the son of a bitch—one shot, point blank—and then himself. There would not be a single reason to draw a single breath afterward. She was his life.

"What's going on now?" Byrne asked into the headset, into his three-way connection.

"Static shot," Mateo replied. "Just the . . . just Colleen against the wall. No change."

Byrne paced. Another row house. Another possible scene. Jessica rang the doorbell.

Was this the place? Byrne wondered. He ran his hand along the grimy window, felt nothing. He stepped back.

A woman opened the door. She was a stout black woman in her late forties, holding a baby, probably her granddaughter. She had gray hair pulled back into a tight bun. "What's this about?"

Walls up, attitude out front. To her, it was another invasion by the police. She glanced over Jessica's shoulder, tried to hold Byrne's gaze, backed off.

"Have you seen this girl, ma'am?" Jessica asked. She held up the picture with one hand, her badge with the other.

The woman didn't look at the photograph right away, choosing instead to exercise her right not to cooperate.

Byrne didn't wait for an answer. He bulled his way past her, looked around the living room, ran down the narrow steps to the basement. He found a dusty Nautilus machine, a pair of broken appliances. He did not find his daughter. He charged his way back up and out the front door. Before Jessica could utter a word of apology—including the hope that there would not be a lawsuit—he was banging on the door to the next row house.

THEY SPLIT UP. Jessica would take the next few row houses. Byrne jumped ahead, around the corner.

The next residence was a shambling three-story row house with a blue door. The nameplate next to the door read V. TALMAN. Jessica knocked. No answer. Again, no answer. She was just about to move on when the door inched open. An elderly white woman opened the door. She wore a fuzzy gray robe and Velcro-strap tennis shoes. "Help you?" the woman asked.

Jessica showed her the picture. "I'm sorry to bother you, ma'am. Have you seen this girl?"

The woman lifted her glasses, focused. "Pretty."

"Have you seen her recently, ma'am?"

She refocused. "No."

"Do you live—"

"Van!" she shouted. She cocked her head, listened. Again. "Van!" Nothing. "Musta gone out. Sorry."

"Thanks for your time."

The woman closed the door as Jessica stepped over the rail onto the stoop of the adjoining row house. Beyond that house was a boarded-up retail space. She knocked, rang the bell. Nothing. She put her ear to the door. Silence.

Jessica walked down the steps, back across the sidewalk, and almost ran into someone. Instinct told her to draw her weapon. Luckily, she did not.

It was Mark Underwood. He was in plainclothes—dark PPD T-shirt, blue jeans, running shoes. "I heard the call go out," he said. "Don't worry. We'll find her."

"Thanks," she said.

"What have you cleared?"

"Right up through this house," Jessica said, although the word *cleared* was less than accurate. They had not been inside and checked every room.

Underwood looked up and down the street. "Let me get some warm bodies down here."

He reached out. Jessica gave him her rover. While Underwood made the request of base, Jessica stepped up to the door, put her ear against it. Nothing. She tried to imagine the horror for Colleen Byrne in her world of silence.

Underwood handed the rover back, said: "They'll be down here in a minute. We'll take the next block."

"I'll catch up with Kevin."

"Just tell him to be cool," Underwood said. "We'll find her."

KEVIN BYRNE STOOD IN FRONT OF THE BOARDED-UP RETAIL space. He was alone. The storefront looked as if it had housed a variety of enterprises over the years. The windows were painted black. There was no sign over the front door, but there were years of names and sentiments carved into the wood-framed entrance.

A narrow alleyway cut between the store and the row house to its right. Byrne drew his weapon, walked down the alley. There was a barred window halfway down. He listened at the window. Silence. He continued forward, emerging into a small courtyard at the back, a courtyard bounded on the three sides by a high wooden fence.

The back door was not covered in plywood, nor padlocked from the outside. There was a rusted dead bolt. Byrne pushed on the door. Locked tight.

Byrne knew he had to focus. Many times in his career, someone's life had hung in the balance, someone's very existence riding on his judgment. Each and every time he had felt the enormity of the responsibility, the weight of his duty.

But it was never like this. It wasn't supposed to *be* like this. In fact, he was surprised that Ike Buchanan hadn't called him in. If he had, though, Byrne would have thrown his badge on the desk and gotten right back out on the street.

Byrne took off his tie, undid the top button of his shirt. The heat in the confines of the courtyard was stifling. Sweat laced his neck and shoulders.

He bulled open the door with his shoulder, entered, weapon held high. Colleen was close. He knew it. *Felt* it. He pitched his head to the sounds of the old building. Water clanging through rusted pipes. The creak of long-dried joists.

He stepped into the small entrance room. Ahead was a door, closed. To the right was a wall of dusty shelves.

He touched the door and the images slammed into his mind . . .

. . . *Colleen against the wall . . . the man in the red monk's robe . . . help, Dad, oh help hurry, Dad, help—*

She was here. In this building. He had found her.

Byrne knew he should call for backup, but he did not know what he would do when he found the Actor. If the Actor was in one of these rooms, and he had to draw down on him, he would pull the trigger. No hesitation. If it was not a clean shoot, he didn't want to put his fellow detectives on the line. He would not draw Jessica into this. He would handle this alone.

He pulled the earpiece from his ear, turned off the phone, and stepped through the door.

JESSICA STOOD OUTSIDE THE STORE. SHE LOOKED UP AND DOWN the street. She had never seen so many police officers on one detail. There had to be twenty sector cars. Then there were the unmarked vehicles, the tech vans, and the ever-growing crowd. Men and women in uniforms, men and women in suits, their badges glinting in the gold sunlight. To many of the people in the crowd, this was just another siege of their world by the police. If they only knew. What if it was their son or daughter?

Byrne was nowhere in sight. Had they cleared this address? There was a narrow alleyway between the store and the row house. She walked down the alley, stopping for a moment to listen at a barred window. She heard nothing. She continued on until she arrived in a small courtyard behind the shop. The back door was slightly open.

Had he entered without telling her? It certainly was possible. She thought for a moment about getting backup to enter the building with her, then thought better of it.

Kevin Byrne was her partner. It may have been a department operation, but it was his show. It was his daughter.

She made her way back to the street, looked both ways. Detectives and uniformed officers and FBI agents were at either end. She walked back down the alley, drew her weapon, and stepped through the door.

He moved through a lair of small rooms. What had once been an interior space designed for retail commerce had many years ago been remodeled into a maze of nooks and alcoves and cubbyholes.

Designed just for this purpose? Byrne wondered.

Down the narrow confines of a tight hallway, gun waist-high. He felt a larger space open before him, the temperature dropping a degree or two.

The main room of the retail space was dark, crowded with broken furniture, retail fixtures, a pair of dusty air compressors. There was no light streaming through the windows. They were painted with thick black enamel. As Byrne ran his Maglite around the large space he saw that the once brightly colored boxes that were stacked in the corners held a decade of mildew. The air—what air there was—was fat with a stagnant, bitter heat that clung to the walls, to his clothes, his skin. The smell of mold and mice and sugar was dense.

Byrne clicked off his flashlight, tried to adjust to the dim light. To his right were a series of glass retail counters. He could see brightly colored paper inside.

Shiny red paper. He had seen it before.
He closed his eyes, touched the wall.

There had been happiness here. The laughter of children. All of that stopped years earlier when an ugliness entered, a morbid soul that devoured the joy.

He opened his eyes.

Ahead was another hallway, another door, its jamb chipped and splintered years earlier. Byrne looked more closely. Fresh wood. Someone had recently brought something large through the doorway, damaging the jamb. Lighting equipment? he thought.

He put his ear to the door, listened. Silence. This was the room. He felt it. He felt it in a place that did not know his heart or his mind. He slowly pushed open the door.

And saw his daughter. She was tied to a bed.

His heart shattered into a million pieces.

My sweet little girl, what have I done to you?

Then: Movement. *Fast.* A flash of red before him. The sound of fabric snapping in the still, hot air. Then the sound was gone.

Before he could react, before he could bring his weapon up, he felt a presence to his left.

Then the back of his head exploded.

9 0

With dark-adapted eyes, Jessica edged her way down the long hallway, moving deeper into the center of the building. Soon she came upon a makeshift control room. There were two VHS editing decks, their green and red lights glowing cataracts in the gloom. This was where the Actor had dubbed the tapes. There was also a television. On it was the website image she had seen at the Roundhouse. The light was dim. There was no sound.

Suddenly, on screen, there was movement. She saw the monk in the red robe move across the frame. Shadows on the wall. The camera lurched to the right. Colleen was strapped to the bed in the background. More shadows, darting and scurrying over the walls.

Then a figure approached the camera. Too quickly. Jessica couldn't see who it was. In a second the screen went to static, then to blue.

Jessica tore the rover from her belt. Radio silence no longer mattered. She turned up the volume, keyed it, listened. Silence. She banged the rover against her palm. Listened. Nothing.

The rover was dead.

Son of a bitch.

She wanted to fling it against the wall, but thought better of it. There would be plenty of time for rage very soon.

She flattened her back against the wall. She felt the rumble of a truck pass by. She was on an outside wall. She was six to eight inches away from daylight. She was miles from safety.

She followed the cables coming out of the back of the monitor. They snaked up to the ceiling, down the hallway to her left.

Of all the uncertainties of the next few minutes, of all the unknowns lurking in the darkness around her, one thing was clear. For the foreseeable future, she was on her own.

HE WAS DRESSED LIKE ONE OF THE EXTRAS THEY HAD SEEN at the train station—red monk's robe, black mask.

The monk had struck him from behind, taken his service Glock. Byrne had fallen to his knees, dizzied but not out. He closed his eyes, waiting for the thunder of the gunshot, the white infinity of his death. But it didn't come. Not yet.

Byrne now knelt in the center of the room, his hands behind his head, his fingers interlaced. He faced the camera on the tripod in front of him. Colleen was behind him. He wanted to turn around, to see her face, to tell her it was going to be all right. He couldn't risk it.

When the man in the monk's robe touched him, Byrne's mind reeled with the images. The visions pulsed. He felt queasy, light-headed.

Colleen.
Angelika.
Stephanie.
Erin.
A field of torn flesh. An ocean of blood.

"You didn't take care of her," the man said.

Was he talking about Angelika? Colleen?

"She was a great actress," he continued. He was behind him now. Byrne tried to calculate his position. "She would have been a star. And I don't mean *just* a star. I mean one of those rare supernova stars who captures the attention of not only the public, but also the critics. Ingrid Bergman. Jeanne Moreau. Greta Garbo."

Byrne tried to trace his steps into the bowels of this building. How many turns had he taken? How close was he to the street?

"When she died, they just moved on," he continued. "*You* just moved on."

Byrne tried to organize his thoughts. Never easy when there may be a gun pointed at you. "You . . . have to understand," he began. "When the medical examiner rules a death accidental, there's nothing the Homicide Unit can do about it. There's nothing *anyone* can do about it. The ME rules, the city records it. That's how it's done."

"Do you know why she spelled her name that way? With a *k*? Her given name was spelled with a *c*. She changed it."

He wasn't listening to a word Byrne was saying. "No."

"*Angelika* is the name of a famous art house theater in New York."

"Let my daughter go," Byrne said. "You have me."

"I don't think you understand the play."

The man in the monk's robe walked around in front of Byrne. In his hand was a leather mask. It was the same mask worn by Julian Matisse in *Philadelphia Skin*. "Do you know Stanislavksy, Detective Byrne?"

Byrne knew he had to keep the man talking. "No."

"He was a Russian actor and teacher. He founded the Moscow Theater in 1898. He more or less invented method acting."

"You don't have to do this," Byrne said. "Let my daughter go. We can end this without any more bloodshed."

The monk put Byrne's Glock under his arm for a moment. He began to unlace the leather mask. "Stanislavsky once said: 'Never come into the theatre with mud on your feet. Leave your dust and dirt outside. Check your little worries, squabbles, petty difficulties with your outside clothing—all the things that ruin your life and draw your attention away from your art—at the door.'

"Please put your hands behind your back for me," he added.

Byrne complied. His legs were crossed behind him. He felt the weight on his right ankle. He began to lift the cuff of his pants.

"Have you left your petty difficulties at the door, Detective? Are you ready for my play?"

Byrne lifted the hem another inch. His fingers touched the steel as the monk dropped the mask onto the floor in front of him.

"In a moment, I will ask you to put on this mask," the monk said. "And then we will begin."

Byrne knew he could not take the chance of a shootout in here, not with Colleen in the room. She was behind him, strapped to the bed. Crossfire would be deadly.

"The curtain is up." The monk stepped to the wall, flipped a switch.

A single bright spotlight filled the universe.

It was time. He had no choice.

In one smooth motion Byrne drew the SIG-Sauer from his ankle holster, leapt to his feet, turned toward the light, and fired.

THE GUNSHOTS WERE CLOSE, BUT JESSICA COULDN'T TELL WHERE they came from. Was it this building? Next door? Upstairs? Had the detectives outside heard it?

She spun around in the darkness, Glock leveled. She could no longer see the door through which she had entered. It was too dark. She had lost her bearings. She had traversed a series of small rooms, and she had forgotten how to get back.

Jessica sidled up to a narrow archway. A musty curtain hung over the opening. She peered through. Ahead, another dark room. She stepped through the opening, her weapon out front, her Maglite over the top. To the right, a small Pullman kitchen. It smelled of old grease. She ran her Maglite along the floor, the walls, the sink. The kitchen had not been used in years.

Not for cooking, that is.

There was blood on the side of the refrigerator, a wide fresh swath of scarlet. The blood streaked toward the floor in thin rivulets. Blood splatter from a gunshot.

Beyond the kitchen was yet another room. From where Jessica stood it looked like an old stockroom, lined with broken shelves. She continued forward, and nearly tripped over the body. She knelt down. It was a man. The right side of his head had been almost taken off.

She shone her Maglite on the figure. The man's face was destroyed, a wet mass of tissue and shredded bone. Brain matter slithered onto the dusty floor. The man was wearing jeans and running shoes. She moved her Maglite up the body.

And saw the PPD logo on the dark blue T-shirt.

Bile rose in her throat, thick and sour. Her heart kicked hard in her chest, rattling her arms, her hands. She tried to calm herself as the horrors piled up. She had to get out of this building. She had to breathe. But she had to find Kevin first.

She raised her weapon out front rolled to her left, her heart hammering in her chest. The air was so thick it felt like liquid entering her lungs. Sweat poured down her face, salting her eyes. She wiped at them with the back of one hand.

She summoned her courage, slowly glanced around the corner, down the wide hallway. Too many shadows, too many places to hide. The grip of her weapon now felt slick in her hand. She changed hands, wiped her palm on her jeans.

She glanced back over her shoulder. The far door led to the hallway, the stairs, the street, safety. Ahead of her lay the unknown. She stepped forward, slid into an alcove. Eyes scanning the interior horizon. More shelves, more cases, more display counters. No movement, no sound. Just the clock-hum of silence.

Staying low, she moved down the hall. At the far end was a door, perhaps leading to what was once a stockroom or employee lounge. She edged forward. The doorjamb was battered, chipped. She slowly turned the knob. Unlocked. She threw open the door, scanned the room. The scene was surreal, sickening:

A big room, twenty by twenty . . . impossible to clear from the entrance . . . bed to the right . . . a single overhead bulb . . . Colleen Byrne tied to the four posts . . . Kevin Byrne standing in the middle of the room . . . kneeling in front of Byrne is the monk in the red robe . . . Byrne has a gun to the man's head . . .

Jessica glanced into the corner. The camera was smashed to bits. No one back at the Roundhouse, or anywhere else, was watching this.

She reached deep inside herself, to a place unknown to her, and stepped fully into the room. She knew that this moment, this brutal aria, would score the rest of her life.

"Hey, partner," Jessica said, softly. There were two doors to the left. To the right, a huge window, painted black. She was so disoriented that she had no idea onto what street the window faced. She had to turn her back on those doors. It was dangerous, but there was no choice.

"Hey," Byrne replied. He sounded calm. His eyes were cold emerald stones in his face. The monk in the red robe was motionless, kneeling in front of him. Byrne had the barrel of a weapon to the base of the man's skull. Byrne's hand was firm and steady. Jessica she could see that it was a SIG-Sauer semi-auto. It was not Byrne's service weapon.

Don't Kevin.

Don't.

"You okay?" Jessica asked.

"Yes."

His answer was too fast, too clipped. He was operating on some untamed energy, not reason. Jessica was about ten feet away. She needed to close the distance. He needed to see her face. He needed to see her *eyes*. "So, what are we going to do?" Jessica tried to sound as conversational as possible. Nonjudgmental. For a moment, she wondered if he had heard her. He had.

"I'm going to put an end to all this," Byrne said. "This all has to stop."

Jessica nodded. She pointed her gun at the floor. But she didn't holster it. She knew the move was not lost on Kevin Byrne. "I agree. It's over, Kevin. We've got him." She took a step closer. Eight feet away, now. "Good work."

"I mean all of it. It all has to *stop*."

"Okay. Let me help."

Byrne shook his head. He knew she was trying to work him. "Walk away, Jess. Just turn around, go back through that door, and tell them you couldn't find me."

"I won't do that."

"Walk away."

"No. You are my partner. Would you do that to me?"

She had come close with that, but she hadn't reached him. Byrne didn't look up, didn't take his eyes of the monk's head. "You don't understand."

"Oh, I do. I swear to God, I do." Seven feet. "You can't—" she began. Wrong word. *Wrong word.* "You . . . *don't* want to go out like this."

Byrne finally looked at her. She had never seen a man so committed to an action. His jaw was set, his brow narrowed. "It doesn't matter."

"Yes it does. Of *course* it does."

"I've seen more than you have, Jess. A lot more."

She took another step closer. "I've seen my share."

"I know. It's just that you still have a chance. You can get out before it takes you down. Walk away."

One more step. She was five feet away now. "Just hear me out. Hear me out, and if you still want me to walk, I will. Okay?"

Byrne's eyes shifted toward her, back. "Okay."

"You put the gun away, no one has to know," she said. "Me? Hell, I didn't see a thing. In fact, when I walked in the room here, you were putting him in cuffs." She reached behind her, dangled a pair of cuffs on an index finger. Byrne didn't respond. She tossed the cuffs onto the floor at his feet. "Let's bring him in."

"No." The figure in the monk's robe began to shake.

Here it comes. You've lost him.

She reached. "Your daughter loves you, Kevin."

A flicker. She'd gotten to him. She stepped closer. Three feet, now. "I was there with her every day when you were in the hospital," she said. "Every day. You are loved. Don't throw it away."

Byrne hesitated, wiping the sweat from his eyes. "I . . ."

"Your daughter's *watching.*" Outside, Jessica heard sirens, the roar of big engines, the screech of tires. It was the SWAT team. They'd heard the gunfire after all. "SWAT's here, partner. You know what that means. Ponderosa time."

Another step forward. Arm's length. She heard footsteps approach the building. She was losing him. It was going to be too late.

"Kevin. You have something to do."

Byrne's face was laced with sweat. It looked like tears. "What? What do I have to do?"

"You have a picture to take. At the Eden Roc."

Byrne half-smiled, and there was a world of heartache in it.

Jessica glanced at his weapon. Something was wrong. There was no magazine. *It wasn't loaded.*

She then saw movement in the corner of the room. She looked at Colleen. Her eyes. Terrified. Angelika's eyes. Eyes that were trying to tell her something.

But what?

Then she looked at the girl's hands.

And *knew* as—

—time jogged, slowed, crawled, as—

Jessica spun, weapon raised, two hands. Another monk in a blood-red robe was nearly upon her, his steel weapon high, pointed at her face. She heard the click of the hammer. Saw the turn of the cylinder.

No time to bargain. No time to deal. Just the shiny black mask in that tornado of red silk.

I haven't seen a friendly face in weeks . . .

Detective Jessica Balzano fired.

And fired.

93

THERE IS A MOMENT, AFTER THE TAKING OF A LIFE, A TIME WHEN the human soul weeps, when the heart takes harsh inventory.

The smell of cordite hung thick in the air.

The coppery scent of fresh blood filled the world.

Jessica looked at Byrne. They would be forever linked by this moment, by the events that had occurred in this dank and ugly place.

Jessica found that she was still holding her weapon out, a two-handed death grip. Smoke seeped from the barrel. She felt the tears dam up behind her eyes. She fought them, lost. Time passed. Minutes? Seconds?

Kevin Byrne gently took her hands in his, and eased the gun out.

BYRNE KNEW THAT JESSICA HAD SAVED HIM. HE WOULD NEVER forget. He would never be able to pay her in full.

No one has to know . . .

Byrne had held his gun to the back of Ian Whitestone's head, mistakenly believing he was the Actor. When he had shot the lights out, there had been noises in the darkness. Crashes. Stumbling. Byrne had been disoriented. He couldn't risk firing again. When he lashed out with the butt of the pistol he had connected with flesh and bone. When he turned the overhead light on, the monk was on the floor in the center of the room.

The images he had gotten were from Whitestone's own blackened life—what he had done to Angelika Butler, what he had done to all the women on the tapes they had found in Seth Goldman's hotel room. Whitestone had been bound and gagged beneath his mask and robe. He had tried to tell Byrne who he was. Byrne's gun had been empty, but a full magazine was in his pocket. If Jessica had not come through that door . . .

He would never know.

At that moment a battering ram crashed through the painted picture window. Dazzlingly bright daylight flooded the room. Within seconds a dozen very nervous detectives spilled in after, weapons drawn, adrenaline raging.

"Clear!" Jessica yelled, holding her badge high. "We're *clear!*"

Eric Chavez and Nick Palladino stormed through the opening, got between Jessica and the mass of divisional detectives and FBI agents who looked a little too eager to cowboy up this detail. The two men held up their hands, stood protectively on either side of Byrne and Jessica and the now prostrate, sobbing Ian Whitestone.

The blue womb. They were sheltered. No harm could come to them now.

It really was over.

TEN MINUTES LATER, as the machine that was a crime scene investigation began to rev up around them, as the yellow tape unspooled and the CSU officers began their solemn ritual, Byrne caught Jessica's eye, the one question he needed to ask on his lips. They huddled in a corner, at the foot of the bed. "How did you know Butler was behind you?"

Jessica glanced around the room. Now, in the bright sunlight, it was obvious. The interior was covered in a silken dust, the walls patchworked with cheaply framed photographs of a long-faded past. Half a dozen padded stools lay on their sides. And then there were the signs. WATER ICE. FOUNTAIN DRINKS. ICE CREAM. CANDY.

"It isn't Butler," Jessica said.

The seed had been planted in her mind when she read the report of the break-in at Edwina Matisse's house, when she had seen the name of the responding officers. She hadn't wanted to believe it. She had all but known the moment she had talked to the old woman next to the former candy store. Mrs. V. Talman.

Van! the old woman had yelled. It wasn't her husband she was yelling for. It was her grandson.

Van. Short for Vandemark.

I came close once.

He had taken the battery from her two-way radio. The dead body in the other room was Nigel Butler.

Jessica walked over, peeled back the mask on the dead man in the monk's robe. Although they would wait for the ME's ruling, there was no doubt in Jessica's mind, or anyone else's for that matter.

Officer Mark Underwood was dead.

BYRNE HELD HIS DAUGHTER. SOMEONE HAD MERCIFULLY CUT the rope from her hands and feet and put a suit coat over her shoulders. She shivered in his arms. Byrne thought of the time she had defied him when they had gone to Atlantic City one unseasonably warm April. She had been about six or seven. He had told her that, just because the air temperature was seventy-five, it didn't mean the water was warm. She had run into the ocean anyway.

When she'd come out, just a few minutes later, she had been a pastel blue. She had quivered and quaked in his embrace for almost an hour, teeth chattering, signing *I'm sorry, Dad,* over and over again. He had held her then. He vowed to never stop.

Jessica knelt down next to them.

Colleen and Jessica had become close after Byrne had been shot that spring. They had spent many an afternoon waiting out his coma. Colleen had taught Jessica a number of handshapes, including the basic alphabet.

Byrne looked between them, and sensed their secret.

Jessica raised her hands, spelled the words in three clumsy hand-shapes:

He's behind you.

With tears in his eyes, Byrne thought about Gracie Devlin. He thought about her life force. He thought about her breath still inside him. He glanced at the body of the man who had brought this latest evil to his city. He glimpsed his own future.

Kevin Byrne knew he was ready.

He exhaled.

He drew his daughter even closer. And it was in this way they comforted each other, and would for a long time to come.

In silence.

Like the language of film.

THE STORY OF IAN WHITESTONE'S LIFE AND DOWNFALL WAS THE stuff of movies, and at least two of them were in the preproduction stages even before the story hit the papers. In the meantime, the report of his having been involved in the porn industry—and perhaps involved in the death, accidental or otherwise, of a young porno starlet—was dripping red meat for the tabloid wolf packs. The story was surely being readied for publication and broadcast all around the world. How it would affect the box office of his next picture, along with his personal and professional life, was yet to be seen.

But that might not be the worst of it for the man. The district attorney's office was looking into opening a criminal investigation into exactly what had caused the death of Angelika Butler three years earlier, and what role in her death Ian Whitestone might have played.

MARK UNDERWOOD HAD been seeing Angelika Butler for almost a year when she had drifted into the life. The photo albums found at Nigel Butler's house depicted a number of photographs of the two of them at family functions. When Underwood had kidnapped Nigel Butler, he had defaced the photos in the albums, as well as gluing all those photographs of movie stars onto Angelika's body.

They would never know exactly what drove Underwood to do what he did, but it was clear that he knew from the start who was involved in the making of *Philadelphia Skin,* and whom he held responsible for Angelika's death.

It was also clear that he blamed Nigel Butler for what *he* had done to Angelika.

There was a good chance that Underwood had been stalking Julian Matisse the night Matisse killed Gracie Devlin. *I secured a crime scene for him and his partner in South Philly a couple of years ago,* Underwood had said of Kevin Byrne at Finnigan's Wake. On that night, Underwood had taken Jimmy Purify's glove, soaked it in the blood, and held it, perhaps not knowing at the time what he would do with it. Then Matisse went away for twenty-five to life, Ian Whitestone became an international celebrity, and everything changed.

A year ago Underwood broke into Matisse's mother's house, stealing the gun and the blue jacket, putting his strange and terrible plan in motion.

When he learned that Phil Kessler was dying, he knew it was time to act. He had reached out to Phil Kessler, knowing the man was strapped for money to pay his medical bills. Underwood's only chance of getting Julian Matisse out of prison was to trump a charge against Jimmy Purify. Kessler had jumped on the opportunity.

Jessica learned that Mark Underwood had volunteered to work the film shoot, knowing it would put him close to Seth Goldman, Erin Halliwell, and Ian Whitestone.

Erin Halliwell was Ian's mistress, Seth Goldman was his confidant and co-conspirator, Declan was his son, White Light Pictures was a multimillion-dollar enterprise. Mark Underwood tried to take away everything that Ian Whitestone cared about.

He had come very close.

THREE DAYS AFTER THE INCIDENT, BYRNE STOOD AT THE FOOT OF the hospital bed, watching Victoria sleep. She looked so small beneath the covers. The doctors had removed all of the tubes. Only a single IV drip was left.

He thought about the night they had made love, how right she had felt in his arms. It seemed like so long ago.

She opened her eyes.

"Hi," Byrne offered. He hadn't told her anything of the events in North Philly. There would be time enough.

"Hi."

"How are you feeling?" Byrne asked.

Victoria weakly butterflied her hands. Not good, not bad. Her color had returned. "Could I have some water, please?" she asked.

"Are you allowed?"

Victoria glared at him.

"Okay, okay," he said. He skirted the bed, lifted the glass with the straw to her mouth. She sipped, laid her head back on the pillow. Each movement caused her pain.

"Thank you." She looked at him, the question poised on her lips. Her silver eyes were touched with hazel in the early-evening light streaming through the window. He had never noticed that before. She asked. "Matisse is dead?"

Byrne wondered how much he should tell her. He knew she would learn the full truth eventually. For now he said, simply: "Yes."

Victoria nodded slightly, closed her eyes. She bowed her head for the moment. Byrne wondered what the gesture meant. He couldn't imagine that Victoria was offering a blessing for the man's soul—he couldn't imagine that anyone would—but then again he knew that Victoria Lindstrom was a better person than he could ever hope to be.

After a moment, she looked back up at him. "They say I can go home tomorrow. Will you be here?"

"I'll be here," Byrne said. He peeked into the hallway for a moment, then stepped forward, opened the mouth of the mesh bag over his shoulder. A wet snout poked through the opening; a pair of lively brown eyes peered out. "He will be, too."

Victoria smiled. She reached out. The puppy licked her hand, his tail thrashing around inside the bag. Byrne had already decided on a name for the puppy. They would call him Putin. Not for the Russian president, but rather Rasputin, because the dog had already proven himself a holy terror around Byrne's apartment. Byrne had resigned himself to buying his slippers by the case from now on.

He sat on the edge of the bed, watched Victoria as she drifted off to sleep. He watched her breathe, grateful for every rise and fall of her chest. He thought about Colleen, how resilient she was, how strong. He had learned a great deal about life from Colleen in the past few days. She had reluctantly agreed to enter a program of victim's counseling. Byrne had arranged for a counselor who was fluent in sign language. Victoria and Colleen. His sunrise and sunset. They were so much alike.

Later, Byrne looked at the window, surprised to find that it had gotten dark. He saw their reflection in the glass.

Two damaged people. Two people who found each other by touch. Together, he thought, they might make one whole person.

Maybe that was enough.

THE RAIN WAS SLOW AND STEADY, THE TYPE OF GENTLE SUMMER storm that could last all day. The city felt clean.

They sat by the window overlooking Fulton Street. A tray sat between them. A tray bearing a pot of herbal tea. When Jessica had arrived, the first thing she noticed was that the bar cart she had seen the first time she had visited was now empty. Faith Chandler had spent three days in a coma. Doctors had slowly brought her out of it, and predicted no lasting effects.

"She used to play right out there," Faith said, pointing to the sidewalk beneath the rain-dappled window. "Hopscotch, hide and seek. She was a happy little girl."

Jessica thought of Sophie. Was her daughter a happy little girl? She thought so. She hoped so.

Faith turned to look at her. She may have been gaunt, but her eyes were clear. Her hair was clean and shiny, pulled back into a ponytail. Her color was better than the first time they'd met. "Do you have children?" she asked.

"Yes," Jessica said. "One."

"A daughter?"

Jessica nodded. "Her name is Sophie."

"How old is she?"

"She's three."

Faith Chandler moved her lips slightly. Jessica was sure the woman had silently said *three,* perhaps recalling the toddling Stephanie running through these rooms; Stephanie singing her *Sesame Street* songs over and over, never quite hitting the same note twice; Stephanie asleep on this very couch, her little pink face angelic in slumber.

Faith lifted the pot of tea. Her hands were shaking, and Jessica considered helping the woman, then decided against it. When tea was poured, and sugar stirred, Faith continued.

"My husband left us when Stephie was eleven years old, you know. He left a house full of debts, too. Over a hundred thousand dollars."

Faith Chandler had allowed Ian Whitestone to buy her daughter's silence for the past three years, silence about what happened on the set of *Philadelphia Skin.* As far as Jessica knew, there were no laws broken. There would be no prosecution. Was it wrong to take the money? Perhaps. But it was not Jessica's place to judge. These were shoes in which Jessica hoped never to walk.

On the end table was Stephanie's high school graduation picture. Faith picked it up, ran her fingers gently over her daughter's face.

"Let a broken-down old waitress give you a piece of advice." Faith Chandler looked at Jessica, a gentle sorrow in her eyes. "You may think you have a long time with your daughter, a long time until she grows up and hears the world calling her. Believe me, it will happen before you know it. One day the house is full of laughter. The next day it's just the sound of your heart."

A lone teardrop fell onto the glass picture frame.

"And if you have the choice between talking to your daughter, or listening," Faith added. "Listen. Just . . . listen."

Jessica didn't know what to say. She could think of no response to this. No verbal response. Instead, she took the woman's hand in hers. And they sat in silence, listening to the summer rain.

JESSICA STOOD NEXT to her car, keys in hand. The sun had come out again. The streets of South Philadelphia steamed. She closed her eyes for a moment, and despite the punishing summer heat, the moment took her to some very dark places. The death mask of Stephanie Chandler. The face of Angelika Butler. Declan Whitestone's tiny, helpless hands. She wanted to stand beneath the sun for a long time, hoping the sunlight would disinfect her soul.

"Are you all right, Detective?"

Jessica opened her eyes, turned to the voice. It was Terry Cahill.

"Agent Cahill," she said. "What are you doing here?"

Cahill wore his standard blue suit. He no longer wore the sling, but Jessica could see, by the cant of his shoulders, that he was still in pain. "I called the station house. They said you might be down here."

"I'm fine, thanks," she said. "How are you feeling?"

Cahill feigned an overhand pitch. "Like Brett Myers."

Jessica assumed that this was a baseball player. If it wasn't boxing, she was clueless. "You're back at the agency?"

Cahill nodded. "I finished my stint with the department. I'll be writing up my report today."

Jessica could only wonder what would be in it. She decided not to ask. "It was good working with you."

"Same here," he said. He cleared his throat. It appeared he was not very good at these sorts of things. "And I want you to know that I meant what I said. You are one hell of a cop. If you'd ever consider the bureau as a career, please give me a call."

Jessica smiled. "You on commission or something?"

Cahill returned the smile. "Yeah," he said. "If I bring in three new recruits I get a clear plastic badge protector."

Jessica laughed. The sound seemed foreign to her. It had been awhile. The lighthearted moment passed quickly. She glanced up the street, then turned back. She found Terry Cahill staring at her. He had something to say. She waited.

"I had him," he finally said. "I didn't take him down in that alley, and a baby and a young girl nearly died."

Jessica had suspected he felt this way. She put a hand on his arm. He didn't draw away. "No one blames you, Terry."

Cahill looked at her for a few moments in silence, then turned his gaze toward the river, to the heat-shimmered waters of the Delaware. The moment drew out. It was clear that Terry Cahill was gathering a thought, searching for the right words. "Do you find it easy to go back to your life after something like this?"

Jessica was a little taken aback by the intimacy of the question. But she was nothing if she was not bold. She wouldn't be a homicide cop if it had been any other way. "Easy?" she asked. "No, not easy."

Cahill glanced back at her. For an instant, she saw vulnerability in his eyes. In the next instant, the look was replaced with the steel she had long associated with those who choose law enforcement as a way of life.

"Please give Detective Byrne my regards," Cahill said. "Tell him . . . tell him I'm glad his daughter was returned safely."

"I will."

Cahill hesitated briefly, as if to say something else. Instead, he touched her hand, then turned and walked up the street, toward his car, and the city beyond.

FRAZIER'S GYM WAS an institution on Broad Street in North Philadelphia. Owned and operated by former heavyweight champion Smokin' Joe Frazier, it had produced a number of champions over the years. Jessica was one of only a handful of women who trained there.

With her ESPN2 bout set for early September, Jessica began her training regimen in earnest. Every sore muscle in her body reminded her how long she had been out of it.

Today she would get into the sparring ring for the first time in months.

As she stepped between the ropes, she thought about her life as it was. Vincent had moved back in. Sophie had made a WELCOME HOME sign out of construction paper worthy of a Veterans Day parade. Vincent was on probation in Casa Balzano, and Jessica made sure he knew it. So far, he had been the model husband.

Jessica knew that reporters were waiting for her outside. They had wanted to follow her into the gym, but you just don't walk into this place. A pair of young guys who trained here—twin heavyweight brothers who tipped in around 220 each—had gently persuaded them to wait outside.

Jessica's sparring partner was a girl from Logan, a twenty-year-old dynamo named Tracy "Bigg Time" Biggs. Bigg Time had a record of 2–0, both knockouts, both coming within the first thirty seconds of the fight.

Jessica's great-uncle Vittorio—a former heavyweight contender himself, a man who held the distinction of once having knocked down Benny Briscoe, at McGillin's Old Ale House, no less—was her trainer.

"Go easy on her, Jess," Vittorio said. He slipped her headgear on, fastened her chin strap.

Easy? Jessica thought. The kid was built like Sonny Liston.

As she waited for the bell, Jessica thought about what had happened in that dark room, about making the split-second decision that took a man's life. There had been a moment, in that low and horrible place, when she had doubted herself, when the quiet violence of fear had owned her. She imagined it would always be this way.

The bell rang.

Jessica moved forward and feinted a right hand. Nothing overt, nothing flashy, just a slight movement of her right shoulder, the sort of move that might go unnoticed to the untrained eye.

Her opponent flinched. Fear grew in the girl's eyes.

"Bigg Time" Biggs was *hers*.

Jessica smiled, and launched a left hook.

Ava Gardner, indeed.

EPILOGUE

HE TYPED THE LAST PERIOD ON HIS LAST REPORT. HE SAT BACK, looked at the form. How many of them had he seen? Hundreds. Maybe thousands.

He recalled his first case in the unit. A homicide that had started as a domestic. A Tioga couple had gotten into it over the dishes. Seems the woman had left a piece of dried egg yolk on a plate and put it back into the cupboard. The husband beat her to death with an iron skillet— poetically, the one in which she had prepared the eggs.

So long ago.

Byrne pulled the paper from the typewriter, placed it in the binder. *His last report.* Did it tell the whole story? No. Then again, the binder never did.

He rose from the chair, noticing that the pain in his back and legs was almost gone. He hadn't taken a Vicodin in two days. He wasn't ready to play tight end for the Eagles, but he wasn't hobbling around like an old man, either.

He put the binder on the shelf, wondering what he'd do with the rest of the day. Hell, with the rest of his *life*.

He put his coat on. There was no brass band, no cake, no streamers, no cheap sparkling wine in paper cups. Oh, there would be a blowout at Finnigan's Wake in the next few months, but today there was nothing.

Could he leave it all behind? The warrior code, the joy in the battle. Was he really about to leave this building for the last time?

"Are you Detective Byrne?"

Byrne turned around. The question came from a young officer, no more than twenty-two or twenty-three years old. He was tall and broad-shouldered, muscular in the way only young men can be. He had dark hair and eyes. Good-looking kid. "Yes."

The young man extended his hand. "I'm Officer Gennaro Malfi. I wanted to shake your hand, sir."

They shook hands. The kid had a firm, confident grip. "Nice to meet you," Byrne said. "How long have you been on the job?"

"Eleven weeks."

Weeks, Byrne thought. "Where do you work out of?"

"I'm out of the Sixth."

"That's my old beat."

"I know," Malfi said. "You're kind of a legend around there."

More like a ghost, Byrne thought. "Believe half of it."

The kid laughed. "Which half?"

"I'll leave that up to you."

"Okay."

"Where are you from?"

"South Philly, sir. Born and raised. Eighth and Christian."

Byrne nodded. He knew the corner. He knew all the corners. "I knew a Salvatore Malfi from that neighborhood. Cabinetmaker."

"He's my grandfather."

"How is he these days?"

"He's fine. Thanks for asking."

"Is he still working?" Byrne asked.

"Only on his bocce game."

Byrne smiled. Officer Malfi glanced at his watch.

"I'm on in twenty," Malfi said. He extended his hand again. They shook once more. "It's an honor to meet you, sir."

The young officer began to make his way to the door. Byrne turned and looked into the duty room.

Jessica was sending a fax with one hand, eating a hoagie with the other. Nick Palladino and Eric Chavez were poring over a pair of DD5s.

Tony Park was running a PDCH on one of the computers. Ike Buchanan was in his office, working up the duty roster.

The phone was ringing.

He wondered if, in all the time he had spent in this room, he had made a difference. He wondered if the diseases that infect the human soul could be cured, or if they were merely destined to patch and repair the damage people did to each other on a daily basis.

Byrne watched the young officer walk out the door, his uniform so crisp and pressed and blue, his shoulders squared, his shoes buffed to a high gloss. He had seen so much when he had shaken the young man's hand. So much.

It's an honor to meet you, sir.

No, kid, Kevin Byrne thought as he took off his coat and walked back into the duty room. The honor is mine.

The honor is all mine.

TRANSLATION OF THE DEDICATION:

The essence of a game is at its end.

ABOUT THE TYPE

This book was set in Perpetua, a typeface designed by the English artist Eric Gill, and cut by the Monotype Corporation between 1928 and 1930. Perpetua is a contemporary face of original design, without any direct historical antecedents. The shapes of the roman letters are derived from the techniques of stonecutting. The larger display sizes are extremely elegant and form a most distinguished series of inscriptional letters.